THE SORCERER'S WHORE

Pages of Darkness Book Two

SAMANTHA GROSSER

SAM GROSSER
BOOKS

The Sorcerer's Whore

Cover design by Elena Karoumpali at L1graphics

https://samgrosserbooks.com

London

1632

Chapter One

SOMETHING WICKED THIS WAY COMES

It was pleasant on the bench in the autumn sun, and the river flickered and glinted silver as it shifted with the tide in the late-afternoon light. It was the last gasp of summer, the clouds high and breezy, the sun still warm and bright. Mary rolled her head back against the wall and, with her eyes closed, lifted her face to the warmth, watching the flecks of orange behind her eyelids. It was a quiet afternoon. The playhouses had not yet turned out their hordes, and she was enjoying the respite from work.

A lone cloud stole across the sun, and she shivered in the sudden chill of the shadow. Pulling her shawl closer about her shoulders, she opened her eyes and blinked them back into focus. On the river a pleasure boat was rowing steadily past, music and laughter drifting to the shore in snatches on the breeze. Ladies in fine silks reclined on cushions while gentlemen lolled at their feet. Mary smiled at their pleasure, luxuries unknown to most on Bankside, though sometimes she tried to imagine such a life. But even in the growing cool of the oncoming evening, she was reluctant to go inside, and so she lingered a while longer, holding her shawl tight and enjoying the sharp salt tang of the river in her nostrils. She would be working soon enough, she thought, when the theatre crowds arrived, their passions roused by the emotions of the play and searching for pleasure.

A wherry drew in at the landing stage below Goat Steps and two young bucks stepped onto the quay, grazing their eyes across the row of brothels, eager but undecided. Mary assessed them with a professional eye: merchants' sons, she guessed, with money to spend and little experience. Rising from the bench, she let the shawl slip off her shoulders to the bends of her elbows, revealing the low-cut gown and pushed-up breasts, her nipples barely hidden. She stepped forward with a smile, and the two men turned towards her, interest written in their faces. She was about to call out when a scream sliced the air between them – a woman's cry from the brothel behind her. She spun towards it, panic running through her blood, and a man brushed past her from the doorway, his arm colliding with her shoulder with a force that almost knocked her to the ground.

Recovering her balance, she stared after him as he strode to hail the wherry that had brought the two bucks. She had seen him earlier, she recalled, when he wandered in. He had been alone and there had been an untrustworthy look about him. Briefly, she watched as he dropped out of sight into the boat. Then, forgetting all about the young men, she turned and ran inside, skirts lifted, taking the stairs two at a time to the corridor where the girls did their business. All the doors were open, girls and men in various states of undress hanging in the passage, waiting, gawping. Whispers of curiosity filled the air, like leaves that shifted in the wind. She pushed past the crowd, and in the doorway to Rosalind's room she halted, breathing hard as she took in the scene before her. The room was in disarray; her friend's few belongings were scattered across the floor, the bedclothes awry, and Rosalind lay sprawled on the bed with her skirts around her hips. Her wrists were bound to the head of the bed, drawn tight with a belt, and her eyes were open wide with fear.

Mary paused for a heartbeat, trying to still her ragged breath. One of the other girls was crouched on the ground beside the bed, sobbing, and it was the only sound in the silent room. Pushing past her, Mary ran to the bed, and scrabbled to untie the belt that held

Rosalind's wrists. It was wound tight and she struggled to loosen it, but as soon as she had worked it free, Rosalind drew up her legs and curled herself into a ball, still silent with fear and shock. Mary stroked her hair, gently.

'What happened?' she murmured.

Rosalind shook her head, still too numb to speak, and Mary sighed. Wanted more than he paid for, she guessed. It happened: she had dealt with such men before. She turned to the girl who was still sobbing on the floor.

'Go find Madam,' she ordered.

The girl stared and made no sign she had understood. Mary rose from the bed and went to her, then squatted down. 'Get up!' she hissed, taking the girl's arm and shaking it. 'Go find Madam. Now!'

At last the girl nodded, dragged a hand across her eyes to dry them, and scrambled to her feet. At the door she turned back to look once more and gave another squeal of fear before she disappeared. Mary heard her footsteps running on the boards of the passage and the thud of her shoes on the staircase. Then she went back to sit on the bed, resting a reassuring hand on Rosalind's shoulder. Her friend was shaking now, shock setting in, and Mary hauled the blankets up to cover her before she reached for the belt and wound it into a coil. The leather was soft and supple in her hands – it was an old belt and well cared for, and she guessed the man would regret he had left it behind.

She turned to the little crowd that had gathered at the door. 'What happened?'

'We heard a scream,' one of the men said. 'By the time we got here, he was halfway down the stairs.'

'Did you see him?'

The man shook his head with a shrug. 'Grey hair, stocky. More than that I couldn't tell you.'

The crowd shifted back as Madam Putana pushed her way through, and Mary stood up from the bed to face her. It was hard to say how old Madam was – guesses ranged from forty to sixty – but she ran the brothel with a rule of iron, and such things rarely happened in her house. She stood now at the end of the bed, looking down at the shaking girl under the covers, appraising in one glance. 'Get everyone out of here,' she said to Mary, 'and back to work.' A ripple passed through the gathered crowd, and she swung round to address them herself. 'The show's over,' she said, a hardness in her tone that brooked no dissent, 'and there's nothing more to see.'

The group at the door shuffled reluctantly away, and when she closed the door behind them Mary could hear the chatter in the passage, no longer hushed. A shriek of laughter and a door banging shut. Normal business being resumed. Madam had taken a seat on the bed where Mary had sat, and her hand rested on Rosalind's shoulder as Mary's had done.

'What happened?'

The girl shook her head, and Madam sighed and shot a glance of exasperation to Mary, who lifted her eyebrows in response.

'He tied her hands with a belt,' she said. 'That's all I know.'

Madam lifted her hands in confusion. 'That's all?' She gestured to the terrified girl. 'Then why all this?'

Mary shrugged.

'Well, there must have been something,' Madam said. She peered into Rosalind's face and smoothed a stray hair back from her temple. Then, lifting her head, she said, 'Stay with her, and tell me anything else you discover.'

Mary nodded and slid into the chair that was close by the bed as the door clicked shut. She heard the rhythmic tap of their mistress's boots on the boards, the steady tread on the stairs. The crowds from the playhouse would be making their way to the brothels now, she thought, and Rosalind's terror would soon be forgotten. One more damaged whore that no one cared about.

No one except Mary. Mary cared, and the image of the man who had almost knocked her to the ground burned behind her eyes. It was a face she vowed never to forget.

In Rosalind's room the hours passed in slow boredom as the light grew dim with the dying of the day and the sunset flared briefly beyond the tiny window. With the darkness Rosalind ceased her trembling and fell instead into fitful sleep, eyes flickering with dreams, limbs twitching. Downstairs and in the passage beyond the door, Mary could hear the business of the brothel going on uninterrupted by Rosalind's distress. Footsteps and laughter, and now and then the thud of a body against the door as couples groped and chased each other along the passage. She knew each woman's laugh, each woman's footstep. It was a busy night.

As the night drew in, Mary climbed under the covers beside her friend for warmth and wondered what images were troubling Rosalind's dreams. What had the old man done to so terrify her? She was a Bankside whore, after all, and no blushing flower to be so easily bruised and frightened.

Still turning over the possibilities in her thoughts, Mary slid into a restless sleep that was lit with her own strange dreams, images half-recollected from childhood – she saw a forest and a straight-backed lady who led her through the trees in the dark. An ancient yew, and a great black dog who lay beside her and kept her warm as she slept amid the old tree's roots.

A heavy thud of boots on the boards outside the door woke her from her doze, and she turned to look beside her. Rosalind was still sleeping next to her, quiet now, and as Mary stared up into the dark, her mind trailed back across the memories the dream had evoked. She hadn't thought of the straight-backed lady in years, and the details of the stern face had long since been lost to memory. But the woman she had only ever known as Aunt had picked Mary out from amongst all the other girls at the orphanage, in spite of her curse and her deformity, to take her sometimes to the forest, where she talked about a goddess called Hecate. A protectress, Aunt had told her, who would keep her safe. A goddess more ancient than the god of the Christians. Mary never understood why the woman had chosen her, but for a while it had given her a hope for her humanity, and a new understanding that another world existed beyond the harsh and unrelenting discipline of the orphanage.

After Aunt had ceased to come, Mary had gone sometimes to the forest alone to seek refuge from beatings for now-forgotten transgressions, but she could no longer recall if the dog had truly come to keep her safe or if it were merely the creation of a childish mind. She hoped it was true – the magic of the forest had imbued those days with a small flare of light in a dark and loveless world. Remembering the hope the woman had given her, she murmured a prayer now to the goddess for protection, and for revenge on the man who had hurt her friend.

Then she turned her head on the pillow to look at Rosalind again. Her friend seemed at peace now in her sleep, her breathing deep and even, but Mary stayed all the same. She had seen the terror in Rosalind's eyes, and she was reluctant for her to wake alone.

Chapter Two

T oby Chyrche had woken in the early hours to his mother's hand against his shoulder, struggling to open his eyes and meet the flickering candle flame that lit the darkness.

'Toby.' His mother's voice, calling him from the depths of strange forgotten dreams. 'Your father grows worse. You should come to him.'

Still half-asleep, he tipped himself from the bed and followed his mother down the narrow wooden staircase from the attic to his parents' chamber on the floor below. At the door he paused to ready himself, blinking the sleep from his eyes. He ran a hand through his hair. Was this the last time he would do this, he wondered, the last chance to reach across the divide that had always lain between them? Shrugging back his shoulders, he took a deep breath and went inside.

The chamber was stifling with heat and the sour smell of sickness, and he felt the sweat break out beneath his arms and along his spine. Trees of candles lent the room an air of brightness, and the fire danced merrily in the fireplace, oblivious to the drama before it. His father lay in the big double bed, propped up by pillows to ease the labour of his breathing, and each hollow breath was a momentous effort, a victory over the pain. Toby went to the bed and sat on the edge of it, taking his father's hand in his own, the narrow fingers calloused and rough from the long years in the tailor's shop downstairs.

'Father,' he said. 'It's Toby. I'm here.'

His father's hand tightened briefly on his own, but there was no strength left in the grip any more and their fingers rested gently intertwined. Toby lifted a glance to his mother, who had moved to the chair at her husband's head where she had made her home these last few weeks. Tucking a stray strand of hair back behind an ear, she tried to offer her son a smile, but Toby saw the weariness beneath the movement and realised with a jolt of guilt that he cared more for his mother's distress than for the oncoming death of his father. He gave her a small smile in return and turned his attention back to the dying man.

Did his father even know he was there? he wondered. Did he care? The old man had rarely shown much interest in his company before: though they worked long hours each day side by side in the tailor's shop, they had only ever talked of matters of business. He was a cold father, an unloving husband – Toby had grown up in a house that seethed with tension, some unspoken resentment at the heart of it, and a veneer of civility he had never dared to peer beneath. As a boy he had believed his father hated him, but now he understood it was indifference, and in some ways that was harder to bear.

A log cracked and shifted in the grate, sending a shower of sparks into the room, and Toby awaited his father's passing with the same lack of interest, wondering what he might have done different: he had only ever sought to please. Even when his spirit had chafed at the life of a tailor and he dreamed of escape to a different world, he had kept his thoughts well hidden and gone to his work with good grace. What more should he have done to win his father's love? He sighed – it was too late now to change. Caressing the bony hand in his fingers, he could feel his father's hold on life begin to slacken, the desperate rattle of each breath growing weaker as, beyond the curtains, the church bell tolled the slow passing hours. Once, they heard the nightwatchman, calling out that all was well. He lifted an ironic eyebrow and the gesture raised a smile on his mother's face.

But mostly they sat in silence in the heat and stuffiness, the only sounds the dying breaths and the crackle of the fire. Minute by slow minute the night passed, time measured by the rhythmic rattle of his father's chest.

As the dawn rose unseen behind the curtains, the servant girl, Frances, trod softly across the boards to tend the fire, then returned a little later to bring them ale and bread, which lay untouched on the tray on the cupboard. Though he knew it was wrong to wish for it, Toby prayed the end would come soon: his limbs screamed with the stillness.

But the morning had already lit the window with a rim of light that was bright around the edges of the curtains before his father drew his last breath. No rattle, no sigh of his passing, just no more breaths to come. For a while they simply sat on in the silence afterwards, neither knowing quite how to be: the emotion that overwhelmed him now was relief, not sorrow, and he guessed his mother felt the same. Lifting his head, he looked at her, sitting dry-eyed across the bed, weary with the long days and nights of vigil at her husband's side. Had she loved his father ever? he wondered. He had never seen any sign of it, but perhaps she had, long ago, before he was of an age to remember.

Finally, he let his father's hand go and stood up, stretching out the stiffness in his back from the long hours slumped at the bed, spine crunching with the movement.

'What happens now?' he asked. 'What should we do?'

She gave a half-shrug. 'Go to the church? Let the vicar know?' She shook her head in uncertainty. 'We'll need to organise a funeral.'

He nodded, but said nothing. He wanted to offer her some comfort, to say something to let her know he cared and felt for her weariness, but he could think of no words and the moment passed. She got up from the chair and crossed to the window, drew back the curtain and looked out and down into the street. 'It's full day already,' she said.

'I'll go to the church,' he replied.

'Thank you.' She turned from the window and gave him a smile. 'Thank you.'

On an impulse, he went to her and took her hand in his, squeezing gently. There was a moment of hesitation, then he put his arm around her and drew her into him, her head just against his shoulder, her arm curled loosely round his back. He had no memory of the last time they had held each other – not since he was just a child – and after a while she drew back. But she held on to his hand a little longer, prolonging the rare and precious moment of affection, and he was glad.

Then he said, 'I should go.'

She nodded and let go of his hand, and he felt her gaze follow him across the room and out of the door as he headed out into the morning.

At first glance the church was deserted, and the air inside was cool and hushed. He rarely came here outside of Sunday services, and his presence seemed an intrusion into the peace. But the solitude was in keeping with the dullness inside of him: no grief, no sense of loss, had yet disturbed his spirit, and he wondered at his lack of feeling. His father had died: surely he ought to feel something? Moving further into the church, he ran his fingers across the edges of the pews. The wood was warm against his fingertips, worn smooth with the touch of countless pious hands. He should pray, he thought, but the urge fled as quickly as it came, and so he wandered on towards the altar. There was no sign of the priest.

A sound from the little side chapel startled him – a footstep on the flagstones, and he turned to look. A young woman emerged from the chapel entrance, a soft smile on her lips, eyes radiant with the joy of her prayers. Judith Tooley. His heart missed a beat and a sudden warmth rushed through his blood. She had not yet noticed him, still absorbed in her contemplation, and he used the moment to observe her: the strong features and dark eyes, the full lips and smooth olive skin. Tendrils of hair had escaped from the plait that hung down her back, and his fingers itched to stroke them back from her face. Then she lifted her head, and her smile brightened into pleasure at the sight of him, a flush stealing across her neck. She bit at her lip in her self-consciousness, and Toby's breath quickened. She was lovely, he thought, and he wanted her for his own.

'Master Chyrche,' she said, and though her voice was soft it sounded loud in the quiet church. 'What brings you here at this time?'

'I was looking for the vicar.'

'He's not yet here,' she answered. 'You'd best go to his house.'

He nodded, but neither of them made a move to leave.

'Is something the matter?' she asked.

'My father passed away in the night.'

She lowered her head away, ashamed perhaps of her feelings for a grieving man. 'I'm so sorry. I know he was very ill.'

'It's a blessing,' he said. 'He suffers no more, and he's in God's hands now.'

She stepped closer and laid a hand on his arm, more confident now as comforter. 'If there's anything I can do …' She smiled up at him, and he placed his hand over hers.

'Walk with me a ways,' he said. 'I could use some air.'

'Of course.'

They left the church through the side door by the chapel and stepped into the gathering breeze of the morning. The day was mild and the freshness helped dispel the fog of sleeplessness behind his eyes. Judith walked close beside him as they wound southwards away from the church and the waking busyness of the morning streets, skirting the farm carts on their way to the market, and the villagers with their baskets of onions and watercress, blackberries and pears. Briefly, he remembered he had eaten nothing, but the feeling passed, his hunger forgotten in the presence of Judith at his side.

For a long while they walked through the streets in silence. Then, as the streets and houses gave way to a lane that cut across the fields, he spoke again.

'Do you go to the church so early every day?'

'Most days,' she answered. 'I like the peace at that time: I can sense the prayers of all those who have prayed there before me. It's when I feel closest to God, and I take that joy with me all through the day.' She turned to smile at him again, and he sank a little deeper in the passion in her gaze.

'I envy you,' he said. 'For myself, I've never found much joy in my prayers.'

'Perhaps you're doing it wrong,' she said, and he laughed.

'Perhaps.'

Brought closer by the laughter, she looped her hand in his arm, and with her touch his desire lifted again. A sliver of guilt flickered through him. He should be grieving, he thought, instead of hoping for a kiss.

When they came to the edge of the woods, they were breathless from the slope, so they turned to sit on the grass and look back across the fields to the city they had left. Southwark sprawled along the river beneath a haze of woodsmoke, and the tower of St Saviour's loomed above the jumble of houses and shops that lived cheek by jowl with the brothels and theatres, the tanneries and prisons. Their own church spire they could just glimpse above the expanse of roofs, and beyond it all, the great bridge that led across the river into London itself. He had only rarely crossed it – Southwark had always been his whole world, though his dreams had long been filled with the hope of other places.

He turned to Judith. Her skin glowed rosy with the exercise, and more hair had worked loose from the ribbon, strands blowing over her face. Without allowing himself to think, he lifted his hand and gently teased them away with his fingers. She made no protest but lifted her head to look at him, and when he had finished with her hair he let his hand linger on her cheek. Then he bent towards her and placed his lips on hers.

For a moment she froze, holding her breath before her mouth began to soften under his, and her hand reached behind his head to caress his neck. Slowly, he reminded himself, gently, though his whole body burned with desire. The kiss ended too soon but her hand remained against his neck, her fingers trailing through the hair, and he laid his forehead on hers. Then, at last, she raised her head, and he could see the question in the depths of her eyes, the wonder that he would make love to her on the day of his father's death, and the doubt of his intentions.

'I must go,' she said. 'Before my mother grows concerned. I'm not usually so long at my prayers.' She stood up, a dark form against the brightness of the sky, and he watched her, shading his eyes with a hand, before he got to his own feet. They stood together, awkward now after the passion of the kiss. She was shy again and her head was turned away, but he had felt the rise of her desire, and he knew now that she wanted him too. He offered her his arm, and she took it with a nervous laugh that was delightful. Then they wandered back across the fields towards the church, and he was aware only of her warmth beside him as her skirts brushed against his leg, her arm shifting lightly against his as they walked together along the path.

At the church he bid her farewell, and though he wanted to kiss her again, the street was busy and she kept her face lowered to avoid the temptation. He watched her stride away through the morning until he could see her no more. Then he turned back to the church and went to find the priest.

On the day of Simon Chyrche's funeral a chill autumn breeze shook the leaves from the trees in the graveyard of St George's, scattering the mourners with cold drops of water. The weather had turned in the last few days, summer sliding into autumn. Chyrche's widow stood at the graveside as the vicar's voice ebbed and flowed with the wind, the words hard to catch. But it made no difference. It was not her church, not her vicar: it had been Sarah's one rebellion throughout their marriage to attend a different, less puritan church. And all she wanted now was to get this over with. She felt no grief, no sorrow, just the same detached numbness she had known when her husband had still been alive. A life half-lived. A life without joy, feeding on the memory of those brief days before her marriage, when her brother Tom had still been alive and she had been a seamstress for Shakespeare's playhouse. Briefly she allowed her thoughts to linger in the past, but she was aware of Toby next to her beside her husband's grave, her head close to his shoulder, almost touching, and she let her eyes wander over the little crowd of mourners on the other side of the grave. Most of them she barely knew – customers to the tailor's shop, men from the Guild, people her husband had known from church, all of them huddled in their cloaks against the gusting wind and eager for the warmth of the wake to follow.

Sarah dropped her eyes to the dark dug earth at their feet, the soil black and moist. It was almost inviting to climb inside herself, and her thoughts slid away to another grave at the Cross Bones graveyard a few streets away, unconsecrated ground where the bodies of the whores and the sinful were laid to rest, and the body of her brother. In her mind she pictured the sapling of yew she had planted long ago to guard the grave amid the weeds and grass that grew untended all around. It had been too long since she visited last, though she still thought of him often. She would go again soon, she decided, to mourn the man she had truly loved.

The vicar's voice had ceased and a moment of silence settled, no one moving in the cold afternoon. Reluctantly she drew her thoughts away from her brother and brought them back to rest on the funeral before her. Toby nudged her arm and she looked up at him in surprise.

'The dirt,' he murmured. 'You have to throw in some dirt.'

She nodded and squatted easily to gather up a handful of soil to throw onto the grave. It was damp and dark against her fingers, and she could feel the grit beneath her fingernails as the earth landed with a thud against the coffin. Then Toby did the same, and the vicar's voice began again – a prayer she paid no mind to.

Finally, it was over and, with her arm linked through her son's, she stepped away from the graveside and prepared herself to face the mourners. They approached her in ones and twos, offering the expected words of condolence, and though she replied with nods and smiles of thanks, her thoughts were elsewhere, lost in the memory of a different burial.

Then a figure from the past stepped before her, and the wall of detachment she lived behind was stripped away in an instant, emotions suddenly exposed and raw. It was all she could do to stay upright, and she grabbed at Toby's arm to stop herself from falling.

'Master Tooley,' she breathed.

'Mistress Chyrche.' He dipped his head in a small of bow of respect. 'I'm sorry for your loss.'

'Thank you.' The words came automatically, but her mind groped to make sense of her feelings, and to master them.

'It's good to see you after so many years,' he said.

She nodded. He was still a handsome man, she thought, though the redness of the beard was flecked with grey these days, and the cheeks had grown more gaunt. But he had kept the old actor's charisma, and his eyes were still bright with sad intensity. She remembered the brush of his beard against her cheeks, his mouth against hers, and old passions lurched up in her belly. She slid her eyes away, exposed. It had been many years since she had felt such things. Why was he here? she found herself wondering. Why now?

'You remember my wife?' He gestured to the small pinched woman beside him. 'This is her church too – she knew your husband well.'

'Mistress Tooley.' Of course she remembered. Becky. Nick's sour and Puritan wife who had once called Sarah whore. 'I remember.' She lifted her eyes to Nick's with a small smile of complicity that he answered in kind. He had not changed then, and in the glance that passed between them she recognised the old familiar light of desire.

The other woman gave her a nod, but the hatred still burned in her look of contempt. Then she said, 'I didn't realise *you* were Master Chyrche's wife. We never saw you here. I assumed he was a widower.'

'I worship at St Thomas's,' Sarah said, though it had not been her choice. She had wanted to go to St Saviour's with the players and the whores, amid all the lively characters of Bankside, but her marriage had put an end to such a life and the church of St Thomas had been a compromise. She turned to her son. 'This is Toby,' she said to Nick, 'my son.'

Becky smiled her greeting. Toby had worshipped alongside his father: this was his church, and Mistress Tooley had known him since he was a boy. But Nick still went to St Saviour's, the actor's church, and this was their first meeting. 'Master Tooley is an old friend.'

The two men bowed, but she saw the understanding cross Nick's face, the surprise, and the half-spoken name on his lips. 'Tom.'

She said nothing, and an awkwardness fell till Toby stepped into the silence in his new role as host. 'You'll come back to the house for the wake? It's nothing grand but you'd be very welcome.'

Becky started to shake her head to demur but Nick said, 'Of course we'll come, though just for a short while – I'm playing this afternoon,' and Sarah had to suppress a smile, the old sense of mischief returning. She remembered how Becky had hated the play-house, and how she had refused to live with an actor husband until she was given no choice. She wondered if the hatred still burned, or if time and proximity had forced her to relent.

The Tooleys moved away, and though Sarah was aware of the unspoken questions on Toby's lips, another man had taken Nick's place in the line of mourners, so there was no time to answer them, and she was glad. For how could she tell her son the truth about his birth that Nick had seen so easily? Or about the love she and Nick once shared? But she knew that sooner or later he would ask, and so, as she resumed the mask of the grieving widow and thanked the other mourners for coming, her mind began to turn on the story she might tell.

Chapter Three

'TIS PITY SHE'S A WHORE

At the brothel the players had just arrived, fresh from the triumph of a new play.

'What's it called?' Mary asked, sliding onto the lap of one of the men at the table. He was in his forties, she guessed, with grey flecks in a reddish beard and hungry eyes that were sad. She passed an arm around his neck, and his left hand rested on her thigh. She liked the players: they were always good for entertainment and often had a sensitivity about them that was rare in the apprentices and artisans who made up their audience.

'*'Tis Pity She's a Whore*,' the player said, and Mary laughed.

'So it's about me, then?'

He laughed and squeezed her leg. 'Come see it tomorrow,' he said. 'We play for three more days.'

'Perhaps I shall,' she replied. She liked the playhouse, and though most of the girls went there only to pick up trade, Mary loved it for the magic of the drama, an escape from the drudgery of her life. She ran the tips of her fingers across the muscles of his arm. He was strong, and the muscles were hard and taut. Sometimes, she thought, being a whore was not so bad. Then, 'Does it end well for the whore?'

He shook his head.

'So it's true to life.' It was not a question.

'Truer than you can imagine,' he answered, and slid his eyes away in some kind of sadness she could not know.

To distract him and bring him back to her, she ran her hand inside his shirt, combing the chest hair with her fingers, wrapping it lightly around them. 'What is your part?' she asked.

He turned his head towards her again with a smile, the memories apparently safely buried once more and the mask resumed. 'The cardinal,' he said, and she laughed again. It was hard to imagine him pious and celibate, a man of God. Her fingers slid deeper inside the shirt and she felt the shift in his attention, the slight heave of desire. Then his hand crept beneath her skirts, rubbing gently on the skin of her thigh. Strong hands, she thought, as they spread across the muscle in her leg, kneading. Hands that could hurt if he had a mind to. She stayed wary, mindful of Rosalind, who was still frightened of her shadow, working now as a drudge for the other girls and all but useless as a whore.

Mary smiled and moved herself closer, her lips close to his face. 'Shall we go upstairs?' she whispered.

He shook his head. 'It's early yet and I would like to drink my ale.' But he kept his hand beneath her skirt, still holding her thigh as he reached for his cup, and though she wanted now to move away and find another customer, he did not let her go. One of the other girls had fared better and was leading her man away from the table. They caught eyes for a moment and the other girl laughed: it was a predicament they all knew too well.

'Tell me more of the play,' she said, taking his cup from his hand and draining the last few mouthfuls before reaching across to pour him more from the jug.

'A brother seduces his sister,' he replied, 'and they beget a child. But then the brother kills the sister ...'

She waited for him to go on, but he said nothing more, only sipping at his ale, his attention miles away, apparently lost in the story. She rubbed her hand across his chest again and he flicked his eyes to her, as if surprised to see her there. She said, 'It sounds sad.'

He nodded, taking his hand away from her thigh, and she knew she had lost him as a customer. There were other things on his mind, a private pain, and she was sorry for it. She liked him, and for once her job would have been a pleasure. Disappointed, she scanned her eyes across the room to search out another prospect, and near the door she saw a young man alone who had just come in. In his mid-twenties, he was tall and wiry, with a narrow face and wavy hair that would have been blond as a child but was darkening now. Men alone were a rarity, and Mary lifted herself from the player's lap without a word and crossed the room towards him, straightening her skirts as she went and glancing down to check the line of her bodice across her breasts.

'Good evening, sir,' she said, a coy curtsey, a shy smile.

'Good evening.' He answered her with a smile of interest that lit the blue-grey eyes.

'May I interest you in a jug of our finest ale?'

'You may.'

Smiling, she reached out and took his fingers in hers, before she led him to a table away from the players, quieter in the corner. Then she lifted a hand to gain Rosalind's attention to bring the ale, and sat on the bench close beside him, his fingers still wrapped in hers.

'Did you go to the play?' she asked. *'Tis Pity She's a Whore?* I hear it's a sad one.'

He shook his head and gave her a wry smile. 'I buried my father today. I have no need for sad plays.'

She nodded her understanding. 'I'm sorry.' Then, 'I never knew my father. I don't think my mother knew him either ...' She gave a little shrug for comic effect and it raised the smile she had hoped for. Then Rosalind brought the ale and almost spilled it setting it down in her haste, so that Mary had to slide her hand from the man's to steady it. The man gave the girl tuppence, and Mary poured for them both.

They held their cups up in toast. Mary said, 'To your father.'

'And to yours,' he replied. 'Whoever he may be.'

She laughed and they drank, then sat for a moment in silence. He did not seem to her like a man who was grieving, but there was a sadness about him nonetheless, a loneliness.

'Did you love him?' she asked.

He thought for a moment, as if he had never considered it before. Then he said, 'No, I don't think I did. And I would wager a large sum of money that he had no love for me.'

She said nothing – it was hard for her to imagine the love of parents or the lack of it, and she could think of no words to say. To break the silence she said, 'May I know your name?'

'Of course,' he said, with a tilt of his head. 'Toby Chyrche, at your service.'

'Mary Sparrow,' she replied. 'Well met, Master Chyrche.'

They sat for a moment in a pleasurable silence. He was quite beautiful, she thought, with his high cheekbones and sad eyes, and as a new warmth caressed her heart, she realised she liked him for more than the business she could get. The knowledge unsettled her, her usual ease of banter sinking beneath unfamiliar and unwelcome feelings. Then a shout from the players' table drew their attention towards it.

'Toby? Toby Chyrche?' It was the player from before, calling out to the man beside her, who slid her a small sidelong glance of apology before he replied.

'Master Tooley.'

'Come join us. You can bring the girl.'

'Shall we?' he asked. And though she understood it was not her decision, she liked him more for his courtesy.

'If you like,' she agreed, and hoped he would not see her disappointment.

Taking her hand, he led her across the floor as if she were a lady, and they drew up stools at the long table where the players were seated. The player poured them more ale, slopping it onto the table, and she realised he was starting to feel its effects – he had been drinking hard since he got there. Drowning unknown sorrows, it seemed, and there was a recklessness in him now that made her cautious. She had learned from experience how fast drink can change a man.

She turned brightly from one to the other. 'So how do you two gentlemen know each other?'

The player answered. 'My wife knew Toby's father. They worshipped at the same church. We met at the funeral today.'

'And Master Tooley knew my mother – long ago, I believe?' He lifted his eyebrows in question to the older man, who nodded in agreement before he turned to Mary to explain, though she guessed from the tension that Toby knew little more than she did.

'Toby's mother was a seamstress at the playhouse before she married. I knew her then.'

'Knew her well?' Toby asked, and Mary sensed the edge to his tone. Family history he did not know, and resentment at finding it out from the mouth of a player in a brothel.

Nick hesitated. 'You should ask your mother,' he said, and drained off another cup of ale. 'It's not for me to tell you her story.'

Toby's hand on the table curled into a fist. Mary laid her own hand on his forearm and she could feel the heat of his anger as it shimmered on his skin.

'It's your story too,' he murmured.

'But you are her son,' Nick countered. 'And it's her decision what she tells you about herself.'

Toby nodded reluctant assent and took long gulps of his ale. Mary slid closer and let her fingers creep up his arm, brushing the soft pale skin of the inside of his elbow with her fingertips. Gently he placed his other hand on hers, caressing.

Then Nick leaned across the table and grasped her other wrist. 'Now we can go upstairs,' he said. 'I've drunk enough.'

'She's with me,' Toby answered, softly but with a steel in his voice that checked the other man. 'You had your chance.'

Nick's grip tightened on her wrist. 'She's a whore,' he growled. 'You can have her when I'm done.'

Toby fingered the cup in his free hand, watching the movement of his fingers while he considered. Mary sat rigid, her wrist smarting from the pressure of the player's fingers – she would have bruises there tomorrow – and her other hand still rested on Toby's forearm. She was reluctant to go with the player now: he was battling some daemon of his own, anger pulsing in the working of his jaw, and she was afraid to be the target for his rage. She flicked a silent plea for help to Toby, who touched her fingers with his own in reassurance.

'Let her go,' he said, coaxing, reasonable. 'Don't let's fight about a whore.'

The muscles in Nick's cheek twitched with his tension, his whole body tight with unspent anger. Because of Toby's mother? Because of the dredged-up past? Perhaps, Mary thought.

Slowly he loosened his hold on her wrist. Then he lurched forward across the width of the table to thrust his face within an inch of the younger man's. Toby jerked backwards in surprise, recoiling, and almost tipped from his stool.

'You are too like your father,' the player hissed. 'Take her and go!' Then he slumped back into his seat and roared for more ale to be brought. Rosalind, flustered and frightened by the loud voice, dropped the jug she was carrying with a crash.

For a moment Toby made no move, and Mary was half-afraid he was going to fight back, but then he took her hand and rose from the table, unhurried, unafraid, and led her towards the stairs.

'Are you like your father?' she asked him in the room.

'Not in the slightest,' Toby answered. 'But I don't think Tooley even knew my father.'

'Then?'

He shrugged, and she waited, unsure if he wanted to talk some more, or if she should get down to business. She wanted to please him beyond the desire for a satisfied customer, she realised, hoping to earn a place in his affections. She had lusted for customers before

– she would have taken pleasure with the player – but this was something different: her spirit lifted inside of her with his company, and every look he turned her way felt like a caress. The sudden wash of feeling was bewildering, stripping her of her usual easy way with men. Like a virgin, she thought, awkward and uncertain, and gave a wry smile.

Toby said nothing more, still standing close to the bed, so she lay back and lifted her arms in invitation. He looked down at her as though he were considering, then kicked off his boots and lay close beside her, hand lifting her skirts to find the skin beneath, pausing midway on her thigh. The tips of his fingers were rough and calloused, tickling as they brushed the delicate skin, and her breath tightened in her chest with his touch. She liked him too much already, a joy that went deeper than her senses. He paused, teasing, enjoying her pleasure, and she wondered if he knew it was unfeigned.

Moving his weight across her, he touched his lips to hers, and though she rarely let men kiss her, this time she lifted her head to meet his mouth, eager for the taste of him. His lips were soft and warm and sweet, and she sighed as his hand coaxed one breast free of the bodice and his fingers teased the nipple. Then, taking his mouth from hers, he slid down her body, teeth biting lightly at the pale skin of her neck, tongue tracing the dip between her breasts, finding her nipple, sucking. Her back arched in response, desire billowing out to her limbs, and there was no need for pretence, desire for him in every fibre of her being. When he rolled up her skirts to touch his lips to her thighs, tongue flicking at the soft warmth between them, she came with an explosion of light through her blood, her whole body pulsating with sensation. Then he was above her once again, entering her, hard and strong and good until he convulsed in his own climax, shuddering inside her.

Afterwards, they lay facing each other, heads close on the pillow, knees touching, his hand caressing her cheek, her shoulder, her arm. She smiled and reached to touch his face, smoothing back the wayward hair from his forehead. Then she berated herself for caring. She was just a whore to him, a quick fuck to slake his lust. Don't fall, she warned herself. Don't you dare fall. Just because he gave you pleasure means nothing. He's a paying customer, no more. But though her head repeated the warning over and over, her body and heart were already in freefall, and she had no defence against it. She could only hope the landing would not break her.

Confused by the unfamiliar feelings, she rolled away from him to lie on her back, staring up into the darkness of the ceiling as it shimmered in the shifting light from the candle. The room was better in the dark, she thought, its meanness hidden, the rough wood and walls unseen. In the comfort of the bed in the candlelight, it was possible to imagine they were far away from the squalor of Bankside, the only place she'd ever known.

After a moment he took her hand, winding his fingers in hers, counting. Then he said, 'Six fingers. Six perfect fingers.'

So he had noticed at last. 'I was cursed at birth,' she said. 'They say 'tis the Devil's mark, a symbol I belong to him.'

'And do you?'

She gave a half-laugh. 'You see the life I lead: *by their fruits ye shall know them ...*' Scripture, drummed into her at the orphanage before she ran away from the beatings and half-starvation to take her chances on the street. Then she recalled her dreams of Hecate and the tall, straight-backed woman who had taught her, and thought that in the church's eyes, she did indeed belong to the Devil.

'I see no evil in you,' Toby said. Then, smiling, 'A little sin, perhaps. But who amongst us isn't a sinner?'

'What sins do you commit, Master Chyrche?'

'I'm here with you for one,' he laughed. 'But I have pride. And ambition. And a desire to be more than what I am.'

She was silent, aware that he had shared something private of himself with her. Men did that sometimes, confessing sins and fears to a whore they barely knew, truths they would tell no one else. She had learned just to listen.

In the silence the bell at St Saviour's tolled the hour. It was late, and other customers would be waiting. She wondered if Tooley was still downstairs – if so, he would be wretchedly drunk by now, and incapable. She hoped he had long since gone home. She should go down, she thought again. Madam would be growing impatient. But it was warm in the bed next to Toby, stolen moments imagining a different life, and she did not want to leave.

Footsteps thudded on the boards of the corridor outside the door. A man's boots and the lighter scuff of a girl's slippers. Laetitia, she guessed, one of the youngest among them, still fresh with an innocence that was fading fast.

She turned to Toby, who was lying on his side, watching her, fingers still linked with hers. 'I have to go down. I have to work.'

'Stay a while longer,' he said.

She hesitated, torn.

'I'll pay extra.'

She smiled. As long as he was paying she could stay. 'What would you like me to do?' she asked, 'I'll do anything you ask, since you're paying.'

'You wouldn't do it otherwise?'

She hesitated, unsure if he was teasing, or if he understood her feelings. 'I'm a whore,' she said. 'I do it for money.'

'Pity,' he replied, and she wished she had said something different.

In the silence she ran her hand inside the loose shirt, fingers trailing over the hard, lean body, finding the narrow trail of hair that led down inside his breeches. They were still undone and his cock was easy to grasp, standing tall with her touch.

'Use your left hand,' he said. 'Six fingers.'

She shifted position and changed hands without a word – she was used to men who liked the feel of six fingers. He lay back with a groan, and though she had not planned it, she slid down the bed to take him in her mouth. He was warm and hard and the taste of him was sweet as she used her hand in rhythm with her tongue to bring him to his climax in her mouth. Then she moved back up the bed to

SAMANTHA GROSSER

lie beside him, and with his arm holding tight around her shoulders,
he lowered his head to kiss her.

'That wasn't for the money,' she whispered.

'I know,' he replied. 'And I thank you for it.'

Then they lay for a long while, arms wrapped around each other,
and Mary allowed herself to dream of being loved.

26

Chapter Four

WHAT IS PAST IS PROLOGUE

In the morning Toby rose with the first light of day to go downstairs and open up the tailor's shop for the first time since his father's death. Black mourning cloth was still draped across the window, and he took it down with relief. It was a prosperous shop with three full-time tailors, but the missed days would take time to recover from and for the next while they would be working all hours to fill the orders. The other tailors arrived, and once he had settled them into the work of the day, he left them, without explanation, and ignored the exchange of irritation in their looks behind his back. Then he trod back up the narrow stairs to the first-floor chamber to break his fast.

And to confront his mother.

She smiled as he stepped through the door. 'Good morrow, Toby. Did you sleep well?'

'Aye. Thank you. I was late home, but yes, I slept well.'

'You went to the tavern?' she asked.

He nodded, unsure how to broach the questions he needed to ask. She looked tired, he thought. The weeks of his father's illness had been a strain, and her eyes were dark and sad, her features drawn. A part of him recoiled against distressing her further, but he needed to know – his own history wrapped in her past. Taking some bread and ham from the cupboard, he sat at the table across from her. She was picking at a wedge of cheese without interest.

'The players were there,' he said, and observed the change that crossed her face, colour rising, eyes brightening with interest. She dropped the cheese back to the plate and waited for him to go on. 'I talked with Master Tooley.'

'What did you talk of?' she asked. Her voice was casual, but he saw the effort of control it took. Her gaze was fixed on him with a new and eager intensity.

'He said he knew you from the playhouse, years ago. That you had been a seamstress to the players.'

She nodded, lowering her gaze once again to her food, picking crumbs from the cheese. 'Yes. For a short while before I married.'

He took a deep breath. 'Why did you never tell me?' He was envious, he realised, his own life bound by the confines of the tailor's shop, a narrow world without risk or passion, and a long future that stretched out unchanging till death came to claim him. She must have known Shakespeare and Richard Burbage, he thought. Famous men, and excitement in a world he would never know.

She hesitated, eyes still lowered. Then she lifted her head and held his gaze with her own. There was a light in her look he did not recognise, a woman with a life and secrets he had never suspected.

'Your father hated the theatre,' she said softly, 'and I was forbidden to go again after our marriage …' She lifted one shoulder in half a shrug and gave him a rueful smile.

'Puritan to the core,' Toby said. Though he had worshipped at the same church as his father, it was only custom that took him there each week. He had to worship somewhere, he reasoned, and the church of St George was just down the road. And lately, of course, there was Judith Tooley, Nick's daughter, with her brown eyes and slim hips, to attract him.

Sarah smiled. 'Indeed.'

'Why did you marry him?' he asked then. She had been barely sixteen, and even as a young child he understood there was no love between them, no passion. They had lived in a circle of restrained civility, everything that mattered unspoken, and he was only now beginning to realise there might have been secrets untold, a history he did not yet know.

She let out a laugh to cover her unease. Then she said, 'He was your grandfather's choice. Your father was the apprentice in the shop, being groomed to take over – it was only natural I should marry him.'

'But you were so young.' He had no memory of his grandfather – the old man had died when he was just a small boy.

'They both of them wanted me away from the playhouse …' She trailed off and he knew for certain there was more to tell.

Curiosity burned in his gut, and even as he warned himself to tread gently, he heard himself asking, 'How well did you know Nick Tooley?'

'Why do you ask such a question?' she said. 'Did he say something to you?'

'I saw you with him yesterday at the funeral, and I saw the way he looked at you. My father never once looked at you that way.'

She gave a small shake of her head and, picking up her plate, she got up from the table. Then she turned to look down at him. 'It's ancient history, Toby,' she said. 'Leave it be.'

For three beats of his heart he said nothing, filled with uncertainty, then he lifted his face towards her, still standing at the side of the table with her uneaten breakfast in her hands. 'He said something else,' he said at last. 'He said I was too like my father. What did he mean by that? Even a fool could see there was no resemblance at all between us. Everything I am I inherited from you …' He stopped as the possibility of a new and unwelcome truth curled itself around his thoughts. Could it be, he wondered, that he was not Simon Chyrche's son but another man's? That his mother had whored herself at the playhouse and got herself with child?

'You are your father's son,' she answered, which told him nothing. Then she strode swiftly from the room, skirts swinging, and the door rattled on its hinges as she slammed it shut behind her.

Late in the afternoon, after long hours in the shop that he thought would never end, he sought out his mother to make peace again between them. He had not meant to upset her, but the need to know more burned in his innards, and he had thought of little else all day. He found her in the attic room across the passage from his own that had been her chamber as a girl. It served now mostly as a storeroom for those items they had nowhere else to keep: spare blankets and quilts, a broken chair, outgrown clothes and old dresses she had not bothered to alter, documents tied and sealed with wax. He had rarely ever been inside.

The late-afternoon sun filled the window, dust motes floating in the bar of light that fell across the room. Sarah was sitting on the rug before the unlit fireplace, and the floor was strewn with linen and papers and faded bundles of herbs, their scents lost long ago. She looked up at him with a smile as he entered. 'I've been meaning to sort through these old things for a long while. Now seemed like a good time.'

'A new beginning?' he asked.

'Something like that.'

'Would you like some help?' He sat on the edge of the bed to one side of her and leaned forward, elbows resting on his thighs as he scanned the scattered mess. She had made little headway, and still she was unpacking things, adding to the confusion.

'Your company would be very welcome,' she said. 'But I'm not sure how much help you can be.' She held up a child's jacket. 'This was yours when you were little,' she said. 'For a while it was all you would wear. I had to repair it over and over.' She ran her fingers across the much-darned fabric, and a sad smile touched her mouth for the memories it evoked. 'Do you remember?'

He shook his head. 'But I remember you made me a scarlet cloak that I loved. I thought it was the kind of cloak a king would wear.'

She nodded, smiling. 'You were a little bit older then, and all you wanted was to be a warrior king. You had a knife as a sword and you slept with it under your pillow. I don't know what happened to it,' she said. 'But you could try the trunk over there, under the window. It's been years since I looked in there.'

He nodded and swung himself off the bed to kneel at the trunk. It was ancient; heavy oak slats with a great iron key that turned in the lock with surprising ease. He had expected it to have rusted with disuse. The lid opened with a creak and a dusty fragrance of old lavender.

His mother came to kneel beside him and together they peered inside. It was packed with clothes that had been carefully wrapped in calico, and he lifted each packet out one by one. Girlish linen, and petticoats, a skirt she must have worn as a child. Then his fingers brushed against something hard, and he leaned over to look. Nestled in amongst the linen was a book, an old book by the feel of it, the leather cover worn and smooth in his hand.

'What's this?' he turned to his mother with a smile of curiosity, but she was staring with horror, frozen, all the colour leached from her face. For a moment he thought she was going to collapse in front of him, and he lifted a hand to her arm to steady her. But she did not fall, and he withdrew his hand.

'Mother? What is it?'

Her eyes flicked up to his and they were pale with fear. The same eyes as his, he had always been told, changing grey-blue, but now they were full of pain. She held out her hands for the book and he placed it into them gently. She was scarcely breathing, and her fingertips caressed the soft leather with the tenderness of a lover.

'What is it?' he asked again, but softly this time, aware he had uncovered something infinitely precious.

She gave a little shake of her head, still unable to find her voice, and her eyes remained locked on the book.

'May I see?' He was curious to know what manner of book could provoke such feelings, the history behind it, and he reached out his hand to take it, but she snatched it away from him, clutching it to her breast, arms wrapped around it.

'Mother?' He was at a loss to understand: he had never known her to be so irrational, so strange, and when she finally lifted her head, her face was wet with tears. His heart turned in pity, for though he had no understanding of the cause of her sorrow, her pain was raw and palpable.

'What did I find?' he murmured, coaxing, tender. 'What is it?'

She lifted the book away from her body to look at it again, but her fingers still gripped it with all the strength they possessed, as though her life depended on not letting it go. Then she turned her face at last to look at him. 'It belonged to my brother,' she whispered. 'It belonged to Tom. And its power helped to change his fate, the fates of us all.'

'You had a brother?' He had never heard of him; his uncle's name had never been uttered in his presence.

'A half-brother,' she replied, her voice still breathy with emotion. 'Tom Wynter. And this was his.' It was as if the finding of the book had shattered her resistance to his questions, the past opening wide before them and all its secrets revealed.

With a half-sob, half-sigh, she held it out for him to take, and instinctively he held it with care, understanding it was no ordinary book. His fingers brushed the covers as Sarah's had done, and he realised that once upon a time the leather had been red, though time and use had darkened it now to a warm and burnished brown. The book's title was indecipherable; the remnants of lettering once stamped on the front had long since worn smooth, and it was heavier than he expected – a small book but weighty just the same. As he felt the heft of it against his palm, an image of Mary flickered at the edges of his thoughts, the sweet bow of her lips and the sad brown eyes, the cursed six-fingered hand. Shaking his head to shift her figure to the back of his mind, he brought his thoughts to bear once again on the volume in his hands.

Tentatively, and with great care, he opened the cover, aware of his mother's breathless attention beside him, watching as he flicked through the pages gently. Fine parchment slid between his fingers, soft and creamy, but at first glance the words that covered them were hard to understand. There were pages of Latin that he half understood, and passages in other tongues too: Greek and Hebrew scripts he recognised, among others he did not know. Long sections were filled with unfamiliar symbols in patterns – circles and stars, and a chart that seemed to track the phases of the moon. That it was ancient, he had no doubt. That it contained great power he felt in the centre of his soul, his heart beating quick with the knowledge, his blood aquiver in his veins.

'A book of magic,' he breathed, more to himself than to Sarah.

Next to him, she nodded, and as he lifted his gaze to study her, he began to understand her reluctance to visit the past. She was watching him as though to read his soul, and he dropped his head under such intensity. 'I never knew what happened to it after he died,' she said. 'I guessed he had hidden it somewhere ...' She shrugged and slid a glance to the chest, open and empty now before them. 'I never imagined it was here.'

'And if you had?'

'I would not have touched it.' Her answer was swift and definite. She laid a hand on his forearm, her touch light and cool. ''Tis a book of great power, Toby,' she said, her voice so low he could barely hear her. 'It teaches the words and rites to raise creatures from other realms, daemons to cause great harm.'

'You know this?' He had heard tales of such books, manuals that show a man how to raise the Devil's minions and how to harness their power, but he never thought he might one day hold one in his hands.

'It was a strange time, foul forces at work. Master Shakespeare awoke them first with the magic of his words, though he did not mean to. Tom ... your uncle ... we ...' She was struggling to find the words to tell him, perhaps wondering if she should. 'We did rites together and set ourselves on a path we could not turn away from, a path that led to Tom's death.'

'How did he die?'

Her mouth tightened, lips compressed against the desire to cry, eyes growing dark with tears. He saw her then as the young girl she must have been – a different person from the mother who had raised him. With a deep breath, she forced herself to speak. 'He was hanged as a witch,' she said, 'and I was forbidden to speak of him again.'

He was silent. Dear God! No wonder Tom's name had never been spoken, his very existence denied and erased from the story. Toby had guessed there were untold secrets in the family, and he had wanted to know the truth. But nothing could have prepared him for this. His whole world was rocking underneath him, splintering, and the long years ahead in the tailor's shop that were all he had ever seen for himself fractured now into fragments like the shattered pieces of a mirror. Everything had changed with the finding of the book, and everything he thought he knew about himself was cracking open, fissures of light and possibility against the darkness of his fear and doubt.

At the window, the light shifted as the sun moved round with the drawing down of the day. Without it the room grew dark and was suddenly cold, and he shivered as his fingers smoothed the page that was open before him. A circle marked with unknown figures shimmered as he ran his hand across it, and he felt a ripple of its energy pass along his arm. Mary trod once more across his mind, and this time he allowed his thoughts to follow her.

'Toby?' his mother's voice called him back from dreams of the whore to the darkening room, and he turned to her with a smile. 'You're a grown man,' she murmured, 'and I cannot tell you what to do – I can only beg you to be careful. Tom had a teacher for his magic for a while, and still he could not contain the forces he awoke ...'

Toby laid a hand on his mother's arm. 'Do not fret. I promise I'll be safe.'

She gave him a sad smile and he knew she didn't believe him. Perhaps Tom had once told her the same. But even so, he could hardly refuse the gift the book was offering: an escape from the constraints of the tailor's shop, a new possibility, and the power to dream of a different life.

∽

That night Sarah slipped from the house not long after Toby, stepping out into the cool evening dark to stand beside the torch that stood sentinel at the door, allowing her eyes to adjust to the gloom. The street was quiet at this time, families all safe inside, and as she stepped away from the shelter of the house, she felt the old thrill of the night's possibilities, though it had been many years since she'd walked the Southwark streets after dark. Time was when it had been her world, when Tom was still alive and her life still brimmed with expectation. But now the dark made her nervous, and though she squared her shoulders to shrug off her fears, in truth she knew the night-time streets were an unsafe place for a woman alone.

Drawing her cloak closer around her and lifting her hood to cover her hair, she strode along the lane, eyes wide with vigilance and her heartbeat quick with nerves. The way was well known: a right turn at the church, and across the High Street. Glancing north towards the river, she could sense the life that lay that way – the taverns and inns that would be filling now with travellers who had arrived too late to cross the bridge, and locals, enjoying the company. Shadows with torches moved in the distance. But she was taking a different road that led away from the liveliness and laughter, towards a lonelier destination.

She cut through the inn yard at the Falcon, footsteps light and quick, her hood drawn down to hide her face. A drunkard lurched across her path, having lost his way back from taking a piss, but he meant no harm and she sidestepped him easily, hurrying on. The dark closed in around her in the lane between the buildings, and with no moon to light her way, she had to slow her pace, feeling her way with a hand along the wall beside her, conscious of the rough, uneven earth underfoot. She could hear her own breath, and with every other noise she jumped. She should have gone the long way round, she thought, and stayed on the road, instead of cutting through between the buildings. It would have given more light and been safer for it.

Then she was turning right onto Red Cross Street, where bright torches flared in doorways and a rising half-moon strove to glisten through the clouds. A few minutes more and she had reached the gate to the pauper's graveyard, the resting place of whores and thieves, the burial ground for witches. She visited rarely these days, the years of grief too heavy a burden, but now she regretted it for this place was her last connection to Tom, the only place she knew where to find him. Though she had loved her son well through all the many years that had passed since then, she still sometimes questioned the choice she had made, her heart still raw with Tom's loss, her love for him undimmed.

She pushed open the gate with a shove, and the swollen wood caught on the untended ground beneath it. She had no fear of the graveyard – the dead scared her less than the living – and she cut along the well-known path between the unmarked mounds towards the plot by the wall that was Tom's. It was overgrown and untended, but the yew tree she had planted long ago was growing well, its branches casting their shadow of protection across the grave. She smiled to see it: it was an offshoot of the tree from the Grove and sacred to Hecate, their protectress. Among its roots the shewstone lay buried but not forgotten. For the first time in years she felt its call – a vision offered, a fate foretold. For a moment, she closed her mind against it, reluctant to know. Then, on an impulse, she knelt and began to scrabble in the dirt until her fingers found the hard, smooth surface of the stone. Prising it from its place, she swallowed with a sudden wash of apprehension. But as she brushed the soil from its surface, the pleasure of its touch brought an unexpected smile to her lips – memories of a different time, a different life, filled with love and hope and magic.

Still smiling, she remembered the reason she had come, placed the stone gently on the ground beside her, and laid her hand on the cold earth of her brother's grave.

Forgive me, Tom, for staying away so long ... You know well it's not through lack of love. I ache for you every hour of every day. I wake and think of you, I sleep and think of you. But such a love can be hard to bear, and sometimes I must turn to the world of the living to survive it. I've seen

Nick again and all the old feelings are still there, so perhaps I will find some love again after all. Perhaps.

But I come to you now with a heart full of fear.

Toby has found the book that you left and I'm afraid for him. It led us to dark places, Tom, and he has no one to aid him as you did. He is all that I have left of you, and I could not bear to lose him.

Guide him, I beg of you. Help him, and keep him safe.

She breathed deeply, hand still resting on the grave, eyes closed, hoping to sense the connection. But she felt no answering breath of love, no chill from his realm of the dead as she once used to do. Perhaps too many years had passed to call his spirit back, perhaps he was at peace at last in the underworld. With a sigh of resignation, she sat back on her heels, still reluctant to leave, some residue of his presence here even if she could no longer sense it.

She sat for a long time in the dark as the night grew old, knees growing stiff, but she could not bring herself to leave, drawing some little comfort from this last remaining connection. Voices floated out of the blackness across the graveyard, a man and a whore's exaggerated moans, bringing her back to the world around her. She could hear the animal noises of their sex a few graves away. But they were oblivious to her presence and she knew that Tom would have laughed to hear them.

Finally, she leaned across the grave and kissed the earth in farewell before she stumbled to her feet, legs grown numb, and, taking a different path to avoid the lovers, she made her way back to the gate, the shewstone held close to her breast. Then, with one final glance at the grave that held all that was left of her brother, she turned and ambled home on weary legs.

Chapter Five

LOVE'S WOUND

✤

ary had waited for Toby to return to the brothel, eager and hopeful, but aware even so that she was a fool for wanting him. It was unlikely to end well, she knew, for what man wants anything more from a whore than a few hours of entertainment? There were stories, of course, that the whores told amongst themselves of girls who had been taken from Bankside and wooed and wed, stories of rags to riches – handsome men, rich men, kind men. But it was always the tale of friend of a friend of a friend, and she knew of no one herself who had ever escaped the brothel that way. But even as she told herself that her longings for Toby were pointless, her heart still quickened at the thought of him and the memory of the pleasure he had given her. And so she waited each night for him to come with a sense of hopeful trepidation.

Tonight the brothel was quiet – it was strange how some days the men just failed to come, no rhyme or reason to it, just the way the business flowed – and she sat at the table by the cold grey hearth and settled to her sewing, a linen shift that had ripped. It was Rosalind's job now to do such mending, but she was a poor and careless seam-stress and Mary had some skill with a needle – it was one of the few useful things she had learned at the orphanage. She liked the quiet demands of the work, and now and then she raised her eyes to glance around. A few men sat drinking in the company of a couple of the girls, and Rosalind sat beside her, staring into the hearth. Mary had given up asking what had happened that night with the old man: the girl's wits had never fully recovered, and she would merely shake her head at the questions and turn her face away. Mary tried not to think of the merry girl she had once been – a woman with hopes and dreams and a wicked way with words that could bring a whole room to laughter in a trice.

One of the girls led a man upstairs, and Mary followed them with her eyes. He was young and drunk, and she guessed it would be over quickly. He was the kind of customer she preferred: young and healthy men came quicker, and most of them only wanted the swift satisfaction of the fuck. It was the older men who tended to demand more, and as long as they could pay for it, the girls had to comply, whatever they were asked to do.

Lowering her attention from the stairs, she scanned the room around her again, alert as always. Then Toby ducked through the low door from the street and her breath stopped short in her throat. She was on her feet in a moment, shoving the sewing back into the basket at the hearth, straightening her skirts, checking her hair and adjusting the neckline of her bodice, small breasts pushed up and on display to their best advantage. She waited by the hearth, a coy smile on her lips and her head tilted in invitation. He saw her straight away and made his way towards her, and the little light of hope inside burned brighter. He had come, not for any girl, but for her.

'Ale, Rosalind,' Mary ordered to the other girl, who still sat staring at the unlit fire. Rosalind turned towards her, frowning in question. 'Get us ale,' Mary told her again, and eventually the girl got to her feet and headed out the back to where the barrels were kept.

'Master Chyrche.' She dropped her best curtsey, and he returned it with a bow.

'Mistress Sparrow.'

They sat at a small round table beside the fireplace, and he looked around the empty room. 'Where is everyone?'

She shrugged. 'Elsewhere.'

'Then I'm glad,' he replied. 'Because it means I can have you all to myself.'

She laughed, taking pleasure in the pleasantry. 'I am all yours, Master Chyrche.'

He took her left hand in his, and began to caress the extra finger, gaze intent on the movement of their hands. Then, looking up, his eyes fixed hers in question. 'Are you truly cursed, Mary Sparrow?' he asked. 'Does the Devil suckle at night on this finger?'

She gave him an uncertain half-smile in answer. Why was he asking the same questions again? 'I cannot rightly say,' she murmured. 'I hope not.'

Lifting her palm to his mouth, Toby kissed it, then briefly, discreetly, slid the extra finger between his lips, his tongue warm and moist as it curled around the tip. Her breath lifted in response, warmth in her gut. Then Rosalind returned with the jug of ale and Toby let her hand go. Mary poured for them both and she drank, unsure of him now. She had met men before who made a fetish of her fingers, but Toby's sudden interest disconcerted her. She lowered her cup and looked at him. He was watching her closely, eyes grey and pale in the candlelight, and she was self-conscious under his scrutiny.

'Perhaps I'm your Devil,' he said.

'Perhaps,' she replied, but she had no understanding of his meaning. He must have seen the confusion in her eyes, though she tried her best to hide it, because then he gave her a smile that made her fall a little deeper.

'Forgive me,' he said. 'It has been a strange day, and I am not myself.'

'Grief can take you by surprise,' she said.

He tilted his head in question.

'Or so I've heard …'

He laughed then, and seemed to set aside his strangeness. They finished their ale and she led him once more upstairs to her room. A single candle guttered low on the window ledge, and she took two more from the table and lit them from the dying flame, casting ghoulish shifting shadows on the walls as the new flames surged and ebbed. Toby stood at the window, looking out into the darkness of the yard behind. In daylight it was a foul mess of broken things that stank of excrement and piss, but at night from the window you could imagine a garden – trees and flowers and a bench to enjoy the sunlight in the afternoon.

Mary went to stand beside him, and he lifted a hand to cup her face before he kissed her. A weight of desire shifted inside her, all other thought effaced by her need for him, her fingers scrabbling at the buttons of his jacket, eager to touch the cool skin beneath. But he stayed her hands with his own and, slowly, taking his time, he unthreaded the laces of her bodice until it gaped at the front, exposing her breasts and her belly. Then he untied the cord at her waist that held her skirt so that it slipped down her legs to the floor, and knelt at her feet to roll down the only pair of stockings that she owned, lips brushing against her inner thighs. The suspense was both delicious and a torment, and she wanted only to be with one him, to feel their bodies interlock in union, pleasure shared.

When at last she was naked before him, he allowed her to undress him too, and though she had undressed a man a thousand times before, she could only fumble with the ties and buttons, and it seemed to take an age until they were standing close together face-to-face, skin on skin. Tilting her head, she found his mouth again with hers, and as they kissed he turned her till her back was against the wall, the wooden boards rough against her shoulders and her buttocks as he leaned into her, pinning her with the weight of his body. She wrapped one leg around his hip as with one easy move-ment he lifted her up, and though she felt the scrape of the wood against her skin she did not care, all sensation focused on the places where their bodies met.

It was over quickly, and when her feet touched the ground again she rested her head against his chest, her arms draped around his shoulders. Then he shifted his weight to free her and immediately she was sorry. She had liked the hardness of his body against hers, the smell of him filling her senses, so she took his hand and led him to lie with her under the covers of the bed. They were quiet with each other, no need for words, but they lay with their limbs wrapped together and her head resting on his shoulder, fingers gently twisting in the fine hair that snaked across his belly. The closeness was exquisite.

After a while she realised he was watching her, and so she moved away from him to lie on her belly beside him as he propped himself up on an elbow and trailed his hand along her back. Within moments, he had noticed, his fingers finding the lines of the scars that crisscrossed the skin. They were old now and healed, and in the light they showed as pale pink weals.

'What happened?' he said.

'The Clink,' she replied. 'The house of correction …'

'How long …?' She could hear the pity in his voice as his fingers still traced the pattern of marks.

'I was fourteen,' she said. 'And still an innocent – fetching and carrying for the older girls, sewing their linen. But I was a girl in a brothel and they made no distinction when they raided the place. And by the time I left prison I was no longer innocent. It's an odd world that punishes whores with rape.'

He was silent, no answer he could make.

She shrugged. 'It was a long time ago.'

'But you still carry the scars.' He smiled, his fingers caressing her back, marking out the haphazard lines. 'They're beautiful.'

'They're an ugly reminder of an ugly life,' she said, shaking her head. 'No more nor less than that.'

'What do you dream of, Mary?' he asked her then.

She gave a half-laugh of surprise and pleasure at the question, that he liked her enough to ask. 'What does any whore dream of?' she answered. 'I dream of a man who will take me to some other place, to some other life, before I'm too old and diseased for the brothel and they throw me out to sell tricks for pennies in alleys dark enough that men can't see my age and my ugliness.' Mostly she refused to think of it, but it was the end of most whores who survived the hard years in a brothel and didn't die young from disease or violence or childbirth.

He left off his caresses and lay on his back, staring up into the flickering dark, and she turned her head to watch him. 'Are you married?' she said. Though he wore no ring, she still had to ask.

He shook his head.

'A sweetheart?'

'There's a girl at church,' he replied, 'Judith. But she's pious and chaste and I've little hope of anything more than a kiss without a wedding first.'

'Does she like you?'

'I think perhaps she does.'

Mary was silent, thinking that love was a cruel trick of the gods, for what were the chances of loving the person who would love you back? She remembered the aunt from her childhood, with her knowledge of herbs and potions. She would have known how to make Toby love her, Mary thought. She had known spells and cures for most things. But Mary had no garden of herbs to choose from and she had never learned the words that gave the spells life. She should pray to Hecate as Aunt had taught her, but she was reluctant to frame the words, for how should she, a Bankside whore, disturb the most powerful of goddesses for a love that was well-nigh impossible, however much she wanted it?

She turned her head to look at Toby once more as he lay in the bed beside her. He was so beautiful, she thought again, with his grey-blue eyes and the creases at the corners when he smiled, the sharp cut of his jaw. How could any girl deny him? Contempt for Judith's stupidity rippled through her, even as a part of her was glad – she could nurse her slender hopes a while longer. She touched his shoulder with her fingers, the muscles smooth and hard, and he turned to her and smiled. Then he said, 'I should go.'

She nodded with a smile so he would not see her disappointment, and he ran a hand along her arm, squeezing her fingers. 'I'll come again,' he said, so it seemed he had seen her feelings after all.

She shrugged – putting the wall back in place, returning to reality. Taking the cue, he rolled out of bed and she watched him as he dressed, covering the long, clean limbs, the pale skin bright in the changing light of the candles. She wanted him again, but in a way she knew not even sex would satisfy, and when he was almost finished with his clothes, she got up too and dressed with practised speed.

He looked up from tying his boots. 'How much?'

'Sixpence,' she said, and he took a shilling from his purse.

'You don't have to do that,' she said.

'I know.' He got up and stood before her, tucking loose strands of hair behind her ears, neatening. 'But I want to.'

'Then I thank you.'

Slipping the coin into the pouch at her waist, she followed him into the passage and down the wooden stairs. The place had filled somewhat – clusters of men sat drinking, the other girls flitting to and fro between them. Someone shouted an obscenity to the youngest whore, and there was a roar of laughter.

At the door Toby squeezed her fingers a final time, and then he was gone, the tall figure swallowed by the evening gloom. Sadly, she turned back inside and came up short when she saw at the hearth the man who had robbed Rosalind of her wits. He was watching her and nursing his ale, and her breath stopped, heartbeat hammering in panic. Desperately, her eyes searched for Madam, finally lighting on her figure in the corner, flirting with one of her favourites – a ship's captain, whose many gifts from faraway places over the years took pride of place in Madam's chamber. The older woman would not welcome an interruption. But still … Keeping her gaze lowered and away from the old man, Mary wove between the tables, aware of his attention.

'Madam?' She stood at a respectful distance, and the older woman looked up with an impatient question in her eyes. 'A word?'

Madam nodded.

'The man at the hearth,' she breathed, '… is the man who addled Rosalind's wits …' She could barely bring the words to her mouth, and she knew without turning that his gaze burned into her back.

'I am aware of it,' Madam said. She sighed. 'But Rosalind's mind

44

was ever weak, and you are made of sterner stuff.'

'Please, Madam?' She had never once asked for this, never shirked her duty, but her blood sang with fear of him, the knowledge of the darkness he contained. 'Please?'

For a moment she thought the Madam might relent in a rare moment of compassion, but in the end the head for business won. 'Do as he asks you,' Madam said. 'That is all.'

Mary nodded her understanding and backed away, a cold chill of dread threading through her veins like a sickness. For a moment she paused, her back still towards the man, dredging deep for her courage, finding a brave face with a smile to mask her terror. An image of Toby's smile touched her thoughts and gave her strength. Then, with a quick breath for courage, she turned and tripped across the floorboards to join him.

He smiled at her approach and held out an arm to greet her, sliding it around her waist as she moved in beside him, her arm resting lightly across his shoulders. She could feel the power of his muscles beneath her arm: though he was grey and ageing, his body was still strong. She swallowed and searched for the automatic patter of her trade, but no words came to mind and so she stood in silence, aware of the weight of his arm around her, holding her fast.

'You must be Mary,' he said. 'The six-fingered whore.'

'That's me.' She smiled, and let her fingers caress his shoulder. 'And may I know your name, sir?'

'You may,' he answered. 'I am Doctor Robert Alexander, scholar, physician, and astrologer.' His voice was low and soft, and there was a music in it that oozed with charm.

'Scholar of what?' she asked.

'You don't really care to know that, do you?' Contempt dripped from his lips, and his hand shifted from her waist to find its way under her skirts, rough fingers rubbing against the skin of her thigh, then forcing her legs apart. She moved to lean forward and pour herself some ale, a distraction, but he stopped her with a look. So she stood close beside him with her legs apart and let him slide his fingers across the tender skin, hard and ungentle, hoping to hurt. She was aware of him watching her but she stared ahead, lips firm and jaw set tight, refusing to give him the pleasure of seeing her pain.

'Do I frighten you?' he asked.

She flicked a look towards him and caught for an instant the cold, grey eyes that regarded her with cruel enjoyment. 'A little,' she admitted. 'I remember what you did to Rosalind.'

'Aah,' he said. 'The weak-minded girl ... Is she not yet recovered?'

'She is not.'

He gave a half-laugh. 'Then I am sorry for it. And you're afraid I'll do the same to you?'

Fear and hatred tangled in her gut, and she had to fight the urge to pull away from him, to strike out. In the corner Madam's attention was still with the captain – Mary could expect no help from her. She gave him no answer, and in irritation at her silence, he pinched her inner thigh so hard that she stumbled forward into the table.

'Answer me,' he said.

'Yes,' she said. 'I'm afraid of that.'

He nodded his satisfaction with her answer, and his fingers gentled in their movement against the skin of her legs, but now and then they just brushed against the openings between them, a reminder to obedience. She stood rigid and trembling. She had met many men of violence, men who had frightened her, men who had hurt her, but this man was something different – a darkness and a cruelty that smacked of Hell. Perhaps the Devil did exist, she thought, incarnate in this man who sat beside her. Then she thought again of Hecate, the mistress of her own dark realms, and her blood was charged with a little of the power of the goddess. She drew strength from the connection, and her fear began to wane.

Perhaps he sensed the change, because he dragged her suddenly onto his lap, her hip banging hard against the table, spilling the last of the ale, which dripped off the far side of the table onto the floor. 'I think it's time we went upstairs,' he said. 'So you can earn your daily bread.'

Shoving her off him again, he gripped her arm and together they headed for the stairs.

In the end he only wanted a simple fuck, taking his pleasure from her fear of him, the glimpses he had shown her of his darkness. When it was done she rolled off the bed straight away to squat above the chamber pot. It helps to stop a child, the other whores said, but whether or no, it was good to feel his seed drain out of her. When she had finished, she stood up and straightened her skirts, tucked her breasts back inside her bodice and sat on the stool at a distance from the bed. Alexander rolled onto his side and watched her, lust still in his eyes. She waited, aware there was more to come.

'The man who went before me,' he said, after a while.

Toby, he meant, and her senses quickened.

'What do you know of him?'

She shrugged. 'Nothing.' The lie was instinctive, and she would have said the same to any man who asked.

He smiled then, and she saw a whisper of a different man. 'Of course you don't.' He heaved himself to the edge of the bed and sat for a while, taking his time to straighten his clothes. Then he looked across at her and smiled again. 'You're a good whore, Mary Sparrow,' he said, passing across the coins he owed. She took them with a nod of thanks.

But she remained at her place on the stool when he walked to the door and she did not watch him leave. It was only much later she thought to wonder how he had known her name.

Chapter Six

THESE NECROMANTIC BOOKS ARE HEAVENLY

Toby slept with the book beneath his pillow, loath to let it from his sight. He understood by instinct that it was an infinitely precious thing, a rare gift, and before he slept he held it in his hands again, taking pleasure in the softness of the pages. Though the words and symbols made little sense, still they spoke to him, a spark that travelled through his fingers to his heart and mind, lighting the first shards of understanding.

He would study, he decided, and learn to unlock the secrets it contained. Perhaps he too could find a teacher, as his uncle had, a scholar who could read the arcane signs, though how he might find such a man he could not think. But he vowed to keep the book hidden; he would make copies of the pages if he had to ask for help. For surely no man how who understood the words would resist the book's temptation? Men would kill to learn its secrets, he was sure, and as he smoothed his hand once more across the cover, he could sense the history behind it, the many lives the book had touched. Lives made and ruined, acts of love and violence, riches won and lost. He smiled at the thought of it, the power in his hands, and though he was reluctant to set it aside, the night was almost done and he was tired. So he slipped it under his pillow, lay his head above it and quickly slid into his dreams.

In the dream he is shrunken, a tiny naked figure of a man no bigger than a poppet, and he is standing on the pages of the book, in the centre of a circle drawn in ink. Around the circle's edge are other people, tiny as himself, all of them reduced to inhabit the dimensions of the page. He does not stop to wonder how such a thing could be – within the dream anything is possible.

Slowly he turns to look around him, and the parchment is soft and warm against his soles.

He sees Mary first, to the north, with her hand outstretched towards him, inviting him closer. Desire rises – he has never felt so much for a whore. For a breath he is tempted to go to her, but some instinct calls him to turn away and look instead to the south. Behind him is Judith, her hands clasped in supplication, a prayer on her lips. Her body is lean and strong and boyish. The two women in his life, both beckoning him towards them.

He turns again.

To the west is an old man in the robes of a scholar, watching, and as Toby slowly wheels full circle, he sees in the east a man who can only be Tom Wynter. Like a mirror of himself, with changing blue-grey eyes, his uncle.

Uncertain what to do, he spins until he is almost sick with giddiness, and when the spinning stops he finds himself in front of Judith. She smiles and reaches out to touch his cheek. With her touch he grows hard, impossible to hide in his nakedness, and she drops her hand and turns her head away from him in sorrow and shame.

He spins again. To Mary this time, who kneels before him and takes him in her mouth. Sighing with pleasure, he watches the lines of ink lift from the page at his feet to form a doorway that leads to a forest behind her. A great black dog stands guard on the path.

Then he is spinning once more, and when it stops he is thrown at the feet of the old man, who lifts a boot to pin Toby's wrist to the page. He looks to see, and where his hand lies on the parchment the letters of Hebrew start to coalesce into meaning – invocations to

God, a summons to the Devil, words flowing through his mind. The man's boot presses harder, hurting, and all around him the ink lines lift and shimmer in the air: everything is clear and bright and sharp, all knowledge is his – he understands it all. Power surges through his limbs and he shakes the man's foot from his hand. Then he is spinning once more, and when he comes to, he is kneeling at the feet of his uncle.

For a moment there is stillness and he waits, uncertain, until Tom places his hand on Toby's head in a gesture of benediction. A love he does not understand surges through his blood like fire through a forest, scorching, cleansing. A new beginning. He rises to his feet and stands face-to-face with his uncle, who smiles.

Then the ground beneath their feet begins to shudder and they stumble and fall as the book snaps shut. He wakes, sweating and breathless as his thoughts grope after the images before they steal away and are forgotten.

Sunday morning and Toby and his mother went their separate ways to church. With his thoughts still turning on his dream, Toby's footsteps were slow and the service had already begun when he got there. Sliding inside, he stood at the back of the silent congregation, eyes scanning the sea of heads for a glimpse of Judith. She was in her usual place, a head taller than her mother, who stood squat and round beside her, and as the minister expounded on God's love for the chaste and the abstinent, Toby sidled through the worshippers to take a place where he could see her better.

Then, oblivious to the words of the service, he turned his eyes to look at her. She was in profile to him now and though her hair was hidden by the plain wool scarf, he could just see the fullness of her mouth and the dark line of her eyebrow. If she noticed him, she showed no sign, her attention focused fully on the minister. She dressed modestly, a good Puritan girl, and though there was little skin on display, he could trace the line of her breasts and narrow hips beneath the coarse wool.

Nick Tooley's daughter, he knew now, which explained why she came to church without him. The player, he imagined, would worship at St Saviour's with all the other denizens of Bankside: this Puritan, joyless church would hold no appeal for an actor – it despised everything the playhouse stood for. He had assumed till now that she was fatherless, but he remembered the player's hostility towards him at the brothel and understood the game had changed to something different now.

The minister stopped talking, and as the congregation began to mumble the confession, Judith turned her head and saw him. He smiled, and though an answering flush of pleasure flared across her cheeks, she shook her head and turned her face away. A weight of disappointment shifted in his gut – their exchange of looks and smiles, the brushing of hands, had become a ritual these last few weeks, the beginnings of a courtship, so why had she turned away now?

He observed her, bewildered. A few days since they had walked together arm in arm to the edge of the forest, and he was certain he had not mistook the delight in her smile at his company: he had hoped he might win another kiss today. She was quick and bright, with her dark eyes full of promise, and he thought he might fall in love with her. Remembering the touch of her hand, the long, cool fingers wound in his as they wandered through the fields, he felt again the turn of heat inside him.

The minister droned on, unheard by Toby, and it seemed that years had passed before the service ended at last. His fingers twitched with impatience and, as the congregation milled and chatted, he made his way towards her. Her mother stood close by, engaged in conversation with an elderly couple from down the street.

Judith raised her face to look at him, and in the almost black of her eyes, all he saw was regret. 'I'm forbidden to speak with you again,' she breathed.

'For why?' Nick's doing? It seemed unlikely.

She slid a glance towards her mother. 'Your mother was a whore …' she murmured, and with a light press of her fingers against his, she moved away.

'But …' he tried to say, but she was already gone, exchanging brief words with others as she passed between them towards the door. He watched her go, lit with bewilderment and fury, frustration churning in his gut. Then he turned to see her mother, still standing close by, her mouth a tight line of hatred and her eyes full of judgement. He tilted his head and smiled in greeting – they had known each other many years after all – but she turned her back on him and walked away, following her daughter to the door. When she was gone, he slipped out through the side door, halfway along the church's length, and strode out into the mist of the autumn morning to make for the row of brothels along the river on Bankside.

The brothels still traded on Sundays, the beadles well bribed, but the door was closed and he had to knock for admittance. The place was quiet in the mornings, and he guessed most of the girls had taken themselves to church as the law required. St Saviour's, no doubt, in the same company as Nick Tooley. Would his mother go there too, he wondered, now that she had no Puritan husband to stop her? From the doorway he scanned the room: a cluster of men were playing dice in silence beside the unlit fire, and in the corner a solitary old man nursed his ale and stared into space.

Throwing himself onto the bench beneath the window, he called for ale. The half-witted girl hurried to fetch it, and when she returned with the jug she hovered awhile, as if she would ask him something more. But he waved her away: her anxious jitters jarred on his nerves.

He poured himself a cup and drained it off. His throat was tight with anger but the ale did nothing to ease it. He drank some more, and a wooziness began to lighten his head: he was unused to drinking more than a little small beer in the morning. He thought of Mistress Tooley with the new hatred for him in her eyes. What did she know of his mother that was unknown to him? Why had she called her a whore? Then he recalled the look in Nick Tooley's eyes when he talked with his mother at the funeral; it was a look he knew well. He shook his head to clear it of the conflict in his thoughts, but it made no difference, and instead he drained another cup of ale.

Letting his eyes wander the brothel, he hoped to see Mary, but his gaze lit instead on the old man in the corner. He was familiar from somewhere, with his silver hair and keen pale eyes that were staring at Toby now with interest, and for a moment Toby puzzled, trying to place him. Then his hand throbbed with sudden pain and he remembered the man's boot on his wrist in the dream, and the new knowledge his submission had brought.

He raised his eyes to meet the gaze and wished he had drunk less ale – his thoughts were drifting and distant, and it was hard to pin them down. The man got up from his place near the hearth and, with a word to the girl who shrank away from him in terror, he came towards Toby's table.

'May I?' he asked, and, without waiting for an answer, he eased himself onto the stool opposite.

The girl brought more ale and fled, and the old man poured for them both, but Toby left his where it stood – his thoughts were muddied enough already. Undeterred, the old man lifted his cup in toast. 'To old friends,' he said. 'And fathers.'

His voice was soft and deep, with the shadow of an accent from the west. Wales, perhaps, Toby thought, though he couldn't be sure. But there was a melody in its tone that was beguiling, and he tensed himself in defence against its charm.

'We are not old friends,' Toby said. 'And my father is dead.'

The lined face broke into a smile. 'Yes, yes, I know. But you look just like him, you know. It's uncanny … From over there I could have sworn you were the man himself.'

'I am nothing like my father,' he replied. 'In looks or character.' It was almost a point of pride.

The old man took a mouthful of ale and tilted his head. Then, looking up, fixing Toby's gaze with a level stare, he said, 'Then your father is not the man you think he is. And your mother was a whore.'

Toby was silent, reluctant to admit the possibility of it even as he knew that it was true. But if he were not Simon Chyrche's son ...

'You knew my father?' He did not want to ask, his blood cold with distrust, but the urge to know was overwhelming.

'He was my pupil for a time.'

'Pupil in what?' he heard himself ask even as with a sickening lurch in his gut he realised he already knew. He heard his mother's voice. *Tom had a teacher for a while ...*

His uncle was his father.

It was not only Nick Tooley his mother had whored herself to. She had borne a child by her brother, and he was that child. His gut heaved, vomit rising, and in one swift movement he was up and out of the door, spewing his guts onto the dirt outside. The ale burned his throat and left a foul taste, and his belly pained with the violence of the contractions. He breathed deeply, and only when he trusted that there was no more vomit to come, he wiped his mouth with the back of his hand and wandered to the water's edge, taking in the rank salt tang, his thoughts caressed by the slap of the tide against the quay, the river unchanging, uncaring. Perhaps his father stood here too, he thought, watching the river heave and turn on its endless journey out to sea. But what witchcraft had he done to end his days with a noose around his neck? What crimes had he committed beyond the seduction of his sister, the begetting of a child?

Lifting his face to meet the warmth of a weak morning sun that glimmered behind the shifting clouds, Toby recalled his father's hand upon his head in the dream and the promise of protection contained within his blessing. Taking a deep breath, he filled himself with the vitality of the river, the life of ages in its air, and turned back towards the brothel to learn more about Tom Wynter.

The old man's eyes watched him with curiosity as he slid back into the bench by the window, his back against the wall. Toby took a mouthful of ale to shift the acid taste from his throat.

'You are so very like him,' the man said again.

'Who are you?' Toby asked. 'And what do you want with me?'

The man smiled. 'I am Doctor Robert Alexander.' The man who taught his father the secrets of the magic that had killed him, Toby thought. 'And I can teach you as I taught your father.'

'Teach me what?'

'To gain whatever you desire.' He drank, placed his mug on the table and leaned forward. 'What do you desire, Toby Wynter?' he asked. 'What do you want from your life?'

Answers, Toby thought. And to be more than what I am. To know. To feel. To love. Then he thought of Judith at the church that morning, the shy desire in her eyes that might never be fulfilled, and the look of smug satisfaction on her mother's face. It was as good a place to start as any. 'There's a woman,' he said.

Alexander laughed. 'Ah, you are indeed like your father ...'

'Can you help me?'

'Of course.' The older man tilted his head in agreement. 'There are many ways to win a woman. What is it you want from her? Her love? Her virtue? Her soul?'

He was silent for a moment, recalling her smile and her hand in his, the heave of desire with her touch. He wanted her love, he thought, in spite of her mother's law. Perhaps this was a way to win her regardless. But he wanted her virtue also. She filled his mind often when he was alone at night, the wide, full lips and dark eyes, the narrow, boyish tilt of her hips. Her legs would be lean and strong beneath the plain wool skirts, he guessed, her belly flat. And he knew she nursed the same latent desire. Was it possible to win a woman's soul?

He shrugged. 'Her love. And her body.'

'She is forbidden to you?'

Toby looked up sharply. How could the old man know that? He nodded.

'Then come to my rooms tomorrow night – I rent the attic at the sign of the Wounded Raven, two streets back from the river, beside the glove maker's shop. Will you find it?'

'I know it,' he said. He knew most of the streets in Bankside, and he had drunk at the Wounded Raven as an apprentice. It was a low sort of place, but cheap. Evidently, Alexander's skills had not made him rich, whatever claims he made for his power. Then he said, 'Why would you wish to teach me anything? Where is the profit for you?'

Alexander's mouth twitched into the semblance of smile, but his eyes remained on the cup of ale he was holding. 'Let's say for old times' sake,' he offered. 'In memory of your father.'

Toby said nothing, but he knew already the old man was not so generous. There was something he would want in return and a price to pay, Toby was sure. He remembered the pressure of the boot on his wrist in the dream, and despite his curiosity and his desire to learn the old man's secrets, the blood in his veins rippled with trepidation.

Later, with a headache from drinking too much ale in the morning, he wandered home, reluctant to face the confrontation with his mother, uncertain how to broach it, how she would react. With tears, he guessed, and regret. But he needed to know the story, his history contained with it, and he could not let it go.

He went to her straight away and found her sewing by the light of the window in the first-floor chamber that was the heart of the house. The room was cool and the fire unlit, but she seemed oblivious, needle flicking in and out of the soft linen of a shift. He had always liked to watch her sew – a nimbleness in the stitches he had never mastered in all the years he had learned the trade of tailor. She looked up at him with a smile that faded as soon as she saw his face.

'What is it, Toby?' she asked, laying the shift aside, turning away from the window towards him. 'What's happened?'

With the light behind her, her eyes were in shadow and he could not read her face as he would have liked. He slid onto one of the stools at the table, keeping a distance between them. His mouth was dry and the words he had rehearsed on the slow walk home failed to come to mind. It seemed like the ravings of a madman to accuse his mother and her brother of such lurid things, a plot from the pen of a playwright. And yet …

He swallowed, his eyes on the rush mats that covered the boards at his feet, and he was aware of their fragrance, a scent of herbs that would always take him back to his childhood. He could not bring himself to look at her.

'Toby?'

He heard the misgivings in her voice, and found the courage at last to raise his face to meet the question in her gaze. 'Tom Wynter was my father,' he said. It was not framed as a question, and he heard his mother's sharp gasp of breath. She must have dreaded this moment his whole life, he thought, always waiting and afraid of his discovery of the truth.

She nodded.

'And you married my father to hide it.'

She said nothing, and a sudden fury swelled in him that she had lied for so long, that his whole life was a lie.

'Tell me!' he demanded. 'Tell me the truth. All of it. I have a right to know.'

Sarah nodded again, passing the tip of her tongue across her lips, searching to find the right words, but he felt no sympathy: he simply wanted to know.

'I'll try to keep it simple,' she said, giving him a small smile – hoping, he guessed, for encouragement – but he could not bring himself to answer it, impatience gnawing at his innards, his guts still heavy and churning.

'We loved each other.' She shrugged, as if that was all there was to tell.

'And Nick Tooley too?'

Surprisingly, she laughed. 'Yes. And Nick Tooley too.' With her laughter the tension seemed to break, and he could imagine how she might have been all those years ago, young and pretty, full of life and love. 'I loved them both. We lived in the world of the playhouse. Nothing was real and all was possible, all was magic ...'

'What happened to him? Why did he die?'

The smile left her face as swiftly as the laughter had risen. 'To save me,' she said, the pain still clear in her eyes. 'I was accused of bewitching a boy in the Company, and Tom took the blame to save me.'

Toby stared, all his preconceptions overturned by this unexpected truth. True love, he realised, to make such a sacrifice, and not the sordid lusts he had imagined. His anger ebbed and, uncertain now what to feel, he shifted forward to take his mother's hand.

'Did my father know?' Simon Chyrche, he meant, the man who had raised him as a son.

'I don't know,' she replied. 'For a long time I thought not. But as you grew you were so like Tom, it was hard to believe anyone could think anything else.' She shrugged. 'But nephews sometimes look like uncles, so perhaps he allowed himself to be deceived.'

'He never loved me,' Toby said. 'I was never good enough, however hard I tried.'

'I loved you,' she said, turning her hand in his. 'I still do.' Then she lifted her head to look at him, and he saw the apprehension in her eyes. 'Can you forgive me?'

He gave a half-smile, thoughts still roiling in his head, confused, his heart uncertain. But even in the centre of the turbulence, a part of him was glad: an altered past opened up a different future, new paths to follow. He had always felt like a cuckoo in his father's house, and now at last he understood the reason – another man's blood flowed in his veins. He squeezed his mother's hand. 'Of course I forgive you.'

Her face coloured with relief, and she smiled at him through the tears that brimmed in her eyes. 'Thank you,' she breathed. 'I couldn't bear to lose you too.' Then, winding her fingers more tightly in his, she said, 'Be careful, Toby. Please?'

He nodded, understanding she meant the book and the magic it contained, the magic she claimed had led to Tom's death. Then he wondered how much of it she knew, and if the charges of witchcraft against her had been based in fact: his father a sorcerer, his mother a witch. No wonder he had felt like a cuckoo, he thought, growing up in a Puritan house. For a moment he said nothing, half-tempted to ask her about it before he realised that he did not want to know. His father's magic was enough and he had no need of witchcraft.

Gently, he slid his hand away and drew back from her. 'You've no need to fret,' he said. 'I'll be safe.' But even as he said it, his thoughts turned to Alexander, and he rubbed an automatic hand to ease the throbbing at the wrist where the old man's boot had rested in his dream. He had no illusions about the risk he was taking, but the lure of the knowledge Alexander offered was too great a temptation to resist.

Chapter Seven

THE ACTORS ARE AT HAND

It was years since her footsteps had taken her this way, and though the building itself had been destroyed by fire and rebuilt in the intervening years, the sight of the playhouse looming into sight, white and solid in the morning sun when she rounded the corner, still took her breath away. Sarah halted, casting her eyes across it, every detail almost the same as the original and perfectly remembered in her imagination. It had been her world for a time, a world she had shared with Tom and with Nick, and they had been the last days of happiness she had known. In her mind's eye she climbed the outside stair to the wardrobe-keeper's rooms below the roof where she and Tom had worked on the costumes, and where they had lain together. Grief swelled, unexpected and ferocious, and she had to put a hand against the wall of the alehouse beside her to steady herself. Even after all these years, the pain could still fell her in a moment.

She stood and breathed deeply, supporting herself against the wall, and when she thought she could trust her body again, she pushed away from the warm stone and strode towards the playhouse door, quickly, so she could not change her mind on the way. Sliding inside the building, she paused in the doorway, and in spite of everything, the sudden wash of memories raised a smile. The Company was rehearsing and the small group of men on the stage was engaged in earnest discussion. She flicked a glance around the balconies until she spotted the man she was looking for: Nick, in the ground-floor gallery watching the stage, alone.

Taking a moment to gather her courage, she straightened her skirts and ran a hand across her hair to neaten it. Then, with a last deep breath, she stepped up into the gallery and trod across the boards towards him. He turned at the footsteps without interest, but when he saw who it was his eyes brightened with delighted surprise, and he was on his feet in a moment to welcome her.

'Mistress Chyrche!' he said. 'It's truly a pleasure to see you. But what brings you to the playhouse?'

'Sarah,' she murmured, shy now and doubting. Perhaps she should not have come after all. 'No more Mistress Chyrche. Please call me Sarah.'

He smiled with a tilt of his head in understanding and gestured to the bench. They sat, close together but not touching, and for a moment neither spoke. Then he turned to her and said again, 'What brings you here, Sarah? Why have you come?'

She heard the slight regret in his voice, and remembered how they had once been with each other: in love, happy. They could have made a good life together if the Fates had been kinder. Without his wife. Without Tom.

She gestured with her head towards the stage. 'What is the play?'

'*'Tis Pity She's a Whore*,' he said. 'Some changes to the staging … You should stay for the afternoon performance. It's a good play.'

She smiled. 'Perhaps I will.' Then she said, 'Have you time to talk awhile?'

He turned to her, green eyes light with interest. The lines at their corners were deeper than they used to be but he was still a handsome man, and she felt the old familiar lift of desire in her belly, a feeling she hadn't thought to know again. 'Of course,' he replied. 'Here? Or should we walk to the river?'

'The river,' she said. It would be easier to talk away from the weight of memories that the playhouse held, a more neutral ground.

They got up and she followed him into the cool autumn sunshine outside. When he offered her his arm, she took it, and it seemed the most natural thing in the world to stroll to the water's edge with him. She couldn't imagine how so much time had passed since she had last held his arm, nor how she had got through the years in between in such loveless loneliness.

By tacit consent they wandered eastwards, away from the brothels of Bankside and towards the church of St Saviour's, and they came to a stop just before they reached its shadow, close by the landing stage before it. It was high tide and the water smacked against the wall of the quay with the passing of the boats. It was pleasant to stand in the morning sun, and its light was warm on their faces.

Nick turned to face her, sliding his hand along the length of her sleeve to hold her own, and with the touch of his fingers her breath began to tighten in her chest, suddenly aware of the maleness and strength of his body, his scent. 'What's happened?' he asked. 'What is it you want to talk of?'

Lightly, she bit the tip of her tongue between her teeth as all the words she needed spun out of order. Then, forcing them into sense, she lifted her face to look at him.

'Toby has learned the truth,' she said. 'He knows he's Tom's son …'

Nick nodded. 'It could only have been a matter of time – the likeness is uncanny. 'Tis clear as day to anyone who ever knew your brother.'

'I know,' she said, turning her gaze towards the water, following the line of a wherry as it sped east with the turning tide. 'But still …'

He was silent and she wondered what he was thinking. His last words to Tom had been in anger. 'I needed to tell someone,' she said, lifting her head to look at him again. 'And there's no one else I can tell.'

He gave her a wry smile.

'And,' she said, with a shrug, a slight smile, 'it gave me a reason to see you.'

'Do you plan to bewitch me again?' he asked, and her breath stopped for half a heartbeat, until she realised he was teasing.

She said, 'Do I need to? Or will you come to me of your own free will?'

He lowered his face closer to hers, his lips almost brushing her cheek, so that she could feel the warmth of his breath against her skin. Her whole body was warm with the knowledge of his nearness. 'You never had need to bewitch me, Sarah,' he murmured. 'Nor do you now.'

She swallowed, conscious of the promise in his words. Then she turned her head to meet his, her mouth against the bristles of his beard, tickling. For three breaths they did not move until the sudden awareness of the busy quayside around them forced them to move apart.

'Not here,' he said.

'Then where?'

They hesitated: his wife at his house, her son at hers.

'An inn,' he said then, and taking her hand, he led her towards the High Street, hurrying through the crowd as they cut through the warren of the market, senses assailed by the clamour and the stink. They stopped at the George, and at the door she paused, pulling back on his hand for a moment, beset by memories. The Company drinking here to celebrate success. Finding Will Shakespeare to ask for his help. Tom with his beauty and his recklessness in the centre of it all. But Nick tightened his grip on her hand and kept going, and so she followed him inside to wait at the window, looking out into the street while he found them a room.

He was back for her in moments, taking her hand once again to lead her upstairs and outside onto the gallery above the stable yard, counting off the doors they passed until they came to their own. He bent to unlock it and looked up at her with a smile of such excitement she could not help but return it, despite her terror at what they were doing. She had lost the boldness of her youth, she thought, when love was all that mattered. But inside the chamber, she had no time to think of anything more as his mouth found hers, one hand cupping behind her head, the other loosening the laces of her bodice, seeking out the flesh of her breasts beneath. Briefly, she hoped he would not be disappointed – her body was no longer so young and lean as it was. She had softened with years and childbirth, and was rounder now. But if he cared he showed no sign of it, his desire for her bright and hard, and as he laid her back across the bed, lifting her skirts, her own passion rose to answer his, fingers grasping the still-strong muscles of his back beneath his shift, legs parting, hunger in her kiss.

Her back arched with the pleasure as he entered her and they moved together on the bed, quick and passionate and urgent, his muscles hard and firm in her hands as she remembered them, beautiful in his strength. When it was over, he lay against her with the weight of his body, their faces touching, and she remembered how much she had loved him. Tears formed behind her eyes for all the loveless years that they had lived apart, and as she tried to blink them away, Nick lifted his weight onto his forearms and looked down into her face, tucking back the strands of loosened hair. 'Don't cry,' he whispered. 'We're here now, together ...'

She sniffed and nodded and lifted her mouth to kiss him, gentle now, every touch of him delicious and perfect. Then as he finally withdrew and lay down beside her, the tears came harder. Nick held her to him and her head rested on the firm muscles of his shoulder, her fingers caressing his chest. She could feel his lips against her hair, and finally she lifted her head to look at him.

'Forgive me,' she said. 'It's been such a long time since I loved ...'

'For me too,' he replied with a smile, fingertips tracing the tears from her cheeks.

'Your wife ...?' she ventured.

He shook his head, a wry smile curling his mouth. 'Not since Judith was begotten. And even then, there was little pleasure in it.'

'Puritans ...'

'There was always more to it than her faith,' he said. 'Though that's part of it. She hated me, and still does, for being the man who took her innocence and fathered her child, and for being a man she cannot understand. So she's devoted her life to nursing that hatred, and ensuring our children hate me too. I've not seen our son these many years.'

'She must have loved you once.'

'Until she found herself with child and had to marry me.' He combed back her hair from her forehead with his fingers once again, tender and wonderful. She could have lain there forever in the warmth of his affection.

'And you?' he said then. 'What was your marriage like?'

'We never hated each other,' she replied. 'It was always polite. But it was cold and without love, nothing but the fact of our marriage between us. So I gave all my love to Toby.'

'He is so like Tom ...'

She gave him a rueful laugh. 'Yes. And I fear for him because of it.'

The mention of Tom's name broke the moment's perfection – Nick had hated her brother, and a shiver of darkness settled between them. He rolled away from her to stare up at the ceiling and she felt the distance open up.

'I still think of it sometimes,' Nick said. 'Those days of madness, all of us in thrall to some dark bewitchment.' He turned his head on the pillow to look at her. 'Do you still ... are you still ...?' He trailed off, unable to utter the words.

'Am I still a witch?' She finished the question for him with blunt directness.

He nodded.

'I gave it up when Tom died,' she said. 'I lost the heart for it. I still have my herbs, of course, a little healing here and there, but no, I no longer call to Hecate under the moon, and I've not scried since the day I foretold for Master Shakespeare.' When it all began, she thought, when she saw the spectre of death that set them on a path they could not turn from.

'Do you miss it?'

She gave a half-laugh, surprised by the question, and realised he understood her better than she thought. 'Sometimes,' she answered. Witchcraft had been her faith, her connection to the world of spirits and the light that gave life meaning. But she had shared that light and faith with Tom, and when he left she could not bring herself to visit it again. She regretted it now, a void inside her all these years that the spirits might have filled, a darkness too long unlit by the joy her witchcraft once had given her.

'Perhaps you should take it up again,' he said, as though he were reading her mind.

'I thought you hated that part of me.'

'I used to think so too, and I blamed it for everything that happened. But I know now that there were other forces at work, some power of evil that was woken by the play.'

Macbeth, he meant, the play she had warned Master Shakespeare to abandon.

'You've played it since?'

'Many times, and I've hated it always. Something dark hangs around the playhouse each time those fateful hags come onstage, and always I wait for the worst.'

She was silent, remembering that first production, the fate of the play entangled with her fate and Tom's, the link inextricable, destined. The writing of it opened doors to forces better left undisturbed, and Tom had paid the price. Then, tearing her thoughts from the pain of the past, she turned once more to the man beside her in bed. 'What happens now?' she asked. 'Is this to be our life?'

'Is that what you wish?'

'I don't want to be alone any more,' she replied. 'And you … I always loved you, Nick.'

He observed her, green eyes intent on her face as if unsure he should believe her. 'You loved Tom more, I think.'

She swallowed. 'Tom was part of me, in my core: it was a connection bound in blood and darkness and magic. I had no choice but to love him. But the love I bore for you was the natural love of a woman for a man, an earthly love. We would have made each other happy if fate had given us the chance.'

He was silent, considering her words. She had been as honest as she dared, and though the force of her love for Tom would burn inside her always, scorching and painful, urging her towards her death to meet with him again, she knew it could live alongside her love for Nick as it had once before, and the joy they could give each other.

She waited, hope pulsing with the beats of her heart, and it seemed an age before he rolled onto his side to face her once again. He said nothing, but lifted his hand to caress the line of her cheek, and shifted forward to kiss her. She moved into his arms, limbs light with the pleasure of his touch as his mouth moved down across her neck and her breasts, tongue and teeth teasing the delicate skin of her belly, and on down till she lost herself once more in the ecstasy of his embrace.

This was her life now, and she was glad.

Chapter Eight

A DEED WITHOUT A NAME

❧

In the early evening of a lazy day, Mary flirted with a party of gentlemen. They had noticed her fingers and each of them wanted a turn to touch.

'Such a good firm grip,' one of them said.

'Such dexterity ...'

'You should play an instrument ...' And the rest of them guffawed at his wit.

Later, she guessed, she would play them all in turn: easy money to beat off a trio of rich young men who enjoyed the novelty of six fingers round their cocks.

One of them, the ringleader of the group who seemed to be some kind of lord, cocksure and arrogant, took her hand and slid the extra finger into his mouth, his tongue wrapping warm and wet around it. After a moment he let it go with a laugh. 'A tasty wench indeed!' he pronounced, and she suppressed the urge to wipe his spittle from her fingers on her skirts.

The others laughed again, and briefly she scanned the room above their heads, always wary, always alert. But her gaze landed on Toby, watching her from his place at a table close by the door. He smiled and raised his cup, and with his attention she felt the colour flush her neck, her breathing quicken. Instinctively, she wiped her hand across her skirt, then turned to make her excuses to the gentlemen.

One of them lunged to grab her as she went, but she twisted away from him with practised deftness, and though she was aware of the abuse they hurled at her back as she left them, and the trouble she would catch from Madam, she did not care. She would serve Toby instead and it would not be work. She sashayed across the floor towards him, hips swaying, breasts tilted upward, a coy smile on her lips, and though she saw Toby rise from his seat and heard the beginnings of the shouted warning, she wasn't quick enough to avoid the blow to the side of her head that came from behind her and sent her crashing to the floor.

'Don't you turn your back on me, whore!'

She spun on the boards to see her attacker, and scrabbled backwards away from him. She could feel the blood that trickled from her nose, and briefly she pressed it with the back of her hand. Her head was swimming and her vision blurred, but she could still see enough to know the man was standing over her, and she braced herself for the kick to her guts that he threatened. But it did not come. Instead she heard Toby's voice, loud in the sudden hush that had fallen over the room, all eyes turned to the unfolding drama.

'Leave her be.'

He had moved in close to the gentleman, and the knife he wore at his belt was unsheathed and in his hand, ready.

'What's it to you?' The gentleman stepped back instinctively, one hand reaching to search for the sword at his hip. But Toby's knife was close to his guts and so he let the hand drop. His mouth was ugly with defeat and he was breathing hard. 'She's just a whore.'

'Get out!' Toby said. 'All of you.'

The three men took their time to leave, sauntering as if they were leaving of their own free will, desperate to retain their dignity before the crowd that was watching. At the door one of them turned and threw coins into the straw at Toby's feet for the ale they had drunk. Then they stepped out into the night and the door slammed shut behind them. Toby squatted down next to Mary.

'Are you hurt?'

She pushed herself up to sit, head reeling with the movement, and he touched a gentle finger to her face, wiping away the ooze of blood. Her cheek was already swollen and sore where the blow had landed, and her head throbbed where she had hit it when she fell. The world around her seemed very far away. She said nothing, unsure how to answer, and he waited, watching her with eyes that even in her haze seemed very blue.

'Can you stand?'

He put an arm across her back and helped her to her feet as she staggered against him, head still woozy. But he held her fast, supporting her weight against his body, and though she felt as though she were falling, as in a dream, she was not afraid, sure that Toby would catch her. One of the other girls came to see.

'Help me take her to her bed,' he said to her, and between them they half carried, half dragged her up the wooden staircase to her room. Then they laid her down, and when they had made her comfortable Toby sat on the edge of the bed and placed a hand on her shoulder.

'My mother is a healer,' he said. 'I'll bring her.'

She tried to nod, but with the movement pain shivered through her.

'Stay with her,' he said to the other girl, and then he was gone, hurrying homeward through the darkening evening.

Later, Sarah halted outside the brothel with a hand on Toby's arm. She had come here once before, she remembered, long ago, searching for her brother, though she had no memory of why. To warn him of their father's wrath, perhaps? It had been at the very beginning, she recalled, when the world of Bankside was still unknown to her and she had been afraid.

She ran her eyes across the front – the peeling whitewash that was turning grey, and the painted letters that were large enough to see from a boat on the water. The Cardinal's Cap. Then, turning with a nod and smile to her son, they stepped forward and she followed him inside through the tangle of tables and stools, winding amongst the hum of drinkers' conversations and the high laughs of the whores. Though it had been many years since she inhabited this world, it still felt like home, and she would not have been surprised to see the Company of players with Will Shakespeare in their midst and her brother, Tom.

Upstairs, the girl was lying in the bed as Toby had left her, but she was alone and even in the light of the solitary candle that flickered by the bed, her eyes seemed unnaturally bright against a ghostly pallor. She was shivering.

'I need more light,' she said to Toby, and he turned and left to find candles.

'Mary?' She took the girl's hand in hers and the skin was clammy and cold. She took off her cloak and laid it over the top of the covers. 'My name is Sarah Chyrche. I have some knowledge of healing and I'm here to help you. Can you talk?'

Mary mumbled something that Sarah could not catch. Running skilled fingers across the girl's head, examining, she found the swelling lump beneath her hair. With her touch Mary flinched.

'Forgive me,' Sarah said, 'but I need to find where you're hurt.'

Mary said nothing, eyelids flickering as she drifted in and out of half-consciousness. A thin ooze of blood still trickled from her nose, and Sarah rummaged in her basket, though it was hard to see the different vials in the gloom. Then Toby returned with more candles, and she found the oil of cypress she was looking for, sprinkled drops on a cotton pad and held it to Mary's face.

'This will stop the bleeding,' she said.

Drops of arnica to Mary's temples and her neck – vapours to help with shock, and a cold compress of hyssop and comfrey to ease the swelling. Then Sarah took the girl's hand again in her own and noticed the extra finger. She flicked a look to Toby, who was sitting now on the other side of the bed, a comforting hand on Mary's shoulder.

'They told her as a child that she belonged to the Devil,' he said.

A long-forgotten memory filtered through Sarah's mind of a six-fingered child she had helped her mother to deliver many years ago, and she recalled the woman's curse before she abandoned it. Could it be the same girl? Sarah wondered. Perhaps. She would be about the same age.

Mary shuddered and though the room was quite warm, they could hear her teeth chattering. There was nowhere to light a fire, and there seemed to be no more blankets amongst the sparse furnishings.

'Lie beside her,' Sarah said to Toby. 'Warm her.'

Toby obeyed without question, sliding under the covers and holding Mary close. As the girl nestled in his arms, Sarah wondered how many times before he had lain in this bed, if Mary was a favourite or if they had only just met. It was hard to think of her son lying with whores, and she dragged her mind away from the images that threatened.

Mary's shivering eased with Toby's warmth against her, and as her eyelids closed in a more peaceful rest, Sarah shifted from the edge of the bed and sat on the stool beside it, watching awhile. Beyond the door she could hear the laughter and shouts of couples, and footsteps in the passageway, but the girl slept on, content, and her skin slowly began to lose its clamminess. Next to her, Toby seemed to doze too, his eyes closed, his breathing soft and deep. She smiled to see it – she had always loved to watch him sleep as a child.

Outside the window the bells at St Saviour's tolled the hour, the chimes lifting and fading in the breeze, and Toby stirred, eyes flicking open, taking a moment to remember where he was. Then he saw his mother and smiled. 'Will she be all right?'

Sarah nodded. 'Yes. I think we can leave her now to rest. I'll come back in the morning to see how she does.'

Gently, so as not to disturb her, Toby slipped from the bed and rearranged the blankets to keep her warm. Then, with a backward glance towards the sleeping girl, they stepped out through the door and into the passage. A whore and her partner slid them a curious look as they passed, and then they were out on the street where the heady smell of the river and a damp autumn mist wrapped them in their clasp.

Toby walked with his mother towards home, her arm linked through his, moving carefully through the dark, and though he had planned to be at Alexander's an hour ago, he could not leave her to face the dangers of the night-time streets alone.

'You are fond of her?' Sarah was asking.

He smiled. 'A little. But she is just a whore, after all. And not a girl to love.'

'Still, I am proud of you for caring for her, for fetching me. It was an act of kindness.'

'Like you say,' he replied. 'I'm fond of her.'

He saw her to the door of the house and said farewell.

'You're going back to see her? She needs to rest.'

'Not to her. To see a friend.'

For a moment she observed him, head tilted to one side in consideration so that he thought she was going to ask more, but then she wished him a good night and turned away. When the door had shut behind her, he strode back towards the river, towards his meeting with Alexander. In all the events of the evening there had been little time to think of it, but now his thoughts gathered into focus as his heart knocked briskly in his chest. His breath came quick with expectation, and with fear. The book he had left at home, instinctively reluctant to bring it near to Alexander.

He found the place with ease. The ground floor, with its doors flung open to the street, still housed a down-at-heel alehouse as he remembered. Like many another drinking hole it was a widow's shop, an old lady trying to make a living. A single group of men were playing cards in silence at a table, and they paid him no mind as he walked past them and put his foot upon the stairs, climbing the steep wooden steps that wound through the dark to the attic, past the closed doors to a dozen rented rooms. At the top of the stairs he paused for a moment on the small wooden landing to regain his breath before he knocked on the single door in front of him.

'It's open.' Alexander's voice called out from inside. 'Come in.'

Toby turned the handle and entered, and the quickness of his heartbeat owed nothing to the stairs.

Inside was brightly lit with candles, and the window was open to the night sky where a wan half-moon peeped through shifting clouds. The night breeze set the candles to fluttering, and in the ever-changing shadows they cast it was hard to see the edges of the room around him in any detail. But in the centre a large table was covered in papers and books, and in the far corner was a narrow bed. A large empty space occupied the floor where he stood now, and the old man was seated on a stool at the table with a book open before him, his fingers following the lines of the words. Toby ducked his head to pass beneath the roof beams that crisscrossed above him as he moved further into the room.

'I thought you had changed your mind,' Alexander said, lifting his eyes briefly from his study. ''Tis late.'

'There was some trouble at the brothel,' he said. 'I stayed to help.'

'Ah. I see. The six-fingered whore.'

Toby said nothing, not daring to wonder how the old man knew. He waited, senses alert, wary. He was still uncertain what might lie before him, and his throat was dry with nerves.

'So!' Alexander closed his book with a snap, and turned on the stool to face his visitor. Toby swallowed.

'You wish to learn the way to win a woman's love.' He tilted his head. 'Am I right?'

He nodded.

'And she will not come of her own accord?'

'My company is forbidden to her. Her mother is Puritan ...'

'But she would be willing otherwise?'

He hesitated. Judith was fervent in her own faith. But he had seen the desire in her eyes when he kissed her, and he knew that she wanted him, in spite of that faith. 'She desires me,' he said.

The master nodded. 'And you are prepared to obey me in my teaching?'

Toby swallowed, unsure what such obedience would mean.

'Your father was willing.' He paused as if remembering. 'And he was an apt and eager pupil, though he was younger than you are now of course, and reckless with his youth … But you have his eyes and his beauty, and you've been touched by the spirits as he was.'

'I will obey,' he said, but there were slivers of doubt in his thoughts: his father's willingness had led to his death, and for a heartbeat he thought of running. But the life that waited for him at the tailor's shop was no life at all: the man he had once called his father had been shrunken, hunched, miserable – all the days of his life bent over a workbench. What, really, did he have to lose?

'Will you swear in blood?' The dagger in the old man's hand was richly wrought: the ruby in the hilt caught the candlelight and glimmered.

For the space of a breath Toby hesitated, afraid to bind his fate to the sorcerer's. Then he held out his hand and the blade sliced through the flesh on his palm to drip into the cup Alexander was holding.

'Do you swear to obey me?'

'I swear.'

The old man cut his own hand, and they watched the blood mingle before they each lifted the cup to their lips and drank. With the first taste of the blood on his lips, he felt the changing quiver of energy inside him, a nascent power, a connection to something beyond himself he did not understand. Alexander gave a small laugh of recognition, and Toby met the laugh with a smile. He was ready for whatever lay ahead.

They spent the night in preparation. Casting the circle, Toby learned the words that would protect them from the daemons they would conjure as he chalked out the symbols around the circle's edge. As he wrote each one, Alexander explained its meaning and its purpose in the rite to follow. Toby murmured the sacred phrases over and over beneath his breath, committing them to memory, and their power began to flicker in his mind, lighting his thoughts with a new and unexpected understanding.

When the circle was ready at last, they retired to a washstand in the corner to wash and purify themselves, and as they stood naked beside each other, Toby was aware of the lust in the old man's eyes, and the twitch of his cock with desire. He turned his head away and forced himself to focus on his own ablutions. But he wondered if the nakedness was truly a part of the rite or merely a whim of the old man's to feed his appetites. He could feel Alexander's attention, the burn of his gaze against his thighs and buttocks. Was it for this the old man had agreed to teach him, for the promise of a fuck? What about purification? The cut on his hand stung with the touch of the water.

Clean and dry, still naked, they entered the circle at last, and he knelt as he was told to do beside the quill, inks and parchment that the old man had prepared. Made from the skin of a female dog, Alexander had told him, though it seemed much like any other piece of parchment to Toby. Then he listened as the sorcerer paced the boundary of the circle, cutting the air before him with the blade of the knife, words of Latin prayer tumbling from his lips. Toby strained to understand, striving to recall the grammars of his school days, and though many of the words were unknown to him, he understood enough to follow the meaning.

'When we enter herein with all humility, let God Almighty enter into this Circle by the entrance of eternal happiness. Let all daemons fly from his place, especially those who are opposed to this Work, and let the Angels of Peace assist and protect this Circle, and let discord and strife fly and depart ... Sanctify, O Lord our God, our humble entry herein ...'

Then Alexander too was on his knees, head bowed in mumbled prayers that seemed to have no end. Toby's attention threatened to wander. Thoughts of Mary. Thoughts of Judith. Thoughts of Tom.

Finally, the sorcerer raised his head and the work began.

'On the parchment,' Alexander said, 'draw the naked body of the woman.'

He did as he was told, and the figure that he drew surprised him in its likeness. He felt his own lust begin to rise.

'In your own blood write these words …'

Taking up the knife, he cut the other palm, flinching with the pain of it, and dripped the blood once more into the cup where it mixed with the ink. Then he wrote, *I draw Judith Tooley, whom I wish to have, in the name of these spirits …*

Inscribing the names of each daemon, he touched drops of his blood to her head and her limbs and her heart as he called out to the spirit that governed each part of her body. Then he began the conjuration Alexander had taught him while they were preparing. The words came easily, his whole being focused, blood surging in his veins with an unfamiliar power. He raised his head to the realms beyond his sight.

'I conjure you, all you daemons inscribed on this image, by your lords to whom you are bound in obedience, that you should inflame Judith Tooley to love of me, so that day and night she will think of me and hope for me, until she fulfils my will with ardor. As your names are fixed on this image, may you dwell in her as you dwell herein, until I have had my desire of her.

'I conjure you daemons to whom is given the power to seduce and bind in the love of men to make it so …'

And so it was done.

He turned to Alexander, his body pulsing with energy, as if he could leap a hundred feet in the air or run a hundred miles and never tire, filled with a lust for life he had never known before. He wanted to race and dance and fly all at once, his blood singing with celebration.

The old man grinned. 'And now you begin to understand …'

He laughed. 'Indeed I do.' Then, energy started to slide to desire and his cock began to stiffen. He said, 'How long must I wait?'

It was Alexander's turn to laugh. 'Next time you see her …'

'May I bring her here?' In his passion he could think of nowhere else they might go.

'Of course, though the bed is narrow.'

Toby cast a look to the bed, then at the circle around them. He said, 'But the floor is spacious ...'

They sat awhile, still in the circle, basking in the aftermath of the rite until finally the sun crested the edge of the skylight and flooded the room with a sudden warmth.

Exchanging a final smile of complicity, they both got to their feet, and the old man's knees cracked loudly in protest. Opening the circle with a gesture of his knife and words that Toby did not hear, Alexander stepped outside of it, and as Toby followed him to the basin in the corner where they had left their clothes, he was conscious that Alexander's eyes never left his nakedness, but he no longer cared. He would have let the sorcerer take him if he'd wanted, desire for life in all its forms flooding through his limbs, an awareness of the sacredness of everything in Heaven, on earth and in Hell.

After they had dressed they went downstairs together, and Toby's guts growled with hunger. The alehouse was closed, too early yet for customers, but a boy in the street was selling pies that were still warm from the baker's oven, and the sweet scent of meat and pastry seemed to Toby like manna from God. He bought two and, bidding farewell to Alexander as the old man went away to who knew where, he stood in the street to eat them beneath a warm autumn sun that lit the edges of the clouds.

In the street, all of Bankside seemed to be abroad. He shifted back into the lea of the alehouse to let a carter drive a flea-bitten horse along the lane, and watched as two children tried to catch a hen that had got away. Its squawking filled the morning, and a dog, tied to a post, snarled and barked, throwing itself against the length of its rope. A couple of whores wove homeward, their make-up smeared, skirts askew. One of them had lost a shoe. They grinned at Toby as they passed, and briefly he was tempted, hunger for life still beating through his blood. But he wanted Judith more and though he had no plan of how to see her, he stuffed the last of the pie in his mouth, wiped his lips with the back of his hand, and set off through the bustle of the morning towards her house.

Chapter Nine

WHERE THE WILD THYME BLOWS

he sun was already high when Mary woke, a square of light behind the curtain at the window, but the brothel was quiet beyond her door. She liked the peace of the mornings when half of Bankside was still asleep, though mostly she too was taking her rest after a night at her trade. Drifting in the languor of her sleep, she let her mind come slowly to wakefulness, and then she remembered: the gentlemen, Toby, his mother. With the memory her head began to throb, and she lifted gentle fingers to probe the swelling on her face, wincing with the pain of it. She could feel the split lip with her tongue. Later, she would look at her face in the glass and try to judge the damage, but for now it was enough to feel the tenderness. She would be wearing the bruises for a while, she guessed, but the world at least was clear again. She turned lazily in the bed and stretched, then settled down to sleep some more.

The next time she woke was to find Sarah at her bedside. She sat up quickly, disliking the sense of helplessness that came with lying in bed, and the sudden movement sent a slice of pain across her head. She blinked to clear the blur from her vision, and waited for the pounding to subside.

'You slept well?' Sarah asked.

She nodded, carefully, and the knock settled into a dull aching throb.

'Here.' Sarah passed her a cold compress. 'Press this to your cheek awhile, it will help.'

Mary took it and held it to her face. It was icy cold against her skin, and she shivered as Sarah sat back and observed her. The look was not unkind but it was still an appraisal of sorts, and Mary shifted her gaze away, resentful of the scrutiny.

Sarah said, 'Toby tells me you were cursed at birth. Because of your hand.'

Mary lifted her hand to examine it, turning it this way and that. Each finger was perfect and as a child she had often wondered which one the Devil had claimed as his. 'They told me at the orphanage it was a sign I belonged to the Devil,' she said, raising her eyes to Sarah with a rueful smile.

'Did you believe them?'

'For a while,' Mary answered. It was hard to form the words through the swelling of her lip. 'Sometimes I still do. But there was a lady that used to visit me when I was just a girl who told me I belonged not to the Devil but to Hecate, and once or twice she took me to the forest.'

Sarah smiled. 'I think the lady was my mother.'

Mary stared, the ache in her head forgotten. There had been times through the years when she thought the lady had been no more than a trick of her mind, a child's desperate dream of escape. But now she knew for sure it had been no trick, and the knowledge aroused a warmth inside. She tried to smile and flinched.

'She and I brought you into the world,' Sarah said. 'It was my mother that took you to the orphanage when your own mother cast you away.'

'What happened to her? Your mother?'

'She died,' Sarah said, and slid her gaze away, sadness in her eyes.

'She promised to teach me herblore when I was older,' Mary said. 'And healing. But she never came back after that, and I missed her. She was the only person who ever showed me kindness.' And now her daughter was here and offering Mary the same benevolence. Toby's mother. Surely the connection was fated. With a rush of sudden hope, Mary said, 'Will you teach me in her place?'

She saw the older woman's face close down, and the instinct to refuse.

'Please?'

Sarah hesitated, eyes searching across the much-darned coverlet and the bare boards of the floor for an answer. Had she asked too much? Mary wondered, and she waited, barely daring to breathe.

'Please?'

Sarah raised her gaze to meet hers, and with sigh and a smile, she nodded. 'Very well. I'll teach you what I know.' Then she said, 'Do you feel well enough to walk a ways this morning?'

Mary shrugged. The prospect of a walk held little appeal. The yew tree in the forest was the furthest from Bankside that she had ever ventured. 'To where?'

'To my garden, to see the herbs. It isn't far. And we may as well start straight away.'

She hesitated: she had not thought to begin so soon. Then, understanding the privilege she was being offered, she forced her mouth into a smile. 'I would like that very much.'

'Then get yourself dressed,' Sarah said, 'and I'll meet you outside.'

Mary watched as Sarah got up from the bed, intrigued by this handsome woman in her fine wool dress, so out of place in the brothel, and wondering why she had agreed. But Mary had learned long ago to take kindness without question when she found it, so as soon as the door had snapped shut, she swung her legs out of bed, poured some fresh water from the jug into the little washbasin and began to make her ablutions.

They strolled from Bankside, enjoying the fine autumn sunshine, the cool breeze. It was a beautiful day: bright puffy clouds scudded across a sky as blue as Toby's eyes, and there was a freshness in the air that blew from the river, the creak and thud and splash of the boats still in their ears even when they turned their backs to the water to cut through the market. They trod carefully, lifting their skirt hems to step over the refuse and mud that littered the path. The air was ripe with the stink of meat and fish, and rowdy with the shouts of the traders vying for their business as they passed. The ache in Mary's head shifted forward.

But they did not hurry, content to wander through the morning, and in time they turned off the High Street at a church she had never been inside, to walk along a lane of well-to-do houses with shops that faced the street. At the tailor's shop they stopped, and the sign swung above them with a creak in the breeze. Toby's shop. A shiver of pleasure at his nearness rippled through her: she had never thought to be a guest in his house.

Her eyes were drawn irresistibly to the shop, and as Sarah opened up the door to the house, she wondered if she would see him today, and how he would be in his life away from the brothel. Most men would shun a whore if they met her anywhere else, reluctant to admit to their pleasures in the broad light of real life. The brothel was a world of its own, and men entered it to escape their day-to-day lives – wives, children, business, hardship, all forgotten in the seamy pleasures of the stews. Would Toby be any different? It was hard to say. Forcing her mind away from thoughts of him, she followed Sarah along the dim passage, where the air was sweetly scented with the herbs that were woven into the mats underfoot.

The garden behind the house was wondrous – she had never seen so many herbs, such a profusion of scent and colour, and she wandered between them along the stepping stone paths, just brushing the leaves with her fingertips as she passed, and gathering a residue of fragrance in the weave of her skirts that she would catch at odd moments much later, bringing her back from wherever she might be to the memory of this moment in the garden. She had never imagined that a garden could be so beautiful.

Sarah smiled at her delight. 'It was my mother's garden first – I learned to help her tend it as a girl. She taught me well and I've grown it in the years since then.'

The straight-backed woman, Mary thought, who had led her to the forest as a child and told her stories of Hecate. Had she told her daughter the same wondrous tales? She wanted to ask, eager to learn spellcraft as well as herbs, but she did not dare – the label of *witch* was not to be suggested lightly, and the daughter may not have followed in all her mother's footsteps.

Sarah said, 'Are there any you recognise?'

Mary turned slowly in the midst of the garden, running her eyes across the myriad plants around her, searching for something she knew. Seeing nothing, she followed the path a little way to a bed that was sheltered by a low stone wall, basking in the morning sun. She pointed to a bush that seemed familiar. She reached a hand to touch it, then lifted her fingers to her face. The sweet scent filled her senses. 'Rosemary?'

Sarah nodded. 'A herb of protection. We use the oil for fevers,' she said, 'and to clean a cut.'

The girl nodded her understanding, and as they wandered through the beds, Mary was delighted with how many of the leaves she recognised. Kitchen herbs mostly, familiar from the cook's store at the brothel, or the market. And with each one, the older woman explained a little of its use.

At last they came upon a bench with a wall at its back, and a crab apple tree that swayed in the breeze of the autumn morning, dappling them with its shade as they sat side by side in the warmth. Sarah said, 'What is it you would learn first of all?'

'How best to prevent a child,' Mary said, without hesitation. It was the first fear of all whores: the orphanage was full of the ill-begotten offspring from the Bankside brothels. Her own birth, she guessed, had been the same, and though she had been lucky so far, there were other girls who had been less fortunate.

'Come,' Sarah said, 'I'll show you.'

She got up and Mary followed her through to the end of the garden and a low cottage almost hidden by the foliage. Inside, the place was filled with herbs hung from the rafters to dry, and bottles and jars, and pots and tools and a hundred other bits and pieces that made Mary laugh with pleasure as she wandered through the gloom. Her fingers brushed along the shelves before she turned to Sarah in delight, her sore head all but forgotten.

Just before noon, the two women returned to the house to take their lunch. A simple meal – cold pork with bread and cheese, some beans from the garden in a butter sauce. Toby and the tailors from the shop came to join them at the big table in the kitchen, and she had to turn her face away to hide the blush of pleasure his company aroused. The other men turned glances of curiosity her way, and she wondered what they thought of her – a battered harlot at their master's table – but neither Sarah nor Toby offered them an explanation. She had paid Toby little mind through the morning, her attention fully wrapped in the herbs, but now he was sitting right before her and all her thoughts were filled with him.

He was different, though, from what she knew of him at the brothel. More serious and sober, master tailor and head of the household, and though he met her eyes more than once across the table, there was little more in his glance than a kind and passing interest.

What had she expected? she scolded herself. That he would flirt and make love to her before his mother and his workers? She was a Bankside whore for God's sake, and just to be in his house was a rare privilege she had no right to expect. Disappointment heaved in her gut and robbed her of her appetite, even though she knew she was being absurd, and she spent the whole meal unaware of the conversation, head bowed to the table to hide her face and the feelings she was sure were written plain across it.

In the afternoon, she wandered back towards the brothel with the little paper parcel of herbs clutched to her chest, her new knowledge light inside her. The day had grown cool. A ponderous bank of clouds that was heavy with rain had rolled in from the east and obscured the warm sun that had lit up the morning. She was in no hurry to go home. Her day at the Chyrche house had shown her a different way of life – the beauty of the garden with its abundance of herbs, dinner in a family kitchen. Simple, wholesome pleasures that exposed the void at the heart of her life in the bawdy house, where life was cheap and the cheer was ephemeral.

For the brothel was not real life for the men who came there. There, a man could be king for an hour or a night with a girl to do his bidding, his pleasure paramount, and all his worldly cares forgotten. It was only real life for the girls who lived there, and until today she hadn't truly understood. Now all she wanted was escape – a garden of her own to tend, a kitchen table, and a man who was not ashamed to smile at her.

Toby, she thought. She wanted Toby, and the life that he could give her.

Chapter Ten

THIS PRETTY TOY CALL'D MAIDENHEAD

🙰

Toby went that night to the brothel, and found Mary by the fireplace with her face turned to the wall to hide the swelling and bruises that were turning now to livid purple and yellow-edged, her right eye half-closed in spite of the compresses his mother had given her. It was early yet, the lull between the workers who sought brief pleasures on their journey home from work – a cup of ale and a meal, perhaps a quick fuck – and the more serious seekers of pleasure who spent whole nights in its pursuit.

He sat beside her and called for ale, and a boy he had not seen before with grubby hands and a stupid smile placed it down so carelessly it slopped and spilled, dripping off the edge of the table. Toby moved his legs out of its path and shook his head, eliciting a wry smile from Mary. She was pleased to see him, he knew from the flush that coloured her unbruised cheek and the way she would not meet his eyes. Her coyness aroused him – different from the usual flirting of a whore, a shyness born of feelings that seemed genuine. Was it love? he wondered. Or was he simply a favoured customer? He could not say. But she had been treading through his thoughts all the afternoon since he sat across from her at dinner, distracting him from work, and the memory of the sweetness of her mouth around his cock had made the hours seem long till he could be with her again.

He drained a cup of ale, then reached to take her hand. 'Bed?' he said, and she nodded her acquiescence as though he had asked her for a dance, giving him her hand with a flourish.

They wove between the tables towards the staircase, passing a game of cards where an argument was beginning to flare. A pretty young whore was draped across the oldest player. A fat man, and ugly, with greasy hair and rotting teeth. No wonder Mary was eager to take him, Toby, to her bed, when such men as that were the alternative. Briefly he pictured it, the young girl beneath the grunting man, but the image revolted him and he shook it away, turning his mind again to the woman who was holding his hand, her hips swaying on the stairs before his face. Anticipation flared through his limbs as heat, and the slow tread up the steps behind her was sweet torture.

In the room she knelt at once before him, fingers deft to undo his breeches, mouth warm around him, hands caressing in the pleasure he had dreamed of through the day. But when his legs threatened to give way beneath him, he drew her back up to standing and took her to the bed.

Afterward they lay together, her head on his shoulder and her hand resting lightly on his chest, while his fingers traced the lines of the scars across her back. For all the world like lovers, he thought; he had never lain so with a whore before. Mostly, he couldn't wait to leave their company, lust sated, the business done. But with Mary it was different: the sex was only part of the transaction.

'Tell me about your girl at church,' she said then, lifting her head from his shoulder to look at him.

He turned to her in surprise. 'For why?'

She shrugged. 'I'm curious to know what kind of woman you like.'

'You know what kind.' He lifted his hand to smooth back the hair from her face, tucking it behind her shoulder.

'I know what kind of whore you use to please you. But that's a different thing … This is not real life for you.'

He gave her a half-smile, unsure what more to say. She was right, of course: Mary belonged to a different world, and she was as different from Judith as two women could be.

'So,' she persisted. 'Tell me about her.'

He laughed then and rolled in the bed to face her, their faces close on the pillow. What could he tell her of Judith? He thought of the parchment drawing that was imbued with his blood and hanging now at the window in his chamber at home to catch the breeze so that its power would be carried on the air. Had she felt the effects of it yet? he wondered. Had the spirit he had conjured begun to fill her up with desire for him? Even in the bed with Mary, a warmth filled his groin at the thought of it, desire beginning to stir.

'She is very unlike you,' he said, and Mary turned her head away to hide the hurt, biting her lip, so that he regretted his words immediately. 'I mean that she is dark-haired,' he said quickly, 'and olive-skinned, and her body is boyish: lean and strong.'

But he said nothing of the quick intelligence in the near-black eyes and the fullness of her lips, the pleasure of the touch of her hand against his, nor the passion of her love of God. He had watched her often when he should have been at prayer, excited by her fervency: such passion turned towards a man would surely be a gift.

'But she has been forbidden to speak with me,' he said, 'so I think there is little future for us.' The lie was instinctive. Mary's jealousy was clear in her question, and though she was a whore, he had no wish to hurt her. So he made no mention of the hopes he still nurtured, nor of the magic to achieve them.

'Forbidden why?'

'A Puritan mother …'

'Even a Puritan girl must wed.'

He gave her a wry smile. But the truth was that being forbidden, he wanted her more.

'Do you love her?' Mary asked, and though her tone was light and casual, he understood the gravity of the question.

'I don't know,' he replied, which was the truth. Desire, regard, hope for a future together: did these things equate to love? It was hard to say. Perhaps when he had lain with her and tasted the sweetness of her flesh he would know more surely.

'I need a wife,' he said. 'I'm a householder now, a master tailor ...'

'And you think a Puritan wife will bring you happiness?' She wrinkled her nose in distaste. 'Those people find their only joy in God – they take no pleasure in the world. Your marriage bed will be a loveless place.'

He was silent, aware there may be truth in Mary's words. But still he wanted her, his desire for Judith hard and bright. Soon the magic would do its work, he thought, and her passion would turn from thoughts of God to him. Then he would teach her the joys of earthly love, God-given pleasures to be shared by a man and a woman.

'You'll regret it,' Mary said.

'Perhaps.' He shrugged.

Then he lowered his head to kiss her, slid his body over hers, and in the pleasure Mary gave him, Judith was all but forgotten.

In the morning Toby went early to church but not to pray. Taking a seat on a bench with his back to the wall, he kept his eyes fixed on the door, hoping Judith had got the message he had bribed the servant to give to her, and that she would come.

It was cold in the church, but the morning light fell pleasingly through the unadorned windows, bars of sunlight striping the flagstones. With a shiver, he got to his feet and moved to stand in the warm shafts of light, but his gaze never left the door, and he willed her to walk through it, muscles tense with nerves. Finally, when the bell had chimed the half hour and he was sure she would not come, the door opened at last with a groan of misshapen wood as it dragged on the stone floor beneath it. He held his breath when a slim form squeezed through the gap and then he saw that it was her.

Relief surged through him, ripening swiftly to desire, and he stepped across the nave towards her with a smile of welcome.

She slid the hood of her cloak from her head, and her hair gleamed dark in the sunlight, but her face was stern and her mouth was set tight with an emotion he could not name. He stopped an arm's length away from her, and her eyes tracked his movements, wary, like an animal at bay. He was aware of the rapid rise and fall of her chest, and his own breath quickened with anticipation. He reached a hand towards her, still smiling, reassuring, but she jerked back from his touch.

'Why have you summoned me here?' she demanded in a whisper. 'What do you want?'

Surprised by her hostility, he gave a small shrug in response. 'I wanted to see you,' he said. 'And I could think of no other way …'

'To see me why?' she asked, shaking her head. 'I am forbidden to meet with you. There can be nothing between us however much we wish for it …'

He answered quickly. 'You wish for it?'

She swung her head away from him, saying nothing, and he stepped in closer. This time she did not move away. Her skirts brushed against his leg, and the sweet scent of Castile soap filled him – the smell of her. Lifting a hand to her face, he turned it towards him, and for a moment they stood in the pause of his hesitation. He could feel the knock of his heartbeat in his chest, his breath coming quick. He turned his hand to let the backs of his fingers caress her cheek, and she tilted her head against his touch like a cat, a small smile beginning to soften the sternness. Then, running his hand behind her head to hold it gently, he lowered his mouth to hers for a kiss.

For a long moment she did not respond, her lips unmoving, and he wondered if she would still refuse him after all, but then she lifted her own hand to brush against his cheek and her mouth softened under his, tentative and uncertain, but no longer resisting. Her first proper kiss, he reminded himself, and though his blood roiled with desire, he forced himself to move gently and savour her innocence –

for all the force of his want for her, he had to remember to win her with softness.

A woman's shout that carried on the breeze from beyond the door brought them back to awareness of the day around them. She stepped away from him, her eyes searching his face as she tried to make sense of her pleasure in the kiss. He could see the puzzlement in her look, and he guessed she had come there to see him with a different intention. Smiling, he took her elbow in his hand and guided her across the nave and to the side door that led out into the graveyard beyond.

In the doorway she stopped abruptly and snatched her arm away from his hand, as though she had recovered from the shock of her desire for him. As she tipped her head back to look at him, he saw the passion of before had faded – there was only reluctance now in her eyes. Tread softly, he reminded himself. Give her no cause for fear.

'Where are you taking me?' she whispered, with a glance back inside the church. No one had come in. No one had seen them.

'Put your hood on,' he said. 'We'll walk awhile.'

For the moments of her hesitation, he held his breath, wondering if perhaps she would still find the will to refuse, before she finally lifted the cowl of her cloak over her head, taking time to adjust it so that it fell low across her forehead, her face well hidden, and he breathed again.

Then they stepped out of the gloom of the church and into the morning sun.

They walked southwards out of the city and towards the stretch of forest that bordered it. The life in the streets slowly dwindled as they cut through the city's outskirts, traders and shops giving way to fields where rows of women were bent double to harvest carrots and onions, their babies strapped to their backs. One of them was singing as she worked, and her voice carried clear and sweet through the cool autumn air with a mournful folk tune he did not recognise.

They had walked the same road together the day the tailor had died, when he had been still innocent of the truth, and Judith's mother had yet to discover whose son he was. Then, they had strolled in ease and friendliness, taking pleasure in discovery. They had talked of everything and nothing, and she had been bright with the pleasure of his company. Now, she would not look at him, eyes resolutely trained on the ground before their feet, and though he sensed her tension in the angle of her shoulders, he could not rightly read her feelings. It seemed a long way to walk in the unease of her silence, and when the notes of the folk song had faded in the air behind them, he was aware of the rapid swish of her skirts as she strode beside him, and the quick rise and fall of her chest.

They reached the shelter of the line of trees, sycamore and ash still green and verdant, the leaves not yet turning with the change of the season, and he felt the sudden breath of cool as they stepped beneath the canopy, the scent of dark earth and age in his nostrils as they followed the track further in. He had no thought for where they were going – last time they had halted in the lea of the forest edge, turning to sit and look back at the town – but instinct guided his steps. He had only ever lost his way once in these trees to spend a cold night curled at the roots of a tree, and he had no fear of it, in spite of the stories of ghosts and witches he had heard as a boy. They walked in single file, her footsteps quick and light behind him, and he could just hear the shush of her breath above the screech of a jay flying low overhead.

Finally, they came to a clearing. An ancient yew tree stood sentinel with low, gnarled branches that draped across the carpet of leaves at its roots. He stopped and looked around him, and though he knew he had never been there before, there was something familiar about it, something he liked. He turned and, behind him, Judith had slipped the hood from her head. The dappled light that filtered through the leaves lit the sleek darkness of her hair so that it glistened, and in the deep brown of her eyes he thought (hoped?) he saw a gleam of desire.

'I recognise this place,' he said, 'though I could swear I've never been here before.'

Judith shivered and hugged her arms together beneath her cloak. 'There is something strange about it …'

'I was here with my father …' he started to say, meaning Tom, his real father, which was impossible.

'A dream, perhaps?'

'Perhaps,' he answered, though he knew it had been more than a dream: the memory was visceral, in his blood. He shook his head to clear it of the thoughts, and ravelled his attention back to the girl.

In the freckled light he looked at her, and noticed for the first time the darkness of the skin beneath her eyes, her pallor, as though unwelcome dreams had kept her from her sleep. Reaching out his hand, he took her fingers in his and drew her closer to him. She took a willing step towards him, head tilted up, a smile at the edges of her lips that was almost coy.

'I have dreamed of you these last few nights,' she said.

Warmth shifted in his gut, and his fingers tightened on hers. A shard of the same power of life he had felt in the rite cut through his blood, and his body seemed to swell and grow, imbued with all the light and dark of the forest, the ancient knowledge of its age. 'What did you dream?'

She slanted her eyes away with a small half-laugh that delighted him. 'I cannot say.'

'No?' He touched his hand to her chin and turned her head back towards him. 'Why is that?'

She slid the tip of her tongue across her lips, a moment of hesitation, and her eyes remained restlessly away from his. He could feel the touch of the air on his skin, and the eyes of the spirits all around him.

'Tell me,' he coaxed.

'Dreams that have made me spend my days in prayer to beg for forgiveness …' She lifted one shoulder in a half-shrug.

'And has God forgiven you?'

'Ah, who can tell?' Then, with a sweep of her arm that encompassed the forest all around them, she said, 'Why have you brought me here?'

'You know why,' he answered.

She drew in a deep breath and lowered her eyes, searching the leaf-strewn earth at their feet as though to find an escape, but her hand remained in his. He stepped nearer, their fingers still entwined and their bodies almost touching. Her skirts brushed again against his thighs as she moved. Lifting his hands, he loosened the cord that held the cloak at her neck and it fell from her shoulders to the earth with a sigh. Her dress was modest, her breasts hidden, but he could see the valley at the base of her throat, the skin smooth and nut brown as he traced the line of the bone with his fingers, drawing the bodice away from her shoulder, exposing more of her skin.

She shuddered, with desire or with fear he could not say, but she made no move to pull away as he began to work free the laces that tied her bodice, exposing the flimsy linen shift underneath. As his hand cupped the small and perfect breast, and her back arched in pleasure, she sighed, 'We cannot ... It is forbidden ... I am a maid ...'

But he cut off the rest of her words with his mouth on hers as he lowered her gently to the ground, one hand behind her head, the other searching beneath her skirts, finding the strong, lean legs underneath, the skin soft against his fingers as he sought out the silky flesh between her thighs, rubbing, caressing, opening. Exactly as he had imagined in his own dreams, though he had begged no forgiveness for his.

She seemed to give way beneath him, melting into him without a word as he entered her, as though they were two parts of a whole that were made to fit together, and her legs wrapped tight around his hips, pulling him deeper, fingers clutching the muscles of his back as he moved his body in hers, fingernails digging deep.

'Is this what you dreamed?' he whispered, his face close to hers, her breath warm against his ear.

'This and more,' she answered, and her words lit the passion brighter, heat burning through him as he quickened towards his climax.

Afterwards, they lay close together on the carpet of leaves. Somewhere beyond the clearing they could hear the rustle of an animal – a deer perhaps – and Judith's head rested on the muscle of his chest, his fingers caressing her arm. He drew her cloak across them against the cool of the morning, but their skin was still slick with the sweat of the sex, blood still running warm in their limbs. In his embrace he could feel her quivering. For a long time they were silent: there seemed to be nothing to say.

Then, finally, she lifted her head from his chest and turned her head to look at him. He couldn't read the expression in her eyes. 'What have you done to me?' she said.

He smiled, smoothing the loose hair back from her forehead. 'Loved you.'

She jerked back, and with a swiftness that took him by surprise brought the flat of her hand hard across his face. He lifted his own hand to his cheek, stinging from the force of the blow as she rolled away from him and stood up, covering herself, straightening her skirts, retying the laces of her bodice. Then she was running through the woods away from him, her cloak carried carelessly, dragging in the dirt. He did his best to run after her, struggling with his breeches and following her narrow back as she wove at random amongst the trees, taking them deeper into the woods, though he guessed she thought she was heading for home.

He called out after her but for a long time she did not slow, and they had wound themselves deep into the forest before he finally caught up with her, laying his hand on her arm and swinging her round to face him. Her face was striped with tears, and the pain in her eyes almost took his breath away. He let his hand fall away from her arm. This was not what he had wanted – she had wanted him, he knew, as he wanted her, and he had thought the magic would light her passion and her love, and free her from the reluctance of her faith.

And yet ...

He had known, and had lied to himself.

'What have you done to me?' she repeated. She wheeled away from him, lifting her hands in bewildered resignation, eyes scanning the carpet of leaves at their feet.

''Twas your desire,' he said. 'Your love ... Did you not find pleasure in it?'

For a moment she made no answer, then slowly she turned once more to face him. 'Pleasure?' she whispered. 'Aye, I took pleasure. And for a moment of pleasure I am undone, a sinner in the eyes of God and men. My mother ... oh dear God, my mother!' She bit her lip and shook her head as if to rid herself of such thoughts.

'Your mother need never know,' he said. 'No other man need ever know. It was something we shared, you and I, something precious, and secret. We are bound now.' He reached a hand to take her fingers, but she snatched her arm away and took three steps back from him, her body shifting and bending with emotions she could not express, wracked with guilt.

He watched her, and Mary's words trod unbidden through his thoughts.

Those people find their only joy in God – they take no pleasure in the world. Your marriage bed will be a loveless place.

'I trusted you,' she murmured. 'I thought you were a good man.'

'You came willingly,' he answered. 'I did not force you.'

You'll regret it.

She swung away from him again, leaves clinging to the hem of her dress as she moved, and said nothing. He waited, uncertain. A trickle of remorse filtered through him. She seemed very small and alone in the clearing, all the fire and joy he had loved in her snuffed out by her sorrow. He took a step towards her. 'Forgive me, Judith,' he said. 'I meant not to hurt you. I thought your feelings were as mine ...'

'Feelings?' Her head snapped up and she spat the word towards him. 'What have our feelings to do with it? We are sinners before God, caving in to the lusts of our flesh.'

He was silent: he did not fear God as she did, untroubled by the weight of his sins. He watched her, waiting, uncertain what else he could say, and though some small part of him understood the demands of her faith, the greater part could see little evil in what they had done: two people, loving each other.

'I will make you my wife,' he said.

'And you think that makes it right?' She shook her head. 'To make me your wife now, after you have defiled me? You should have made me your wife beforehand. I will go to my marriage bed impure, an unchaste woman. I am a sinner.'

He swallowed. He had no other reply to give her, and he was beginning to lose his patience. He should have left her alone after all, he thought, and waited till they were wed as she wished. All the pleasure of lying with her was waning in the fallout of their argument. He should have asked more questions of the sorcerer – he had not thought beyond the act itself.

'What more would you have me do?' he asked with a shrug, voice gentle, moving closer. 'What's done is done – I can only try to make things right from here.'

She nodded and said nothing, jaw clamped tight against the desire to cry, though her cheeks were wet with her tears, small sobs still escaping.

'Come,' he said then, 'I'll see you safely home.'

But when he took her arm in his hand to guide her, he felt her shift beneath his touch, the sharp, quick intake of breath, the sudden tension of her desire. She squared her shoulders against it, kept her eyes away from his, but the energy between them had begun to throb once more. They had gone only a few steps when he stopped.

'Look at me,' he said.

She turned her body towards him but kept her head lowered, eyes restlessly grazing the depths of the forest. Her whole body heaved with her breathing, and he could feel the latent tremble beneath his hand. Around them the forest seemed to quieten – the birdsong died, and the breeze no longer rustled in the leaves overhead. The spirit had returned when he touched her, he realised, reawakening a passion she could not deny. Darkness filled him, a new need.

'Look at me.' He touched his hand to her chin, tilting her head.

'What have you done to me?' she asked again. Her lips were close to his cheek, her breath warm, and his senses were filled with the scent of her, Castile soap and lavender. She made no protest when his lips found hers, and his body pressed close against her, shifting her a pace or two until her back rested against the trunk of a tree, its leaves and branches a canopy above them. Then his hand sought beneath her skirts once more and she cried out to the empty forest with the pleasure of his touch.

When it was over, they sat in a mossy hollow between the roots of the tree, their backs against the rough and gnarly bark. She was still trembling from the pleasure he had given her, and he smiled as his mind trailed back across the shudders of her body, the surprise in her cries.

'Now do you understand?' he whispered, his lips brushing the top of her head, loose strands of her hair tickling against his face.

She sat back and tipped her head to look at him. For a moment, he was uncertain if she would rail and cry at him again, her eyes dark with unknown emotions. Then her lips curled at last into a small and unexpected smile.

'I didn't know,' she murmured. 'I just didn't know …'

He laughed, and smoothed back the hair from her temple.

'And now I want all of you, again and again and again …' She lowered her head to his shoulder once more, and her hand on his belly slid under the still-unfastened belt of his breeches. He closed his eyes as her fingers wrapped around him, exploring, caressing it back to hardness.

'May I see?' she asked.

'Of course.'

He wriggled himself free of his breeches, then watched as she ran her fingertips across him, searching, seeking to understand a man's body for the first time, his cock and his balls, lightly probing the tight pucker of his arse. Then he held his breath as she shifted her body down until her face was level with his cock, examining it as though it were an unknown fruit she had been asked to try. She touched it with her lips, unsure, and he shuddered. She slid him a glance, uncertain if she had done wrong, but he smiled his encouragement and so she returned her mouth to its tip, flicking her tongue across it, exploring, until finally she took him into her mouth. He came quickly, the pleasure sharper for being unexpected, and though he waited for her to pull away, she did not flinch at the spurt of warm juice in her mouth, instead moving back up and across his body afterward to kiss him, so that he could taste himself on her lips.

They stayed a long time in the shelter of the tree, wrapped in each other, still exploring as he taught her the secret places, the hidden corners that could offer joy, and it was as though she were drunk on her new understanding of the pleasures of the body. But he remained wary, still mindful of the blow she had given him and the depth of faith that had possessed her until now, still lurking beneath the surface, waiting with its burden of guilt.

The sun was well past its height when at last they wound their way back through the trees hand in hand towards the life of the city – their real life, far from the freedom of the forest. They parted at the church.

'When next?' she asked, her fingers caressing his, reluctant to let him go.

'Tonight?'

She nodded. 'I can creep out late, after Mother is in bed.'

'I will come for you at ten.'

They stood for a moment in silence, hands still linked, and he wanted to tip back her hood and kiss her farewell in the street, but instead they parted only with a smile and the promise of the next time.

Chapter Eleven

QUICK BRIGHT THINGS COME TO CONFUSION

The sorcerer said, 'You have possessed her?'

'I have,' Toby answered. 'Many times.' He saw the old man's lips curled in prurient interest at his answer, and he slid his gaze away.

'And she is pleasing to you?'

He nodded. Each night since the day in the forest, he had taken her to the small room behind the shop that had once been home to the tailor's apprentice. Simon Chyrche had lived there before his marriage, and another man since, but when Toby became the apprentice the room slid into disuse as anything more than an office and storeroom – a desk that was littered with samples of cloth, ledgers and files. But the narrow bed in the alcove had remained, and it was here that Toby took his pleasure each night with Judith when she came to him, eager and burning with a passion so intense that no act was forbidden, no path to pleasure taboo. A week ago he could not have imagined doing such things with anyone but whores, least of all with the modest Puritan girl he had liked from church. But in the darkness of the old apprentice's room there was no corner of her skin he had not tasted, no part of her he had not entered, and in the aftermath as he walked her home through the early hours of the morning, his whole body sang with the joy of her:

every fibre was sated, every inch of him ringing and alive with satis-faction.

'But you've not brought her here ...' Alexander narrowed his eyes.

'We found another place,' he said. 'More convenient ...'

'Pity.'

He tilted his head with a smile. He felt no need to apologise, and he liked it better that Alexander should not come near her. Lust still glimmered in the old man's eyes. Then he said, 'How long ...?'

It was Alexander's turn to smile. 'Until you are done with her ...'

'And if I am never done?'

'The girl will weary in the end – the spirit that possesses her burns her night and day, inescapable, unending. No human being can withstand such possession for long.'

'How then do I release her?'

'Another rite' – Alexander shrugged – 'to dismiss the spirit. When the drawing is burned, her body will be free.'

'And afterwards?'

'Ah. That depends. Some women stay fallen, unwilling to give up the pleasure in the lusts of the flesh they have discovered. Others repent, and still others ... well ...' He shrugged again and trailed off, turning away to his desk.

Toby stepped forward and touched his hand to Alexander's arm, wanting the answer the old man had been reluctant to give. Alexander turned to him with another shrug. 'Some women are driven to madness ...'

He thought of Judith as he had left her that morning, reluctant to leave him, desire in her eyes and mouth, even as he said farewell. Did she burn for him now? Still? He had not thought of the hours between their trysts, his own desires spent by the ardour of their coupling. Was she thinking of him, seeking pleasure on her own as he had shown her, her mind turning only on her lust? He could barely imagine her in her life without him – she had not talked of her family again, nor told him how she spent her days.

'Come tomorrow,' Alexander said, 'if you would release her. And I will show you what you must do ...'

Toby nodded and bowed his farewell, but as he thudded down the wooden stairs, he wondered again what the old man stood to gain by helping him, and rubbed at his wrist where Alexander's boot had rested in the dream.

Toby did not come to the brothel, and Mary pined, fighting off the urge each day to find some excuse to visit Sarah in the hope of seeing him. Had she angered him? she wondered, with her talk of Puritan women and her warnings. Did he seek his pleasure elsewhere now with a whore who asked no questions? His absence burned as slow pain inside her, an ache she could not shake off, and as she laboured each night on her back, she hated every man who wasn't him.

Saturday morning, and Sarah Chyrche sent a message for her to come. So she dragged herself from the lazy comfort of sleeping alone and sauntered by the river, shielding her eyes from the shards of sun as they glinted on the tide, the air cool and fresh against her face. Then she bent her footsteps through the early hubbub of the market, ignoring the shouts of the traders, turning her head away from the calls and whistles of men she had not refused in the night. She felt their eyes on her back as she walked away from them, and swung her hips a little more before she threw a smile back over her shoulder and disappeared from their view.

She strode down the High Street, sweat in the runnel of her spine and on her neck, nerves quickening her heartbeat. Would she see him today? Would he turn his eyes towards her with a smile that could break her heart? She barely thought of Sarah or the herbs she had learned before – all her thoughts were of Toby. The morning streets were busy – shoppers and workers, and servants sweeping the steps or inspecting the hawkers' wares – and just off the High Street she had to step into a doorway to let a washerwoman with an overloaded basket on her hip go past her. She slowed her pace as she neared the house, observing every passer-by that might be him with a hopeful glance. Then in Narrow Lane, she paused before the house and cast her eyes across it.

Three solid stories of brick and timber loomed above the tailor's shop, and the sign creaked lightly in the breeze above her. *Chyrche & Son – Master Tailors*. They needed a new sign, she thought, now that the older Master Chyrche was dead. Beneath the sign the shutters were open, the shop windows thrown wide to the morning, and it took all the strength of her will not to peer inside to see if he was there. But the knowledge of his nearness – his house, his shop, his life – threatened to turn her inside out, and she had to force herself to breathe in slow, deep draughts of air to steady herself. Infuriated by her weakness – he was only a man after all – she gave a small lift to her shoulders, set her jaw and lifted her hand to knock.

The morning passed slowly, and though she tried to pay attention and remember all that Sarah was telling her, her mind wandered again and again towards the tailor's shop at the front of the house, and the possibility of breaking bread with him at noon.

Halfway through the morning, Sarah lost her patience.

'Where is it that you'd rather be?' she asked. They were kneeling on the soft grass of the path between two beds of herbs, cutting leaves for a tincture to ease the pains of childbirth. Above them, small puffs of cloud drifted in a sky of summer blue, and the sun was warm against her shoulders.

'Forgive me,' Mary said. 'I am tired, merely ...'

'If you do not wish to learn, do not come ...' The older woman observed her with shrewd grey eyes, and Mary dropped her head away from the scrutiny, ashamed to have met Sarah's kindness with such ingratitude.

'I want to learn,' she said, lifting her head again, fingers running gently along the length of the stems she held in her hand. It was the truth. She loved the garden and the scents that surrounded her, the soft velvet of the petals against her fingertips, the knowledge she was gaining. And she understood too the privilege of being here. But she could not shake Toby from her thoughts, and his image hovered in her mind, his shadow over everything. Damn him, she thought, for spoiling this with Sarah. And damn her own stupidity for falling for him. 'Please, forgive me. I'll be more attentive.'

Sarah lowered her eyes to the dainty purple petals of the skullcap plant, knife deftly trimming the leaves. 'You'll see him at dinnertime,' she murmured. 'Until then, your attention please.'

Mary sucked in a quick breath of surprise. Had her feelings been so plain in her face? She was used to hiding her emotions, a mask in place for most of her days and nights, and she had not thought to have given herself away so easily. Sweat prickled in the nape of her neck and she rubbed at the leaves in her fingers.

'Be gentle with them,' Sarah warned. 'Or they'll crush.'

Mary flicked her gaze to meet the other woman's, expecting censure, or disapproval, or perhaps disappointment that her pupil could harbour such pointless longings. But there was only a sad smile of kindness behind a gentle sigh. 'I recognise the symptoms,' Sarah said, 'and I've no right to judge you. I've loved unwisely also ...'

'You think me unwise?'

'I see little hope for the future in your feelings.'

'Because I'm a whore.'

'Yes. Because you're a whore,' Sarah agreed, though it had not been a question.

'Sometimes,' Mary said, still stroking the wilted leaves in her palm, 'men do marry us, and give us a new life.' She looked up at Sarah with a hopeful smile.

'Have you ever known it to happen? Or is it simply a story you tell yourselves to ease the hardship of your lives?'

Mary was silent, aware of the wisdom in Sarah's words, though the truth contained within them cut sharper than a knife. She was right, of course. There was no hope. He might take her to his bed, enjoy her company, even spoil her with a kindness or two. But she would never be more to him than a girl at the bawdy house. She had been fooling herself with the dreams of a lovesick virgin. If the vicissitudes of her life had taught her anything, she should have learned by now that hope was nothing more than a cruel deception, an illusion like the dramas at the playhouse. She flushed with shame at her folly, and tears pricked behind her eyes. She sniffed and turned her head away, embarrassed.

Sarah laid a gentle hand on the bare skin of her wrist. 'Don't berate yourself,' she said. 'It's not given to us to choose who we love.'

Dragging fingers across her face to wipe away the tears, Mary lifted her head to regard the older woman, and saw the flicker of sadness in her eyes, eyes that changed in the light like her son's. 'Do you have regrets?'

Sarah's face creased into a rueful smile and she shook her head, though she did not meet Mary's gaze of question. 'Some,' she admitted. 'But I've no regrets for the men I've loved. Those things I wouldn't change for all the world.'

Mary nodded, touched by the other woman's trust in her, the sharing of a secret. She smiled, and she was no longer ashamed of herself.

'Now,' Sarah said, 'throw away those stalks that have died in your hand, and let's cut some more.'

Lowering her eyes to the withered leaves, she laughed, and tossed them onto the small pile of discarded plants on the path. Then, taking up her knife, she leaned forward and cut a new stalk on the angle, as Sarah had shown her.

At the table at noon she was quiet with nerves. Beyond the world of Bankside, she was uncertain how to act with a man, so she said little and kept her eyes lowered, only peering up from her dinner now and then to feast upon the sight of him – the quick and ready smile, and eyes that glowed grey in the dim light of the kitchen. She watched his hands as he broke his bread, fingers calloused on the tips from his trade, and turned her mind from the memory of their touch, the gentle caress of their roughness against the scars on her back. Had those fingers touched another woman's body in the days since she saw him last? Had his hands delivered pleasure to someone else?

The thought of it conjured an ache in her throat, and she struggled to swallow the meat on her plate, washing it down with an ale that was sweeter than the stuff they drank at the brothel. He barely acknowledged her, a brief bow of greeting, a slight smile in her direction, and then nothing more. And though it might have simply been the indifference his mother would expect him to pay towards a whore, to her it felt like coldness, and resentment began to fester. For they were not at the brothel now: she was his mother's pupil, a guest at their table, and she was owed at least his courtesy as her host.

Buoyed by anger, she said, 'How goes the tailoring business, Master Chyrche?'

He paused in the cutting of his meat and met her look across the table, a quizzical smile creasing the corners of his eyes, lips parted. 'Very well, thank you, Miss Sparrow. And how about the business of learning herbs? What have you studied today?'

Sensing mockery in his tone, she wished she had kept her silence, but now she had to answer him. With an evenness of tone that came from a life of practised duplicity, though her heart was racing with pain and fury, she said, 'I'm learning the herbs to ease the pain of childbirth: which ones to use, and how to prepare them. There is much to learn.'

'I'm sure my mother is a very able teacher.'

'And Mary is a very apt pupil,' Sarah said.

Toby nodded, but there was little sign of interest in his eyes, and though the others returned their attention to the meal before them, Mary could stomach no more. She was nothing to him, and she wanted only to get out of his presence so she could nurse the heartache in private. Twice, she was aware of Sarah's glance towards her, a question in her eyes, but she pretended not to see: it did not help to recall the older woman's warning, and she did not want her pity.

Later, she sauntered back towards the brothel, pausing in the market now to chit-chat with the traders, many of them customers, flirting, forcing herself back into the life she had so briefly thought to escape. This is it, she thought. This was her life until the end of her days. She would serve these men on her back till her body gave out, then die as a beggar on the streets. All of the instincts of her youth cried out against the prospect – a miserable end to a sordid life. Surely life had more to offer – a chance at happiness at least, hopes of a better future. No wonder she had dreamed her dreams of Toby. There had to be another way.

A meat trader hailed her as she passed his stall. A fat man with boils on his nose.

'See you tonight, my lovely?' he called. 'I've been saving my pennies ...'

She remembered him above her at the bawdy house with his belly wobbling, and turning her head away from the stink of his breath. She suppressed the sigh the sight of him aroused and swallowed down the revulsion that rippled inside her, forbidding it to show its face. Her whole life she had kept her feelings secret, hidden, locked in a chamber inside her she dared not visit. From the earliest days at the orphanage, when even a wrongly turned glance could earn a beating, she had learned to show nothing on her face, to smile with compliant obedience whatever she felt, to serve, and flirt, and keep her counsel. It had become a habit of mind to dissemble and bury the truth, walls of falsehood she presented to the world. It was the only way to survive the hardships of her life. But now Toby threatened to breach those walls with his changing eyes and a smile that could undo her, and without them in place to protect her she felt as though she were skating on ice so thin it was only a matter of time till it cracked.

Switching into her role with a mighty effort of will, she forced herself to swing her hips and tilt her head in coy encouragement. 'I'll look forward to it, handsome,' she murmured. 'Till later,' and blew him a kiss. He turned to the barrow boy beside him with a grin of delighted anticipation, rubbing his fat hands together in satisfaction.

Men were so stupid, she thought for the thousandth time, so easy to take in. Did he really believe she wanted him, with his skin that shone with grease and his pudgy, bloodstained hands? And she still in the flush of her youth. Could he really be such a fool? Yet the bawdy houses were full of such men who deceived themselves, sure of the whores' desire for them, their own attraction.

She despised them all. Spitting into the dirt between the stalls, she kept walking, back towards her life at the brothel.

Chapter Twelve

A POISONED CHALICE

Toby slid the book from its hiding place. He had resisted its call the last few days, his hours wrapped up in thoughts of Judith – her body, her lips, the heave of desire each time he saw her. But tonight in the cool of the early-evening darkness, he was drawn to it again, running his fingers across the soft leather cover. Despite the chill in the air, the book was warm to touch, and the unexpectedness of it lit a smile. He had never owned something so rare and precious, and it was weighty in his hands. Ignoring the memory of his mother's warnings, he opened it, gently, carefully, and with a sense of reverence.

Tom Wynter, he read again, inked in black across the top of the very first page. His fingertips traced the letters, lingering on this connection to his father, and after a moment he raised his head to look beyond the window and into the darkness of the sky beyond, searching for Tom's presence. A memory of his dream filtered through his thoughts, and though he was wary of the power the book contained, he felt Tom's blessing like a talisman.

Turning the pages one by one, he searched for words and phrases he might understand. Passages he recognised as Greek and Hebrew were interspersed with diagrams – circles and pentagrams, and symbols he could barely even guess at. There were charts in Latin –

lists of days and hours and phases of the moon against the names of the angels and spirits that governed them – and though he had not revisited his lessons from school in many years, he was encouraged: it was not an impossible task to decipher a language he already half knew. The Greek and Hebrew would take longer, but there was knowledge to be had without them and he was eager to begin, so many secrets waiting to be discovered.

Brushing each page with his fingers as though he might read the meaning through his touch, he recalled his oath of obedience to Alexander, and the cut on his palm began to tingle and sting. He turned his hand over to examine it, holding it close to the candle. It was healing well, a fine scar across the heel of his hand that would be a permanent reminder of the pact he had sworn. Had his father pledged the same oath? he wondered. Had he honoured it? A sense of disquiet seethed inside him, a memory of Alexander's boot on his wrist in the dream. Though his fate was bound to the old man's, he could not yet say for what purpose. Had Alexander learned somehow that the book had come to him? Then why had he not simply demanded it? Ah, Toby thought finally, who knew what games the old man was playing, what convoluted paths he had chosen to walk.

Turning his attention back to the pages, he found a passage in English that had been transcribed in a different hand from the ones that had gone before. Tom's writing? he wondered, before he dismissed it as impossible. His father had been a student merely for a while – it was unlikely he ever learned enough to transcribe his own rite. But then again …Toby's eyes followed the densely packed words across the page. Even in English the writing was hard to decipher, and the rite bore no title, so he could not tell its purpose. But the instructions for the circle were familiar, the calling to the quarters and the different names of God inscribed around the circle's edge. A diagram showed their positions and the places of the pentacles to be drawn between them.

A man and woman, he read, prepared and purified, to kneel naked in the circle.

The sigil of the spirit written on her skin.

The words of conjuration spoken as they lie together, the moment of power as they climax.

He let his eyes drift away, unseeing, across the rugs at his feet. *We did a rite together,* his mother had said. Was this the rite they did? Was this how he was begotten – in the conjuring of a spirit? For what infernal purpose had he been brought into the world?

Lifting his eyes to the darkness beyond the window, he saw a starless, moonless night, the clouds thick and riding on the autumn wind. Somewhere out there in some realm beyond his senses, Tom Wynter's spirit was watching. Toby remembered his dream again, and his father's benediction. Was he truly protecting him, he wondered, or was it merely the wishful fantasy of restless sleep?

Along the street, the church bell struck the hour of ten with a mournful toll. Closing the book with reluctance, Toby slid it back into the trunk at the foot of the bed, turned the key in the lock, and, buttoning his doublet as he went, he trotted lightly down the narrow stairs and out into the street.

The night was cool. The season was turning, and soon the daytime sun would no longer hold any warmth: the evenings already held the promise of winter's chill. Toby turned up the collar of his doublet and wished he had brought his cloak, but he warmed quickly as he strode towards the river where the air hung damp and rank with the tide. Skirting the brothels that lined the bank, he cut along the back of them, and recalled the reproach in Mary's look at dinnertime. With the thought of it he shook his head. What had she expected? She was just a whore after all, however much he liked her.

Judith was already waiting when he arrived, hidden in the shadows beside the house with her face covered by the hood of her cloak. She was moving lightly side to side, shifting her weight one foot to the other, restless and impatient. She must have been waiting awhile. She tipped back her hood when she saw him, but she remained in the lea of the house and so he stepped into the darkness, sliding one hand around her waist beneath the cloak, touching his mouth to hers in greeting.

'I was almost caught tonight,' she breathed. 'My father coming home from the tavern. We met on the stairs, and I told him I had left my sewing by the hearth.'

'He believed you?'

'I think so. But ...'

He couldn't see her face in the shadow of the house, but he could feel her restlessness against the arm that held her. 'But ...?'

'We cannot keep on like this.'

'Then marry me, and we'll not have to hide any more.' He had asked her once before, but she had given him no answer, diverting him from thoughts of marriage with the pleasures of her body. They had been naked in the narrow bed, limbs entwined, and he had been easy to distract.

'I cannot,' she hissed. 'My mother ...'

'Your mother be damned!' he replied. 'You are of age, and she has no power to stop you.'

'She is my mother and I owe her my duty. This must be the last time.'

For a moment he was silent, aware of the strength of conscience that might yet defeat the spirit that possessed her. Then he said, 'You would give me up to please your mother?' He had hoped to gain her promise while the throes of her passion still outweighed her sense of obedience.

'And to please God,' she replied. 'I cannot go on sinning this way. I cannot.'

'Even though you love me?' He moved in closer, his body pressing on hers, heat between them, and he felt the lift of her breath with her want for him.

'Even though I love you,' she whispered.

He smiled. Perhaps he could still win her after all, love overcoming duty. 'It would be no sin if we were wed,' he murmured.

'We will never be wed,' she answered. 'And this will be the last time.'

For a moment he was silent. Then, tightening his hold on her waist, he stepped forward, moving her with him so that her back was against the wall of the house, trapped with his weight against her, her breasts soft against his ribs. For a single breath he paused, aware of the sin of what they were doing himself, but then her mouth sought his as her fingers fumbled with the buttons of his breeches, and all hesitation was forgotten. Gathering up her skirts, his hand found the cool, smooth skin underneath, heat flaring through him. She wrapped a leg around his hip and he lifted her, supporting her weight against the wall as she, practised now and no longer shy, guided him inside her.

They had never been so bold before, fucking in the lane beside her house as if she were a sixpenny whore. If her mother only knew, he thought, and in the dark he gave himself a smile. They came quickly, excited by the risk and the lewdness of it, crying out together in muted ecstasy. Then they stood awhile, still joined, and he felt the ebbing shudders of her body as they dwindled to a tremble, and his own blissful aftermath. Somewhere down the lane a dog began to bark. The sound brought them back to their surroundings, and reluctantly, he took a step away. The night air was cold against his cock after the warmth of inside her, and he shivered. Soon he would release her from the compulsion of the spirit that possessed her, and it was not for him to foretell what might happen then.

'Come,' he said. 'Let's go.'

They took barely a moment to straighten their clothes, and then he was leading her towards the old apprentice's room at the tailor's shop to spend a final night in pleasure.

Chapter Thirteen

WILL ALL GREAT NEPTUNE'S OCEAN WASH THIS
BLOOD CLEAN FROM MY HAND?

Sunday afternoon at the brothel, and it was still quiet. A table
of regulars threw dice in the corner, betting for pennies, and,
with nothing to do, Mary wandered out onto the quay to
watch the river awhile. The weather had changed in the night. The
soft autumn sun of the last few days had given way to rolls of cloud
that brought a moisture to the air. A light mist hung above the water,
muffling the sounds of the boatmen, and the bank across the river
was shrouded and grey so the towering outline of St Paul's seemed
washed and ethereal. But it was still beautiful for all that. Winter on
its way, she thought, as the dampness touched the bare skin of her
shoulders and made her shiver. She wrapped her arms around
herself. But still, it was good to be out of doors, a brief respite from
the world of the bawdy house when for a time she could picture
herself on a boat on the river, heading away to a new life somewhere,
anywhere.

A wherry pulled in at Goat Steps and she watched as two middle-
aged merchants in thick, rich velvets struggled to get out of it, unable
to get their balance as the boat rocked hazardously in the current.
Then they stumbled up the stairs, and on the solid ground of the
quay at last, they paused a moment to steady themselves before they
brushed down their clothes and headed west along the bank towards

who knew where. She watched them go, their cloaks swinging out behind them, boots ringing loud on the stones of the quay. Then, with an upward glance towards a sky that promised rain, she shivered again, and turned back into the close and heady warmth of the brothel.

She saw him as soon as she ducked through the low doorway, and the throb of her heartbeat quickened in her chest. He was at the same table as before, close to the hearth, and someone had already brought him a jug of ale and two cups. Was he waiting for someone? Or was the cup for her? He must have walked right behind her on the quay while she was gazing at the river. He lifted his eyes from the cup in his hand and, seeing her, he smiled.

'Ah, Mary. You are returned.'

'Doctor Alexander.' She gave him a small dip in greeting. 'I just stepped out for some air.'

'I saw you,' he said. 'Planning your escape.'

She moved closer but stayed out of the reach of his hand. She still wore the bruise on her thigh from the pinch he had given her, and she had not yet forgiven him for Rosalind. She whispered a silent word to Hecate, a reminder of the vengeance she had sought. It seemed a long while since then, but perhaps the justice of gods took time. The hope that it would come buoyed her and she gave him a smile.

'Come sit with me, girl,' he said, patting the empty seat on the bench beside him.

She slid into place and tucked her skirts firmly under her legs, a trick learned long ago. Alexander poured her a cup of ale, and though they clinked cups, she took only a sip: she wanted her wits about her, all her senses prickling and wary.

He lifted his cup and gestured with it at the room around them. ''Tis quiet today.'

'Sunday,' she replied, with a tilt of her head. 'We're closed …'

He laughed, and she saw a glimpse of the man he might have been before life had turned him cruel. Lines creased his cheeks and in his eyes there was merriment, a twinkle that might have been bewitching once. She steeled herself to caution, to remember Rosalind.

'So I see.' Then, pointing to her cup, he said, 'Drink.'

Hiding her reluctance with a smile, she lifted the cup and did as she was told. He filled it again and repeated the order.

'You wish me to be in my cups?' she asked. 'For why? I work better sober.'

He smiled but there was no merriment this time. She felt herself judged and appraised as his eyes travelled over her face and body, lingering on the line of the bodice that just covered her breasts.

He lowered the jug to the table and inclined his head. 'If you say so,' he conceded.

Then she wondered if it might have been better to drink after all – a drug to dull the pain and blur the edges: it had served her well in the past. She said, 'And you do wish me to work, do you not? That is why you've come?'

He nodded but his gaze remained levelled at the jug in his hand, his fingers rubbing at the handle. Then, abruptly, he turned to her with eyes dark with lust, and let go of the jug.

'Yes. I wish you to work.'

Swiftly, she slid from the bench and led him across the boards to the staircase, aware of the heat of his gaze on her arse as she climbed the steps ahead of him. She swung her hips a little more to please him.

Inside the room, he was on her in a moment – she couldn't have said how she even came to be on her back. But as he thrust himself inside her and began to move, she was grateful for the simplicity of his desires. She had expected him to want all manner of perversion, but, as before, he seemed content with a straightforward fuck, and her fear of him ebbed a little. But she remained on her guard, still aware of the darkness that lurked.

Afterward, she lay on her back in the bed, and he propped himself up on one elbow, observing her, his free hand tracing patterns across her breast. 'And how is your boy?' he said.

She turned her head on the pillow to face him. 'My boy?'

'Tall, pretty, grey eyes, nice arse.'

She knew who he meant of course, but why did he want to know? 'I haven't seen him in a while,' she replied. 'He hasn't visited.'

'No. I thought not.' Alexander turned on his back, and clasped his hands on his chest, staring up at the open beams of the ceiling. Like a corpse in a coffin, she thought, dead.

'Why do you ask?'

He turned his head to look at her. 'He has a girl now, so he has no need of whores.' Which did not answer her question.

'The girl at church,' she murmured, and hated her.

'Indeed,' he agreed. 'The girl at church. A good girl, virtuous.'

She said nothing, thinking the girl might not be so virtuous if Toby had no more need for whores. A thread of jealousy wound around her heart.

Alexander said, 'You like him?'

She gave a half-shrug – her feelings for Toby were her own concern. 'What is it to you?'

He observed her, appraising once again, and though she was used to the judgement of men, his scrutiny unnerved her. He had slaked his lust already – what else did he want from her?

'Would you like him to love you?' He rolled once more to face her, and ran the backs of his fingers up and down her arm, eyes following the movements. She held her breath to stop herself from flinching, and Alexander looked up at her with a smile she did not trust. 'Instead of the girl at church?'

Moving onto her side, she looked at him more closely, barely understanding what he was asking. His fingers moved to trace the line of her throat, and she was aware of the strength in his hand and the frailty of her neck. She held her breath.

'I can make him love you,' he went on, 'and not simply lust, or desire. You can rouse that in him yourself. I mean love, such as makes a man wed a woman, spend a life with her.'

'Why would you do that for me?' she demanded. It seemed impossible that her fate could turn so easily.

He laughed. 'Most women would ask how before they ask why,

but I will answer you just the same, Mary Sparrow. It's really very simple. He has something of mine that I want. Something that was stolen from me many years ago. I win his love for you, and you get me what I want.'

She was silent. Toby's love in exchange for a betrayal. Part of her rebelled at the thought of it, but the prize Alexander offered was hard to resist. She said, 'What is it he has?'

'A book.'

'A book?' She was incredulous he would go to such lengths to obtain something so small as a book. Surely there was an easier way to get it. 'What manner of book?'

'An ancient book of Greek and Hebrew and Latin.' He waved a hand dismissively. 'A book your boy could not even make a start to understand. It's worthless to him, but more precious than jewels to me.'

Her heart beat quick with possibility and, despite her reluctance to comply, she knew she had no will to refuse. A life beyond the bawdy house, a life with the man she loved. A tailor's wife, a respectable woman. She could learn to be a healer, the same as Sarah. Briefly, she saw herself again as mistress of the house in Narrow Lane – a family, servants, a husband who would love her. A book seemed a small price to pay. A book he could not even read.

'How will you make him love me?' she asked. Was it possible? She thought of the herbs in Sarah's garden and tales of witchcraft the girls told amongst themselves on quiet nights, potions mixed to win a man's devotion, spells murmured in the moonless dark. Then she thought of Hecate, and the power of the goddess. Nothing was impossible, she realised – it only needed faith.

'A simple rite of conjuration,' he said, 'that I learned many years ago.'

'Then he will love me?'

He nodded. 'Then he will love you.'

'Why should I trust you?'

'I will give you the man you dream of. Once he's yours, you give me the book.'

'What if I cannot find it?' In her mind she searched Toby's house for books, and found only the collection of recipes in Sarah's kitchen. But perhaps he kept it hidden away in his chamber – she had not yet explored the rooms in the attic.

'I will take his love away from you as easily as I gave it.' Alexander snapped his fingers and gave her a smile that left no space for doubt he had the power and will to do as he said.

'I will do it,' she said, and he laughed.

The rite to release Judith from the spirit was simple, and Toby was glad to do it. Seeing Judith in the morning light at church had shocked him: in the candlelit dark of their night-time pleasures, he had not noticed the ghostly whiteness of her skin and the sunken cheeks. Like the tailor before he died, he thought, the grey skin stretched too tight across the bones, the beginnings of death in life. He still thought of her as olive-skinned with cheeks that were plump with youth and health.

Once or twice across the aisle, her eyes had sought him out, bright with the unnatural light of fever, and in their depths a look that spoke of realms of darkness, knowledge of worlds no living man should glimpse. But he saw desire also, in spite of her claims it was over, and he had to turn his head away, ashamed of what his lust had brought them to, touched by remorse for the pleasures he had taken: he had meant only to loosen the strictness of her faith awhile so they might love each other freely.

Now, standing in the circle he had prepared in Alexander's attic, he held Judith's image above the fire, uttering the words that would rid her of the spirit, and as he dropped the parchment into the flames, a great howl split the silence, like the bay of a hound at the hunt. The room filled with an evil-smelling smoke that stung his throat and eyes, almost blinding him, and he struggled to pronounce the final words that forbade the spirit's return.

Then it was done. The smoke cleared as though it had never been, and the fire died. He shivered, and remembered the surge of power he had felt the last time, the life that had flowed through his blood in the following days, but this time he felt nothing but weariness, and a ripple of relief that Judith was free. He was aware of Alexander's eyes on his body as he moved to the edge of the room to wash the smoke from his face and to dress himself, but he felt no trace of answering lust. All he wanted now was the softness of his bed to sleep, though he could have lain on the floorboards and slept just as soundly.

''Twas well done,' the old man said.

'You showed me what to do.'

'Aye,' Alexander agreed. 'I did. But it takes a rare skill to command the spirits, and few men possess it.'

With a wry smile, Toby sat on the stool to pull on his stockings and boots. 'Perhaps it's in my blood,' he said.

'Oh indeed it is,' the old man answered, and he did not return the smile. 'I have no doubt of it.'

Toby finished dressing and leaned back against the wall behind him. The old man had not yet put on his clothes, and Toby ran a dispassionate eye across the ageing body, the papery skin and the rolls of his belly, the spindly legs. His cock was semi-hard, and twitching. Alexander ran his tongue across his lips, and his gaze never left Toby's body. Was he about to demand his payment? Toby wondered. He should have said so earlier, before Toby put on his breeches: he would need to take them off again. With a sigh, he waited, too weary to really care.

Then the sorcerer turned away and began to dress himself. Toby watched, lazily, and wondered again when the old man would ask him for the book.

Chapter Fourteen

THE COURSE OF TRUE LOVE NEVER DID RUN
SMOOTH

I n the morning Sarah went to the playhouse and slid onto a bench in the downstairs gallery to watch the rehearsal in progress. Like old times, she thought, and the ache of its absence from her life rippled through her. So many wasted years. The playhouse had been a second home once, and the Company of players as close as family. Why had she given it up so easily? She could have come to watch a play now and then at least, she thought. No one would have known. But she had kept her side of the bargain that was made – a husband and father for her child and no more life on Bankside. So she had kept her memories buried deep and visited them only in the darkness of dreams and sleepless nights across the years, and the daytime mask had remained carefully in place. To have returned to the playhouse would have threatened that mask, offering another possibility.

Nick was onstage, and she recognised the play immediately – an old comedy of Master Shakespeare's, a muddle of love in the forest, fairies and potions, a happy ending won through magic. They were rehearsing: Nick as Oberon, preparing to play a trick on Titania.

> *Yet mark'd I where the bolt of Cupid fell:*
> *It fell upon a little western flower,*

Before milk-white, now purple with love's wound,
And maidens call it love-in-idleness.
Fetch me that flower; the herb I shew'd thee once:
The juice of it on sleeping eye-lids laid
Will make or man or woman madly dote
Upon the next live creature that it sees...'

She watched in delight – it had always been one of her favourite plays, full of light and magic and laughter. They finished the scene, and Sarah waved as Nick's gaze turned outward from the stage. He saw her straight away, his face brightening into a smile. With a word to the other players, he hurried down the steps, crossed the yard and sat on the bench beside her.

Their hands met, and she watched their fingers entwining, his strong fingers against the smallness of her hand, but she was aware of his gaze on her face and after a moment she raised her head to meet it.

'*A Midsummer Night's Dream*,' he said, with a glance to the stage. 'Do you remember it?'

'Of course,' she replied. 'Love and magic and mayhem. I always loved it.'

'It was the first play I ever saw,' Nick said, 'when the players came to my father's inn to perform.'

'I remember the story.' She smiled. 'You wanted to be Puck, and when the players moved on, you went with them.'

'Aye.' He returned the smile. 'And here I am.'

On the stage the rehearsal began again – the two Athenian lovers, arguing – and for a moment they watched it together. Then Nick pressed his hand around hers.

'Come to the play this afternoon,' he said. 'And afterwards we can … talk.'

She laughed, and he dropped his head away with a smile that was shy and beautiful.

'You know …' he murmured, lifting his eyes to her again.

'I know,' she replied. And though the conversation was over, their hands remained linked on the bench between them, and she was aware of the pressure of his fingers against her palm and the promise they contained.

Finally, he took his hand away. 'I've got to get back,' he said, gesturing with his head towards the stage. 'I'm on again in a moment.'

She nodded, and watched his back cross the yard away from her, the broad shoulders and narrow waist, the slightly uneven stride. Then he was in character on the stage, the Fairy King, and she could not look away from him, absorbed in the illusion of the play once again.

For the first few nights after he had let Judith go, Toby still went to the house to wait for her, hoping she would still come to him, out of love, perhaps, if not desire. But each night he waited in vain, standing in the cold autumn dark, gently stamping his feet for warmth, his arms wrapped around himself under his cloak. Twice, he had to duck into shadow as her father came or went. But the house remained silent, no sign of the women within, and when he heard the distant striking of the bells, he gave up his vigil and turned his steps for home.

It was only on the third day that he thought to look for her at church, with the sudden recollection that she used to go there in the early mornings for peace to pray and reflect. As he'd hoped, he found her in the chapel, and, absorbed in her prayers with her eyes closed and filled with tears, she did not notice him even when he took his seat next to her on the bench.

'Judith,' he said.

At the sound of his voice she swung towards him, and the terror in her eyes at the sight of him almost stopped his heart.

'Get away from me!' she spat.

He raised his hands in a gesture of peace. 'I came to see how you are,' he said. 'That is all.'

'I am as you see me,' she flung back. 'Broken, fallen, a whore …
the Devil must be pleased with you.'

His breath quickened under her attack: he had not expected such
hatred. Anger, perhaps, and regret, but not this naked loathing.

'What did you do to me?' she snarled. 'What spell did you work to
tempt me to sin as I did? What deal with the spirits of Hell?'

'We only loved each other,' he answered. And still he hoped to
coax her back. 'I would make you my wife if you'd have me.'

'Loved each other?' Contempt dripped from her words. 'That
wasn't love. That was depravity, the lusts of the flesh, the work of
Satan. How can you call that love?'

'There are many who love each other so – all things come from
God, do they not? Why then should such things be forbidden? I
swear that for my part, I did nothing but love you.' It was only the
truth, he thought, his desire bound up with the promise of love, a life
together.

She stared at him, eyes cold with disbelief, and he remembered
the look on her mother's face at his father's funeral, the same ugly
expression of contempt. *Your marriage bed will be a loveless place –*
Mary's words played across his thoughts and he shook them away.

'You are in thrall to Satan if you call that love …'

'But you felt it too … Did you not take pleasure in our nights
together? Did you feel nothing?'

She slanted her eyes away in a moment of hesitation. Then she
lifted them back towards him and he could see no love in them, only
the same hard denial. 'I felt pleasure,' she conceded. 'But it was the
pleasure of the flesh and not the spirit.'

He touched his fingers to her arm, sensing a softening, and she
flinched. But she let his hand stay, and he could feel the quiver of her
tension, her chest heaving with her breath.

'Then I beg for your forgiveness,' he said. 'I meant not to hurt you,
Judith. I only hoped to love you more. Forgive me.'

She turned her head away from him towards the altar and the
plain wooden cross that was the symbol of Christ's sacrifice. 'It's not
my forgiveness you should seek,' she said, 'but God's. We were

tempted by the Devil and we must confess and repent. *The body is not for fornication, but for the Lord: and the Lord for the body.'*

'And what of us?' he asked, with a last gasp of hope. 'Will you be my wife after all?'

'There is no us,' she said, and her mouth hardened into a thin, tight line, so that there was no trace left of the soft, full lips that a few days ago had caressed his whole body with delight. Now she seemed to be a different person altogether.

'Now go,' she spat. 'And do not come again. There is too much of the Devil in you, and I trust you not.' Turning from away from him, she closed her eyes and clasped her hands at her breast, her lips moving in murmured prayer.

He watched her awhile, observing her profile, his gaze travelling across the small breasts that lifted rhythmically under her bodice and the line of her thighs beneath the plain wool skirt. The thought of it stirred him, wanting her again as he had before, memories of her nakedness on the narrow bed behind the tailor's shop, bodies entwined and pleasure given and taken: he had hoped for a lifetime of such pleasure with her. A sliver of shame passed through him for harbouring such lustful thoughts in church as she confessed her sins to her Maker, sins she had committed with him.

Perhaps she was right, he thought then. Perhaps there was too much of the Devil in him. Shades of his father, he guessed, the blood of witchcraft in his veins. Getting up from the bench, he briefly adjusted himself in his breeches and, with a small bow of farewell that she did not notice, he took his leave and strode across the flag-stones to the door.

Chapter Fifteen

KEEP WELL MY HEART

Autumn had turned to winter by the time Toby went again to the brothel, and he strode through the chilly damp, his cloak pulled close around his neck against the cold. He had stayed away these last few weeks, spending his evenings instead in study from the books that Alexander lent him, learning the movements of the stars and the letters of Greek and Hebrew, the properties of plants and stones and herbs, their correspondences. Once or twice he had visited the old man to ask him questions, and little by little the arcane secrets began to open up their magic.

He barely slept. Each night when his study was done, he would slip the book from its hiding place in his chamber, and though his progress seemed painfully slow to him, each night he could unravel a little more of the meaning in its pages. But he rarely felt tired, his spirit fired by his knowledge and the new understanding of his place in the universe.

Now, needing a distraction from the demands of study, he ducked through the low door of the Cardinal's Cap to look for Mary. The night was in full swing when he arrived. Someone was playing a fiddle in the corner, and a couple of the whores were dancing with a variety of men who switched in and out of the dance, breathless and laughing. His eyes searched the throng for Mary, and he found her at last on the lap of a young gentleman, her arm around his neck, his hand up her skirt. Remembering the last time and in no mood for a fight, he turned away and took a seat in the corner where she could not see him unless she turned right around. The girl with the addled wits brought him ale, and he nursed the cup gently between his fingers, the glaze rough against his skin. Cheap glaze, he thought. Watery ale. He wondered why he came here at all. Except for Mary. Habit, he supposed. He had come here as a young man with other young men of his acquaintance, losing their innocence in time-honoured fashion, goading each other on. He could barely remember the face of the whore he had slept with first, though he could still recall the touch of her fingers on his cock, and the exquisite pleasure of that very first discovery of sex.

He smiled at the memory and took another mouthful of the bitter ale, but his eyes never left Mary's back, catching glimpses of her profile now and then as she turned her face full towards the gentleman, lips against his beard, laughing. Then she was on her feet and leading the young man towards the stairs, and Toby watched her go, surprised by the ball of jealousy that gathered in his gut, and feeling so much; she was only a whore after all. But in his head he followed them to Mary's room, a fly on the wall as the gentleman laid her on her back across the bed and undid his breeches. An urge to rush upstairs and stop them barrelled through his innards and he tensed against it, forcing himself to watch instead as the images unfolded across his thoughts: Mary's thighs wrapped around the young man's hips, her face contorted in the pretence of arousal. His own desire rose at the thought of it, and he shifted on the stool, uncomfortable.

They seemed to be gone a long time, and he wondered what favours the man had paid for, seeing all the possibilities in his mind. Jealousy writhed in his veins as he watched, twisting and tumbling with desire. He was growing impatient for his turn. For something to do he ordered more ale, and when the idiot girl brought it she took a seat on the stool beside him and poured into his cup.

'She won't be much longer,' the girl said, lifting her eyes towards the stairs. 'He's a regular.'

He turned to her in surprise. 'How did you know I was waiting?'

'I've seen you before,' she replied. 'Though not for a while. You like her.'

He smiled. 'I do.'

'Be good to her,' the girl said. 'She's my friend, and the kindest girl I know. Don't let her end up like me.'

'What do you mean?'

'The old man comes here to see her,' she said. 'The old man that took my mind. She thinks I don't notice, but I see everything, and I know.'

The old man, Toby thought. Alexander. He stared, surprised and disturbed by the girl's warning.

'He wants only her. He waits for her as you do. But he dances with devils and I'm afraid for her.'

'I'll be good to her,' Toby said. 'I promise.'

She nodded her thanks and left him, and he watched her slip easily between the tables, fetching more ale and avoiding the groping hands that reached for her as she passed. He drained his ale and lifted his attention again to the stairs, waiting.

In the far corner the fiddler had stopped his playing, and the group of dancers dispersed to their tables, laughing, the chatter loud in the hush that had fallen when the music finished. Impatience filled him. He should have danced when he could, he thought. It would have passed the time and the movement might have soothed his jangled nerves. Instead he poured himself more ale and drank it down. It did little to help, but it gave him something to do with his hands while he waited.

Finally, finally, he heard a door open at the head of the stairs and footsteps on the boards of the passage. Looking up, he saw the gentleman as he thudded down the steps, and Mary following behind, holding her skirts carefully. In the unguarded moment when she was at the gentleman's back, he saw the hard set of her mouth and jaw that curled up into a ready smile as they reached the bottom and the man turned to her again.

He had not been kind to her then, Toby thought. He had hurt her.

Automatically, he reached for the knife at his belt, fingering the hilt, tempted. But it would do no good and he knew he would get no thanks for it, so he let it go, returning his hand to caress the cup. The gentleman, having done what he came for, gathered his attendants and made for the door. Mary watched them go with a small smile that Toby knew to be fake, then she turned away and went to the Madam's room to hand over the coins. She still had not seen him, and only when she stepped back out did she notice him at last. This time the smile was genuine, and he saw the lightness in her step as she wove between the other customers to sit beside him.

'Master Chyrche.' She nodded her head in greeting as she drew up a stool, and Toby poured her some ale.

'Did he hurt you?' he said, gesturing to the stairs with his head. 'The gentleman.'

She shrugged. 'No more than most.' She lifted an eyebrow and gave a sigh of resignation. Then, 'Where have you been? We've missed you.'

'We?'

She laughed. '*I* have missed you.'

'I've missed you too,' he said, and realised that he meant it. It was simple with Mary: no games, no lies. Everything was as it seemed, and he felt no guilt for wanting her as he had done with Judith. Except now, of course, there was Alexander, tainting her with the shadow of his daemons.

'Come upstairs,' she said then. 'Let's be alone awhile.'

She took his hand and led him up the wooden staircase, her hips swaying sweetly before his face, her six fingers entwining his hand. In the room, with the door closed, she sat on the bed and he sat beside her. But he was aware of the smell of other men in the bedclothes, the presence of the man who had only just left.

'What did he do to you?'

She shook her head and smiled. 'Nothing. He was just rough, is all. Gentlemen tend to be; it's a question of power. And oft-times they don't want to pay – they think it's their right to have us, that we should be their slaves.'

'What happens then?'

She shrugged. 'Madam has ways of getting their money ... They rarely refuse to pay twice.'

He did not doubt it. He had seen on his travels through Bankside the odd gentleman curled in the dirt, blood on his face and clothes ripped, and sometimes his arse hanging out where the brothel's men had chosen to take payment in kind.

She laid her hand on his thigh and trailed it upward lightly. Heat turned in his belly as desire, and he forgot about the odour of the other men, the wish from a moment ago to take her elsewhere, somewhere nicer. As she slid her leg across him to straddle his thighs, he closed his eyes and let her undo his breeches and gather up her skirts. Then he shuddered as she guided him into her, warm and sweet, and surrendered himself to the pleasure.

Afterward, they lay together half-undressed in the tumble of the bedclothes, and he remembered again the parade of other men who had shared her bed. He should take her to the tailor's shop, he thought, and have her to himself. Turning his head on the pillow, he looked at her: she was watching him with those light brown eyes as her fingers caressed the fine hairs on his belly. A slight smile curled her lips.

'How is your girl at church?' she asked.

'Are you jealous?' He tucked a stray strand back over her shoulder, fingertips lingering on the smooth, cool skin.

She tilted her head evasively and slid her fingers lower on his belly. His pelvis tilted to meet her touch. 'Perhaps,' she answered after a moment. 'A little.'

'You have no need to be,' he said, but he was pleased to know she cared – he was not just another customer after all. 'It's over.'

'How so?' He heard the surprise in her voice, and the pleasure.

'I ... offended her, and now she hates me.'

'Offended her how?'

He hesitated, uncertain how much truth to tell, and though he was aware that Mary would not judge him, a prickle of warning warmed his skin, Alexander's shadow looming. But he had taken too long to answer.

'You seduced her,' she said, laughing. 'You took her to your bed, your Puritan girl at church. So now she believes she's a whore and bound for Hell.'

He gave her an uncertain laugh in reply.

'And she thinks that you are an agent of the Devil …' She gave him a grin of pride at her deduction. 'Am I right?'

'You are right,' he said, and swallowed. 'But I'm not proud of it. She was a sweet girl and I've hurt her.'

'I bet she loved every minute of it,' Mary said, and there was no laughter in her now. 'She should be thanking God for you, and for the gift of a life that offers such a choice. Does she not understand her privilege? One man, one bed, and a lifetime of repentance? Does she really think God cares that much? 'Tis nothing more than self-importance … These people sicken me.' Then, looking up at him, abruptly coquettish again, 'Was she good?'

He smiled at the question, and thought of Mary's mouth around him, her six-fingered hand, and Judith, trying too hard in the eagerness of her passion. She had been a slave to her desires, and to his, her body offered up in sacrifice. Submissive, he realised now, wanting only to please him. 'She was … willing,' he said.

Mary nodded, content with his answer, and snuggled closer into him as he held her tight, his lips pressed to her hair as it caught in his beard and tickled. Next time, he thought, he would take her to the shop, and keep her to himself for the night. Even if she was just a whore.

Chapter Sixteen

HOW STRANGELY WOMAN'S FORTUNE COMES ABOUT!

After the performance, Sarah waited in her seat in the lower gallery as the crowds filed out. They were lively with chatter of the play, and though the afternoon was turning cold, clouds darkening above the open roof and threatening rain, she was content, her thoughts still wandering within the world of the drama she had seen.

She didn't have to wait long. Changed and fresh-faced from scrubbing off his make-up, Nick came up from behind her and surprised her with his hands across her eyes. She squealed in shock and jumped but turned to him straight away to meet his mouth for a kiss, laughing. He slid onto the bench beside her and took her hand.

'Did you like it?'

'I loved it,' she said. 'I can't imagine how I've lived so long without all of this ...' She lifted her head to gaze around the playhouse before she brought her eyes back to his: they were watching her with bright intensity. She said, 'You were wonderful. The Duke of Florence.'

'It's a good play, a good part. Middleton was a formidable playwright.'

'Almost as good as Will.'

He smiled. 'No one is as good as Will.'

'Nor ever will be.'

They sat for a moment in comfortable silence, hands still together on the bench between them.

'Would you like to go backstage?' he asked then. 'For old times' sake? They made a few changes with the new building – I think you'll approve.'

She took a deep breath, uncertain. So many memories were tied to the playhouse, Tom's ghost in every corner, and she wasn't sure if she could face it. But Nick was already on his feet, drawing her down into the yard towards the stage, and she could find no will to refuse. On the stage she turned to look out – the actors' view – and shivered with nerves. Even though they were completely alone, she still felt exposed up there onstage. Three floors of galleries towered around the yard where people paid a penny to stand, and above her the stage was covered with painted heavens: a golden moon and the constellations against a night-blue sky. She said, 'Do you never feel afraid up here, before all those people?'

He considered a moment, then shook his head. 'Not afraid. Nervous, always. Every time. But never afraid.' He cast his eyes across the playhouse, in shadow now with the drawing down of the day, before he turned to her again. 'But the nerves always fade with the first words I speak, and the magic takes over. I wouldn't give it up for the world.'

She smiled, caught up in his love of the stage, remembering it had once been her world too. A different viewpoint perhaps but wrapped in the magic all the same, and she envied him that his whole life had been in its thrall.

'Come,' he said, holding out his hand, and she followed him through to the tiring house at the back of the stage where the players dressed and waited for their cues. She had spent many hours in the dim glow of this room, the play taking place just beyond the curtain, the players coming and going, last-minute repairs, whispers and the hushed laughter of mistakes unnoticed by the audience. But most vivid was a memory of the last time she had been here: her brother Tom, beautiful as Macbeth's Lady and awaiting his entrance, and Nick's hatred simmering and dangerous. She halted and closed her eyes for a moment to let the recollection come and go.

'You're remembering,' Nick said.

'How could I not?' Even here with Nick, who she loved, grief for her brother still had the power to knock the breath from her body.

He stepped closer to her, his hand still tight on hers, and she was aware of his warmth and strength, his shirt brushing against her bodice, his breath against her hair. 'We should make a new memory,' he said. 'A different recollection.'

She laughed and he moved to stand before her, sliding one hand behind her back, the other tucking under her chin to lift her face. They kissed, warm and gentle, and the old ache of desire rippled through her. In Nick's arms she felt safe and loved, and the memories filtered to the background of her thoughts as he turned and led her to a small room off the tiring house that had not been there in her day. Inside, there were costumes strewn everywhere: a silk dress of peacock blue had been discarded across the floorboards, and a velvet doublet lay in a heap beside it. Pairs of breeches and hose littered the floor, and the seamstress in her wanted to tidy them away to keep them fresh and neat for tomorrow's performance. How could the wardrobe-keeper allow such precious things to be treated so carelessly?

Then Nick undid the laces of her bodice and touched his fingers to her breasts, and the costumes were forgotten.

They stayed at the playhouse late into the evening, the solitude too precious to give up. Lying on the couch wrapped in each other, they talked of mundane things, and though they visited the past, they were careful of the paths they took and Tom's name was not mentioned.

Then, as the church clock in the distance struck the hour of nine and she thought that at last they should go, Nick pushed himself up to sit on the couch's edge, elbows resting on his knees, hands clasped lightly between them, head bowed. She sat up too, aware there was something he wanted to say, something difficult, and she touched a gentle finger to the muscle of his arm so that he flicked a glance to her.

'What's wrong?' she said. 'What is it you would say?'

He lifted his eyes to the ceiling is if searching for inspiration, and ran his tongue across his lips.

'Nick?'

Taking a deep breath, he turned towards her and said, 'My daughter is with child.'

For the space of three heartbeats she was shocked into silence. His Puritan daughter, devout and chaste. Becky's girl. Then she said, 'Who is the father?'

He gave a wry smile and shook his head. 'She refuses to say. My wife is beside herself. She wants me to beat the girl into telling ...'

'How is she? Judith, I mean.'

'She is ... distraught. She spends every hour of the day at church, every hour of the night in prayer. She doesn't eat, doesn't speak ...'

'Oh, Nick, I'm so sorry.'

'And though I know she hates me for the life I lead, she is still my daughter ...' He shook his head, unable to say more, but Sarah understood.

'Can I help?'

He looked at her sharply.

'With herbs, I mean,' she clarified. 'There are ways to be rid of a child.'

'D'you think my wife would let you near her?'

She dropped her head away. 'No,' she admitted. 'Of course not. I didn't think.'

He nodded and patted her hand, still resting on the muscle of his forearm. 'I know,' he said softly, 'and it would have been an answer.'

'What will you do?'

'There is nothing can be done, unless we can find her a husband. But I would not wish her as she is now on any man ... She is half-crazed with penitence.'

History repeating, she thought. Nick forced to marry Becky for just the same reasons. 'Have you any clues as to the man? Why would she refuse to name him?'

He shrugged. 'Who knows what goes on in a woman's mind?' He turned to her with a shake of his head. 'It's beyond me to imagine.'

Beyond the playhouse walls the clock struck the half hour. 'The evening grows late,' he said. 'We should go.'

They stood up and straightened their clothes, and she was reluctant to go out into the night and back to her house to spend the night alone, without him.

'I'll walk you home,' he said, and she took his arm as they strolled through the chill of the night, but she did not care about the cold, only aware of his body beside her, the hardness of the muscles under her hand. They barely spoke, but when they reached her house, they risked a farewell kiss in the darkness of the street.

'Till next time,' he murmured, with a touch of his fingers to her cheek. Briefly, she rubbed her head against his hand, then wrenched herself away from him and stepped up to the door.

'Till next time,' she replied, turning back.

He dipped his head in a bow, and she stood and watched him be swallowed by the darkness as his footsteps faded in the night.

In the morning she broke bread with Toby, and they talked in desultory conversation of their plans for the day and the events of yesterday – the small, inconsequential talk of a family. She knew he told her little any more of what mattered to him, and though she understood – she was his mother after all – the loss of trust still hurt. As a boy he had told her everything, no detail too small, and she had shared his world with love and wonder. But it was how the world worked, and perhaps she did not truly want to know.

'I saw Nick Tooley yesterday,' she said. 'I went to the playhouse.'

'What was the play?'

'*Women Beware Women*. It was wonderful.'

'How is Master Tooley? I've not seen his wife and daughter at church these last few weeks.'

'He is well,' she replied. But there was something in the tone of Toby's question that lit a sense of foreboding in her gut: the way his eyes remained lowered, a studied casualness in his voice. She swallowed, heat across her skin, an almost-panic that trembled in her blood. She hardly dared to go on. She had not planned to tell him – she had seen no reason he should know – but now it seemed she must. Lifting her eyes to look at him, she waited for him to meet her look. Reluctantly he raised his head, something guilty in his eyes.

'Did you know his daughter is with child?' she said.

The colour leached from his face in a moment, cheeks paling to a sickly shade of grey, and his eyes filled briefly with tears before he blinked them away, turning his head to the side, furious with himself. When he had regained control of his emotions he lifted his gaze to hers. 'I did not know,' he whispered.

'She has refused to name the father.'

There was a silence and she watched him struggle, jaw set tense, breath coming quick: she had given him the chance to deny it and he had but a moment to decide.

'I would marry her,' he said at last, and his voice was still low and hard to hear above the roar of the fire in the hearth at his back, 'but she will not have me.'

'Oh, Toby,' Sarah breathed. 'What have you done?'

He gave her no answer, and though neither had finished their food, they sat together in the silent room and ate no more.

Chapter Seventeen

SO FOUL AND FAIR A DAY

'The girl is with child.' Toby was barely through the door of Alexander's, his cloak dripping on the floorboards. It was a filthy night outside with solid sheets of rain that showed no signs of abating. He ruffled his fingers through his hair and sent a spray of drops across the room.

'Is she now?' Alexander turned from his perusal of a book at his usual place at the desk and observed his visitor calmly. 'Did you not take precautions?'

'The usual,' he answered. Pulling out, he meant, or taking pleasure in ways that could not lead to a child.

'You should have been more careful,' Alexander said, and his condescension was like oil on the flames of Toby's anger.

'Don't tell me you haven't left a host of bastards running round behind you. I won't believe it.'

'Me?' He shook his head with a smile. 'Not me. I prefer boys,' he said. 'So no patter of little bastards' feet for me.'

For a moment Toby stared. Then the anger washed out of him in a wave, and he let out a laugh of disbelief. Alexander smiled in return as Toby slid out of his cloak and slumped onto the stool at the end of the desk, elbows on his thighs, leaning forward.

'She has refused to name the father.'

'Good,' Alexander said. 'So you're off the hook.'

Then, the question that had worried him all day. 'Will the child be normal?' Being the child of a daemon, he meant. A child born of magic.

The old man shrugged. 'Ah,' he said. 'Who can say? Perhaps. Perhaps not. Only time will tell, eh?' He returned his attention to the book that was open before him.

Toby watched and thought again of his mother's warning, his father's death. Had it started like this? he wondered. With the promise of pleasure? Had it all begun with Alexander's careless handing out of knowledge? 'Tell me about my father,' he said.

Alexander lifted his head again. 'What would you have me tell you?' he asked. 'That he was brilliant? Gifted? A man of integrity and virtue? That I saw all these things in him and so I picked him for my student?' He swung round on his stool to face the younger man. 'Well, I can tell you he was none of those things. He was a reckless, careless youth with an almost desperate greed for life, and I liked his pretty face and the tightness of his arse, and so I taught him for a while, as I teach you. Only I got something more in return from him.'

'You've never asked for it from me,' Toby snarled, though he had often seen the old man looking and the lust in his eyes. He could feel the rapid thud of his heartbeat, anger flaring and his breathing ragged. 'Why is that?'

The old man inclined his head, considering his answer before he spoke. Then he said, 'I've other plans for you.'

'What plans?' He balled his fists, knuckles white, containing the urge to grab the old man's shirt front and disrupt the nonchalance of his arrogance with violence. It would be so easy, he thought, to knock him to the ground and beat him senseless. He set his jaw against temptation. He knew the pleasure of the violence would quickly dissipate and that it would do no good: he would only have made an enemy of a man who possessed great power. It would be the action of a fool.

'Set aside your anger, Toby,' Alexander said. 'We have work to do.'

'What plans?' Toby repeated.

'All in good time.' His calmness was infuriating, and Toby flexed his fingers and balled them again, still fighting the instinct to hurt. 'Come. There's a drying sheet on the rail in the corner. Dry yourself and get warm by the fire. Have some wine. Then you may bring me your questions.'

Toby drew in a deep breath, forcing down his ire, but the blood was still racing in his veins when he got up and went to get the towel, and even when he was warmed and dry and had taken his place beside the old man at the desk, he was still aware of the quickness of his heart, and the pulse of his anger just beneath the skin. He learned very little that night.

In the morning Toby left the shop in the care of the other tailors and, ignoring the furtive exchange of glances that flashed between them, he went again to the church, hoping to find Judith. The rain had eased to an insistent drizzle that settled on his hair and crept inside his cloak, and though the way was short he was still glad when he reached the shelter of the church. Scanning the dim interior from the doorway, his eyes passed over the hard wooden benches and the plain altar at the front. A few candles flickered bravely but they made little headway in the gloom, and the light beyond the windows gave the lie to the day. Shaking the rain from his hair, he made for the chapel to look for Judith, but it was empty save for a beggar woman taking refuge from the weather. He gave her a penny and went back out into the graveyard.

It was a desolate place in the rain: the clouds glowered dark overhead and the bare winter branches dripped on the scattered mounds. He cast a glance towards the tailor's grave by the north wall, and sighed. He should pay his respects, he thought, but now that he knew the truth of things, the man he had once called father seemed to be a stranger, and he felt little call to go. As he hesitated, inclination vying with a sense of duty, a movement near the wall caught his eye. A woman was huddled by the brickwork, arms wrapped around herself, rocking to and fro. Judith.

He half ran towards her, skirting easily around the graves, and squatted down. Her hair was slick to her head from the rain, and she was wearing no cloak. Her whole body was shivering with cold. 'Judith?'

Her head jerked up at his voice, and she skittered backwards along the uncut grass away from him until the bushes by the wall behind her stopped her short. She stared at him, eyes dark against chalk-pale skin. One cheek bore the purple stain of a bruise as though someone had struck her. 'Get away from me!' she spat.

He lifted his hands in a gesture of peace. 'You're half frozen to the bone. Take this.' He unclasped his cloak and leaned forward to drape it across her shoulders. She made no protest, and he sat himself down on the wet grass beside her. 'What are you doing here?'

She slid her eyes away from him and shook her head as if it were beyond her to give him an answer, and he watched her, searching for the right words to say. There seemed to be nothing left of the bright girl he had loved in the woman before him, and his heart turned in shame and pity that he had brought her to this.

'Judith,' he said gently. 'Shall we go into the church? 'Tis warmer in there, and dry.'

She shook her head.

He bit at his lip and tried again. 'I heard you are with child.'

She lifted her eyes to meet his at that, and for the first time there was something of her old self in the look she gave him. Contempt, perhaps? Sorrow? 'I am.'

'Then marry me,' he said.

She dropped her head away and stared out over the graveyard. He followed her gaze across the mounds. It was a bleak place, the winter trees bare and the leaves wet underfoot, and the dead offered him no comfort. 'For your good name,' he said. 'And so the child will have a father.'

Slowly she raised her head and fixed him with a look that was hard to meet. He forced himself not to turn away.

'The child already has a father,' she said. 'And he is a denizen of Hell. It is a monster that I carry, begotten in madness, spawn of the Devil, and I can feel its evil growing inside me. You think I care for my good name?'

Another cursed child, he thought. Would it have six fingers like Mary? Or was it truly a monster, as Judith said?

'Whether or no,' he replied. 'It will need an earthly father too. And you must have a husband to care for you.'

'As my father cared for my mother?' The bitterness was unmistakable.

'You have never wanted for anything,' he said. 'Whatever you may think of his livelihood.' Then he wondered why he would defend Nick Tooley – for his mother's sake, perhaps? 'You cannot raise the child alone.'

'I can give it away,' she answered. 'Same as all the other whores do with their ill-begotten offspring ...'

'You are not a whore.'

'The things we did? What else could I be?'

He looked out across the graves again, searching for inspiration. Then he remembered Mary's recriminations. 'You surrendered yourself to one man,' he said, 'and he would be your husband. How does that make you a whore?'

She drew in a deep breath and turned away as though to consider his words, and a brief hope lit inside him that maybe she would come to him after all. But the hope withered when she swung her head back towards him: her eyes were cold and hard, and he read only utter contempt for him within them.

'I would rather live and die a pauper – I would rather die – than spend a single night as your wife. *Blessed is the man that doth not walk in the counsel of the wicked, nor stand in the way of sinners.* You brought me to depravity, to acts against God, against nature. The blood of Hell runs in your veins.'

He drew back from her venom, putting distance between them. What more could he do? he wondered. 'And for this you've kept my name secret?'

She nodded. 'So they cannot force me to have you.'

He was silent, disturbed by the depth of her hatred, and no more words to say to her.

'Leave me,' she said then. 'Go about your sinful life and remember me when judgement comes.'

He swallowed and got to his feet, brushing the wet grass from his breeches. His eyes tracked across the mounds of the dead all around them. Were they good souls in Heaven? Or did they cry out in the pains of eternal agony? He shook his head, the burden of it all weighing heavy. He should have listened to his mother. He should have tossed the book aside and given Alexander no quarter. *Reckless, careless and a desperate greed for life,* Alexander had said of his father. The same flaw in his own blood – would it lead him the same way? Looking down at Judith, still curled around herself, he said, 'I never meant you harm. I only wished to love you, and for all that has happened I am truly sorry.'

She raised her head to look at him, blinking in the drizzle, but she said nothing. Then, lifting his cloak from her back, she held it out for him to take. 'You'll need this,' she said. 'The day is cold.'

He reached out a hand to take it and opened his mouth to speak, but she had already turned herself away from him, eyes closed, hands clasped in prayer.

'May God forgive us both,' he murmured.

Then he swung the cloak across his shoulders, fastened it at the neck, and strode away from her between the graves and out into the street.

At the Cross Bones graveyard he couldn't tell which grave was Tom's, and he wandered through the overgrown grass and weeds on the path that soaked his legs, looking for some sign to help him. A memory of his dream murmured in his thoughts; his father's image and the surge of love within the blessing he had given. A sense of the connection ripened, his father's spirit hovering close. Most of the mounds were unmarked – this was the resting place of the unloved and unwanted, the sinners of the world who were denied a Christian burial. Here and there a rough-hewn cross stood sentinel over a grave, and on one someone had planted rosemary. He ran his fingers along the leaves, inhaling the scent that lingered.

What would his mother have planted? he wondered. What herb to mark the passing of her brother-lover? He scanned the graves a second time. By the wall was a yew tree, dark leaves and bright berries, and he made his way towards it. It seemed a fitting marker for a witch's grave, the tree that was sacred to Hecate, a gateway to the underworld. Was this where his father's body lay? Perhaps. But it was close enough, and he sat at the graveside on the untended grass, the damp soaking through his breeches once again, barely noticed.

He could think of nothing to say. He had thought he would pour out his heart to this man he had never met whose blood he shared – of all the souls in the world, he knew that Tom would understand. But no words came, so he sat in silence instead, and though he grew cold in the haze of rain, he was content simply to be in his father's company, drawing strength from the connection.

Later, at dinner with his mother, he said, 'I visited my father's grave today.'

She lowered the hunk of bread in her hand to the plate, and her face grew still, set hard against her emotions. She said nothing.

'I found the yew tree.'

She smiled at that. 'When he died I took a cutting from the tree in the Grove, where we used to go,' she said. 'Ancient, sacred …'

'It's growing well.' He would ask more about the Grove another time, he thought, curious now about this different facet of magic. He would ask her to take him there.

'Did he come to you?' She lifted her eyes to his. They were very grey today in the dim light of the main chamber, and filled with sadness.

He shook his head. 'We exchanged no words, but he was there, I would swear it.'

'He used to come to me often, for a while,' she said.

'In your dreams?'

'And in spirit.' She hesitated. Then she said, 'For a long time I wanted to go with him, to follow him into death – a life without him seemed not worth the living. But he had given me you and so I stayed.'

'Forgive me,' he said. For though he could barely begin to imagine the pain of her grief, he understood the sacrifice.

'You are Tom's son.' She smiled, and he caught a glimpse of the beauty of her youth, when she was loved and all seemed possible. 'How could I do anything but love you?' Then, the smile fading, 'And I will be with him soon enough – a mortal life lasts barely a moment …'

Thoughts of death edged away the brief flush he had seen of her girlhood, and the years marked her once again with sadness. But still, it was hard to think of her in the cold, dark earth with her kind eyes closed for the final time and her skin leached pale of blood. All these years she had been waiting, he realised, and when Death came finally to take her, she would go with him willingly to take her place beside her brother. They would meet again in Hecate's realm of death, he knew, not the Heaven and Hell of Judith's faith. He would bury her at the Cross Bones beside her brother, he decided – she needed no Christian rites to speed her soul on its way. He said nothing, and they finished their dinner in silence.

~

He woke abruptly in the early hours of the morning with a chill inside him that ran deeper than the winter night. He sat up, eyes searching the darkness, and jumped, startled, when he saw a shadow move against the paler square of the curtain at the window. Silently, he reached for the knife beside the bed, the handle slipping in the sweat of his palm. He held his breath, heartbeat hammering, throat parched. He had never been so afraid, never known such cold before – the chill of death, reaching into his bones, ice in his blood. Was this how it felt to die? Tightening his grip on the knife hilt, he strained to see through the dark.

Set the knife aside.

He heard the words but not the voice – something, someone, speaking inside his head. He swallowed and tightened his grip on the knife.

I come not to harm you but to help.

His father, he realised. Come to him in spirit, as he used to visit Sarah. He loosened his hold on the handle of the knife but did not let it go, fear still running in his veins. The shadow moved closer, and he shivered in the deepening cold.

You found your way to Alexander, as I did. But he wants far more from you. Be wary. He desires the book above all things, but it's protected by my name in blood and my love for you, so he cannot take it straight from you.

Nonetheless, he needs you – because of me you're bound in its power, and the ritual he craves he cannot work without you. Without your sacrifice. Keep it close. Keep it safe. Write your own name in blood under mine.

'What ritual?' he heard himself asking. His physical voice sounded loud and barbarous against the power of Tom's silent words. 'What rite does he crave?'

A deal with the Devil himself, for the gift of eternal life.

Toby was silent – nothing he could think of to say.

My connection to this realm grows weak ...

'I wish that I had known you.' He found his words at last.

You do know me, Tom answered. *You've always known me. My blood runs through your veins, my spirit is entwined with yours. You've never been Simon Chyrche's son.*

As Toby nodded his understanding, Tom's shade swept closer,

lips brushing Toby's mouth in a kiss of farewell that seemed to wrest the blood from his veins – a touch from the realms of death. Then in a swirl of the darkness, he knew that his father had gone.

For three beats of his heart he waited, just to be sure, then the vomit rose in a bitter gush from the depth of his gut. He found the chamber pot beneath the bed just in time, and heaved his insides into it.

Chapter Eighteen

THE WOEFUL TIME

Sarah awoke from strange dreams that slipped away into the darkness, elusive, as the church clock along the street struck four. In the room above she could hear Toby, awake and restless too, and though his footsteps were light and careful, the boards were warped and it had long been impossible to walk in silence across them.

She lay on her back awhile in the darkness, trying to chase down the memory of her dream, but she could not even catch so much as the tip of its tail, conscious only of the sense that she was missing something she would never recover – something precious that was lost forever. Tom, she whispered, calling out to him as she had done so often over the years. Just the shape of his name on her lips brought him closer, and so she breathed the word over and over, hugging the thought of him close.

Too awake to sleep any more, she swung herself out of bed and shivered as the cold air touched her skin, her feet bare on the rug. She was still unused to the chamber and the bed being hers alone, but she liked it – the sense of solitude, the freedom to light a candle whatever the hour, or to sit by the window to watch the moon. Grabbing the robe from the end of the bed, she wrapped it around herself, then sat in the window seat, looking out at the stars. The rain had moved on, the clouds blown westwards by the wind, and the sky was bright and clear. A perfect half-moon sat high above the roofs of the city.

Above her, Toby's movements ceased, and the house grew quiet again as she leaned against the glass of the window, her arm cold with the chill of it even through her robe. Perhaps he was sleeping now, a brief respite from the torment of his conscience. She had seen the horror in his face when he learned of Judith's child, and the desire to make it right. History repeating, she thought again.

And now she, Sarah, must maintain the lie with Nick. But still, it was strange. A Puritan girl. How had he tempted her to bed, with her so chaste and devout? Magic, she realised. The book. Foreboding turned in her gut, sickness rising. History repeating indeed.

She leaned her head against the glass, liking the cool against her temple, and a glimpse of the shewstone shimmered at the edges of her mind. It was years since she had scried in its surface: she had put away that part of her with her marriage, and the world it belonged to was in her past, hidden in the corners of her thoughts. Scrying was something she used to do, a skill she had all but forgotten, but the more she tried to push the image away and focus on something else, the more her mind refused to be commanded. The stone kept on calling out to her, insistent and demanding.

Long ago, when she was just a girl and Tom was still alive, she had rejoiced in her witchcraft, her ability to foretell. Then, it had seemed like a gift, a boon granted her by the gods. It had made her special, and Tom had envied her the skill. But since his death it had felt like a curse, and it was many years since she had been grateful for it. Swallowing, she took a deep breath, trying to ignore the stone's swelling presence in her mind, its call growing louder.

Whatever the stone wished to tell her, she decided, she did not want to know.

She sat for a long time with her head against the glass, and watched the sky slowly pale above the houses with the coming of the morning, thinking of nothing.

In the morning, Mary ambled through the market. She had woken early, despite the late night, troubled by dreams she could no longer recall. Only the strangeness of them remained, and the sense of dark dislocation they aroused stayed with her through the morning, trailing all her thoughts with a weary sadness she did not understand.

The day was cold, winter beginning to settle in, and her breath billowed in little puffs before her face. But she liked it – the clear, clean crispness and the sun riding low above the roofs, glinting on the puddles and the wet stones at her feet, blinding.

She turned from the market and into the High Street where the constant stream of traffic to and from the bridge filled the road with a lively commotion. Traders, travellers, farmers, beggars, gentlemen, horses, donkeys, carts and herds of livestock all vied together for a path through the crowd. Shouts and laughter, and the odd burst of argument, mingled with the clatter of wheels and hooves on the cobbles and the cries of animals, the calls of the herdsmen.

She halted, for once overwhelmed by the hurly-burly. She should have gone the back way, she thought, along Red Cross Street and past the paupers' graveyard. But she was here now and had no energy to double back, so, cutting through the traffic to the other side of the road with native ease and then keeping close to the buildings, she slipped swiftly through the turmoil, ignoring the calls from the men who loitered in the doorways of the inns, and shaking off the hand that tried to grab her as she passed. Finally, she could turn off into the backstreets, cutting through the yard of the George Inn, the tumult growing muffled behind her. A few more twists and turns and she was at the tailor's shop, resisting the urge to peer in through the window, to catch a glimpse of him. She would see him later, she told herself, and he would fall for her a little deeper. She smiled at the thought of it and lifted her hand to knock on the door.

She helped Sarah through the morning, but neither had much will to work: the older woman seemed weary also, a listlessness about her that Mary had not seen before. She had always seemed strong till now, with an invincible energy like the straight-backed aunt of her childhood. But today Sarah's eyes were dark and restless, and she seemed to struggle with the simplest of tasks.

'Are you quite well, Mistress Chyrche?' Mary asked, when Sarah dropped the small vial of tincture of rose they had finished distilling that morning, glass smashing into a thousand splinters on the stone kitchen floor. The sweet vapours filled the kitchen, heady and intoxicating.

Sarah attempted a smile. 'Tired, merely,' she said. 'I had a bad night with strange dreams, and then I could not sleep again.'

'I had strange dreams also last night,' Mary replied. 'Perhaps it's something in the air.'

Sarah nodded, and slid onto the stool at the long kitchen table to rest, shattered glass still scattered at her feet. Mary fetched a broom and began to sweep as the servant girl set about preparing the dinner at the other end of the table.

Fortune had smiled on Frances, Mary thought, to find her a position in a household where the family was kind, with Sarah as her mistress. A life to dream of. But Frances had come into the world uncursed. A flush of envy prickled over Mary's skin. It was a better life than the bawdy house, a life with a chance at love and happiness, away from the often brutal lusts of men. Dropping her eyes away from the girl's five-fingered hands as she set about dressing the ham, Mary turned back to the shards of glass on the floor by her feet and kept up her sweeping.

In the tailor's shop Toby was just about to lock up the door before the men went in for their dinner. Standing in the passage, he was reaching to the lock with the key when the door slammed open, almost taking him with it. He sprang back in surprise, and though he reached an automatic hand to his knife, he was too slow to stop the man who occupied the doorstep from swinging a fist that sent Toby reeling backwards.

Nick Tooley.

Pain sliced through Toby's head, sharp and blinding. So he had learned the truth – Judith must have surrendered after all. Had Nick beaten her also?

Stumbling from the blow, he struggled to recover his feet as Nick moved in again with a punch to the guts that knocked all the air from Toby's body and sent him crashing to the floor where he lay, curled and helpless, waiting for the boot to follow. Nick's foot found its mark against his ribs with a sickening thud and he writhed. Somewhere above him he heard women's footsteps on the stairs. His mother, he guessed, and Mary.

Then Nick was crouching over him with his fingers pressed into the soft flesh of Toby's throat, palm jammed hard against his wind-pipe. Toby thrashed in panic, clawing at the older man's arms as he struggled for breath. But the muscles were firm and strong, and he could do nothing to lessen the pressure on his neck. Is this how I die? he thought. Is this it? In sudden determination for life, he reached for the other man's face and pushed against his jaw with all the strength in his body, slowly turning Nick's face away. The pressure on his throat lessened just a fraction and he gasped for air, sucking it in. Nick took his hand away.

'I should have known,' he hissed. 'I should have guessed it was you.' He snapped up his head to look at Sarah, standing stricken and pale on the steps above him. 'Your family is poison!' he snarled. 'Your brother corrupted everything he touched … and now … and now this. Your son is no different. The same blood. The same evil.' He got to his feet and aimed another kick, and this time the boot found the tender place between Toby's legs. Pain spiralled through him in a burst of heat, and he twisted to spew on the floorboards beside him. But he stifled the groans: he would not give Nick the satisfaction.

Mary half hurled herself down the stairs to kneel at Toby's head, fingers caressing. 'Leave him alone!' she shouted.

Nick caught her a backhand that sent her sprawling across the floor. 'This is nothing to do with you, whore. Get out!'

Mary scrabbled to sit up and tracked backwards, lifting herself onto the safety of the step by Sarah's skirts and nursing the blow to her jaw with one hand. The older woman touched reassuring fingers gently to her head and then stepped down into the hallway. Her chest was lifting in great deep breaths, but when she spoke her voice was calm. 'Leave him, Nick.'

He ignored her and, squatting down again, he grabbed Toby by the front of his shirt and hauled him up to stand, slamming his back hard against the wall and leaning into him with his weight, holding him upright, face-to-face, close enough to kiss. Toby could feel the man's breath warm on his cheek and see the spittle on his lips. Lips his mother had kissed, he thought, and wished he hadn't. He swallowed, tasting blood, and his hands still tried to drag at the other man's arms, seeking to lessen the weight on his chest. He could barely breathe. But Nick was a big man, and his fury fuelled his strength.

'Did you think she wouldn't tell?' Nick breathed. 'That you would walk away, untouched?'

'I asked for her hand.' The words were hard to say, breath coming short. 'Even before there was a child. But she refused me. Many times.'

For a moment Nick wavered, but somehow he must have understood the truth in Toby's words, because he released his hold and stepped away, hands on his hips, breathing hard as Toby slumped down the wall onto his haunches, watching the other man's back, still wary. Every nerve seemed to be alight with pain.

'Nick, please?' His mother reached a hand to touch Nick's arm but he shrugged her off. 'This does no good.'

Mary sidled in to crouch beside him with a smile of comfort, fingers resting on his thigh. He caught her fingers in his own, just briefly, and squeezed before he let them go. He should have stuck with the whore, he thought, and let Judith be. He wondered that he had ever wanted her – he surely did not want her now.

Heaving himself to his feet, his gut turned in spasm as he tried to straighten up, leaning his back against the wall, his legs still unsteady beneath him. 'I would marry her if she'd have me. I'll make it right,' he said. 'But I think she'll not have me ...' Hoping she would still refuse, for he was afraid of a loveless life with a woman who hated him.

Nick turned once more to face him, and Toby saw the pain in the older man's eyes, lines of grief etched into the corners. 'Why would she refuse you, when she went so easily to your bed?'

He gave a slight shrug. 'I tempted her against her conscience.'

'You seduced her, you mean.'

'Perhaps.'

Nick shook his head. In frustration? Or resignation? 'So like your father, in every way; corruption in the marrow of your soul.' His words dripped with bitterness, his mouth set tight with hate. He turned to Sarah. 'Stay away from the playhouse, Mistress Chyrche, and do not come again. You and I have no more business with each other.'

He stepped to the door, and from the gloom of the passage his form loomed large in silhouette against the midday brightness. 'I will talk to my daughter, and bring her to her senses,' he said, with one last glance into the house, eyes grazing the small group that stood waiting and uncertain. 'And I will come again.'

Then he turned and walked away.

They helped Toby to the first-floor chamber. The smell of dinner drifted through the passage from the kitchen: something meaty with herbs that turned his gut as he let them guide him to the soft cushions of the couch beside the window, where he sank down with a sense of relief. His head was pounding now, and breathing was hard through a nose clogged tight with blood. Pain throbbed as light from his groin and his gut, and when he laid his head on the cushion Mary put for him, he remembered throwing up in the night, the presence of death in Tom's visit.

Mary knelt by the couch and touched a hand to his arm. 'Will she have you, do you think?' she whispered, and he gave a half-shrug in return.

Sarah brought herbs to ease his hurts: arnica for the bruises, tincture of poppy for the pain. Toby submitted himself to their care, and when they were finished he drifted for a while, the poppy filling his head with its strangeness – walking through an unknown land, a brighter sun than England – and though he could still hear the music of the women talking, their words were beyond him to understand.

When he came to again, the pain had softened to a slow, dull ache, but it was still hard to open his eyes, and the grey afternoon light seemed bright at the windows. Touching a tentative hand to his face, he searched gently, wincing as his fingers found the break in the bridge of his nose. Slowly, he pushed himself up to sit. His head swam with the movement and he paused, waiting for the wooziness to subside. The women sat at the table, sewing, and he watched Sarah's needle flicking deftly through the linen of a shirt. For him? he wondered. It was not for Nick Tooley, of that he was sure.

He moved his head from side to side, testing, and the ache shifted a little with the movement but did not worsen. Mary smiled to see him awake. 'There's bread and cheese for you,' she offered, 'and broth in the kitchen if you'd like it.'

'I'm not hungry,' he replied. His gut was still tender, and he got up from the couch with care, uncertain of his strength. He turned to his mother. 'Your Nick Tooley should make a living with his fists.' He attempted a smile, and his face tightened and pained with the movement. He had forgotten the bruise on his cheek. 'He has some skill with them.'

'He's not my Nick Tooley.' She returned the smile, and laid down the linen as he eased himself onto the stool at the table beside her. Mary poured him ale and he sipped at it to chase the sour taste of stale blood from his mouth.

'But he was till today?'

She nodded.

'Forgive me.' He felt for her wrist with his fingers, the bones close beneath the skin, fragile. 'I have robbed you of your happiness.'

She shrugged. 'It wasn't fated to be. Too many things against us.' Then, 'Do you think she will marry you?'

It was his turn to shrug. 'She hates me.'

'Nick's wife hated him, but they still wed.'

He was silent – the misery of Nick's marriage stirred a surge of despair within him. Becky – sour and hostile, turning her children against their father. Would Judith do the same? Or would the child be a monster as she had predicted? He saw his whole life in relief before him. Every day hunched above the tailor's bench to provide for his child, a loveless wife, and no hope for something better.

'I hope …' he began, and trailed off. They knew what he hoped. They understood. There was no need to say the words aloud.

'But even so,' Sarah said, 'the child is still yours and you cannot simply walk away.'

Mary tied off the thread she was sewing and handed it back to Sarah. The older woman took it with a nod of thanks and cast an appraising eye across the stitching.

'It's fine work.'

Mary flushed with the praise. 'They taught us at the orphanage, and it's served me well since then.' She gestured to the bodice and skirts she was wearing, a gaudy striped cotton, wearing thin. It was much repaired, Toby noticed now, but the stitching was cunningly done with bows and ribbons that hid most of the work.

'"Tis your only dress?' Sarah asked.

'I have one other,' Mary answered, and her eyes slid away in shame.

'I may have an old bodice or two upstairs you could have, though they'll need some fancying up. A tailor's wife has little use for bows and stripes. I'll search them out.'

The women exchanged smiles, and Toby watched them talking with pleasure. Mary as the daughter Sarah never had, the two of them comfortable in each other's company. He found himself imagining a life of hours like this – Mary part of the household, his wife. Then a spasm of pain in his groin reminded him of the truth of things and, forcing his mind away from such idle speculation, he drank more of his ale. His head was beginning to clear at last.

Sarah picked up the shift and began to sew again. Toby watched the needle's dance through the fabric, and slowly his thoughts drifted back to the book that lay hidden in the chest upstairs. Back to Tom. He must write his name in blood beneath his father's, he remembered. And he must ready himself for whatever lay ahead. A ritual to raise the Devil himself, a sacrifice. But looming as a shadow over all those thoughts was the dread of what Judith would say – his whole life hanging on her word.

The hours passed slowly. Mary left to return to the brothel, and the usual household tasks of the day went unattended. Twice, he got up from the couch and went to the window to watch the road below, waiting, restless. He began to pace the room as his energy returned, the pain easing.

'Why don't you go back to work?' Sarah asked. 'It'll give you something to do.'

'For the same reason as you,' he answered.

She smiled. 'At least I'm sewing.'

He gave her a small smile in return and felt the bruise stretch and pinch with the movement. He flinched. 'I'll fetch another compress,' she said, and, laying down her work, she left the room. He listened to her boots on the stairs before he turned away from the window to throw more wood on the fire and squatted to tend it, arranging the logs to his liking, poking at it till the new wood caught and began to burn. Then he stood before it awhile, enjoying the heat on his legs and watching the flames till his mother returned.

'Press this to your cheek,' she said.

He took the wet cloth – soaked in arnica, he guessed, and comfrey. The woody scent reminded him of childhood – bruised shins and grazed knees, a black eye from fighting other boys at school. He held it to his face and the coolness was soothing.

The afternoon had almost given way to evening, rainclouds

turning bruised and grey above the roofs and no more sun behind them, when the knock at the door finally came. Even though they had been waiting all day, still the sound startled them and made them jump.

'I'll go,' Sarah said, getting up.

'No.' Toby touched a hand to her arm to stay her. 'Let me.'

She tensed but kept her silence, and he heard her follow him into the passage to wait at the head of the stairs. A scent of vinegar filled the hall, rising from the small damp patch on the boards where Frances had cleaned up the vomit. At the door he paused to order his emotions and to find his courage. Then, with a quick breath, he turned the handle and yanked it open. A boy of perhaps eleven or twelve stood on the street, fingering a folded sheet of paper that was sealed with wax. He was searching the front of the house with his eyes, anxious, and he greeted Toby's appearance with obvious relief, stepping forward eagerly.

'Master Chyrche?'

'I am.'

'Message from Master Tooley.'

Toby held out his hand to take the letter and gave the boy a coin in exchange. The boy gave a cursory bow of thanks and then he was gone with all the swiftness of his youth. Toby watched his back disappear into the growing gloom, swallowed quickly by the oncoming darkness. Then he tapped the letter against the knuckles of one hand, closed the door with a sigh, and trod heavily up the stairs to where his mother was waiting.

She backed into the first-floor chamber and he followed her towards the hearth. It had been cold in the doorway, he realized, and now, back in the warmth, he shivered. They stood side by side before the fire while he dug for the resolution to read the news. Finally, with a deep breath, he coaxed open the seal and unfolded it. A brief message was scrawled in a bold cursive hand.

She will have you, it said. *I will write again.*

He handed the sheet to his mother and turned away to lean against the mantelpiece, staring down at the sparking fire, kicking at the hearthstone gently with the toe of one boot. He felt almost nothing. Just a cold and dark reluctance in his soul. Turning his head towards his mother, he gave her a rueful smile.

'Do you think he beat her too?' he asked. 'To gain her assent?' He shook his head, emotion returning in a roil through his body, anger and regret tumbling over each other, fury at his own stupidity. 'At least I never hurt her,' he said. 'At least I never did that.'

Sarah nodded. 'Perhaps she will soften with time, with a child. Perhaps she will remember that she loved you once.'

He nodded, but he held little hope of it. He had seen her mother, holding tight to her bitterness and hate, contempt for her husband in every look she gave him. He had seen the same look in Judith, a martyr's fate. Had Alexander known, he wondered, where the ritual would lead? Was this part of the sacrifice? An image of his father flickered in his thoughts, a mirror image of himself dancing at the end of a rope. His own throat constricted at the thought of it, and he swallowed.

He needed company, he decided, a distraction. He needed Mary. 'I must leave you now,' he said, and Sarah nodded, surprising him. He had expected protest, a plea that he should rest. But it seemed she understood, because she merely touched a caring hand to his face and said, 'Be careful.'

He took his leave of her with a bow and headed out down the stairs and into the darkening evening outside.

Chapter Nineteen

OUR TEARS ARE NOT YET BREW'D

Mary had hoped he would come whatever the news, guessing that either way he would want her company, for comfort or for celebration. But as soon as she saw him duck through the low door from the street, she knew there would be no celebration. His brow was drawn tight, and his eyes were grey and dull with sadness. Setting down the empty jug of ale she had just collected, she stepped across the floor to greet him.

He took her hand, and gave her a small brief smile that sighed with hopelessness. 'She will have me,' he said.

'I'm sorry for it,' she answered, her own sadness cascading through her heart, surprising her. She hadn't realised that she had held such hope, her feelings feeding instead off the way he had watched her as she sewed with his mother that afternoon, the affection and regard she had seen there. She had spent the hours since she left him imagining their life together: a house and a family, a husband who loved her. And though she had known it was nothing more than an idle daydream, the news that she could never be more than a whore to him threatened to undo her – she had to turn her face away to hide the tears she could not stop from rising. She sniffed, appalled at herself: she had never let a man see her cry in her life. He squeezed her fingers gently.

'You have to marry someone.' She forced a smile. 'It may as well be her.'

'Earlier today,' he answered, 'I hoped it might be you.'

She stared. Had Alexander's magic worked so completely? She had not thought it possible. Or perhaps the love was genuine, the natural reaching of his heart towards a woman who loved him in return. She guessed she'd never know, but the pleasure of his affection flared inside her, and though he couldn't marry her she knew she held his heart.

'Can we go somewhere?' he murmured. 'Somewhere other than here?'

She flicked a glance back over her shoulder, scanning the room. It was quiet. A few regular customers drinking steadily, a rowdy game of dice taking place near the hearth. She had already been with the ones who wanted her – there was no more money to be made from them tonight. A couple of the other girls lounged at a table not far from the door, and Madam was nowhere to be seen.

'I'll pay you for your time,' he said, understanding her hesitation. 'I wouldn't want for you to be in trouble.'

She blinked and set her jaw, nodding, knowing that if she spoke she would cry in earnest. She wished she could refuse and be with him as a normal girl might – the pleasure of each other's company the only exchange. But her time was not her own to spend, and she could do little else but take his money.

Taking her elbow, he steered her towards the door, but she disengaged her arm and doubled back to fetch her cloak from its hook beside the stairs. He helped her with it, draping it gently across her shoulders as a gentleman might do for a lady, and the backs of his fingers brushed her neck: with his touch she shivered.

Then they stepped out into the soft damp of the night, a mist rising on the river and the stars hiding behind the shifting curtain of cloud. On the water, lanterns bobbed, and the plash and thud of oars drifted to the shore as the boatmen laboured against the tide. Bankside was busy – torches flared along the row of brothels, lighting the whitewashed fronts, and groups of men of all classes strolled on the quay in search of pleasure, or hurried to and from the landing stage. Her world, she thought, and she would leave it only for a plot of ground at the Cross Bones, where no one would ever come to mourn her.

With her arm linked through his – for all the world a courting couple – she walked with him along the bank towards the market, pacing swiftly to keep up with his long stride, wondering where he planned to take her. The market was closed now and in darkness, but the shut-up stalls offered shelter and places to hide, and they turned their eyes away from the shadows that moved in the corners of their vision. Even Mary was afraid of the market at night – she rarely walked here alone. She held his arm tighter, and he laid his hand over hers, reassuring, but on the High Street she breathed again. The road fairly bustled with activity – travellers too late to cross the bridge stepping down from carts and coaches and horses to search out a room for the night in one of the many inns that lined the road. Torches flickered in their sconces – the street was brightly lit, and traders with baskets still hawked their few remaining items before turning in for the night, though their shouts held out little hope.

They passed a young beggar girl, offering a single small posy of lavender, and on an impulse, Toby stopped. The girl stared in surprise as he gave her a coin and took the posy, before her fingers tightened over the penny and she fled into the night. They watched her go, the small ragged back enveloped swiftly by the gloom, then Toby proffered the posy to Mary with a bow. She laughed and curtseyed as she accepted the gift, then held it gently between her fingers as they walked on, the sweet scent of lavender breathing in the air around her. No one had ever given her flowers before.

When they arrived at the house in Narrow Lane it was dark and shuttered – nobody had thought to light the torch that usually flickered at the door – but inside, a trio of candles burned. Toby took one from its place and led her along the passage to a small room behind the shop that she had never entered. An office, she thought from the doorway, though in the corner was a narrow bed with a brightly embroidered counterpane.

'It used to be the apprentice's room,' he said, by way of explanation.

'Did you bring her here too?' Mary asked. The words slid from her lips before she had time to stop them.

Toby hesitated, caught off guard by the question, and for the space of a breath his eyes flicked across the floor and towards the corner. An unwelcome image twisted into her thoughts: Toby and the girl who would be his wife, entwined in pleasure on the bed, begetting their child. She turned her head away and drew in a deep breath, trying to still the jealousy. Had he ever bought a posy for Judith?

'I did,' he answered finally.

They were silent a moment. The candle flickered and guttered in the draught that filtered from the passage and threw shifting shadows – their figures stretched and deformed against the wall. He reached out his hand for hers and said, 'Come. We'll go upstairs.'

She let him take her hand and lead her out of the little room and back along the passage that ran from the front of the house to the back. They crept up the stairs, past the first-floor chamber and on upwards, to parts of the house she had never been to before. His mother's bedchamber, and then a narrow flight of stairs that led to an attic where two doors led off a tiny landing.

'My chamber is above my mother's,' he whispered. 'We must be silent.'

She nodded her understanding as he pushed open the door. It was a spacious room, with a sloping roof and a window that looked out on the street. A fire had been laid in the fireplace but was not yet lit, and the bed was hung with an awning for warmth, larger than the narrow cot in the apprentice's room, a good-sized bed with an oak trunk for storage at its foot. Beside the window was a desk that was littered with papers and quills and books, and she remembered the book she was supposed to steal. Stepping to the desk, she ran her fingers across the cool, smooth wood surface, curious, then picked up the first book her hand came to. A Latin grammar, well thumbed, the margins replete with notes.

She lifted her head to him with a smile of puzzlement, but he gave her no answer. Instead, he took the book from her hand and laid it back on the desk, standing close to her, near enough for her to feel the warmth of his body, the sweetness of his breath. She laid the posy on the table, the scent of lavender still on her hands, and Alexander's book was forgotten as Toby's mouth closed on hers and he lifted her onto the desk, careless of the papers underneath, one hand beneath her skirts as she reached for the belt of his breeches.

Their sex was quick and good and silent, and afterwards they remained awhile together as she felt him diminishing inside her, her arms draped around his neck, her head against his collarbone. Finally, he shifted to move back from her, but she held him tighter, reluctant to let him go. Gently, he reached up and unwound her arms from behind his head, but his lips brushed her hair and his own regret was in the sadness of his eyes.

'I should take you back,' he whispered.

'Can we stay a little longer?' she replied. 'Please?'

He smiled, and stepped back, tucking himself back into his breeches before he lowered himself to sit on the edge of the bed. She remained on the desk, her skirts still hitched up around her thighs, skin pale in the candlelight. They were silent, but comfortable with each other. She reached behind her and took up another book. It was a volume on astrology, and she flicked through the pages, eyes glancing over symbols and charts and words she could not read. Alexander's books, she guessed. So Toby was gaining the knowledge he needed. Perhaps the book she'd been asked to steal was not so worthless to him after all. Doubt turned again in her gut.

Toby watched her, waiting for her questions, but she said nothing, afraid to give herself away. Finally, she lowered her skirts and slid from the surface of the desk. Taking a moment to straighten her clothes, she went to sit beside him on the bed, fingers resting gently on his thigh. A bed he would share with Judith soon, she recalled, despite his growing love for Mary. Did it matter then? The book? If Alexander took Toby's love away, what difference would it make?

'We should go,' she said finally. She would have been missed at the bawdy house by now, and though she would have payment for her time, Madam preferred the girls to be under her roof where she could keep an eye on them and keep them safe. Her displeasure was something to be avoided.

He nodded and stood up, and they crept from the room, treading lightly on the wooden steps. It was tempting to giggle, until they rounded the corner into the passage and met Sarah coming the other way, a candle in her hand and her cloak still on her shoulders. Mary dropped into an instinctive curtsey. 'Mistress Chyrche,' she murmured.

'Mary.' Sarah nodded her head in her reply.

Mother and son locked eyes for a long moment, but in the changing light from the candles, Mary could not say what she saw there. Toby said, 'I was just taking Mary home.'

Sarah nodded and opened her chamber door, stepping into its shelter to make way for them to pass her in the narrow passage. They went on their way without another word, and as they hurried back towards Bankside, her arm looped through his, she could think of nothing more to say.

Chapter Twenty

B reakfast, and mother and son ate in silence, neither sure how to broach their meeting in the passage, or if they even should. Toby swallowed the last of his egg and took a mouthful of ale. Then he put down the cup and said, 'I think we should have another servant.'

Sarah lowered her bread to the plate in front of her and smiled. 'Mary?'

'With a wife and a child,' he replied, ignoring the question, 'another pair of hands …'

'Another pair of hands would indeed be helpful,' Sarah agreed. 'But having Mary under your roof is no way to win Judith round.'

He shook his head. 'Judith will never come round, Mary or no. She thinks I dance with the Devil, and there is nothing I can do will persuade her otherwise.'

'And do you?'

He let out a laugh to hide his unease, but it came out high and nervous, and he bit at his lip. 'Hardly,' he said.

'But you used the book?'

He shook his head. 'The book is hard to understand, hard to read. Latin, Hebrew, Greek, and full of symbols that mean nothing to me.' But even as he said it, he knew it was a lie. He had studied hard, an eager student as his father had been: schoolboy Latin easily recalled, and the letters of Hebrew and Greek beginning to coalesce into meaning. The arcane symbols had started at last to make sense, and he had made the book his own with his name in blood beneath his father's as Tom had told him. With his claim on it, the book had responded, beginning to yield up its secrets, pages humming with possibility. He had begun to carry it with him always, a pocket sewn for the purpose into the breast of his doublet.

'How then?' she asked. 'What magic did you use?'

He lowered his eyes, unsure how much to trust to her, how much she understood.

'Tell me, Toby,' she persisted. 'I will not judge you. I only want to help.' She reached across the table and took his hand, a small smile of encouragement curling her lips that he had seen so many times as a boy when she had coaxed out the truth from him. But they had been minor wrongs, the infractions of a child. Could he trust her with this? he wondered. Should he?

'There is an old man,' he said, with a shrug, 'who showed me a ritual ...'

'You conjured spirits?'

He heard the fear in her voice and wished he had held his peace. 'Aye,' he said. 'I did.'

She was silent, eyes lowered to the table between them, turning the knife in her hand, over and over.

'Then I dismissed them,' he added. 'She is free of them now.'

'What's done cannot be undone,' she said, looking up. She shrugged. 'And you must make a life with her.' Then, 'Have Mary here if you wish, if it will bring you some happiness.'

He nodded. 'I'll think on it,' he said, and she smiled.

Then he swung his legs over the bench, got up and headed downstairs to open the shop for business.

In the afternoon Mary went to the playhouse to tout for trade. No wonder the Puritans wanted it closed, she thought with a smile, as the small band of girls paid their penny entrance and fanned out amongst the watchers, flirting, joking, enticing. She pulled her bodice lower to show the tips of her nipples and the winter air lifted the goosebumps across her skin. But she was used to the bite of cold against her chest and she paid it little mind. A shy apprentice bought her a cup of ale and she stood close beside him while she drank it, aware of his sidelong glances at her breasts.

The play began with a crash of thunder that split the air above the audience, and an explosion of smoke billowed through the playhouse. Ale spilled across her hand, barely noticed, and when the smoke cleared the apprentice was nowhere to be seen.

Onstage three dark figures were circling, black-garbed and wild-looking, barely human. Mary watched, entranced, hardly breathing.

'When shall we three meet again,
    In thunder, lightning, or in rain?'

'When the hurlyburly's done.
    When the battle's lost and won ...'

Witches. She remembered Sarah's mother and the Grove, the black dog that had kept her warm. The witchcraft she knew of was nothing like these weird women on the stage – malice oozing with every word. Shades of the same dark she saw in Alexander, she realised, and shuddered. Did he hail from the same hellish realms? But still, she couldn't look away, drawn by the spell of the illusion as a new and murky dark seemed to descend upon the playhouse.

'Fair is foul, and foul is fair,
    Hover through the fog and filthy air.'

Then with another crash of smoke they were gone and the spell was broken. Mary flicked a glance around her, and her eye caught the form of Alexander in a seat in the lower gallery close by the stage. But his attention was not with the play – his gaze was intent and fixed on her, eyes dark with malevolence. Pinning her with a look, his lips parted in the semblance of a smile that chilled her to the marrow, and she hung there, frozen for what seemed an eternity, before the apprentice appeared again beside her and nudged her arm, drawing her back to the world around her.

'Are you all right, miss?'

She stared at him, her mind still groping in the dark, before she turned away in terror and fought her way out of the crowd, oblivious to the curses and grumbles of the people she pushed aside in her haste to escape.

Only when she was beyond the playhouse walls in the open space before it did she stop to breathe in the air in great long gulps, as though she had surfaced from a great depth underwater.

That night Alexander came to the brothel. Mary saw him as she trod down the stairs behind the young man she had just lain with – smooth-skinned and eager, an easy shilling earned. Alexander was in his usual place with his back to the hearth so that he could see the whole place at a glance, nursing a cup of ale between his hands. Her mouth went dry at the sight of him, and her guts clenched: he frightened her still.

Seeing her on the steps, he lifted a hand to beckon her over, and with a final smile and touch to the cheek of the young man, she turned from him and made her way between the tables towards the fireplace.

She stood before his table, and he inclined his head in greeting as he gestured for her to sit. She obeyed, but kept the width of the table between them.

'A pretty one,' he remarked, throwing a glance across the room to where the young man was laughing now with his friends. 'You like them pretty?'

She shrugged. 'Do you?'

He laughed and took a mouthful of ale. He said, 'As it happens, I do.'

She followed his gaze, still tracking the young man, who was telling a story now to his companions, their attention rapt. Pretty was not important, she thought. Kindness mattered more, and sometimes it came from the most unexpected quarters, men she had judged as rough as they climbed the stairs surprising her with unlooked-for gentleness. The pretty ones could be as cruel as any, though the boy tonight had been kind enough.

Alexander brought his attention back to Mary and pinned her with those hard blue eyes that seemed to bore into her soul. She slid her own gaze away and watched his hand where it rested on the cup. Stubby fingers, she noticed, the nails stained with ink. He leaned towards her and she shrank back instinctively, but his hand darted out and curled around her wrist, pulling her closer. Briefly, she tried to twist her arm free of his grip, but his fingers dug deeper and dragged her forward, so that their faces were close above the surface of the table. She could smell the sourness of unlaundered clothes and the bitter ale on his breath, and it took strength of will to suppress a shudder.

'Do you have it?'

She shook her head. 'Not yet.'

'I am not a patient man, Mary.' He tightened his hold on her wrist, hurting, but she set her mouth firm against the pain. 'I have kept my side of the bargain, have I not? He loves you?'

'Perhaps,' she murmured, still reluctant to believe it, for in the end it made no difference – he would marry Judith and she would still die a whore. 'I don't yet know where he keeps it,' she said. 'I need more time.'

'Your time is running out, girl.' He rubbed his thumb along the inside of her forearm, as though considering whether or not to snap the bone beneath. It would be easy enough to do, she thought, and she had no doubt he had inflicted such cruelties before. She took a silent deep breath, trying to steady the quickened beating of her heart, the blood pulsing through her veins beneath his fingers.

Then he laughed and threw her arm back towards her. She nursed it gently with the other hand, and thought briefly of the herbs she would need to tend to the bruises he had wrought – arnica and comfrey, perhaps. She would go to Sarah in the morning.

'Are you afraid of me, Mary Sparrow?'

She nodded. He could do far worse to her than take Toby away. She could end up witless and foolish like Rosalind, or face down in the Thames.

'Good,' he said. 'Then get me the book, and you'll have no more cause to fear me. You'll find me a fair man to my friends.'

She was silent, still gently rubbing at the swelling bruise. She would fear him always, in spite of his claims. He leaned forward once more and took her fingers gently in his own, caressing, like a lover. She tensed and waited for the cruelty behind it.

He said, 'Will you be my pretty boy tonight?' He slid a coin across the table towards her, and though she swept it up with her free hand, she kept her eyes lowered away from him: she did not want to see the lust in his eyes. 'Shall we?' he said, his fingers still entwined in hers, raising her to stand.

She let out a silent sigh, pocketed the coin, and led him through the tangle of tables and chairs towards the staircase and on upwards to her chamber.

Later, Mary wandered out to the quayside, an escape from the fumes of ale and sex that pervaded the brothel, and the echoes of voices raised with drink drifted through the low door after her. Standing at the water's edge, she gazed out into the darkness across the river, lights flickering, the shadow of St Paul's a darkened mass against a velvet sky. Away to the west, the church bells tolled the hour with two mournful strikes, and she folded her arms against the breeze that rose off the water, chilling her, the cool damp curling against the bare skin of her neck and shoulders. She should have brought her shawl.

But it was good to be out by the river, a timeless force that paid no mind to the vicissitudes of men, rolling always onward to the sea, inevitable as death. She felt humbled beside it, and her own concerns seemed less important. But still ...

Could she steal the book? Should she? Fear argued in favour, and she rubbed at the swelling on her wrist that was already turning to mottled purple. Alexander was a man of casual brutality, and she dared not imagine the violence of his anger. But Toby would marry Judith whatever she did, and she, Mary, would still die a whore on Bankside. She was going to lose him anyway – betrayal or no – whatever Alexander promised.

On the river a pleasure boat hove past, oars beating in stately rhythm to the music of a lute and tambor, lanterns blazing and the high voices of women. Would they shoot the bridge, she wondered, taking pleasure in the risk of it? She watched the boat till the lights were swallowed in the mist and dark, voices drifting back in snatches as quietness settled once again across the water – in the small hours few people were abroad.

A shout from the row of buildings behind her, a man's voice raised and querulous, drew her back to the business of the night, and with a sigh, she turned from the river and headed back inside to the noisy dissipation of the bawdy house, the decision still unmade.

Chapter Twenty-One

A DAGGER OF THE MIND

The summons to the Tooleys' took days to come, and Toby spent the time in a sleepless haze of dread, going about his work without care, his mind always turning on what lay before him. The other tailors worked alongside him in the quiet of his tension, trading brief looks of unease, and though they said nothing to their master, he knew they marked the change and wondered amongst themselves.

His mother watched him too. He could see the pity in her eyes, and the sorrow that there was nothing she could do to save him from the loveless dark of his future.

He barely spoke, to her or anyone, his feelings writhing under the weight of his duty and his mind rolling in the constant hunt for some way out, a different ending to the tale. Even in the brief dreams of restless, wakeful nights, he found no relief – images of prison cells, shackles on his wrists and a long walk through jeering crowds towards the hangman's noose. He would wake then in the cold early hours, breathless, skin slick with sweat and his heart knocking quick enough to burst. His father's end, he realised, reliving the death of Tom Wynter. A reminder, perhaps, to be grateful for the mercy that was his life. For with life there must surely be hope. Hope of change. Hope of renewal. It was hard to make himself believe it, and he called to his father often in the chill breath of the dark, but no answer ever came.

The message from the Tooleys arrived as he broke bread one morning, eating in silence with his head turned away from the sorrow in his mother's eyes – her pity was almost more than he could bear. Passing the letter across the table to Sarah, he managed a wry smile. 'I am summoned at last.'

She took it and skimmed her eyes across the words, then looked across at him. 'Should I go with you?'

'To even the numbers?' He shook his head. 'I would take my father if he were here, but no man wants to be seen to need his mother.'

She nodded and gave him a weak smile that did not reach her eyes. ''Tis a betrothal,' she said. 'Not a wake.'

'If you say so,' he replied. Then he got up from the table, lifted his doublet from the bench beside him, and shrugged it on. The book sat neatly against his ribs in its secret pocket, and he took comfort in its presence – his connection to his father, and a gateway to different and unknown realms. If he must be a prisoner in the daylight world, he thought, then he would find his escape in the dark secrets of the night.

His mother watched him go and he saw the struggle with her tears. Did she stand at the window as his back faded out of sight along the street? He guessed so. He walked with purpose, striding along the High Street in the damp cold of the morning, avoiding the puddles in the ruts, boots staining with the mud. The season had fully turned, winter here to stay, and the sky glowered low and dark, full of the rain to come.

~

He arrived too soon and paused to run his eyes across the front of the house. It was a modest house on the end of a terrace of three: the acting trade had served Tooley well enough, but it had not made him rich, as it had some others. Not so long ago it had been the last house in the street, but now others had been built alongside and the path that had led to the fields and woods beyond had widened into a track that was rutted from cartwheels, mud churned into ridges, puddles glistening and treacherous. But his gaze was still drawn to the freedom the road was offering. He could just keep walking, he thought. Away from this life and into another. He had the book, a few coins, his wits and his trade as a tailor. He could step on a ship and be gone into the risk and adventure of a new life within the day. A life where no one knew him. A life where he could begin again. It was tempting. He scanned the landscape. The river was little more than a stone's throw away behind the houses, ships docked at the quayside and ready to sail.

Last chance, he thought, and dropped his head to the dirt at his feet, tightening his lips against the temptation, and fingering the gold ring in his pocket, the metal warm and smooth against his skin. It was a plain, simple band, and uninscribed. For what could he engrave upon it that would not be hypocrisy? He took a deep breath. Judith is with child, he told himself. His child, and he could not just walk away. But still he could not bring himself to cross the lane and knock at the door. He lifted his eyes to the sky and the heavy ridges of cloud, grey upon grey upon grey, leading into infinity. Was Heaven beyond them? A realm of the dead?

What would you do, Tom Wynter? he breathed. *What counsel for your son?*

A breath of wind whispered along the lane, cool against the skin of his face. Then the first drops of rain began to fall, splashing against his forehead, into his eyes. He blinked and lowered his head, gaze coming to rest once more upon the stone front of the house before him. Then, setting his shoulders and taking a deep breath, he strode across the muddy ground and rapped upon the bright-painted wood of the door. The moments seemed long before his knock was answered by an ancient servant, who stared at him in surprise.

'My name is Toby Chyrche,' he said. 'Your master wished to see me.'

She nodded, recovering herself, and backed away to let him in. 'In there,' she said, gesturing to a door off the passage. 'They are expecting you.'

Toby nodded and went through into a low-ceilinged room that was modestly furnished: a table, a sideboard, two chairs and some cushions before a hearth where a fire burned brightly, showering the room in a cheerful light. It was hot after the cool of the day outside, and he was conscious of the sweat that coated the back of his neck. He ran his fingers through his hair and scattered a light spray of water to the rug.

The family sat at the table, and Toby bowed lightly in greeting. Nick rose from his place and nodded in return. If he noticed the bruises that still covered the younger man's face he gave no sign of it. Becky stared at him with ill-disguised hostility, and Judith's gaze was resolutely lowered to her hands, which were clasped together on her lap. He couldn't see her face. No one spoke and the tension hung in the air like smoke from a fire, stifling. Toby waited, still fingering the ring. Amongst the detritus of breakfast on the table – a crust of bread, cups, a jug – he could see the contract of betrothal, the bold lettering in the same hand as the message that had come. He gave a silent sigh – all he wanted now was to get it over with. He gestured to the paper. 'Is that the contract?'

'It is,' Nick replied.

'Shall we?' He turned towards Judith, who had not moved, and still she did not lift her head until her father spoke to her.

'Judith, it is time.'

She rose from her stool and went to stand at the hearth in obedient silence. She had been instructed beforehand, he realised, the process rehearsed to make it easier. He looked to Nick, who gestured with his chin towards his daughter, then he followed her to the fireplace to stand before her, close enough to touch. She kept her eyes on the woven rug at their feet, her face still mostly hidden, but even so, he could see the pallor of her forehead and the gauntness of her cheek beneath the fading bruise. Remorse slid through him. He had never wanted to hurt her – he had hoped only to loosen the fetters of her faith and allow her passion free rein. He remembered the first time he tried to kiss her before he had ever met Alexander, and the want in her eyes as she refused him, the lift of her breath as she forced down her desire.

'Judith?' he said, and reached to touch her fingers, but she snatched her hand away as though he had burned her, and her head snapped up to look at him at last. They locked eyes for a moment, and there was no trace of love or desire for him in her look any more, only blank hostility, and he slid his gaze away, unnerved. What had he done?

'We are to be married,' he managed to say. 'Can we not at least be friends?'

'I will be your wife,' she breathed in reply. 'Because I must, and only that …'

Toby let out a breath between lips pursed tight and abandoned all hope of some kind of compact between them, an agreement to be kind to each other. He said, 'Then let's get this over with.'

She gave a single sharp nod, and he withdrew the ring from his pocket. He had no idea what words to say, and he slanted a glance towards Nick for help. Perhaps his mother should have come after all, he thought. It would at least have wiped the smugness from Becky's face.

'Give me your hand,' he said.

For a moment she hesitated, the last gasp of freedom before she committed herself. Then she raised her arm and let him slide the ring onto her finger. It fitted perfectly, and as she turned it gently with her other hand, she could not help but lift her head and twitch her lips into the beginning of a smile. Hope surged again in his belly – perhaps they could find a way back after all. Then her mother approached and stood at Judith's shoulder and all trace of the smile was gone, her mouth set once more in the same thin line as her mother's. Reluctantly, he held out his hand to receive his own ring, but when Judith tried to slide it onto his finger it refused to fit across the knuckle, in spite of the narrowness of his hands.

She looked up at him again, this time in helpless frustration.

'No matter,' he said, gently, taking the ring from her. 'I will get it altered.' He held it cupped loosely in his palm.

'You need to sign,' Becky said, and gave him the quill.

They stepped to the table and took turns to make their signatures on the document, and then they stood close together side by side, awkward. It was not the betrothal he had imagined, and he raised his head to look at Nick. 'I would like a few moments alone with my bride-to-be,' he said.

From the edge of his eye he saw Becky's mouth open in the beginnings of protest, but Nick simply nodded, and with a hand on his wife's shoulder, he led her from the chamber. The door clicked shut behind them, and he waited for their footsteps on the flagstones of the passage, heading towards the back of the house and what he guessed would be the kitchen.

'So it is done,' she said. 'We are betrothed.'

'By tradition we should kiss,' he said. 'To seal it.'

She gave a small huff that lay between laughter and contempt, then turned away. 'Your lips will never touch mine again,' she said. 'They have drunk their last of that pleasure.'

He was silent, waiting, sensing more to come. Swinging back to him, she said, 'I will be your wife because whatever it is I carry needs a father, but do not think I trust you or forgive you, or that you will ever touch me again.'

He nodded, and the little light of hope that had lit with her smile at the ring was extinguished. There was no more to say. With a bow of farewell, he crossed to the door. She gave him no answering curtsey.

'I'll see you at church on Sunday,' he said, turning back towards her.

She lifted her head and stared, as though surprised at his presence.

'For the banns,' he said.

'For the banns,' she agreed.

Then he stepped out into the rain, and the cold water felt good and pure against his head.

Sarah watched her son go from the window, tracing the tall, narrow back as it disappeared into the morning. For all the world he could have been Tom, she thought. The same lean height and light wavy hair, the same tilt to his shoulders as he walked. The likeness still unsettled her, stirring her memories and her loneliness. And Nick, breaking through the shroud of self-sufficiency she had wrapped around herself through all the years of her marriage, reawakening her need to be loved, to be touched by another. A brief rip that had utterly destroyed her defences, so that now she felt her aloneness with raw and fresh intensity, the same bright pain that Tom's death had raised, sleeping on a pillow each night that was wet with tears. But the pain was proof at least she was alive: in the half-life she had lived with Simon, the only stir to quickness had been her son, and now the whole world in all its mad and baffling wonder breathed again through her blood so that she reeled with its presence.

Standing at the window, Sarah stared at the space in the street that Toby had left, tracing his steps in her mind to Nick Tooley's house. She knew the way well – she had walked the same path many times. Was it truly his fate to marry Judith? To live a loveless life as she had done? It was not the path she had hoped for him, not the life she had prayed to Hecate to give him, and the pain of it was as raw as a salted wound. Tom's boy, his final gift to her, and for all her spell-craft it seemed she had failed to protect him. She raised her eyes from the road to the strip of grey that hung above the houses. The sky was full, almost bursting with its burden of rain, and she made a silent call to Hecate. *Lead him on a different path, Great Goddess. Let him love.*

Turning from the window, she rested her hips against the sill and surveyed the room before her. The same dark and heavy furnishings she remembered from her childhood, the same pewter plates on the table, the faded wall hanging of a forest scene, a white hart in flight. She had always loved that picture – the hart other-worldly and the forest a place of great and powerful beauty, a reminder of Hecate's sacred grove. She let her eyes linger on the image until it deepened, drawing her in. Stepping towards it, she traced the tight stitched lines of the trees with her fingertips and sighed.

She needed to scry. The shewstone had been calling her, filling her dreams and vibrating at the corners of her thoughts. Every surface seemed to offer its secrets – a pail of water, a windowpane, even the dying embers of the fire, although she had never been gifted to read the flames easily. She turned away from the tapestry, reluctant. Her last vision had been of her brother's death and her own, and she was afraid. But the stone was insistent, refusing to be ignored, and she knew that in the end she could do nothing else but look into its depths and see what it foretold.

Tom would not have been afraid, she told herself; Tom would have told her to scry. With sudden determination, she strode to the door, skirts swinging with a whisper on the rush mats that covered the floor. She took the stairs two at a time and in her chamber she retrieved the shewstone from its hiding place, wrapped and buried in the linen chest, though from whom she still needed to hide it she could not have said. Old habits, she guessed, a life of secrets kept.

Kneeling at the open chest, she unwrapped the shewstone from the piece of leather that protected it and took it out. A mirror of black obsidian, highly polished, smooth and cool against her fingertips. It had been a gift from her mother as a child, though whence it came before that she did not know. She should have asked, she thought now. Sarah ran her fingers across its surface, almost a caress, and the connection still hummed in her touch, sensation prickling through skin and bone, her blood quickening. She had thought to go to the Grove to scry in spite of the threatening rain for it was a place of power and memory, but the stone was beckoning now with a new urgency in its call, so she set it on the little table and drew the curtain at the window against the soft morning light. Then, setting a candle to the embers in the fireplace to light, she placed it close by the shewstone, drew up a stool, and readied herself to foretell.

For long minutes she gazed at the stone's dark shine and saw only the reflection of the room about her. Her breath grew deep and long, heartbeat slowing to a steady knock as she became aware of the pulse of the blood in her veins, and her whole body quivered with its flow. Memories flickered through her thoughts, the playhouse, a stage, images of Tom, but she slid them to the darkest corners of her mind and gently trained her focus deep inside the stone.

Slowly – wondrously, it always seemed to her – the black mirror gave way to colour, like clouds against the sky in a swift-blowing wind. Blues, greens, crimson coloured the surface, shifting, the Fates still undecided, futures as yet unknown. She waited, gaze steady and patient, fear at bay. A sweep of deep red coalesced into fleeting images that faded too fast for her mind to grasp – like the dreams that leave a trail on waking but offer no form to hold on to. And as she watched and waited, the stone seemed to deepen and grow, a gateway opening onto another world, a path leading in. Her mind stepped forward to follow a twisting tunnel through rough-hewn rock, until she found herself in a vast dark cave set deep within the earth.

A sorcerer at work, his face hidden.

A globe, and charts, and maps.

A table strewn with books. Candles.

A circle on the ground, and at its centre kneels her son.

Her breath froze as her hand rose of its own accord to reach out towards him, and though it stopped just short of the stone, it was enough to blur the vision so that she felt more than saw the knife at Toby's throat. But she heard the hiss of his blood running into the sorcerer's vial, and the soft thud of his lifeless body to the ground as the blood drained out of him. Her fingers came to rest on the stone's face as though to bring back the images, but with her touch the vision faded into utter obscurity and only a burning heat in the mirror remained to say the image had ever been there at all.

She let her hand slide away, and sat for a long time in silence.

She should have left the shewstone in the earth with Tom. She should have let it be. But things seen can never be unseen, and a fate foretold was hard to turn aside.

Chapter Twenty-Two

THE LOVE THAT FOLLOWS US

When the tailor's shop had closed for the day, Toby went to the Cardinal's Cap, hoping to lose himself in drink and Mary's company, a brief escape from the knowledge of his future. The hubbub from the brothel flooded out into the street through the open windows – men's voices thick with drink, and the brief high shrill of the whores' laughter. Play-goers, he guessed. It was the right time of day, the late afternoon almost darkened into night. Firelight flickered and leapt inside, candle flames dancing in the draught, and he paused in the doorway to scan the crowd for Mary. But his eyes came to rest instead on a table in the centre of the crowded place. The players themselves, and Nick Tooley among them with a jug of wine in his hand, pouring for the others.

Toby bit his lip and for three breaths he hesitated, in half a mind to go elsewhere. But he wanted Mary, so he stepped inside and found a place in the corner that was side on to the players. A girl he had not seen before, pretty and new, swayed towards him and he bid her fetch him wine. He needed more than ale to dull his sorrows tonight. She was back in a trice, sliding onto the stool beside him, pouring wine for them both. 'Where's Mary?' he said.

The girl lifted her head towards the landing upstairs. 'She's busy.'

'Then I'll wait,' Toby replied.

'I can do whatever she does,' she offered.

'Perhaps,' he agreed. 'But I came here for her.'

She sighed and sat back. 'As you like.' Then she refilled her cup from the jug, gave him a wink, and sashayed towards the table of players. Her approach caught Nick's eye and, looking in her direction, he noticed Toby, sitting behind her. For a moment he just stared and Toby held his look, though his gut tightened in anticipation and he lifted an automatic hand to the last traces on his face of the blows Nick had given him.

The player drained his cup. Then, picking up the jug, he lifted his legs over the bench and sauntered over. He was unsteady on his feet, Toby noticed, though he hid it well. He had obviously been drinking hard. Nick set himself down on a stool and put the jug on the small table between them. 'What brings such a newly betrothed man to the bawdy house?' he said. 'Bored of your bride-to-be already?'

Toby gave a rueful smile. 'Having a drink,' he said. 'Same as you.'

Nick shook his head. 'If you're here for the same as me,' he said, 'you're here to fuck.'

He said nothing. What answer could he give?

'Are you not here to fuck one of these fine ladies?' Cup in hand, Nick gestured around the bawdy house, eyes flitting, searching out the girls amongst the men. 'I'm guessing you won't be getting much of it at home. I can recommend the one with six fingers, every one of them with skill.' He brought the cup back to the table with a thud, and the wine inside splashed red drops onto his wrist. Lifting his hand to his mouth, he licked the drops away, tongue pink and dainty. Then he turned his attention to Toby, fixing him with green eyes that were still bright with intensity, in spite of the wine. 'Ah!' he said. 'Who am I to judge you? I did just the same.' He took a mouthful of his drink.

Toby sipped at his own wine and waited, still wary. Nick was in a strange mood, heavy with alcohol, and Toby did not doubt his temper could turn in a heartbeat. They sat in silence for a while, Nick drinking steadily. His father-in-law, Toby thought with wry amusement, and both of them finding their pleasure at the brothel, their Puritan wives at home. Was this to be his life now? He poured himself more wine and drank it off, feeling the blurriness hit his blood and the edges of the world beginning to soften.

Nick observed him across the table, fingering his cup. When Toby lowered his drink and met the other man's look, Nick slid his gaze away. Then he said, 'How is your mother?'

Toby shrugged. 'Sad,' he said. 'Lonely. She's a widow ...'

Nick's jaw worked with tension, and his fingers continued to slide up and down the cup for a while until he lifted it once more to his mouth and drank.

Then Mary was there, sliding her arm across his shoulders, and Toby had not seen her arrive.

'That's the one,' Nick said. 'The six-fingered whore I was telling you about.'

Toby nodded, and lifted a smile towards Mary as he wrapped his arm around her waist. She smiled in return and leaned her body in closer, so that his head was against her breast. He could feel the beat of her heart, her body warm against him, and desire pounded through him, heat and hardness.

Nick passed some coins across the table. 'Have her on me,' he said. 'Think of it as a dowry payment.' Then he laughed, knocked back the contents of his cup and got up. Toby watched as he stumbled back to the table of players, and Mary swept up the coins with a deft movement of her hand.

'What did he mean – a dowry payment?' she asked.

'I was betrothed to his daughter today.' He wondered if she heard the bitterness in his voice, if she cared. He wanted to believe that she did, but didn't every man think he was different? That he was the one the whore truly cared for?

'Come upstairs,' she said, by way of answer, so he had no idea of what she felt.

Then she led him to her room.

She had missed him. He had stayed away for many days and she had worried herself about him, a vague sense of apprehension tainting her blood, his sad eyes watching her in dreams, and never free from thoughts of him. She gripped his hand tighter, grateful for the solid touch of his flesh and his living warmth. Alexander had been again, asking for his book, growing impatient. Instinctively, she touched her free hand to her neck with the memory of the pressure of his fingers, then fought to force him from her mind. She was with Toby now, and safe, for a while at least.

When she closed the door behind them, he let go of her hand and wandered to the window, though there was nothing to see but the blackness of the yard below and the vague flicker of lights behind the curtains of the surrounding buildings. Other brothels for the most part, or taverns and ale-houses. Places men came to escape their real lives. Other women pleasuring other men. Violence being done.

''Tis done then,' she said, crossing to stand beside him, reaching again for his hand. 'You are to be wed.'

He turned to look at her and though his lips lifted in the beginnings of a smile, she could not read the look she saw in his eyes. His fingers tangled with hers. 'I will still come,' he said. 'God knows I will have little satisfaction in my marriage bed.'

Mary tilted her head. 'She is with child ...'

He shifted his gaze back to the world outside the window and said nothing. She could feel the heaviness of his spirit and knew of no way to tease him back to her.

He said, 'Let us have more wine.'

She smiled. 'Of course,' she replied, and crossed to the door to call to the boy who served the rooms upstairs. Then they waited together at the window, Mary's palm resting on his chest, her body close to his, drinking in his warmth and savouring his closeness, and when the boy brought the wine, Toby took the cup she poured for him with a small nod of thanks. She watched him drink before she lifted her hands to unfasten the buttons of his doublet, the leather soft and worn between her fingers, the buttons easy to undo. Sliding her hands inside, she noticed a new pocket sewn into the lining, and something solid and heavy within. Briefly she was curious, but it was forgotten in a moment as Toby set down his cup on the window ledge and lifted her face to kiss her, sliding one arm around her back, the other hand caressing her head.

He tasted sweetly of wine, and as she remembered again that he was betrothed to another, the pain of her lost hopes bristled through her body as desire to make him hers. She wanted him inside her, filling her, all of her, skin against skin, his child in her belly. She dragged at the laces of her bodice, and he, catching her urgency, threw off his doublet and hauled the shirt over his head, shivering as the cold air touched the pale skin of his torso, cool against her breasts.

For a moment she struggled with her skirts until they were on the floor around her feet as Toby stepped out of his breeches and they were naked with each other in the cold room, his cock pressing hard against her. His mouth found hers, one breast cupped in a palm, and as he held her tightly against him he shifted her towards the bed, their mouths still locked, laying her down across the covers until she was beneath his weight. Then he entered her and the pleasure of it sent tears across her face as her back arched up to meet him. He finished quickly with a small cry and a shudder before he laid his head on the bone of her shoulder and she held him, fingers trailing gently across the smooth skin of his back.

They lay a long while, unmoving, and his weight was heavy on top of her, but she did not mind: she felt safe beneath him, not alone, and when finally he rolled away to lie beside her, she felt as though she had lost the part of herself that made her whole. She turned her head on the pillow to look at him beside her, and she saw the traces of tears in the dampness of his lashes, a streak of wet across one cheek. Shifting her body to face him, she lifted her hand and gently rubbed at the spot with her thumb.

He gave her a small sad smile and his eyes flickered closed in the drowsy aftermath of their sex. She smiled in return and let him lie, staring up at the rough crossbeams in the gloom of the ceiling, the shadows from the candles shifting and bobbing across the planks with the draught that crept around the window frame and in under the door. Reaching down, she drew the covers over them. Toby's hand rested lightly on her breastbone, and she caressed it absently. It felt so right to lie beside him, life as it should be, and for a while she allowed herself the illusion: a different path, a kinder fate. Then she remembered the heft of the parcel in the inside pocket of his doublet, and the real world fell through the crack in her thoughts. It had felt like a book, and this might be her only chance.

Turning her head on the pillow, she looked down at the man beside her, peaceful in his sleep. Her eyes traced the line of his cheekbones and the sculpted jaw, the wave of his hair, his long, fine fingers. In her mind she saw the changing blue-grey eyes and his smile, and her guts recoiled at stealing from him. Then she remembered the threat of Alexander's fingers on her neck, the bruises on her wrist, and the urge to life impelled her to do as he had bid.

Lifting Toby's hand from her breast, she placed it gently on the bed between them and slipped from between the covers. The air was cold and she shivered, skin bubbling with goosebumps as she reached for the robe that was flung across a stool. In her haste, she neglected to fasten the tie at the waist, and the gown gaped open as she crouched to the doublet on the floor where Toby had dropped it in the urgency of their passion. She found the pocket easily: it was cunningly sewn to hold the book closely, and she slipped the volume gently from its sheath. Soft leather covers of faded red, just as the old man had described, and even in her ignorance of such things she could sense the age of it, precious years of life that gave it substance, a weight in her hand beyond its size. Beguiled, she opened it, and saw Toby's name in blood-red ink beneath another – *Tom Wynter*. But there was no sign of Alexander's name and doubt seized her. Had it once belonged to him as he claimed? She ran her fingers across the letters of Toby's name, hesitating.

'What are you doing?'

Toby's voice from the bed behind her swung her round and the book slid from her hand to fall back onto the doublet. He was watching her, leaning on one elbow, and she could not tell whether or not he had seen the book.

'Are you stealing from me?' His voice was hard with accusation.

She shook her head.

'Then?' He sat up in one languid movement and shifted across the bed towards her, and she stood up, ready to meet him. Her heart ticked loudly in the silent room, and her mouth felt dry.

'I was curious,' she said. 'I felt something in your jacket before ...'

'You could have just asked.'

'You were sleeping.'

He swung his head away with a sigh, elbows resting on his thighs, and his lips were compressed in thought. She waited, breath coming quick in fear: of what he might do in his anger, of losing him, of being killed at Alexander's hand. There seemed to be no possible path from this moment that did not lead her to the dark. She drew her robe around her and held it tight with her hands, as if it were a shield.

Toby swallowed and looked at her again. 'Tell me the truth.'

She swallowed, panic rising, blood thrilling in her veins. Tears pricked at her eyes, and she dragged a hand across them. Then she threw herself onto her knees at his feet, clasping his hands in her own in supplication.

'He made me do it,' she breathed. The tears were coming in earnest now and she could not hold them back. 'Alexander. He said he would kill me – a long, slow death. Or turn me witless like he did to Rosalind. He said it was worthless to you, that it was stolen from him, and precious ...' She bent her forehead to rest on his knee, waiting for the blow to come, but Toby only tucked back her hair behind her shoulder, gentle.

'Why did you not tell me before?'

She sniffed and lifted her head to look at him. Her cheeks were streaked with tears, and strands of her hair clung to the wetness. She dragged them away. 'I was afraid,' she said.

He nodded, and ran a thumb across her cheek to catch the tears that still fell, and she could not tell his thoughts. She waited, her hand still on his leg, looking up into his face, but his gaze seemed to light on something far beyond the confines of the room, his mind no longer with her.

'Forgive me,' she said at last. 'I'm so sorry.'

Toby hauled his attention back to her, and laid a hand over hers. When he spoke he seemed far away from her, and all the closeness of before had faded into the shifting candlelight.

'It's a good thing I discovered you,' he said, setting her hand aside and rising to fetch the book from its place on the floor. It sat comfortably across the flat of his hand, and seemed lighter in his grasp than it had in hers. He looked down at her, still kneeling by the bed. 'Whatever he told you, Alexander must never have it. He plans to work great evil, and he needs my blood to do it.' He sat beside her on the floorboards, long legs bent up and awkward. 'It belonged to my father once, but now it answers to me.' He turned his head towards her with a smile of pleasure at the knowledge, and his eyes glowed so dark she was uncertain if it were merely a trick of the candlelight or something more.

She said, 'Then he will do as he promised, and I will die a hard death at his hand.'

'He comes to you at the brothel?'

She nodded.

'Then we must take you some place else, somewhere safe, and weave magic to protect you.'

She almost laughed. 'Take me where? Where can I go that will make me safe from him?'

He tilted his head. 'Soon I'll have a new wife at home, and a babe – there will be work for a servant, perhaps even a nurse for the child, if you will take it.'

She swallowed. An escape from the Stews, and the life of a servant to the man she loved. It was not quite all she'd hoped for, but it might be a beginning. 'Your wife would agree?' she asked.

'I need no consent from my wife to hire a servant. She has no say in it.'

'Then I will come,' she said, 'and gladly.'

He stood up and gave her his hand to help her and they dressed in silence, but even once all her clothes were fastened about her, she could feel the chill of the air, as though it still brushed her bare skin. She watched him tuck the book back into its pocket in the doublet, safe against his body. Then, making a meagre bundle of her belongings in a sheet, she let him lead her from the brothel and out into the dankness of the night beside the river.

Mary spent the night in his bed, though she understood that on the morrow she would have to make her home in the old apprentice's room. But tonight he wanted her close, and so they settled under the covers with an affectionate embrace, content in each other's company. She lay facing him, her lips close to his shoulder, her six-fingered hand resting on the muscle of his arm as she slid quickly into sleep, her breathing soft and warm on his skin through the thin linen of his shift.

As though they were wed, he thought, looking across at her sleeping beside him, her face peaceful in the safety of his protection, and though he tried to imagine a lifetime of such nights, he could not hold the image in his thoughts. Mary's features kept sliding into Judith's, and he gave himself a wry smile – he doubted that his wife-to-be would ever lie beside him as Mary did now.

As he rolled in the bed to face her, regret for what could never be stuck hard in his throat. He swallowed but the feeling would not shift. Her face was still, the alabaster skin smooth and soft in the fluttering light of the candle flame. He had never seen her so at peace, he realised: at the brothel the wariness never left her eyes, the constant need for self-protection. Remembering the scars across her back, he reached a hand to tuck a stray hair back from her face, and as her lips curled in an instinctive smile with his touch, he vowed he would keep her safe.

With that thought in his mind he slid from the warmth of the bed, and shivered. The fire was unlit and the night was cold, winter mist trailing through the streets beyond the window amid the threat of more rain. Wrapping a spare blanket around his shoulders, his bare feet chilled against the boards, he freed the book from its hiding place in his doublet and took it, along with the candle, to sit at the window and read.

The pages turned easily in his fingers, the vellum soft and warm, and his eyes scanned the words and symbols. He had mastered much in his short weeks of study and he could mostly follow the pages of Latin now, at least where the handwriting was legible. Many of the symbols had begun to speak with meaning. But he still struggled with the Greek, and the pages of Hebrew he had not yet even tried to decipher.

Flicking through the various rites with impatience, he searched for a ritual that might protect Mary from Alexander's magic. Though she was safe now in his house from physical harm, he knew that distance was no bar to inflicting damage: she needed the protection of the spirits, some way to guard against the sorcerer's malevolence. But he could find nothing that suited – no rites that would shield her. All of it – that he could read at least – he realised, was written from a place of power. The holder of the book wielded the strength of knowledge, and had scant need to avert the magic of others.

With a sigh he let the book fall shut, smoothing the cover with his hand. The leather was warm, and with every touch, he took pleasure in its age and connection to the past. On an impulse he turned once again to the front page where his name was inscribed beneath his father's. Touching a fingertip to the letters of Tom Wynter's name, he traced them carefully.

'What would you do?' he whispered, lifting his eyes to the sky outside. The pregnant moon had lifted herself above the roofs and struggled bravely now to shed her light through the slowly shifting curtains of cloud. A dim glow glimmered towards the east. 'Have you no word of advice for your son?'

Mary stirred in the bed at the sound of his voice – she slept less deeply than he'd supposed. 'Who are you talking to?' she murmured, her words thick with sleep.

'No one,' he answered. 'Go back to sleep.'

She turned and said nothing more, reassured, and Toby sat a long while, growing cold and waiting for a message from his father that never came.

Chapter Twenty-Three

THE CHARM'S WOUND UP

In the morning he searched out his mother early and found her in the garden, collecting herbs still wet with dew in the small wicker basket she had carried ever since he could remember. A childhood memory of playing amongst the fragrant plants flickered through his mind, his mother in tears, and her own mother standing by. He had few recollections of his grandmother – she had died when he was just a boy, but he recalled a stern face and a sense he could keep nothing hidden from the wisdom in her eyes. He shook the memory away, and Sarah turned in surprise when she caught his movement in the half-light of the late-dawning day. 'Toby? What's the matter?'

She laid the knife on top of the herbs in the basket and rested her full attention on his face. He swallowed, aware of his weariness, the sleeplessness starting to thud in his temples, and he could see the concern in his mother's look, the questions she dared not ask aloud. The words he had planned to say failed in his mouth.

He said, 'Mary is here. She needs our protection.'

Sarah was silent, her gaze tracking across the beds of herbs. He waited, uncertain of her reaction until she raised her eyes again to look at him. 'Protection from what?'

Though he had decided in the quiet hours of the night that he must tell her, he still hesitated. She had known too much grief already.

'Toby?'

He sighed. He had no alternative. 'From the sorcerer,' he murmured, casting an instinctive glance towards the house. They were still alone. 'He commanded her to steal the book – Tom's book, under threat of death.'

'And you have no magic to keep her safe?'

He shook his head, and tried to remember the sense of power he had felt the first time he conjured, when he had bound Judith to him in desire. He had believed himself invincible then, all the realms of the universe at his feet, the spirits his to command. How could he have been so deceived? He had merely stumbled onto the path to be shown a glimpse of possibilities, like a child who thinks himself a master of archery because his father stands beside him and guides his hand. He was no match for Alexander, and he slid his gaze away in shame.

His mother smiled, and reached a hand to touch his forearm – a gesture of reassurance, familiar and comforting. 'Have no fear. We'll do magic together to protect her,' she said, looking up into his face. 'Different magic from the sorcerer's, ancient and powerful. We will call on Hecate.'

But when he looked into her eyes, the light in them belied her confidence, and he saw only the same fear that ran in him.

Frances showed no pleasure at meeting her new counterpart when she arrived at the house before the dawn. Knowing Mary for what she had been, the servant gave her little welcome, and the attention Sarah paid the newcomer was salt in the wound. In jealousy and disapproval Frances offered neither help nor friendship, but against Alexander's malice such slights meant little – they were nothing more than domestic matters that Sarah could deal with later, in safer days.

For now Sarah's only thought was to protect her son and the six-fingered girl from Alexander's magic. The visions from the shew-stone still shimmered in the spaces in her thoughts – a fate foretold, but not yet accepted. They had proved the shewstone wrong before – one death instead of two, but she knew the price was high. Others would be called to take their places, those souls unprotected by the goddess, and there was no way to know who: the Fates would gather whosoever they chose.

A full moon.

They would go to the Grove at nightfall.

Sarah spent the day in preparation, gathering all she needed into a bundle: candles and a tinderbox, honey and berries, juniper for incense, rosemary and angelica root for protection. Excitement gripped her – it was years since she had prepared such a basket. Her mother and Tom had yet been alive, the three of them working together. In her mind's eye she gave a smile to them both. Could they see her still? she wondered. Was Tom still watching, caring, loving her? Did he still carry a lamp for her spirit as she carried one for him? She hoped so, remembering how he had used come to her in the night, crossing over from his realm of death, and how she had prayed each time that he would take her with him when he returned. But instead he had given her a child, a life to care for, and the Fates had decreed a different path.

She gave a wistful smile at the memory. Had it been worth it? Perhaps, though Tom's absence still burned a hole inside her with every breath she took. Turning her mind away from the past and into the future, she finished making the bundle. And though now she walked through her life without him, the same familiar quiver rippled through her blood, the same joy of anticipation.

Sarah sent Frances home early, paying no mind to her surly surprise: she simply wanted her gone. The servant needed no second telling, eager to be away, and Sarah watched her walk away from the window of the first-floor chamber, observing the eager stride as she strode from the house. Then she called her son and Mary to her, and told them what she planned.

The way was familiar, heading toward the forest to the south. Above the roofs the full moon tussled with the clouds that tried to cling to her, pouring brightly through the spaces in between and shedding a paler light from behind them, so that they could see their way with ease, though once she used to walk this path on nights far darker. Moondark would have leant their rite more power, but she dared not wait – the full moon also contained the moment of change, a point of transition that Hecate might guard. Sarah held the torch tightly as she led the way, the flame leaping with the movement. They walked in silence, but she was aware of Toby's soft footfalls behind her, and the quick stride of the girl who held his hand.

Skirts swishing, she grew warm beneath her cloak despite the night's chill air, sweat beginning to coat her skin and a trickle running down her back. As the roads narrowed into lanes and the houses dwindled, she kept one hand on the knife at her waist. The people that lived in the poor shacks on these streets dwelt on the fringes of city life and three well-clothed strangers would draw their interest. But all the same, never once had she been attacked on her way to the forest, moving under the eye of the goddess, protected.

The path passed the last of the houses and they came to the forest edge. Before them lay a more ancient world, a place of darkness and magic, free from the rules that governed the city that lay at their backs. Sarah lifted the torch up higher, peering between the branches. The tree line had receded in the intervening years as the city encroached, and it took a few minutes to find the path she needed. Toby and Mary waited, still holding hands in silence.

Then, trusting a sense she could not name, Sarah stepped beneath the canopy of branches that were mostly bare now, and the sudden dark surrounded her like a caress. *'World of spirit,'* she whispered, *'I am returned. May I pass unhindered, as I used to do?'*

The answering silence welcomed her, and she trod softly across the leaves that carpeted the path, heading deep into the trees, putting faith in the instinct of her memory to lead her truly. Behind her, she could hear the rustle of the others' passage through the trees, and somewhere further south she heard the bark of a fox. She found the Grove with ease and a sense of relief. She had trusted to her memory and it had not let her down.

She looked around her, and saw that in the years she had been away the place had barely changed. The soft moonlit dark filled the clearing, and the ancient yew tree still stood on guard. She ran her hands across the gnarled and knotted bark, letting the soft green needles brush across her face and hair. She loved this place, and for all the world she could not think why she had stayed away.

'I know this place,' Mary said. 'The straight-backed lady brought me here.'

Sarah turned from the tree with a smile. 'This is Hecate's Grove.'

Memories flickered in her mind, rituals to the goddess, and the night when she and Tom had conjured another kind of spirit. Brushing her gaze across the clearing, she half expected him to be there again, pale and beautiful as she remembered him. But he was nowhere to be seen, and the others were waiting for her instructions. Dragging her mind away from thoughts of her brother, she let the excitement of the night infuse her once again.

'Gather branches,' she told them. 'And make a circle. We'll prepare a fire.'

They worked quickly, and a fire soon flickered bravely in the forest dark. Standing close before it, they threw in the herbs and incense, which crackled and sparked. Sarah breathed in deeply as the scents began to rise and the fragrance filled her up. She could feel the miracle of her beating heart and the flow of blood in her veins, her breath a gift from the gods. Then, taking her knife from her belt, she gestured to the others to kneel as she began to pace the line of the circle, halting four times to call to the quarters, summoning the spirits of Air and Fire and Water and Earth to protect and guard the circle.

She was surprised at how easily she recalled the words, as though they were a part of her, and in the silence that surrounded them she could feel the spirits' presence, a hush of sacred promise.

Then she raised her arms to the moon above and called out to the goddess.

'Great Goddess Hecate, we honour and love thee.

Accept these humble offerings, and bless the hands that offer them.

Great Goddess, guide and lead us. Show us the way.

I ask nothing for myself – my life is more than halfway done;

Soon I will meet you at the Crossroads and you will guide me home.

But I ask for protection for my son, and for this girl, Mary, from the dark forces that threaten her.

Shield them from evil, and from those who would do them harm.

Bring them happiness, bring them light. Let them live their lives in joy.

Let them love and be loved above all, for a life without love is a life unlived.

These things I ask of you, Great Goddess.'

Sarah lowered her arms and bowed her head, waiting for the answering lift of spirit that signified the goddess's presence. Close by, from the branches of the yew tree, an owl called out to the night, Hecate's messenger, and Sarah felt herself filled with the ecstasy of light, a brightness whose perfection she had forgotten.

Hecate had heard, and their fate was in the hands of the goddess now.

Cradled in the afterglow, Sarah knelt on the soft grass, oblivious to her son and to Mary, and let her spirit rest, peaceful in the lap of Hecate's presence.

The bells of St George were tolling midnight as they made their way home. The sombre chimes carried across the fields, and the moon peeped through chinks in the curtain of clouds so that their path was lit in fragments. They were silent as they walked, and Mary felt the quiver of her body – strange and pleasant ripples in her blood. She recalled the night she once spent at the yew tree with the dog who had kept her warm, and understood that Hecate had protected her before.

Not for the first time, she wondered why a well-to-do tailor's wife had cared enough for a friendless orphan to bring her under the goddess's wing, but whatever the reasons, Mary could only be grateful.

She flicked a glance towards Toby beside her as he walked across the grass, eyes lowered to the path at his feet, his thoughts his own. Did he feel the same quiver inside? Had he too felt the goddess's presence? It was hard to say and he seemed so self-contained, so distant, that she did not dare to question him.

When, finally, they reached the house in Narrow Lane, she waited, uncertain of her place, hoping for Toby's bed but expecting the narrow cot of the old apprentice's room. Neither mother nor son spoke to her, still wrapped in Hecate's mantle of silence as they hung their cloaks on the hooks behind the door. When Sarah put a foot on the stair, Mary said, 'Forgive me, Mistress Chyrche, but where should I go?'

Sarah turned back, one hand resting on the banister. 'My son is master in this house,' she said, but her voice was not unkind. 'Your place is up to him.'

Mary looked to Toby, who answered with a gesture of his head towards the stairs. She smiled, and took his hand in hers as she followed him towards his attic room.

Chapter Twenty-Four

SHE SHALL BE MARRIED

Toby saw no more of Judith until the wedding: she had not come to church for the banns. When he woke early in the dark that morning, he found Mary already awake, curled up and facing him, watching him as he slept. He smiled and touched his fingers to her hair, smoothing it back behind the cold pale skin of her shoulder. The last time, he guessed, that they would wake like this. The coming night he would sleep in the main bedchamber with his new reluctant wife, and his mother would return to her old attic room. He had protested, unwilling to turn her out of her chamber, but she was adamant, and seemed in the end to be eager to leave it.

'It was my marriage bed,' she had explained. 'And the only fond memory it holds is of bringing you into the world.'

Now, Mary snuggled closer, skin on skin, one knee sliding in between his legs, fingers trailing across his chest.

The last time.

He moved his weight across her, mouth meeting hers, her breast in one palm, his cock hard against her thighs. Lazily, she moved her legs apart and in one movement he had entered her, forcing the breath from her lungs in a gasp of pleasure, her lips brushing now against his cheek as he moved inside her, slowly, desperate to make the moments last. He was aware of everything: the cold breath of air across his shoulders where the covers had come off, the roughness of the soles of her feet against his legs, her nails scratching gently as her fingers clutched the muscles of his back, the warmth of her breath and the softness of her breasts against his ribs. Why must this end? Why could he not have this girl he loved to hold for life, instead of a woman that hated him? And though he wanted to blame Alexander, he understood that the fault was his own. He had been a fool: what had he thought would happen?

He climaxed with a shudder that wracked his whole body and brought more pain than pleasure, and afterwards he lay for a long time still entwined with her, his head close to hers and her hair catching in the wetness of his tears.

'I will always be yours,' Mary murmured. 'I need no ring, no words in church to belong to you.'

He laid his forehead against hers so she wouldn't see the tears. But perhaps she would taste them as they fell, he thought, unchecked, onto her face. Finally, when he could trust himself to weep no more, he lifted his head and gave her the best smile he could manage, fingers touching her lips, her cheeks, her brow, drinking in her smooth pale beauty, so familiar now. Then, reluctantly, he slid his body off her and reached for the ring that was on the table by the bed, holding it out to her. 'Marry me instead,' he whispered.

She pushed his hand away. 'Don't,' she replied, and swung her head away. In profile he could see the tight set of her jaw as she struggled not to cry. He lay and watched her through the lessening gloom when she swung herself out of the bed to go to the washstand and sponge herself, gooseflesh rising with a shiver as the cold water touched her skin, nipples growing hard.

He wanted her again, but with a sigh of resignation, he dropped the ring back onto the table and forced himself from the bed. Then, keeping his eyes away from Mary, the sight of her too painful to bear, he washed and dressed and made himself ready for the day.

Wearing the altered ring in church for the first time, it felt awkward on his finger. Perhaps when it was moved to the left hand with their marriage vows it would feel more natural, though he doubted it.

Mary trod across his thoughts, and he had to fight the urge to turn and find her amongst the guests behind him as he stood at the front of the church, twisting the gold band gently, round and round, the symbol of his folly. Behind him people milled and chatted. His own household and the tailors from the shop, a few well-wishers from the church congregation who had watched him grow from boy to manhood, and a couple of passers-by who had wandered in out of curiosity. There was no one yet from the Tooley side, and a little part of him flickered with the hope that she would not come after all.

Then behind him the hubbub of chatter changed in tone, and instinctively he turned to see the Tooleys arrive: father, mother, daughter, and the ancient servant he had seen at the house, shuffling at their backs. His bride walked proud and straight in a night-blue gown with lace at the neck and a spray of baby's breath in her hair. She was beautiful and he remembered why he had wanted her, though he was surprised she had taken such care. But perhaps it had not been her choice. Her head was held high, eyes forward, and he sighed in pity for the effort he knew it took.

She reached his side at the altar steps, and her gaze remained resolutely ahead. Toby shifted closer so that their arms just touched, and with the contact he recalled the passion they had shared, her dark eyes bright with desire when they were on the cusp of love and anything was possible. Regret sidled through him – he had poisoned the bud with his impatience and his lust, and both of them were infected now with a sickness that had no cure, bound in mutual misery.

She flicked a glance his way as their arms brushed, and he met it with a smile of encouragement, but her face remained set hard. As her eyes turned forward once again, it was beyond him to guess if the stoniness was in the effort not to cry, or if it was deliberate hostility.

The priest moved to stand before them, and Toby flinched as a billow of sour breath washed towards them with the opening words of the ceremony.

'Dearly beloved, we are gathered here together in the sight of God ...'

Hush descended on the people at their backs, settling to fidgets and coughs, and though Toby tried to focus on the service, he was conscious of Judith quivering and tense beside him, and his mind wandered from the words again and again, seeking some escape.

'I require and charge you both, as ye will answer at the dreadful day of judgement, when the secrets of all hearts shall be disclosed, that if either of you know any impediment why ye may not be lawfully joined together in Matrimony, ye do now confess it ...'

Toby waited, half expecting his bride to confess the truth, but she was silent. Had she already made her peace with God – this marriage as penance for her sins? Sliding a look towards her, he wondered if he might ever win her back. Not to love perhaps, or even desire. But to friendship? Their life would be a hard road together if they must live as enemies.

'Wilt thou have this woman ...'

He dragged his thoughts back to the priest's voice. It was almost done.

'... and, forsaking all others, keep thee only unto her, so long as ye both shall live?'

'I will,' he heard himself say.

Judith gave him her hand in obedient acquiescence and her fingers were icy in his. He slid the ring across the knuckle and searched her face for some flicker of emotion, but her eyes were cast down, and he could not tell what thoughts were passing through her mind.

'With this ring I thee wed, with my body I thee worship, and with all my worldly goods I thee endow: In the Name of the Father, and of the Son, and of the Holy Ghost. Amen.'

They knelt side by side, man and wife, as the prayers and psalms and sermon droned interminably above his head, barely heard. It was done – irrevocable and binding – and his life seemed to stretch out before him in desolate loneliness. Like his mother and Nick Tooley before him, he thought, though the knowledge he was not alone in his misery offered little comfort.

Mary, he thought, and wished it was she who knelt beside him now.

His knees had begun to ache before it was over, and he rose to his feet with gratitude when the priest spoke the final words of the service at last.

At the celebration at the house, the feast was plentiful. They had worked hard, bringing in other servants to help and serve despite the cost: he had vowed to give the Tooleys no cause to criticise. They had carried the kitchen table to the dining chamber to accommodate all the guests, and borrowed chairs and stools from neighbours. Capons in orange sauce, beef pastries, and sweet chicken pâté vied for space alongside an apple mousse and pears in syrup. And he hadn't stinted on the wine, though only Nick Tooley seemed to be taking full advantage.

Toby sat beside his bride and hoped the guests would ascribe her silence to shyness, though she was well known to many of them, and she had never been shy before. She spoke only when spoken to, with brief and quiet courtesy, and however many times he tried to reach across the divide between them, she kept her eyes away and refused his attention.

When the feast was finished and cleared away, the musicians began to play and one of the tailors took his wife onto the floor to dance. Other guests joined them, and the bride's sullen mood went unnoticed. Briefly, Toby thought that he should dance with her, but she was sitting now with her mother by the window, and he guessed she would not welcome the suggestion.

So he stood at the hearth with Nick Tooley, warming the backs of his legs and surveying the room. Sarah was laughing with the Tooleys' old servant, and the sound pealed brightly across the room, even over the strains of music and the thud of dancing feet.

Nick gestured towards them with his wine. 'Joyce has been with me for many years. She knew your mother as a girl.'

Toby smiled. It was good to see his mother laugh – it was a sight he saw too rarely. Only in the brief weeks when she had found love again with Nick had he ever known her to be happy.

'She misses you,' he said, on an impulse. 'She's been a long time without love.'

Nick took a mouthful of wine, considering, before he turned to look at Toby. ''Tis your fault it ended,' he said.

'It would bring happiness to you both, I think.' He looked across to Becky and Judith at the window, and Nick followed his gaze. Toby drained off his wine. He had planned to stay sober, unused to drinking so early in the day and with the duties of host to perform, but it seemed the celebration needed his attention no longer, and he felt the sudden kick of light-headedness. It made him feel reckless, suddenly, and weary of the charade. He shrugged. 'But it makes no odds to me, either way.'

Mary crossed his line of sight with a jug of wine in her hand, and though they caught eyes only briefly, he saw the warning in them.

'You liked her so much you brought her home?' Nick asked. A brief smile lit his face, and Toby saw again why his mother had liked him. But it was gone in a moment and he said, 'Does my daughter know?'

'What I tell my wife is my affair,' he answered. The wine had made him belligerent, and he could not stop himself.

Nick tilted his head. 'It is indeed. But I know from experience that wives don't appreciate a whore in the house – I tried it myself with your mother.' He lifted his wine in mockery of a toast. 'I will think on your advice,' he said, and strode across the room towards his silent family, joining them to stare down to the street outside.

Toby watched him go, fists balling in impotent fury. He gestured to one of the hired servants, and took more wine, craving oblivion. But even as he started to drink it, he knew he could have no more. He was host at his wedding, and his bride was a terrified girl who was almost three months gone with child. He owed her more. He sighed and put the cup down and crossed the room to pick at the remnants of the food that were laid out on the cupboard.

His mother wandered over to join him. 'What were you talking with Nick about?' she asked, and though her tone was light, he heard the hope and the worry in her voice.

'He doesn't approve of Mary,' he replied, flicking a glance to the tableau at the window, the figures dark and unclear against the light.

Sarah smiled. 'Time was, he didn't used to be so righteous.'

He reached for a small pastry that was alone on a platter. He wasn't hungry but it gave him something to do, and he held it in his fingers. He said, 'How long will they stay? How long until we're rid of them?'

She shrugged. 'Who can say?'

'Can you not put something in their drinks?'

Sarah's head snapped up in alarm.

'It was a jest.'

She laughed and touched his arm, the old gesture of affection. Then she slid a glance around the room at the dancers, and the other guests, watching and laughing. 'It's tempting,' she replied. 'Except the only man drinking is Nick.'

He smiled and put his hand over hers. 'I think you can win him back,' he said.

Looking up into his face, she gave him a look he could not read. She said, 'I'm not sure I want to any more, after what he did to you …'

'You lie,' he murmured. 'He brings you joy, and you've known too little of that in your life. 'Tis a prize to be wished for.'

She lowered her head away with a sigh. 'Perhaps,' she replied. 'Perhaps.'

Then Nick was before them, and, in his attention to his mother, Toby had not seen him approach.

'Mistress Chyrche.' He dipped his head in greeting.

'Master Tooley.'

There was a moment's pause before Toby moved away. With the pastry still in his hand, and no longer standing next to the table, he could do little else but eat it. It was sweet – apple and cinnamon and cloves, and when he had finished it and wiped his mouth clear of grease, he stepped to the window and addressed his new bride.

'Judith.' He bowed, going deep enough to show her respect, and she lifted herself from the stool and returned the greeting with a curtsey, though she kept her eyes away. 'Shall I show you the house?'

She slanted a glance towards her mother, who gave an unwilling nod, mistrust in her eyes. Toby guessed she would have preferred to keep her daughter beside her, but it was not her place to refuse him. He was Judith's lord and master now, and whether she despised him or no, his will was law.

Judith followed him to the door and in the passage he said, 'Shall we start at the bottom or the top?'

Briefly, she lifted her eyes to the stairs, and gave a small gesture upwards with her chin. He smiled. 'Come then,' he said, and, quelling the urge to take her hand, he led her up the first flight of stairs, along the passage and then up again to the small landing between the two rooms of the attic. Pushing open one door, he said, 'My mother's chamber. It was hers as a child, and she says that she has missed it.'

Judith gave the room a cursory glance and said nothing. She did the same with his old chamber, tidy now and bare of his belongings, neatly put away in the chests and drawers of the main chamber below. Her indifference disheartened him – she had always been so vital in the past, so full of vigour. It had been her zeal for life that had excited his desire, lusting for the passion of her nature, and even in her misery till now, her hatred had been fuelled by fervour. This submissive silence was something altogether new. She followed him downstairs, past the little box room and into the doorway of the main bedchamber beside it.

The marriage bed boasted new hangings of a deep red damask, and the panelling had been scrubbed and oiled, the paintwork redone. Sweet herbs freshened the air, mingled with the scent of cedar oil: it was mostly his mother's work, and she could have done no more to welcome her son's new bride. He entered the room with a smile of pride and stood beside the window, watching her reaction, but she stood transfixed in the doorway, eyes wide in horror.

'You do not like it?' he asked, with a sweep of his hand. ''Tis all new painted, new sewn.'

She passed her tongue across her lips and took a small step forward, but her eyes never left the bed. 'We are to share this?'

'Aye,' he said. 'It is our marriage bed.'

Finally, for the first time that day, she raised her eyes to look at him, fire in their depths at last. He still found her beautiful with her dark hair twisted up to show off the fineness of her neck, and the olive skin above the lace of her bodice. He recalled the lean, strong body beneath her dress, ripe now with his child, and he wanted her again.

'We will share no bed,' she told him. 'I will sleep alone. I said as much at our betrothal.'

'You are my wife.'

Her lips tightened and he saw echoes of her mother. She would turn bitter in time, he realised, as Becky had, too full of fear and hate. She said, 'I am the mother of your child, nothing more.'

'You loved me once,' he said, moving from the window to sit on the bed. He patted the coverlet beside him, inviting her to sit, but she shook her head and folded her arms across her chest, refusing to come near. 'Have I changed so much since then?'

'You deceived me,' she replied. 'You are not the man I thought you.'

'You were willing enough at the time.'

'You used some evil means to trick me. I would not have fallen otherwise.' She lowered her eyes to the floor. 'And to fall so low,' she whispered. 'To desire such wickedness, and find pleasure in such sin.'

Toby was silent. There seemed to be nothing more he could say. He had nursed a small hope that time might soften her belief he had used foul means and that she would remember the tug of her own desire, but the hope died with her words: she would never be persuaded now. He could not blame her for it – it was only the truth, after all. He got up from the bed and she took an instinctive step back.

Giving her a weary smile, he lifted his palms in a gesture of peace. 'You have no need to fear me. I'm not going to hurt you, Judith. Or force you against your will. If you wish to sleep alone, so be it. Perhaps once the child is born ...' He trailed off with a shrug. Without the intimacy of a shared bed to bring them together at the end of each day, they would be strangers to each other always, without even the semblance of friendship that had been his mother's marriage.

She said nothing, but moved out of his way as he went to the door.

'Would you like to see the rest of the house?' he asked.

She shook her head. 'Not now.'

He nodded and the door rattled on its hinges as he closed it. Then they went back downstairs to rejoin the celebrations in silent separation.

Sarah watched her son lead his new wife away, then turned once more to the man before her. His face was flushed with wine, but Nick had always held his drink well and his speech was as fluent as ever.

'I wish him luck,' he said. 'I know what lies ahead of him.'

''Tis the way of things.' She shrugged lightly. 'Who among us is loved as would we wish? How many marriages are truly happy? We must take love where we find it and to Hell with the Puritans.'

He laughed. 'Don't let my wife hear you say that.'

Sarah slid a glance to where his wife sat at the window. Becky's face was in shadow, the winter light bright behind her, but from the angle of her head Sarah knew they were being watched. 'She watches us.'

'She's never forgiven you,' he said. 'Or me. And somehow, Judith's condition is our fault.'

'Has she so quickly forgotten her own hasty marriage?'

He gave a small smile and shook his head. Then, taking another mouthful of wine, 'Ah, let's talk of other things.'

Mary approached with the jug, and Sarah took it from her with a smile. But she was aware of Nick's frank appraisal and the ill-hidden interest in his eyes. She waited till Mary had moved away, then poured him more wine. 'She's no longer for rent,' she said. 'She's part of this household now.'

'Pity,' he said. 'She had some skill.'

Sarah turned her face away. How should she answer such a barb? An image of the two of them together at the brothel played across her thoughts – their bodies entwined amongst a tangle of blankets. Had she liked it with him? Sarah wondered. Or had she feigned her pleasure? One of her skills. Perhaps her affection for Toby was just as false, born of the instinct to survive. She said, 'Toby seems to think so.'

'She'll warm him more at night than his wife ever will, I promise you that. Judith is her mother's daughter.'

'She warmed him well enough to get herself with child,' Sarah snapped back.

Nick made no reply to that, and sipped instead at his wine, watching the room over the rim of his cup. They were standing close and she was aware of the warmth of his body, the familiar male smell of him, unchanged. He was still strong: she could see the sinews in his forearm shifting beneath the skin as he moved his arm, and though he was a big man, he was as lean as his younger self. Toby had been right, she thought. She had been lying: she wanted Nick with every beat of her heart.

She lifted her head to look at him, still gazing out across the chamber, eyes seemingly trained on everything and nothing. Catching her movement, he turned with a small smile that crinkled the corners of his eyes in the way that she knew so well. 'Forgive me, Sarah,' he said. 'I am not myself. And I wish things were otherwise.'

'Shall we make them otherwise?' She returned the smile, head tilted in coy question. It was hard to stop herself from reaching out to touch him, desire bright inside her.

The smile broadened, and a soft brief laugh sounded in his throat. 'We shall.'

Her heart skipped and she wanted to jump with excitement like a child. She could feel the flush rushing over her skin.

'The church on the corner,' he said. 'At ten o'clock.'

She nodded, still smiling as he took his leave of her and went back to his wife.

In the early morning dark, creeping past the main bedchamber with the taste of Nick still on her lips, Sarah could hear the new bride crying through the door. She paused. Judith had made no secret of the fact that she would sleep alone, careless of who knew that her marriage was a sham, and Sarah was tempted to let her be. She was eager for her own bed – it had been a long day. Had Toby heard his wife's sobs from his chamber upstairs and chosen to ignore them? Surely he could hear them through the floor. Then she remembered that Toby was most likely downstairs in the old apprentice's room with Mary, and too far away for his wife's distress to reach him.

In spite of everything, she could not help but feel sorry for her. She had known only a Puritan childhood with a mother who was animated by hate and bitterness. Then a brief discovery of the joys of passion before the strictures of her faith had brought themselves to bear again, and she could only feel the sin of it. A memory of her own father flickered in Sarah's mind, his belt across her thighs, the strictness of the life he had forced them to. Puritans. She had always hated their life-denying creed that deemed the human urge to earthly joy a sin. Her own marriage to the tailor had been just as much a sham, though the world was not aware of it.

She stepped to the door and laid her ear against it. Judith was still crying. Sarah knocked, gently, and the crying ceased at once. Silence. She knocked again, and a broken voice called out, 'Who is it?'

'It's Sarah. May I come in?'

She turned the handle and nudged open the door. A candle still burned by the bed, and Judith had not yet undressed. She was leaning at the window, and gazing out as though she hoped to flee beyond it – Sarah knew the feeling well. Judith made no move to turn at the other woman's approach, and Sarah went to stand beside her. The street below was shrouded in the dark and the torches on the houses fluttered and danced against the rain, lighting little of the night around them.

Sarah leaned against the window frame. Across the years she had stood here many times calling to Tom in her mind as her husband slept in the bed behind her. For a long while her brother had answered, but the connection had weakened over time, and now his voice was only a memory that was too painful to visit.

'I married for the same reason as you,' she said. 'And I've often stood here too, dreaming of escape.'

Judith threw her a glance of surprise but said nothing. Her breath was still ragged from her crying – perhaps she could not yet trust her voice.

'But you're here now and we must needs make a home together, all of us. Could you not use a friend?'

She heard Judith swallow in the dark, letting out a long breath to calm herself. Then she turned to face the older woman, and in the changing light of the candle flame and the low glow of the embers in the grate Sarah could see her dark lashes, wet from crying, and the streaks of tears across her cheeks.

'My mother says you're a whore,' she said.

Sarah gave a wry laugh and let her gaze fall back to the torches across the street as they struggled against the downpour. 'I loved your father once,' she said, 'in the days when your mother refused his company and chose to live instead in her father's house. For a long time she was Nick Tooley's wife in nothing more than name.'

Judith stared.

'You didn't know?'

The girl shook her head and Sarah wondered at Nick's silence, when the truth might have won his daughter's affection with a different side of the story.

'Your mother was carrying your older brother when she wed, so you and I are no more whores than she is.'

Judith turned her gaze once more to the outside world. She was quivering with emotion. 'You lie,' she said. 'She would have told me.'

'We all of us have secrets,' Sarah said. 'But you should ask Joyce.' The ancient servant, who had been Sarah's friend. 'Joyce will remember.'

They stood in silence, and Sarah observed her new daughter's profile. She could see what Toby had seen – the glistening hair and dark almond eyes, the full mouth, the lithe, strong body. If only he had waited, she thought briefly, they might have been happy. Then again, perhaps Judith's faith told against it – Toby was Tom's son, after all, with the same vast appetite for life: a pious wife would never have been enough.

'You should get some sleep now. Tomorrow you must begin to learn the life of a tailor's wife, and the day starts early.'

Judith nodded and when Sarah reached the door, she finally turned from the window. 'Thank you,' she said, 'for your kindness.'

Sarah smiled with a dip of her head in acknowledgement, then turned again and left.

That night Tom came to Sarah in her sleep as he used to do in the first days after his death, his spirit returning once more from the realms beyond the grave to lie with her. And though the chill of his presence whispered of the tomb, she scarcely dared to believe he had come to her at last.

'Is it truly you, good brother?' she murmured. 'Or have my wits begun to turn?'

She laid her head close to his on the pillow to feast on his perfection. His pale, gaunt beauty was just as she remembered him from life – only his eyes had changed, darkened now with their ineffable secrets of the dead. Despite her delight to see him, she couldn't help but shiver. Then he smiled his lovely smile and touched his fingers to her cheek, and though she sighed as the chill rippled through her, she felt no fear of him, no horror of the realms whence he came. Tom had come to her again and with him she was complete.

He brushed his fingertips across her throat and breast in a trail of ice that burned with ecstasy. Grief turned inside her, sliding into desire, and when he lowered his mouth to hers, she lifted her head to meet the pleasure of his kiss. All the years of longing fell away in the bliss of their connection, and the taste of death on his lips was sweet. He moved across her body, his cold weight hard against her chest, and she drank him in as he reached between her legs and entered her. The surrender was exquisite, a rapture of love and death: it seemed as though she had waited for this moment all her life. But it was over in a heartbeat, and the woes of the living world bored back into her thoughts with a brightness that was almost blinding. Toby. Judith. Alexander. Tears of want and frustration gathered in her eyes and she could not stop them falling.

'Take me with you,' she begged. 'I've waited so long …'

Her brother lifted himself onto his elbows and looked down into her face, stroking her hair back and away to see her better.

'Not yet, sweet sister,' he breathed. 'Not yet.'

'Then when?'

'Soon.' He rubbed at her tears with a gentle thumb. 'You'll know when it's time. And I'll be waiting for you, as I have all these years.'

She said nothing as he slid off her chest to lie beside her, but she wept in silence, aware of the deathly chill of his body against her living warmth and the taste of her salt tears until she fell at last into a peaceful sleep without dreams.

Chapter Twenty-Five

GIVE SORROW WORDS

Christmastide, and the flow of the Thames was heavy and smattered with ice so that it was hard-going for the boatmen to ferry the revellers who sought their entertainments on Bankside. The playhouse was closed for the season, but it was a busy time for the pleasure gardens and the gambling houses despite the chill and the driving sleet that soaked through all but the thickest of cloaks. Mary was glad she was out of the brothel.

In Narrow Lane, the cold crept around the window frames and under the doors to breathe at the edges of the rooms, and now and then the fires in the hearths would roar as the wind caught in the chimney and whipped up the flames. But the chill in the house reached deeper than the draughts that caught in passageways.

Judith cast a long shadow, with mercurial moods that set the rest of the household to walking over eggshells. Each morning the others would wait in uneasy tension to see how she might be that day – if she would remember her role as the tailor's wife and set about the duties of a housewife, or if she would break her fast in moody silence before returning to the solitude of her room.

Both Sarah and Mary tried to befriend her, and a few times Sarah thought she had succeeded, provoking a smile or a thank you, a word of chit-chat such as any mother might share with her son's new bride. But Mary Judith hated instantly, and though no one was sure if she knew where her husband spent his nights, her rigid moral strictness saw the whore within the servant, and refused her so much as the time of day. Frances, taking her cue from her new mistress, kept her resentment burning brightly, but in the midst of Judith's moods, ill will between the servants for the most part went unnoticed.

It was a brisk time for the tailors – last-minute orders, outfits required for the festivities – and the tailors worked long into the evening, the shop bright with candles, eager for the extra coin the work would bring, for the new year was often lean, a quieter time after the heady twelve days of revels.

Two days before Christmas, evening was settling into night and the men were packing up for the day, their fingers sore and their backs aching from the long hours stooping over the bench, when the door shuddered unexpectedly open. A squat figure with a hood half over his face came inside, and even as Marcus said, 'We're just closing for the day,' Toby knew that it was Alexander.

Carefully, to gain a moment to calm himself, he finished folding the piece of black velvet and set it neatly on the bench. Then he stood to greet the visitor. 'Master Alexander.' The calmness of his voice surprised him when his heart was pounding in his ears and his breath came short and hard. Briefly, he thought of Mary and hoped she was safe and out of sight upstairs. 'What brings you here? 'Tis no night to be walking.'

'Master Chyrche.' The sorcerer slid the hood from his head and, with a deft movement, unclasped his cloak and handed it to Marcus, who took it with an uncertain glance to his master. Toby inclined his head in assent and Marcus hung the cloak on a hook by the door, where it dripped its burden of rain onto the floor.

'I need a new pair of breeches,' Alexander said. 'I thought you might be able to help me.'

The other men hovered, made wary by the sudden tension but still eager to go. The hour was late and the road was dark. Toby nodded his permission for them to leave. 'I'll do it,' he said, with a wry smile. 'Master Alexander and I are old friends.'

'Indeed we are,' Alexander agreed, 'though it's been a while.'

The tailors gathered up their belongings with haste and hurried out into the night. Toby shut the door behind them but he left it unlocked, wary.

'You're working late.' Alexander sauntered closer, fingers reaching to inspect the bolts of cloth and the finished garments that were hung on racks waiting for collection.

'It's a busy time of year.'

'Is that why you haven't been to see me?' The old man left off his testing of the fabrics and turned his full attention to Toby, who met the look with an unflinching gaze, remembering the rite to Hecate, the protection of the goddess.

'One of the reasons. Also, I am newly married, so there is that.'

The old man nodded. 'Congratulations,' he said. 'I wish you every happiness.'

Toby said, 'What colour breeches were you after? They won't be ready now until after Twelfth Night …'

'Plain black. Wool. I have no need of anything fancy.'

'A similar style to the ones you're wearing? Or would you prefer a slimmer cut, as is the fashion now?'

'The same as these. They've done me all my life, and I'm too old to change now.'

Toby reached for his measure, and felt the dryness of his mouth. He was reluctant to kneel before the old man, but he knew of no other way to take the measurements. Uncertain what Alexander wanted here tonight, he was afraid. The old man stood with his feet apart and Toby crouched to measure as he needed, quick and deft and precise, noting the numbers in a notebook.

'So you haven't been to the brothel of late?' Alexander asked, lowering himself onto one of the high tailor's stools that stood by the bench.

'Like I said, I have a new wife.'

'Hmm. The pretty six-fingered whore has disappeared, and no one could tell me where she's gone. However much I asked.'

'Is that so?' Toby feigned concentration on the numbers in his book, but he wondered what violence the old man had inflicted in his search for answers, and who had been hurt. Did he know that she was here, after all? Was that why he'd come?

'You wouldn't happen to know, would you? I remember you were a regular of hers.'

He shrugged. 'She was just a whore.'

'But what a whore.' Alexander smiled. 'With those deft six fingers, and quick pink tongue.'

'I thought you preferred boys.'

'If you turn them over it makes no odds, and she had a pretty little arse, nice and tight. Very like your father's. Of course, he was just a young lad but he learned very quickly.'

Toby swallowed down the bile that threatened to rise, hatred simmering under his skin. But anger would make him careless, and he sent a silent prayer for calm to the goddess. 'What do you want with her?' He made the question sound casual, a mild curiosity. 'She's just a whore, after all – Bankside is full of them.'

Alexander rubbed his chin, as if deciding what lie to tell. Toby waited a moment, then continued to pack away, neatening the tools that lay out on the bench, moving the heavy scissors closer.

'I have a message to give her,' he said finally. 'Perhaps if you see her, you could pass it on?'

'Of course.' Toby shrugged. 'If I see her.'

'Tell her I've not forgotten, and the bargain still stands. She'll understand.'

He nodded and the old man heaved himself off the stool to saunter towards the door. Toby remained at the bench and watched him, impatient for him to be gone. 'I'll send a boy when the breeches are ready,' he said. 'Just the one pair? You're still at the sign of the Wounded Raven?'

'Just the one. And I am indeed still at the Wounded Raven,' Alexander replied, shaking his cloak with a spray of rain before he draped it across his shoulders, reaching up with difficulty, stiffness in his joints. For any other customer Toby would have helped, but a natural aversion kept him far away.

It seemed to take an age before the old man finally left and Toby could shut the door behind him. His heart was still aquiver, his breathing quick, and he did not understand what exactly had passed between them. Locking up the shop at last, he took the stairs two a time and went to find Mary.

In the early hours Toby was startled awake by his mother's shouts. He sat up in the dark, breathing hard, all traces of sleep stripped by the fear he could hear in her voice, and the remnants of strange dreams floated away into the dark. Mary grasped his arm in panic. Scrambling out of bed, they dressed as they ran through the blackness of the passage, heedless of the cold, and up the stairs, bootless, laces flapping, still fumbling with buttons and ties.

The door to the main bedchamber was open, candles lit, and the last gasps of the embers in the hearth lent a shifting glow across the scene before them. Toby's wife lay huddled and sweating in the bed as Sarah wiped her brow with a cloth. She had thrown off the covers and a dark patch of blood was smeared across the back of the white linen shift. He stared, taking a moment to realise before he understood: she was going to lose the child. Pausing, he swallowed, unsure what to do and afraid, but Mary pushed past him in the doorway, and he watched as Sarah gave instructions for the herbs she needed. 'A tea of cramp bark,' she said. 'Can you do that?'

Mary nodded and ran out again.

His mother turned to him. 'Hot water, and linen.'

He took a deep breath and turned to go, and as he hurried down the stairs the thoughts that swam in his mind made him feel ashamed. He shook his head to chase such ideas away, but he couldn't change the fact – without a child, there had been no need for a wedding.

In the kitchen, Mary had already stoked the fire and set a pot to boil. She had not yet lit candles, and shadows from the flames in the hearth cast shifting shadows across the walls in a dance of ghosts. He took the candles from the shelf and lit several at the fire before setting them on the table. Then he said, 'My mother said to fetch linen.'

Mary paused in her search among the jars of herbs that lined the shelves and turned to him. 'The bedchamber. In the oak chest beneath the window ...' Her tone was impatient, and he felt like a fool. Of course, he thought. He should have known. But linen was the preserve of the women, and he had never had to look for it before. He said, 'I'll wait for the water.'

'I'll bring the water,' she replied. 'Go.'

He hastened once more upstairs and found the sheets and cloths in the chest as Mary had said. He passed them to his mother, who took them without a word. Judith was still curled, hands pressed against her belly and, as he bent closer, he could see the slick of sweat on her face and the dangerous pallor of her cheek. She was trembling. Catching his movement from the corner of her vision, she turned her head briefly to look at him with eyes that were both dark and bright.

'Keep away from me!' she whispered. 'This is your doing.' She reached for Sarah's hand. 'Keep him away from me.'

Sarah raised her head to Toby in silent appeal, and he stepped away, crossing to the hearth to tend the fire, where he poked life into the embers and threw on another log. Mary returned with the tea and hot water, and as Sarah tried to coax Judith to drink, Mary tucked clean linen over the clots of blood, using the hot water to mop up the worst of it.

But Judith refused to drink, and Toby turned from the fire to watch.

'I don't want it,' she hissed. ''Tis better if it dies. It's a cursed thing. Let it go. And leave me be.'

'Don't say such things ... drink.' She held the cup to Judith's mouth again.

Judith shook her head, lips compressed in refusal.

'If not for the child, for you,' Sarah persisted. ''Tis dangerous for you to bleed like this ...'

'If it's God's will to take me, then I am ready.'

'God gave us herbs to use,' Sarah said, and Toby could hear the impatience in her tone. 'And He blessed me with the wisdom to heal. Now drink.'

But Judith was obstinate, shaking her head on the pillow, lips closed and firm. Sarah sat back on her heels in frustration with the cup still full of the undrunk tea in her hand, and flicked a glance to Mary. Then, with a sigh, she put the cup on the bedside table and got up, stretching out her stiffened knees before she turned to her son, who was watching from the hearth.

'If she'll not let me help, she will lose it.' She slid a glance toward the bed where Judith lay unmoving, eyes open and staring at nothing. 'But perhaps it's too late anyway.'

Mary sat on the linen chest, hands tucked under her thighs, and Toby went to sit beside her. He could think of nothing to say, and thoughts he did not want to think circled in his head. Sarah lowered herself onto the bed beside Judith, and stroked the girl's hair from her forehead. There was nothing more to do but wait.

The hours passed slowly, measured in the slow chimes of the bells at St George, and Judith said no more, refusing all offers of help with a mute shake of her head. Twice Sarah changed the napkins as they soaked with clots. She had Mary fetch a bucket to put them in, and the metallic stench of blood mingled with the sweet wood smell of the fire. But Frances had not yet arrived for the day when Judith began to convulse, turning in the bed and crying out, though whether in pain or relief Toby could not have said.

Sarah and Mary tended her gently, and Toby wondered if he should he go: childbed was no place for a man, whatever the circumstance, but no one sent him away and so he stayed, too curious to leave unbidden. What slid from between her legs would have fitted in the palm of his hand, yet it had the shape of a tiny child, a head and legs and arms. But even from his place by the window he could see that its spine was misshapen and bent. Sarah wrapped it quickly in linen.

'Show me,' Judith demanded, and reluctantly, Sarah opened up the cloth.

'Deformed,' she breathed, running her eyes over and over the malformed body as if to be sure. 'Cursed. I am glad it's out of me – I could feel its corruption.' Lifting her head, she glared at her husband. 'Conceived in sin,' she spat. 'A child of the Devil. And God has punished us both.'

He dropped his gaze away from the venom in her eyes. 'Forgive me,' he said. 'I never meant to do anything but love you.'

Sarah gave Mary the dead child to hold, and began to wash the blood from Judith's legs, but the girl drew her knees together to stop her. 'Leave it,' she snarled. 'It's the stain of my sin, and it can't be washed away with water.'

'You cannot lie in your own filth,' Sarah said. Her voice was testy. 'It will make you ill.'

'I care not.'

'Well, I care. This mattress was my mother's and I won't let you ruin it.'

There was a moment of silence, a brief battle of wills before Judith's face slid from hatred to despair. She began to weep, a piteous wailing sound, and Sarah went to comfort her, an arm around her shoulders, while Mary took the cloths to wipe her clean.

'It's over,' Sarah said, again and again, holding the girl close, stroking her hair. 'The child is gone.'

'There is still blood coming,' Mary said, from the foot of the bed. 'And clots.'

'Good,' Sarah said, ''tis the afterbirth. Put a napkin there.'

Toby got up from his place on the linen chest. The stench and the blood had begun to sicken him, and the tiny form of his child had swept him with a grief that took him by surprise in its fierceness.

'I'll bury the child,' he said, to no one in particular. 'At the Cross Bones.'

'By the yew tree,' Sarah answered. 'So Tom can guide his spirit home.'

He nodded, and taking up the little bundle, he thudded down the stairs and out into the cold half-darkness of the early morning. The sting of the chill air felt good in his lungs.

Chapter Twenty-Six

UNNATURAL DEEDS DO BREED UNNATURAL TROUBLES

In the early afternoon Mary wandered from the heat of the kitchen into the garden to rest. The winds in the night had blown the rain away, and the winter sun hung low and blinding in a pale blue sky. Facing south, the garden was warm in its light and the leaves still glistened with their sheen of rain. Mary stood on the stepping stone path that led between the profusion of herbs and breathed in the freshness. She had come to love this garden, learning how to tell one leaf from another and the secrets each plant offered. Her fingers searched her skirts for the little poppet of protection that Sarah had given her. It was her talisman now and she kept it with her always, a reminder of her connection to the elements and her trust in Hecate.

She made for the sunniest nook, tucked in against the wall, to sit and rest on the bench, but when she rounded the corner she saw that Judith was already there, eyes closed, face lifted to the sun's caress. Her skin seemed grey, as though the redness of her blood had been stolen away by the child that died in the night, but she seemed peaceful for the first time, sitting here in the winter sunlight. Mary had begun to back away, reluctant to intrude on a rare moment, when Judith's eyes flicked open and she turned her head. 'Oh,' she said. 'It's you.'

Mary nodded, waiting to be dismissed, but Judith simply turned her face back towards the sun, her eyes half-closed, so Mary stepped forward into the light and let the warmth fall deliciously on her head and shoulders. She said, 'Sunshine at last.'

Judith opened her eyes.

'Perhaps it is a sign of better times to come.'

'Perhaps,' Toby's wife said. 'But I think times are good enough already for you. You are blessed with a mistress who loves you, and who teaches you her knowledge of all of this.' She gestured to the garden around them.

'She would love and teach you too, if only you'd let her.'

Judith gave a half-laugh. 'I have no desire to learn the ways of her witchcraft ...'

'Herblore only,' Mary said, quick to Sarah's defence. 'To heal.'

'Do you think me a fool?' Judith turned her body full towards Mary, standing close by, and raised a hand to shield her eyes against the sun. 'Do you think I don't know where my husband spends his nights?'

'Only because he is banished from your chamber.'

Judith's eyes trailed across Mary's body, appraising. It was a look Mary was more used to from a man. 'What does he see in you?' Judith asked. 'You're nothing but a common whore with ambitions for something better. Is he so blinded by his lust he cannot see it?'

Mary swung her head away, taken aback by the casual cruelty. She said, 'He finds love with me. Affection. Understanding. And I do not stand in judgement over him.'

Judith smiled. 'Of course you don't. You're far too clever for that. Why would you risk the life you've made for yourself here?'

Mary shook her head, and the words came out before she could stop them. All the years of biting her tongue in the brothel beneath far worse indignities, but she could not hold her peace now. 'For all your piousness,' she said, 'where is your forgiveness, your charity? Where is your love? All I see in you is hatred and judgement. You have a husband who wants only to love and honour you, a family to welcome you, a chance at happiness. But you wallow in self-pity, and cry you've been ill-treated.'

Judith got to her feet, eyes glinting dark in her pallor, lips curling almost to a snarl. 'You saw the monster he begot on me,' she hissed. 'That was no natural child. In the midst of your own sin you cannot see him for what he is. He needed no foul means to enslave you to him – you go willingly, harlot that you are. But I was not willing and in the days that he bedded me I was not myself but under same strange power he wielded over me. Witchcraft, possession, some evil magic I know not of. And I am not yet free of it – its evil lingers so that I cannot rest: my sleep is uneasy and I dream of hellish things. And you accuse me of judgement?' She spat onto the paving stones, and the small gob glistened in the afternoon sun. 'He's in league with the Devil, and I'm afraid for my soul.'

Mary said nothing, no answer to the other woman's faith. And she was aware of the truth of it, recalling the rite in the Grove and the book, the power of Alexander. Perhaps Judith was right to fear him, after all, a darkness in him he had not shown to her, malign powers at work. But it made no odds: Mary's soul belonged to Hecate, and her death would lead to a different and more ancient realm of death where the Christian Devil held no sway. Closing her eyes, she turned them once more to the sun, eyelids turning red, warmth on her cheeks. It was good to merely be alive.

In the early hours of the morning, Toby woke to the rattle of the latch on the back door. He lay for a moment, staring into the dark as the shadows settled into the familiar shapes of the old apprentice's room. At his back, Mary was breathing lightly and he could feel the warm press of her body against him in the narrow bed. He listened.

The key grated in the lock as it turned – it was a familiar sound – and the latch rattled again as the door that led out to the garden opened with a creak no one ever remembered to oil. He tipped himself out of bed, and drew the covers over Mary so the cold would not wake her. Then he reached for a shift to cover his nakedness, and picked up his knife. The boards were icy on his bare feet as he padded to the chamber door and opened it in silence.

The passageway was crisp with the chill of the night, the back door wide open to a starlit sky. In the distance he could hear the sounds of revellers, shouts and snatches of song, and he remembered it was Christmas morning. He shivered, the thin linen shift giving no warmth against the winter air, and stepped forward to look out across the darkness of the garden. There was no moon. He laid a hand on the door handle, and though he was sure that the door had been unlocked from the inside, he recalled Alexander's visit to the shop, and his heartbeat was light and rapid with wariness. Before him, the outlines of trees were cut-out black against the velvet blue of the sky, but the night had swallowed all sight of herbs and shrubs and vegetables. He peered out, eyes searching for movement until he caught a glimpse of white close to the garden of herbs. Swallowing, he tightened his grip on the handle of the knife, and his palm was slippery with sweat in spite of the cold. Then he stepped out onto the path. He should have brought a candle, he thought, to see the way.

At the break in the wall he stopped, searching the shadows until he caught the flash of white again.

A woman's form in a linen shift, he realised. His wife.

'Judith?' he called softly, but still his voice sounded loud in the night and he jumped, startled, when a fox screamed from somewhere out of sight beyond the wall. The harsh bark sent small creatures scuttling to ground, and an owl hooted in frustrated disgust as his prey found safety for another night.

'Judith?'

She gave him no reply, still moving slowly between the beds of herbs, finding her way, it seemed, by instinct. He lowered the knife, and made towards her across the damp paving stones of the path, legs brushing against the plants he passed and releasing their fragrance into the air around him. When he reached her, he stopped. She was seated on the bench that was placed for the noon-time sun, head lifted as though to catch its warmth. He sat beside her but she seemed not to notice him. Even when he laid a hand over hers, taking her cold fingers between his own, she paid him no heed.

Sleepwalking, he realised. She would not have tolerated his touch otherwise. 'Come inside, Judith,' he coaxed. ''Tis cold out here, and you've left your cloak behind.'

She stood obediently and, with her hand in his, he led her back through the maze of herbs to the house, along the passageway and up the two flights of stairs to her bed. She curled up in its warmth, shivering now with sudden awareness of the cold. Toby stirred the fire into life then turned to stand with his back towards it, heat licking at his legs. In its light he watched her as she slept in their marriage bed – this wife of his he barely knew, who hated him.

Then, with a sigh, he left her to her rest, and went downstairs to the bed of the woman who loved him.

'You must share her bed from now,' Sarah said at breakfast, when Toby recounted what had happened in the night.

Mary tipped a glance over her shoulder from the sideboard, where she was pouring the small beer that accompanied the meal. He met her look with misgiving.

'So that you can stop her if she walks again,' his mother continued. 'What if she were to walk into the street? It was only good fortune that led her into the garden, and that you heard the click of the latch.'

He dropped the piece of bread in his hand back to the table, and as he took the cup Mary gave him, another look passed between them. He could see the worry in her eyes.

'She will not have me,' he said. 'She will refuse.'

The door swung open and Judith came in, pale and tired-eyed.

'Good morrow, wife,' Toby said. 'And the greetings of the season.'

'Morrow,' Judith murmured.

'Come, have some breakfast.'

She shook her head. "'Tis time for church,' she said. 'The bells are ringing.'

'You must eat,' Sarah said, 'to restore your strength.'

'I will feed on God's word,' Judith answered, and Toby saw his mother bite back the words of answer that gathered on her tongue.

'I will come,' he said, getting up, stuffing a last mouthful of cheese in his mouth, a final gulp of beer. He took up a hunk of bread from the table and passed it to his wife. 'Eat this along the way – it will help to sustain you.'

She took it with a reluctant hand and they moved to go, but at the door she turned back. 'Is this house so godless you won't even worship on the day of Christ's birth?'

'We go to St Saviour's, as you know,' Sarah replied. 'And we will leave straight after you.'

Judith said nothing, but the expression on her face was eloquent enough. In another situation, Toby might have laughed.

'Come,' he said to her. 'Eat your bread.'

She slid her eyes towards him with hostile look, dropped the bread to the ground at her feet, and turned and walked away.

At church Judith stood with her mother on the women's side of the church and refused to acknowledge him. He thought of his mother and Mary at the church of St Saviour's. Nick would be there, he thought, with Mary's friends from the bawdy house, and the worship would be boisterous and rowdy, full of the joy of Christmas.

Toby looked around him. No decoration lined the plain and whitewashed walls, at Christmas or at any other time. No winter greenery to decorate God's house. No one smiled beyond the briefest of greetings, all too burdened with the weight of their sins. Where was the love in their worship? The joy? Even on this most joyous of days to celebrate Christ's birth, they seemed conscious only of their unworthiness before God. Yet God had set the heavens alight in alleluia of His son's nativity, and the Magi had brought precious gifts. So why could these people not even raise a smile of celebration? Next time, he would go to St Saviour's with the women who loved him, he decided. He bowed his head, feigning piety to hide the sense of boredom.

When, at last, the service was over, he blinked the sleepiness from his eyes, swallowed down his yawn, and stepped across to the women. They turned as one to face him: mother and daughter, so unlike each other in their physical appearance yet lit by the exact same spirit of martyred righteousness. He rubbed the back of his head, and offered a small smile to his wife.

'Shall we?'

She shook her head. 'I'm going with my mother,' she said.

'You are my wife,' he replied, although the prospect of returning home without her was not without appeal. 'Your place is with me.'

'For a few days only,' her mother added. 'For Yuletide. Then you may have her back.'

He puffed his cheeks lightly, considering. Judith watched him, waiting, and he saw no light of hatred in her eyes now, only misery, and the small hope she would be allowed to go with her mother as she wanted.

'It would be a kindness,' Becky said.

He nodded. 'As you wish.' For what was to be gained by forcing her home? He said, 'One thing. She has taken to walking in her sleep.' Judith's eyes snapped to his in surprise. 'So be watchful. I would have no harm come to her.'

Becky nodded her understanding. Toby dipped a bow to both of them, but only his wife lowered herself into an answering curtsey. Then he took his farewell and left.

The women were already home from St Saviour's when he got there – though the church was further to walk, standing close by the river, the service was briefer. They were in high spirits – the yule log was burning brightly in the fireplace and the chamber smelled sweetly of all the greenery that hung on the walls – ivy and holly with blood-red berries, rosemary and winter savoury. The sideboard was half-laden with the spread of food they had been labouring the last few days to prepare. Brawn and mustard, pies and pastries, jugs of Malmsey wine. In a while, the servants and the tailors with their families would come to celebrate the day, and there would be feasting and games. One of the tailors had some skill with a flute, so perhaps there would also be dancing. Briefly, he wondered how the Tooley household spent the day, but the thought didn't linger long. The women's gaiety was infectious, and once he had explained the absence of his wife, he gave it no more thought for the rest of day.

Chapter Twenty-Seven

OUT, OUT BRIEF CANDLE

He woke in the early-morning dark with a bleared head to the sound of hammering on the front door. It took him a moment to come to, disorientated in his bed in the attic chamber, used to waking now in the hard cot in the old apprentice's room. For a moment he thought he had dreamed it; then it came again and this time it penetrated the fug of Mary's sleep too, and she sat up, listening.

'Who could it be,' she asked, 'at this hour?'

He said nothing and wiped his hands across his face and hair, trying to rub the sleep away, but the heaviness in his head remained – the aftermath of too much spiced wine and a late night of revelry. He slid out of bed and picked up his shift from the floor.

'Be careful,' Mary said, wrapping her robe around her, getting up too.

Picking up his knife, he padded downstairs in the dark. He could hear Mary treading softly behind him, and the rattle of the latch on his mother's chamber door as she came out to join them. When he was almost at the bottom stair, the hammering started again, and his blood quickened with expectation: only bad news ever came this way. With his hand on the bolt, he took a moment to pause, to breathe and draw up his courage. Then he drew back the bolt with a squeal of metal, turned the key and dragged the heavy door open to the night.

'Is she here?' It was Nick, sweating and breathless, his face lit in snatches by the flame of his torch. 'Judith. Is she here?'

'No,' Toby answered, with a shake of his head, dread seeping through his limbs. 'She was with you …'

'She's gone,' Nick replied. 'Vanished from her mother's bed some time in the night and we cannot find her. She has no cloak, no shoes … I thought she may have come here …' He trailed off, and Toby saw the desperation, the fear in his look. He flicked a glance to the women waiting on the stairs. 'Come in,' he said. 'Give me a moment to dress, and I'll come.'

Nick stepped into the hall, closing the door behind him, and briefly Toby remembered the last time, reaching a hand to his jaw in automatic recollection. But there was no time for memories and, turning, he raced up the stairs, brushing past Mary and Sarah, who stepped aside to let him pass.

He was back in just a few moments, still fumbling with the buttons on his doublet. Taking his cloak from the hook, he threw it around his shoulders, before he took the torch that Sarah had lit for him and followed his father-in-law into the night. 'Did you check the church?'

'It was the first place I tried.'

'And the graveyard?' He remembered finding her there before, huddled against the wall in her sorrow and grief.

Nick shook his head.

'We'll split up,' Toby said. 'You check the churchyard and I'll make for the river. We can cover more ground that way. We'll meet back at your house in an hour.'

The older man accepted the direction without a word of resistance, too immersed in his worry, Toby supposed, to protest. At the gate to the church they parted with a nod, and Toby strode on into the High Street, where it was eerily silent. The revellers in the inns and taverns seemed to have taken to their beds, and it was too early yet for the workers who would come with the morning. Torches flickered in doorways, and Toby was glad of their light despite the flame in his hand. An ill-sense of foreboding trickled through his veins: he should have brought her home, he thought, in her rightful place beside him where he could have kept her safe. His mother would have given her herbs to settle her sleep, and he would have heard if she had tried to walk again. Anger lit inside him that her parents had failed to protect her in spite of his warning.

He cut off the High Street and into the darkened maze of Borough Market before he reached the bridge, turning this way and that between the closed-up stalls and lanes, lowering the torch to peer into the corners and calling out her name. Once, he surprised a couple *in flagrante delicto*, which brought a smile to his lips, and twice, beggar children tugged at his sleeve. He gave them sixpence apiece, and one of them bent to touch his feet in gratitude.

At the river he paused. To the east, the towers of St Saviour's loomed in the darkness and to the west stretched the brothels and gambling dens of Bankside. He swung a wistful glance their way towards a world he no longer inhabited, and above the slap of the water on the bank he heard the distant laugh of a woman. In front of him St Overie Stairs led down to the shingle, and on an impulse he took them. The tide was low and the pebbles shifted and crunched under his feet as he walked along them. A couple of wherries were afloat on the current, their lanterns small and bright against the water, but the river was quiet at that hour, and there was no one abroad to disturb him. Still he kept his hand on his knife: he had spent too much of his life in this place ever to drop his guard, and his eyes scanned constantly, searching the shore and the water.

At Goat Steps, he climbed once more onto the quay, then stood awhile, searching the river. She would be frozen by now, he thought, in her linen shift and barefoot, even if no other harm had befallen her. And she was still weak from the loss of her child, her blood not yet restored. Dull dread oozed again in his gut, a sense of helpless urgency to find her, but he could not bring himself to leave the riverside, held there by some unknowable force, and he leaned against the stone wall of the landing stage stairs and peered into the gloom beyond the reach of the torch.

A wherry pulled in and a gentleman alighted, taking the wet steps carefully in his velvet shoes. Toby tracked him as the man stood before the row of brothels for a moment, considering his choices before he decided on the Swan and made his way towards it. Was he married too, Toby wondered, and looking for escape? Or was he just a young buck in search of some pleasure to celebrate the season? Toby shook his head. It seemed a lifetime since he had been so carefree, when his tailor father had yet been alive and the whole world still seemed possible.

He sighed and turned his attention back to the water that lapped at the shingle below. The tide was turning, he realised, a new turbulence in its movement. Leaving the torch on the quay, he made his way down the stairs and let his eyes adjust to the dark, shadows resolving into shapes. Then he continued on his way, wary of the waves lapping closer and mindful of the distance before the next set of stairs. Above him the brothels dwindled out, but beyond them were the gambling dens and pleasure gardens, set amongst a riot of dilapidated tenements, and further on again, there were houses, among them Nick Tooley's, set a ways back from the river.

Ahead of him the dark bulk of Falcon Stairs settled into focus, and he quickened his pace, warm now beneath his cloak in spite of the cold, damp air that blew off the river. A glint of white at the water's edge by the stairs caught his attention, then the movement of a shadow, a hooded man in a cloak, slipping swiftly up the steps and out of sight. With a rush of unwelcome understanding, he shouted to the man to stop and broke into a run, stumbling on the pebbles, agonisingly slow. By the time he reached the stairs the man was long gone, but the white shape he had seen from the distance still remained. A woman's body face down, half in, half out of the water, her hair floating on the changing tide, her shift around her waist and her legs and buttocks exposed to the night. Judith.

Toby ran to crouch beside her, hands reaching out to drag her back from the pull of the current. A few more minutes and she would have been gone, he realised, her body drifting out to sea with the tide, lost. Hauling her onto the safety of his lap, he turned her over and cleared her face of hair and debris with gentle fingers. Even in the darkness he could see the cuts on her cheek and the swelling bruise across her neck. He lifted down the shift to cover her modesty, cradled her in his embrace and wept.

By time Toby arrived at the Tooleys' house with Judith in his arms, his whole body was screaming with the weight of her body. He had sat on the shingle a long time as the turning tide had crept to his boots, unnoticed, only spurred into action at last by the first touch of light above the roofs downriver. He needed to be gone under darkness's cloak: a man with a dead girl would not get far in daylight.

Staggering with her on the bank, he struggled on the steps, falling twice, but it was easier going on the flat path, and though his muscles groaned in complaint he did not stop, holding her cold body close against his warmth as he stumbled through the still-dark backstreets of looming tenements, as yet unlit by the paling sky. He met no one, though once he heard men's voices in a doorway as he hurried past, and waited for the shout for him to halt. But none came, and he trudged on with relief, his steps growing slower with the effort as he neared the house in Water Lane.

When he reached it at last, the curtains were open at the downstairs window and the light inside flickered and faded with guttering candles and a dying fire. Unable to raise a fist to the door, his fingers still desperately gripping onto his wife, he prayed that someone was watching: he was beginning to lose his hold, his muscles stretched beyond the point of exhaustion. He called out. 'Master Tooley!'

The door opened onto warmth and light as his legs began to give way, and he would have dropped his burden onto the flagstones if Nick hadn't stepped forward and taken her weight from his arms.

'Becky!' Nick shouted over his shoulder. 'Wife!'

Toby sank to his knees on the threshold, strength ebbing. He had brought Judith home and he could do no more. In the mist of his weariness he was aware of Nick laying her on a couch near the hearth – did he not realise she was dead? There was no earthly heat could revive her now. Then, raising his head, he saw Judith's mother staring down at him, lips parted in what was almost a snarl.

'Becky,' Nick called to his wife again, and she left him on his knees at the door and bustled to the couch where her daughter lay.

Toby watched the two of them at Judith's body, their growing realisation of her death. Becky's fall to her knees, Nick's anguished pacing. For himself he wanted only to rest, but finally he found the strength to raise himself to stand and, closing the door behind him, he walked on unsteady legs towards the hearth. Nick raised his eyes at his presence, and Toby saw the pain etched in the lines of his face: the other man seemed old suddenly, all the charm and vitality beaten out of him. 'Our thanks for finding her,' Nick said. 'And for bringing her home.'

Toby tilted his head, but said nothing. He wanted no thanks for his part in this.

Becky swung round from where she knelt at Judith's side. 'Thank him not!' she hissed. 'It was him that killed her …'

Weariness slid into anger at her judgement. 'It was your bed she slipped from tonight, your front door she went through … I warned you to be watchful, so you have no right to lay the blame on me.'

Becky's jaw worked in fury. 'This was your doing. You as good as murdered her. And if the law won't judge you, you can be sure that God will. You will end your days in the fire, where you belong. And there will be no mercy for you then.'

'Enough!' Nick's voice was harsh. 'Enough.'

But Becky would not be silenced. 'If you hadn't seduced her, and begotten a monster on her …'

Toby turned his gaze to the fire and thought of the tiny child he had buried with its poor misshapen spine. Not a monster, he thought, but an unloved and unwanted soul that had given up the fight for life before it even began. He hoped it had found some peace in the afterlife, that Tom had eased its way. Tears smarted at his eyes and to hide them he squatted to the fire and poked at the embers, stirring more life into the flames.

'Where did you find her?' Nick asked, lowering himself to the stool at the fireplace edge.

'Below Falcon Stairs. The tide had almost taken her.'

Nick nodded and turned his own gaze to the fire. Toby lowered himself onto the rug, legs aching, and stared into the shifting light. He began to shiver, suddenly aware of his wet clothes, and the cold-ness of the night beyond the warmth of the hearth.

Nick said, 'I'll fetch you a dry shirt and breeches.'

Toby took off his boots and set them to one side, away from the direct heat of the flames. His stockings dripped onto the rug and he removed them too, his feet soft and wrinkled underneath. He wrig-gled his toes, enjoying the heat against the soles, and he could hear Becky's low sobs behind him as she crouched over her daughter's still form. But he could not bring himself to look at her, conscious of the truth in her accusation. Magic or no, he had tempted Judith to his bed, and if he had not done so, she would still be alive.

Nick returned with clean clothes and Toby dried himself and put them on. They were too big, the shoulders of the shift halfway down his arms, and he had to fasten a belt around the breeches. But they were dry and warm and he was grateful for them. 'Should we call the constable?' he asked.

'To arrest you for murder?' Becky spat over her shoulder, star-tling him. He had addressed the question to her husband in a low voice before the spit and crackle of the fire.

'She drowned, wife,' Nick said, without turning. 'There is no murder to answer for.' He raised his eyes to Toby with a silent ques-tion. They had seen the bruises on her neck and both knew she had met a violent end, but an accusation would drag the whole truth into the open, and raise the chance that Toby would be named her killer.

'She was murdered,' Becky said. 'And he ...' She pointed at Toby. 'He murdered her.'

Toby shook his head, too weary to defend himself with any spirit. 'She was my wife,' he breathed.

'And you wanted her gone,' she continued. 'So you could share your bed with that whore. Do you think she didn't tell me? Do you think I don't know?'

'I hoped for a good marriage between us, a family, but she barred me from my bed,' he replied. 'Did she tell you that too?' He shrugged. 'And perhaps I did share a bed with the whore – a man has to sleep somewhere, after all. But I swear to you, I had no hand in her death.'

Becky scowled and turned away, and a flicker of fear ran through him that she would accuse him anyway, and he would die at the end of a rope as his father had done. He shivered, though not from cold, and trained his gaze once more on the soothing lick of the flames. Outside the window, dark gave way to the dull bruised sky of a winter morning, unobserved by any in the house.

For a long time no one spoke, immersed in their grief and shock and sorrow. Toby stared into the flames, thinking of nothing, until the wail and screech of cats squaring up for a fight in the street broke into the silence. Running his hands across his face and hair, and shaking his head to slough off the sleepiness, he turned again to look at Nick. The older man was observing him, as though trying to read beneath the surface of what he saw to some deeper level underneath.

'We should carry her to her bed, and wash her.' He stopped, took a long breath of thought, then said, 'Do you wish to bury her from here?'

Becky snapped round to look at him, attentive.

'She still thought of this as home, and it would seem more fitting …' He trailed off. He had failed her in life in every way. Perhaps in death he could make some small amends.

'People will talk,' Nick said.

'Let them.' He shrugged. 'It matters not.'

Nick turned his head towards his wife. 'Wife?'

For a moment she hesitated, looking from one man to the other. Then, meeting Toby's eyes for the first time, she nodded. 'This changes nothing,' she said. 'And I would still call the constable.'

Nick gave him a quick nod of approval and stood up, stretching out the powerful limbs. Toby watched him, admiring the strength of the other man's body. Then Nick scooped up his daughter's lifeless form in one easy movement, and carried her upstairs to her chamber to lay her gently on the bed.

~

Mary strode through the morning, skirts flapping against her legs and the sun bright in her eyes when her road pointed her towards it. The sky was powder blue above her, and though the air was crisp and clear, there was a welcome warmth in the sun that lit her face. The streets were still quiet – shops were shut up for Christmastide, and though the High Street still bore its share of travellers heading to and from the bridge, there were no farm carts to step around, and few traders hawking their wares.

She cut through the lane by the White Harte and took the back roads, turning right onto Red Cross Street and past the Cross Bones graveyard where Toby had buried the tiny body of his child just two days since. Casting a brief glance towards it she shuddered. She had always hated graveyards, especially this one of sinful souls where she expected to end her days. She fingered the small poppet that she carried at her waist and, tamping down the worst of the thoughts that curled in her mind, she set her gaze to the ground before her feet and kept walking.

So she was unaware of the cloaked man in the shadow of the graveyard trees until he stopped her with a hand on her arm. With a scream of shock, she tried to wrench free, but the man's grip tightened, and in the struggle that followed his hood slid back from his face.

Alexander, she realised, and her skin prickled in fear.

She fought harder, kicking out with her legs, landing blows across his face with her free hand, but he shoved her against the fence that guarded the graveyard, forcing her arm up at an unnatural angle and his body pressing against hers, pinning her with his weight.

'Mary Sparrow,' he breathed, his lips so close to her cheek she felt the warm air of his words against it. 'I have found you at last.'

'What of it?' she replied.

He dug his fingers deeper into the muscle of her arm and lifted it higher: pain screamed through her shoulder and she cried out. She glanced along the street, hoping for rescue, but there was no one and they were alone. *Toby,* she called out silently. *Help me.* Her attacker gripped her chin and turned her face to his. His mouth brushed her skin and her terror of him almost stopped her breath. 'Where is my book?' he said.

She shook her head. 'I cannot find it,' she whispered. 'He keeps it close and hidden. He doesn't trust me.'

'Liar!' He let go of her jaw with a laugh, then brought the flat of his hand hard across her cheek. If he had not been holding her, the blow would have knocked her to the ground. She could taste the trickle of blood from her lip, and she lowered her head away, bracing for the next one.

'Do not think to play games with me,' he said. 'Do you want to end up in the graveyard here before your time? Or face down in the Thames like Master Chyrche's new wife?'

She raised her eyes to meet his at that, fear falling in her belly like a weight of lead. 'You killed her?'

'She is dead.' He shrugged. 'It matters not how.'

Judith had been the price to pay, then, she thought. The life in exchange for Toby's. She was silent, thoughts groping to find a way out, but her mind was soaked with fear of him and she could see no possible escape. Was this how she was going to die? she wondered. For what purpose?

Alexander let out a long sigh and threw a glance along the street, as though considering what to do next. Then he lowered his hand a fraction, and the pain in her shoulder subsided a little. Instinctively she raised the other hand to rub at it, but her eyes never left his face. She wanted to know when her death was coming, and see the murder in his eyes. Swallowing, she waited, sensing his hesitation and the dimming of his rage. Perhaps she was not fated to die today after all, and a small tendril of hope budded inside her. She steadied her breath and stayed wary.

'What do you want from me?' she asked.

He flicked a swift glance along the street before he pressed his face close to hers again and answered. 'Bring me the book,' he snarled, and if you don't, the next time I find you, you will become a five-fingered whore like all the rest of them.' He grasped her hand and bent back the smallest finger until she cried out with pain and the fear he would snap it there and then. 'And then a four-fingered whore ...'

'I will find it,' she answered.

'Good. Then you may stay out of the graveyard for one more day.'

Smiling, apparently pleased with her reply, he let go of her hand with a final cruel twist to her finger which made her gasp. Then he dipped his head in a parody of courteous farewell, lifted the hood up once more, and went on his way. She watched him grow smaller along the street, and her whole arm throbbed with pain.

Mary walked the rest of the way to the Tooleys' house in nervous agitation, jumping at every knock and shout, heartbeat rapid, head light. Shrinking from every passer-by, she cut back onto the High Street, where she felt safer in the bustle. Her whole arm still pained, and she rubbed at her finger gently where Alexander had bent it back.

'Merry Christmas, my lovely.' A man smoking a pipe by the door of a tavern stretched out a hand towards her as she passed, and she ducked out of his reach, pulling her cloak tighter round her. She heard his laugh turn to a cough as she hurried on her way, moving further from the shelter of the buildings, risking the ruts of the road. The hubbub of drunken voices drifted from the doors and windows of the inns and taverns.

Judith was all but forgotten: her fears now were for herself and for Toby. She was not safe from Alexander: wherever she hid he would find her, in spite of Toby's protection. What then should she do? She caressed her extra finger – she had no doubt he would make good on his threat, and the pain still stabbed in warning. Passing through the market, she was wary. She had stolen here herself on occasion, relieving men of their purses when the food at the brothel had not been enough, or she had needed money to pay for medicine or herbs. But it was not theft that frightened her now: her whole body was alive to the prospect of death, and she feared a slow end most of all. One or two familiar faces called out greetings, and she nodded and offered a small tight smile in return. Men she had known at the brothel, men she had hoped to forget.

At last she came out by the river, and from its slow-rolling vastness she drew comfort. She stood at its edge before the row of bawdy houses and breathed in the rich, heady stench. She had spent her whole life a stone's throw from its waters, and the plash and thud of oars and the slap of high tide against the walls calmed her a little, a reminder of life unchanging through the ages, Alexander a mere spot in time. But still, she was afraid of him, and her own poor existence in the vastness of a world that turned unheedful of her plight still mattered to her – it was the only life she had, and she wanted to keep it. Drawing in long, slow breaths to calm herself, she turned west towards where Sarah had told her the Tooleys' house lay, and though there were other routes that were quicker, Mary chose to walk where the roads were busiest and more people were abroad.

She arrived at the house in Water Lane as St Saviour's bells struck midday behind her, and the sombre strikes followed her path along the river. Like a death knell, she thought, and shivered. Then, shaking off the thought with a lift of her shoulders and a deep breath, she raised her hand to the door and knocked. Several long moments passed before the door swung open and Nick Tooley filled the space behind it. She remembered him from the brothel and the wedding: the handsome player. He ran his gaze across her but there was no light of recognition in his eyes. Had he forgotten her, she wondered, or was he too immersed in his grief to care? 'Mistress Chyrche sent me,' she said. 'For news.'

He nodded and stepped back to let her enter, and she found herself in a warm and spacious chamber. Toby was at the hearth and he started to his feet in surprise at the sight of her. 'Mary!' He came towards her.

'Your mother sent me,' she said.

He stopped before her, eyes searching her face with concern. Touching a hand to her cheek, she remembered the blow and the split lip. There would be a welt now, she realised, turning to a bruise.

'What happened?' Toby asked, and she knew that if they had been alone, he would have raised a hand to caress her swollen cheek, a thumb to touch the cut on her mouth.

She shook her head. ''Tis nothing,' she said. 'A fall merely.' She could not explain it here in front of Nick, and hoped Toby would understand. 'What is the news?'

He swallowed and threw a glance towards the other man, who shrugged. Then he turned back to her. 'Judith is dead,' he told her. 'I found her at the river.'

She nodded, unable to say that she already knew. 'I'm so sorry.' She turned to Nick, who had gone to stand by the fire, observing them from a distance. 'I'm so sorry for your loss.'

He acknowledged her condolence with a nod, then turned and bent to tend the fire, though it was already burning well.

Toby said, 'I'll return with you now. There's nothing more I can do here.'

Then, taking his leave of Nick with a bow and a few murmured words, he took his wet cloak from the hook, fastened it across his shoulders and led her back out into the lane.

'What happened?' he asked, as soon as they were out of earshot of the house. They stopped in the street before the silent houses, and Toby touched a gentle finger to her cheek. 'Who did this to you?'

'Alexander,' she said, and told him what had happened, her voice coming in short breathless sentences. 'He killed her,' she ended. 'How else could he have known?'

Toby gazed away towards the town and bit at his lip, hands on hips, considering. She waited, watching him, and she was caught again by his beauty – his eyes, grey now in the dull winter light, and the two-day stubble marking the hard line of his jaw. He must have sensed her scrutiny because he turned from his thoughts to her with a smile at the corner of his mouth. 'Don't be afraid,' he said. 'I won't let him hurt you again. I want you with all of your fingers.'

She smiled then as he lifted her left hand to his lips and kissed each finger in turn, and in the pleasure of his touch and his smile, it was hard to remember their danger. Still holding her hand, fingers entwined, they walked on along the lane.

'What can we do?' she asked, turning her head to look at him beside her. 'How can we stop him?'

'We must use the book against him,' he replied. 'We must do magic ourselves, together, and use the power in the book to undo him.'

She shivered, and tightened her grip on his fingers. 'Will it work?'

'I dreamed of it,' he said. 'And it will work. But 'tis dangerous. Are you game?'

She thought of half-witted Rosalind and of Judith face down in the Thames, and the pain in her arm still throbbed. 'Will he die?'

'I hope to make it so,' he said.

'Then I am game.'

He smiled, and caressed her hand, and she was glad to be by his side.

Chapter Twenty-Eight
UNTIE THE WINDS

At the house in Narrow Lane, they found Sarah in the kitchen, baking. Flour covered her hands and streaks of white slashed her forehead. She looked up from her work as they entered and, wiping her hands, she set the dough aside and fetched ale for them all. 'What news?'

'She's dead,' Toby said. 'I found her at the river.'

Sarah's eyes closed in sorrow. 'She was the price to pay,' she breathed, so quiet that Mary was unsure if she had heard it at all. 'One for one. And there must be another to keep you both. Oh, Toby, what have we done?'

Toby reached across the table and grasped his mother's hand. 'She is with God now.' Then he told her the rest of it, and Sarah got up to find arnica for Mary's bruises, working as Toby talked.

'So we will give him the book,' he said, 'but we will turn it against him first.'

'Hecate?' Sarah finished rubbing the salve into Mary's sore shoulder, and turned to her son.

He shook his head. 'Hecate is too unpredictable.'

Sarah gave a wry smile.

'We must conjure,' he said. ''Tis the only magic the book understands.'

'Together? You and Mary?'

'Aye. At the hour of Saturn.'

'Be careful, Toby. Please.'

He nodded, but Mary only saw the fear in Sarah's eyes, and slid her own gaze away.

∾

In the darkness that night they went again to the Grove. Toby had spent the hours in between in preparation, though Mary had scant idea of what he did, passing her own afternoon with Sarah in household tasks. Frances was still with her family for Christmastide and there was plenty to be done. But when they left he shouldered a great pack, and gave her a small basket to carry.

The night was clear and bright. A sliver of moon reclined above the houses, and bright stars pinpricked the vaulted black while a few high clouds stippled the furthest reaches. Tomorrow, she guessed, there would be more rain. They walked in silence and though a few times she thought to break it, she sensed Toby was deep in his thoughts to prepare his mind for what lay ahead, so she held her peace in spite of the questions that circled in her mind.

When they reached the Grove, Toby set her to making a fire, and while she gathered wood for kindling, she sent her thoughts to Hecate, the guardian of this place, to ask for her blessing and protection. She had little understanding of what they would do tonight. Her only knowledge of sorcery came from the playhouse; *Faustus* and *Macbeth* and *The Tempest*, and fear and excitement tumbled over each other inside her, quickening her heartbeat, skin a-prickle.

Now and then she paused in her labour to watch as Toby laid out two great circles with twine, one within the other, and a smaller triangle a little distance away. When the shapes were made, he placed words and symbols that he had inked onto linen around their edges. How did he know what to do? she wondered. Where had he gained such knowledge? Surely he had not learned it all from the book. Was it innate, a gift from his father, guiding his son from his realm of death? Or did he truly dance with the Devil as Judith had claimed? He had said he had dreamed of it, and she did not dare to ask.

When the circles were finished he turned to help her with the fire, taking time to build it high with branches thick enough that they would hold the heat and not burn away too fast. She was aware of an urgency in his movements and his anxious glances toward the moon as though to check the hour. Far beyond the forest, church bells chimed a single toll, carrying high through the clear winter air. When the fire had caught they stood together for a moment to admire it, though they were both warm from their labour. Then Toby turned to her.

'We must wash,' he said, 'to be pure for the ritual.' Taking her hand, he led her to a stream that flowed just beyond the clearing. Away from the fire the air was cold, but she undressed alongside him at the water's edge, her skin prickling with goosebumps, and though she tried to keep her eyes away from Toby's body close beside her, she was conscious of his pale, lean loveliness and the ripple of muscle under the skin as he moved, the flatness of his belly.

'Shall we?' he said, and stepped into the clear running water.

With a sigh of resignation she followed him in and the sting of the cold snatched her breath away. It was even colder and deeper than she'd imagined, and though she lowered herself into it as he told her to do and rubbed her limbs beneath the water, she could barely breathe with the chill of it. Afterwards she shivered in spasms as they dried themselves on the bank with cloths he had brought, teeth chattering. Then they went again to the circle.

She slid a glance towards him and he smiled. 'Trust me,' he said. 'Come.'

He held out his hand and led her through the opening in the circle's edge. Then he told her to kneel on the rug he had placed in its centre by the fire. She obeyed, eager for its warmth, but her breath was short with sudden fear, and in spite of the heat she still shivered as she watched Toby close the circle. Then she remembered the pain in her shoulder and the danger she was in, and steeled herself to have courage.

Toby began to pace the rim of the circle, tracing the line with a point of his dagger. A heady scent of musk and something oriental she did not recognise danced in the air from burning incense, and her courage ripened, transmuting swiftly to desire. Four times Toby halted on his journey round the circle to call out to unseen forces, and though she had no understanding of the words he spoke, their vibration brought a lifting in her soul, a brightening awareness of the world beyond the seen. Then Toby moved into her eyeline, firelight flickering against the smoothness of his skin, and want for him coursed through her blood. When he turned and knelt on the blanket before her, it took all the strength of her willpower not to reach out to touch him. He must have seen the desire in her eyes because he stilled her with a faint movement of his head, and so her fingers twitched, frustrated, where they lay on her thighs. She could almost taste him already.

He picked up the quill and ink he had lain beside them in readiness, and she flinched as he began to trace a pattern across her chest. The quill nib was sharp, scratching, and she wondered if the ink would leave a permanent mark. She had known sailors sometimes at the brothel who had travelled to exotic lands and returned with markings of ink on their skin that they told her they would keep until they died. She lowered her eyes to watch the quill move to form a strange image, feeling the scrape of its path across her skin.

When it was done, Toby sat back on his heels to check his work. She gazed at it too, transfixed by its sinister beauty, but there was no need for her to look – she could feel every line of the symbol, a heat in the ink, warmth and power soaking through the skin and into the marrow of her being. Like a brand that burned to her core.

She swallowed, surrendering to this new force inside her, and raised her head to meet Toby's look. He gave her a small smile that did nothing to still her fear, then gestured for her to lie back on the blanket. She obeyed, but all she was aware of was the shape of the sigil at her centre, her whole body quivering in its vibration. She could feel the pull of a different, darker realm, and her soul cried out in silent dread. She reached out a hand to Toby to save her from its grasp, and he gripped her fingers, holding her fast.

'You're safe,' he murmured. 'Do not fear. In the circle you are safe.'

She nodded, but she no longer believed him. *He's in league with the Devil.* She remembered again Judith's words in the garden. Was it the Devil's grip that clawed at her innards now? Her soul bound for Hell?

'Trust me,' Toby said. 'You must trust me.'

She brought her gaze to meet his – those changing eyes she loved, searching to find again her faith in him. But the sigil burned in her breast and spread its terror through her blood, and she could feel nothing else. She watched him, unable to move, unable to think, as he slid the book beneath her buttocks. The leather scalded her skin, and the heat rose through her body to meet the brand in her heart.

Then Toby knelt between her legs, and she watched him, her blood humming, transfixed. He began to speak again, words of power that called to the spirit whose sign inhabited her, and she was conscious of the spirit's response, a visceral awakening inside of her. She cried out in terror – was this the possession that Judith had spoken of? She wanted to scream and run, but her body was no longer hers to command.

Toby shifted forward on his knees, still speaking words she did not understand as he thrust himself into her, full and hard. Instinctively her body arched in response as he moved slowly inside her in a rhythm in time with the ritual on his lips. Her whole body seemed on fire, pleasure from the sex circling with the terror and the pain in her breast, a rising violence of ecstasy she had never known before.

Toby's voice swam in and out of her consciousness.

'I conjure you ... I conjure you ... to whom is given the power of life and death over men, that you should obey no conjuror but me.

'Bring harm to others who would summon you, even unto death.

'Turn their desires against them, feed them lies and evil.

'I conjure you in the name of Tom Wynter, who controlled you once, and in the name of the Holy Father, and all his marvellous works; by the heavens, by the earth, by the sea, by the depth of the Abyss, by the winds and the waters of the sea ... by this act of bliss that calls you forth ...'

The music of his words drifted again to the background of her thoughts, all her senses turning on the painful pleasure of her body as her soul writhed in horror as the spirit's captive.

Toby bent closer and briefly the music stopped. 'Think of Alexander,' he whispered, 'and see his death.'

She closed her eyes, and forced her mind to focus and remember the purpose of the rite. A lust for violence engulfed her and it was easy to imagine – she had thought of it many times since that first night with Rosalind. She could see Alexander now, his body floating in the current of the Thames, a trail of red streaming from the slash that slit his throat, staining the water around him. She saw herself with the knife and felt the blade cutting into the flesh, the spurt of hot blood as his last breaths gurgled in the froth.

The heat of the fire beside them turned cold, and even through closed eyelids, she knew a shivering darkness had descended. In sudden fear, she opened her eyes, but the Grove had been plunged into utter black, and though Toby was still thrusting inside her he seemed to be an insubstantial form, as if he had turned into the spirit that possessed her. Terror engulfed her again as all the fire turned abruptly to ice, and the blood in her limbs seemed to freeze. She opened her mouth to scream with the pain of it, but Toby put a hand to her lips.

'Trust me.'

She bit back the cries that gathered in her throat, and the tears flowed unchecked across her face. Toby was still inside her, disembodied but still moving, faster now, and she could feel the ice in her core and the certainty she would never know warmth again. She had always thought that Hell was a furnace. Was this how Rosalind had lost her mind?

Toby took his hand from her mouth and lifted his gaze to whatever being he had summoned. Quivering in fear and cold, she lifted her own hand to stop her cries.

'*Great Duke, I greet thee with respect ... and I ask this of you ... that you let Alexander suffer no daemons to come to him when he calls. Let his magic and sorcery turn to dust, and let his evil be returned upon himself sevenfold. Bring his death upon him ...'*

She forced her thoughts once more to Alexander and sent her own silent plea, closing her mind to all that was around her, Toby's voice ebbing into the silence, her mind filling once more with the sights and sounds of Alexander's death: the slap of the river on the shingle, and the clunk and thud of oars as the sorcerer's body floated past, the redness of the blood on the tide, his robes spread and heavy, the bloodstained knife.

Her sudden, unexpected climax threw her back into the circle, heat pulsating from her belly as Toby shuddered to his own, spasming inside her. She opened her eyes and searched the dark for the spirit that had come, but whatever it had been had departed now, for the ice in her veins had begun to melt and the fire was bright again. In the sudden warmth she shivered, and Toby lay down beside her. 'It's done,' he whispered, running his fingers along her arm.

'What was that?'

'A spirit,' he answered lightly.

'How do you know ... all of this ...?'

He shrugged. 'I studied the book a little, and others too ... I have dreams ...'

She was silent. Toby as sorcerer frightened her. The memory of her terror was still vivid and pulsating, the utter darkness that thing had brought with it, and the certainty that it had been the one inside her. They had been in the presence of something unspeakably evil, and for the first time she began to have some sympathy for Judith. She wanted to wash the sigil from her skin, and she rubbed at it now with her fingers. The ink smudged, running with her sweat, but she knew it would not be so easy to erase its traces.

She turned to look at Toby as he lay beside her. He was on his side, watching her, and she thought again how lovely he was, with his skin so pale and other-worldly in the firelight, and his changing eyes – surely such beauty could admit no evil? He smiled, tracing the lines of the sigil gently with his fingers on her breast, but she wanted none of it. Fear slid into anger and she pushed his hand away and sat up.

With the movement she remembered the book beneath her: it was stuck to her skin with her sweat. She peeled it away. The cover was sticky with their juices and she gave it to him with a grimace, but he smiled.

'It's a good thing,' he said, and took it from her. 'The book is imbued now with our magic, and the elixir contains great power.'

Mary said nothing as he took her hand and helped her to stand. The fire's heat was starting to ebb, and the cold air raised a shiver as it touched the sheen of sweat on her skin. She held her hands out to the fading warmth. The strangeness of all that had happened still sang in her blood, and she glanced across to Toby, pacing the edge of the circle once more, the knife's point tracing the lines. She had seen a different man in him tonight, a man who could conjure the spirits from Hell. Judith had been right after all.

At last Toby opened the circle and they stepped outside its confines together. Mary bent to the water to rub the sigil from her skin, rubbing hard, careless of the chill of it. Then they dressed in hurried silence by the fire where they had left their clothes. He finished first, and when he was dressed he moved to help her with the laces of her bodice. Instinctively, she ducked away from his touch.

'What's wrong?' he asked. 'Why do you flinch away from me?'

She shook her head, unable to find words to explain.

'Tell me.'

He reached a hand to her face and lifted her chin so that she could not help but look at him. She sighed, torn, and her soul turned in restless uneasiness, still in pain from its ordeal.

'That thing,' she murmured, gesturing towards the circle with her head. 'That daemon that you conjured. It was inside of me. It was not in you. It possessed me, and it tried to drag me into Hell.'

He swallowed and was silent.

'Is this what you did to Judith?'

'No!' He almost shouted. 'No,' he repeated more softly. 'It was different.'

She said nothing, watching him in the dying glow from the fire.

Above them, a crescent moon cleared the tops of the trees and spread her ghostly light across the Grove.

He let out a long breath. 'This was powerful magic – I warned you of its danger, but against Alexander ...' He shrugged and trailed off.

She nodded, still uncertain. But when he offered her his hand, she took it. He smiled with relief.

'I thought for a moment I had lost you,' he said.

'It'll take more than possession by the Devil to make me leave you.'

He laughed and bent to kiss her, and she remembered again how much she loved him. Then they walked home, arm in arm, and though she loved him again, the darkness of the spirit trailed behind her like a shadow, and she did not forget it.

'Take it,' Toby said, the following day. The early-evening dark filled the window of his chamber, and his face was pale in the light of a single candle. He held the book in his hands, still reluctant to let it go.

Mary thought of how he'd held his dead child with just the same tenderness, and the shadow passed through her again. He gave her the book and she took it, though with equal reluctance, ready for some jolt or tremor. But it lay inert in her hand, a plain book, and her fear of it subsided.

'It only reacts to its master,' Toby said, as though he had read her mind. 'In my hands it quivers and hums.' Then, 'Go. He will be waiting for it.'

She wrapped it in a cloth and held it close, then made her way downstairs and out into the gathering rain. Outside, it was still busy. Traders in the High Street, calling out the last of their wares, and travellers: horsemen, carts and the weary footsore vying for space on the road. Many had given up the effort to make the bridge before nightfall, taking up residence instead in one of the inns, and the warm conviviality of good food and ale at a journey's end flooded from the windows and doors as she passed.

She held the book tightly against her chest beneath her cloak with both hands. She had never had possession before of anything so precious, and a half-formed thought flickered in her mind that she could escape Bankside forever on its back, a fortune to be made to the right man. Briefly she was tempted. But where would she find the right man? Besides, Alexander would find her no matter where she went. Scolding herself for thinking such things, she thought again of last night's magic – terror and beauty and desire entwined, a heat and cold beyond her wildest imaginings. Would she do it again for that one moment of ecstasy, a transcendence she had not thought possible? She hoped the choice would never come to her again.

A shout from a horseman behind her wrenched her thoughts back to the High Street, and she flattened herself against the wall as he urged his horse towards the river, careless of the danger to those he passed. A gentleman, richly dressed, and full of his own importance. She watched the horse's retreating haunches as they were swallowed in the crowd, and hoped the gates closed before he reached them.

Turning off the High Street, she skirted St Thomas's and the orphanage that she had never once returned to since the day she had left. She could hear the voices of children, chanting a prayer in unison, and pitied them for their unloved lives. With only one wrong turn she came to the alehouse at the sign of the Wounded Raven. It was lively with workers celebrating the end of the day, a poor and run-down place in a street of rotting tenements close to the water. The muddy lane exuded a rank stink as it squelched underfoot, and she freed one hand from the book to lift the hem of her skirt free of its filth. A torch had been lit at the doorway and it threw shifting shadows through the thickening drizzle. She had not noticed how hard the rain was falling, and when she lifted a hand to her face, she realised her hair was slick across her head, quite wet.

On the far side of the lane she paused, running her eyes across the building, searching for her courage. The attic windows, their shutters still wide, glowed with the light of many candles. She swallowed. He was at home then, and there would be no reprieve. An unkempt man with a pregnant belly staggered from the alehouse door, unbalanced with ale, and, seeing Mary, hailed her. 'How much for a fuck?'

She smiled and shook her head. 'I'm not for sale.' Then, evading his grasping hands with deft-footed ease, she slid past him and into the warmth and brightness inside. For a moment she blinked. *Up the wooden staircase,* Toby had told her. *Right to the top.* She glanced around the alehouse, a familiar world, automatically picking out the likely customers against the ones who would play all night but in the end would refuse to pay. Then she set her foot on the bottom stair and with a determined tread made her way into the dark and up towards the topmost landing.

From the top stair she realised that the attic occupied the whole floor, and she hesitated. Was he conjuring inside? Would she walk in on some hellish spirit? She took a silent step forward and pressed her ear to the door, but there was nothing to hear and so she raised her fist to the door and knocked.

Alexander's voice replied straight away. 'Who comes?'

'Mary Sparrow,' she called out.

She heard the scrape of a stool against floorboards and a heavy tread crossing to the door. She stepped back onto the top step to give herself space: she remembered him pressed against her by the graveyard, the hot, stale breath in her face. But when he opened the door and the light from the chamber fell across the landing, he was his most charming self, seductive and kind, a smile at the corners of his eyes. She stayed wary, and when he invited her in, she shook her head.

'I've something for you,' she said, and held out the book.

His gaze caught on the package in her hand, and the kindliness vanished in a moment as his eyes filled instead with an almost desperate lust, his tongue sliding over his lips. She was tempted to drop the book and run, but she stood her ground and held the book steady, so that he was forced to step forward to reach it. Snatching it from her grasp at last, he took one pace back and slammed the door in her face. She heard the key grind in the lock and a heavy bolt slide home. Then, with a dry mouth and her heart still running quickly, she turned and fled back down the stairs and out into the lane.

Chapter Twenty-Nine

THY BLOOD IS COLD

On the day of the funeral it was bitter cold. The earth was frozen underfoot, and the chill air stung Toby's lips and cheeks. The gravediggers would have had the devil's own job to dig the hole, he thought, as the small procession made its way into the churchyard from the gate, the priest at its head. The coffin dug heavily into his shoulder, and he was glad when they laid it down at last beside the grave. He stepped back to stand with the other mourners, Nick close by his side.

A lot of people had come despite the cold, mostly members of the church congregation, and he realised he didn't know if Judith had had any particular friends amongst them – she had never mentioned any names. But he was aware of the sidelong looks from the others. The burial from her father's house hard on the heels of a hasty wedding had aroused their suspicions. He met their looks with brazen indifference – their good opinion meant nothing to him. It had been his church because it was his father's, and if they despised him he did not care.

At the head of the open grave the priest began the service, and his voice carried clear and resonant through the crisp, dry air.

'A man that is born of a woman hath but a short time to live, and is full of misery ...'

Toby nestled his chin deeper inside his woollen scarf. It smelled sweetly of cloves and lavender, the scents of his childhood in winter.

'In the midst of life we are in death ...'

He raised his eyes to the coffin, peering in his mind's eye through the oak to the cold, still body within, and tried to remember her in life; her passion, her quick mind, the reluctant laugh he had coaxed from her so many times. But the images were indistinct. Clearer in his thoughts was the memory of her lifeless body in his arms on the shingle – the shush-hush of the tide on the shore, her body wet against his, his own face streaked with tears. He blinked to force himself to dry-eyed grief, and realised the priest had paused in his liturgy, and beside him Nick and the other bearers had taken a step forward to the grave.

Lifting the strap, he braced, and together they lowered Judith's body into the ground as the priest took up the words again.

'Forasmuch as it hath pleased Almighty God of his great mercy to take unto himself ...'

The coffin landed with a thud and they stepped back as one man. He heard Judith's mother sob before she shuffled forward to throw a spray of rosemary into the grave.

'Earth to earth, dust to dust, ashes to ashes ...'

Other mourners threw other flowers and herbs, and Toby wished he had brought something of his own to offer. He knelt and gathered a handful of cold dirt, and let it drop through his fingers onto the coffin. The dark earth stained his fingers and caught beneath his fingernails. He resisted the urge to wipe them clean on his cloak.

Forgive me, Judith, he repeated over and over in silent appeal. *Forgive me.*

He saw his mother crouch at the grave edge to drop a posy, and she caught his eye with a small smile as she stood up.

'Lord, have mercy upon us,
Christ, have mercy upon us,
Lord, have mercy upon us.'

The first-floor chamber at Narrow Lane was crowded with all the mourners, and the cold morning had given them an appetite. Toby watched from his place at the window as Mary flitted between them, filling cups, and they helped themselves to the spread of meats and pastries that the women had made so much effort to prepare. It was a solemn wake, a godly crowd not much given to levity, and he was careful not to catch Mary's eye, aware of all the watchful gazes and the suspicious Puritan minds, judging.

Nick came to join him at the window. He was nursing an empty cup of ale, and they stood for a long moment, gazing into the busy street below. Some children were teasing another boy, who stood a little distance away, fighting tears. 'Cruelty,' Nick said. 'It's innate.' Then he turned to look at Toby next to him. 'The last time we stood here was for your wedding.'

Toby gave an awkward half-smile to acknowledge the barb. 'It seems a long time ago.'

'Not so long,' Nick disagreed, 'but there was little to celebrate on that day either.'

'I hoped to make her happy.'

'Perhaps, but it seems you failed.'

'Yes,' Toby agreed, with a slight shrug. 'I did.'

Mary approached with the jug and refilled their cups, and she kept her eyes lowered. But Toby saw the judgment in Nick's eyes as he looked her over, as if deciding whether or not to buy.

Nick said, 'Will you marry her now that you're free, and make an honest woman out of her?'

'Perhaps,' he said.

'Ah,' Nick said, taking a long draw of his ale. 'I wouldn't blame you if you did.'

They turned their backs to the gathering and looked once more to the outside world beyond the window. The children had moved on and two washerwomen with baskets on their hips were gossiping in their place. The cackle of their laughter reached them where they stood. They drank in silence until Toby became aware of the other man's gaze, fixed on his face as though he might read Toby's soul. Then he turned, a question in his eyes.

'How did you do it?' he asked. 'How did you get her to your bed?'

Toby half-laughed in embarrassment and shook his head.

'Was it magic?' the other man persisted.

'Desire is its own magic,' he replied. 'And love too. She wanted me as I wanted her, and for those few days she gave in to it …' Until she confessed to her mother, he thought, and the church reclaimed her. It was her sense of sin that had killed her, not the love they had shared.

'No herbs?' Nick asked. 'No spells?'

'No herbs,' Toby confirmed. 'And no spells.'

Nick nodded his understanding and drained off his ale.

The drink was starting its slow ooze through Toby's bloodstream, the beginnings of the release he craved. Wanting more, he turned to scan the mill of people once again to find Mary with the jug, but the first face his gaze lighted on was Alexander's. He was offering his condolences to Becky, for all the world a kindly uncle, eyes crinkled with concern, her small hands held between his fingers.

'Who is that?' Nick asked, gesturing with his cup. 'With my wife.'

Toby said, 'A distant uncle of my father's.' He clarified, 'The tailor …' The lie slipped off his tongue with ease though he could hear the rapid knock of his heartbeat and his mouth was dry. 'He visits now and then.'

They watched the old man move from one mourner to another with a word and a smile until he came to Sarah, who flinched before him, as though she understood instinctively his malice. She slid a glance towards her son, who was at her side in a moment.

'Master Alexander.' He bowed his head in the expected courtesy, aware eyes were watching, curious about the newcomer.

'Master Chyrche. I am sorry for your loss.'

Toby said nothing, all the words that he wanted to say constrained by the company and the occasion.

'It was good of you to come,' Sarah said, to fill the silence. 'Please, eat. There is plenty.'

Alexander bowed his head and moved away. They watched him for a moment and there was no chance to speak before an elderly mourner approached to give her condolences. Toby smiled and thanked her, but his eyes followed the old man's path towards the door with the sudden realisation that Mary was no longer in the room. The old lady prattled on about Judith's virtues and her sure election by the Lord, and Toby had to ball his fists against his impatience, nodding politely, the woman's words barely heard. But Sarah had also noticed Mary's absence, and with a curtsey to the man who was trying to corner her, she ducked away and to the door. Finally, the old woman stopped for breath, and in the pause Toby bowed his thanks for her concern and made his escape.

Neither Mary nor Alexander was still in the house by the time he reached the door. Looking out along the street, he squinted against the watery sun, but he could not find them.

'He's taken her,' he breathed to Sarah. 'But it's me he wants.'

'You can't go yet,' she said, with a glance to the stairs. 'It's Judith's wake and you have a house full of guests.'

'I must.'

'He will wait, Toby,' she said, resting her hand on his arm in the old gesture. 'Trust to Hecate.'

He took a deep breath. She was right of course, but he was filled with an impatience to end it, energy running through his limbs and hard to contain. He hesitated. Then he said, 'I must.'

She nodded, and he chose not to question how she understood so much when he had told her so little. She said, 'Take great care, Toby. He means to offer you up to the Devil. I've seen it.'

'I know,' he laid his hand across hers with a smile of reassurance. 'My father warned me. You have no cause to fear,' he said. 'All will be well, trust me.'

But his confidence was feigned, and as he threw his cloak across his shoulders and headed out into the dark afternoon, he wondered if this day would be his last.

～

Sarah watched him go from the doorway, her heart tight with dread. Upstairs she could hear the mumble of guests, and their footsteps rumbled on the boards overhead. She should be there, she thought, with words of sympathy and a jug of wine, the grieving mother-in-law. It was Judith's wake after all, and it seemed unkind not to mourn her. But her son was striding away towards the fate Sarah had foreseen in the shewstone, and she could not just stand by and let him die. Not after Tom. So, flicking one last glance of regret towards the stairs, she grabbed her cloak from the hook by the door and followed him out into the gathering gloom of the evening.

In the street, the wind gusted at her skirts and billowed her cloak out behind her so that the walk seemed long and hard-going despite her haste. A narrow quarter moon slid now and then from behind the scudding clouds to light her way, but it was full dark by the time she arrived at the graveyard, and there were no torches lit there for the souls of the sinful. Slowing her steps, she picked her way through the shadowy mounds towards Tom's grave, guided by memory and instinct, and stumbling sometimes on the uneven ground. The trees that bordered the place soughed and bent with the wind, but it was more sheltered in the lea of the wall, and when she found the grave at last, she knelt by the yew as it rustled and sighed beside her.

With a smile of pleasure to be near him again, she laid her hand on the cold earth of the grave. 'Tom,' she whispered, though there was no one nearby to hear her – the graveyard was a lonely place tonight, the weather too rough and cold for even the whores who plied their trade amongst the graves. 'It is time.'

A sigh rippled in the wind and she lifted her eyes to the sky as the crescent moon broke through the restless clouds. A silver light brushed across the graveyard and she shivered. 'Tom? Can you hear me, Tom?'

'I am here, gentle sister.'

She lowered her gaze from the shifting sky and he was there before her on the low rise of his grave, just as he had been in life, only pale and bloodless and cold. Once, she would have been afraid of the death she could see in his eyes, but now it seemed to be a gift and it was welcome. He smiled and her heart turned within her, her insides hollowed out with grief and pain and want for him – so long she had waited. He reached out a hand and she took it in hers, and though his touch froze the blood in her veins, the sensation was delicious: she was with him again.

'Toby,' she remembered. 'We must help Toby.'

'One for one,' Tom said. 'The price to pay. Are you willing?'

She nodded. At last, she thought. At last. And it seemed to be no sacrifice to lie beside him again on the cold dark earth, her head on his shoulder as they had used to lie in life long ago, his lips brushing her hair. Her hand rested on his chest, and though there was no rise and fall of breath, no beating heart beneath it, his arm still held her close and with each breath she drew in she felt the chill seeping deeper into her blood, desire rising. She nestled closer, her whole body pressed into his as above them the unquiet wind stilled and dropped, and left the night hanging clear and silver under the waning moon. Somewhere at the edges of her hearing, an owl called. Hecate, come to take her home. Closing her eyes, she was peaceful in Tom's embrace, and she smiled as the cold slowly came to claim her through the passing hours. She was with him at last.

Chapter Thirty

BLOOD WILL HAVE BLOOD

The church bell had just struck five when Toby left the house, and a cold wind had gathered, driving the clouds across the heavens and whipping between the walls of the houses. He drew his cloak tighter round him, but the gusts still bit through the heavy cloth and made him shiver. With an upward glance to the sky, he stepped into the street and set his feet towards the sign of the Wounded Raven.

He strode through the evening, the way lit by the newly-lighted torches that flared at doorways. With the movement his fear abated, resolving into purpose. He thought of Judith in his arms on the shingle, Mary held as hostage. Then a memory of his dream flickered in his thoughts and he saw again the sorcerer's boot on his wrist and Tom's hand on his head in blessing. Would his father come to aid him now? he wondered. Could he reach across once more from the realms of the dead to protect his son? Toby touched his fingers to the tiny poppet at his neck that his mother had given him – Hecate's protection, more ancient than Alexander's sorcery – and hoped his father would hear his call.

The lane outside the Wounded Raven was dark as tar, the over-hanging upper storeys of the buildings shielding the road from the moon's shifting light. Few torches burned at doorways in these poor streets, and the alehouse that occupied the ground floor was shuttered and barred. Looking up, he could see the glow of light through the open shutters of the attic windows. The sorcerer was there, and awaiting him. Toby picked his way across the frozen ruts of mud with care and hammered on the heavy wooden door.

No answer came from inside. He hammered again, and a slat in the door slid back, but the face behind it was enclosed in darkness. 'What do you want?' A woman's voice, rough with drink and sleepiness.

'I have business with Master Alexander,' he said.

The slat closed with a thud before he heard the noise of bolts being drawn, and the door swung open with a squeal of its hinges. Inside, the alehouse hearth throbbed with the dying embers of the fire, and an eerie light filtered across the mess of tables and stools, but the edges of the room were black with shadow and he could barely see the stairs. Briefly, he wondered why it was closed, but the thought passed as quickly as it came.

'Top floor,' the woman said.

Toby thanked her and, placing his hand on the rickety banister, he climbed up into the dark.

At the top of the stairs he halted. Light spilled around the edges of the door, candles burning within. There was no sound to be heard, only the distant barking of a dog that carried on the wind. He swallowed and straightened his shoulders. Then, with a silent vow to trust to the power of the magic and to Hecate, he lifted his fist and knocked.

Mary jumped in startlement at the sudden hammering even though she was waiting for it, ears straining for the sound of footsteps on the stairs, the distant knock on the alehouse door. He had come for her, she thought with relief, and she might yet live through the night.

'It's open,' Alexander called out, without turning from his place at the desk. He had been working for the last hour or so, and his quill scratched rapidly across sheet after sheet of parchment, as though he were writing for his life. He had all but ignored Mary since he brought her here, setting her to make up the fire before binding her wrists with rope and sitting her down on the bed in the corner.

With nothing else to do she let her eyes wander the room, admiring the south-facing windows that must flood the place with light in the daytime. Now they were thrown open to the night, and a narrow moon peeped fitfully from behind the scudding clouds. On the floor were marked painted shapes that she recognised from the night at the Grove, their edges lined with a myriad of symbols she could not read. The sight of them made her shudder, the shadow at her back. The great oak desk where Alexander sat was strewn with books and papers, and amongst them she could see a human skull and a dagger, though she guessed that other, stranger things were hidden to her sight. Charts lined the walls, and everywhere she looked books were scattered in no apparent order. They must have cost a small fortune, she thought. But the book she had brought from Toby was nowhere to be seen.

Now and then Alexander had paused briefly in his writing to stretch out his fingers against the cramp and straighten his back with a sigh, or to take a mouthful of wine from a goblet. She wished he had offered some to her – her mouth was dry, and its warmth would have given her courage.

But now Toby had come to save her, and she watched him close the door gently behind him, tall and pale and determined in the flickering light.

'One moment.' Alexander lifted his left hand briefly while he finished transcribing his thought, and the only sound above the fire was the scrape of the nib. Toby looked across to her with a small and cryptic smile, but she could not read the look in his eyes and she swallowed, nerves pumping in her gut. Alexander finished his work with a flourish and turned to regard his visitor. 'You came,' he said, with a smile of satisfaction.

'You stole my servant,' Toby replied. She saw him cast an eye across the desk in a brief search for the book.

'Your servant? Or your whore?' Alexander regarded her casually over his shoulder. 'And what a whore. Such skill. All those fingers ...'

Not so long ago she would have deemed his words as praise, but now she was ashamed and lowered her gaze away.

'You're repeating yourself,' Toby said. 'What do you want?'

The sorcerer drew in a breath, apparently surprised by the bluntness, but when he spoke, the soft voice exuded its usual mellifluous calm. 'I think you know what I want.'

'Tell me.'

Alexander smiled, and began to fidget with the quill on the desk beside him, turning it this way and that, observing the changing light on the feather. Playing games, Mary thought. Making Toby wait. Then he said, 'There is a ritual for which I need an assistant, a man with some knowledge of magic himself.'

'Why did you not simply ask?'

'I guessed you would refuse.'

Toby nodded, as if in confirmation. Alexander let go of the quill and spread his hands. 'So what was I to do?'

'And if I comply, the girl is free?'

The sorcerer cast another glance towards her and nodded, though the regret was clear in his reluctance. Would he keep his word? she wondered. She doubted it, and a fine thread of vomit gathered in her throat: she thought of Rosalind, and Judith face down in the Thames. Then she remembered the magic they had done together, and that whatever ritual he had planned would not work. Her fear ebbed a little but still she was afraid – Alexander had power enough without the aid of the book to hurt them both. She swallowed down the vomit, and watched and waited.

There was a long silence as each man took the measure of the other, and she sensed a small crack open in the old man's arrogance in the face of Toby's confidence. The fire popped and a log crackled as it fell deeper into the flames and sent a shower of sparks into the room. Neither man seemed to notice, locked in some strange battle of wills she did not understand.

It was the sorcerer who looked away first, and she was glad until he raised his eyes again and she saw the vicious light within them. 'Let us conjure together,' he said. Then he bared his teeth in the semblance of smile.

She knelt within the safety of the circle as Alexander told her, and watched as the men began their preparations. Toby seemed to her to be a different man again. So many facets to his nature – changeable as the light in his eyes: lover, friend, master, magician. All of these men she had met, but she did not know the one before her now, hard and cold, with a secret in his look, and she couldn't help but watch him as he moved, beguiled as always by his beauty. There was no part of him she did not love, and with every aspect he showed to her, she fell a little deeper. He had kept her safe so far, and she had no cause to doubt him.

Alexander moved around her in the circle, preparing what he needed. She saw candles and a silver ring, the pages he had written, incense in a burner and a red-coloured stone she did not recognise. She searched for a glimpse of the book, but there was still no sign of it. Fear began to take hold again as a weight in her gut: a ritual from another source would not carry the same protection.

Then Toby took his place within the circle and stood beside her. He touched her shoulder with his fingertips, and she lifted her head to meet the small smile of reassurance on his lips. But she remembered the terror of the last time in one of these circles, and dread began to gnaw again at her innards. Trust me, Toby mouthed, and she nodded once in understanding, hope beating back her misgivings. Then her eyes caught the glint of the jewel in the dagger in Alexander's hand, and in the other hand she saw, at last, the book. Cold panic oozed through her gut as the sorcerer turned his gaze towards her.

'Not a word from you,' he said. 'Not a word. Do you understand me?'

She nodded, unable to find her voice.

'One sound and I will cut your throat without a moment's pause.'

'I understand,' she managed to whisper. Her gaze was riveted to the blade he held and she was conscious of the thin thread of breath that connected her to life, recalling the pressure of his hand against her neck. One cut was all it would take to break that thread, and she knew he would not hesitate.

He nodded his approval, then began to pace the boundary of the circle. As he called to the quarters, the candles guttered and the fire began to lose its heat until only the embers still pulsed with light and the chamber fell into a shifting gloom. The cadence of the incantation was beguiling, and though she could not understand the words, the rhythm of his voice touched her like a caress. She took a deep breath and hardened herself against the charm. Remember Rosalind, she told herself. And poor dead Judith.

With the circle secured, Alexander faced the east and began his summons to the spirits.

'I conjure you ... and command you by the Father and the Son and Holy Spirit;

'By Him who is everlasting and eternal, and by Him who gave us the Grace not to stand in Hell;

'By your master Astaroth ...'

A pitiless cold descended, and the scar of the sigil on her heart began to throb. Malevolence seemed to fill the space beyond the circle's edge. She stared into the blackness, breath held. Had their magic failed after all? She slid a brief glance to Toby, but he was watching the sorcerer with an intentness she had never seen in him before. Shivering both with fear and cold, she clamped her teeth together so that Alexander would not hear them chattering.

Alexander paused in his evocations and turned to smile at them both, teeth bared again.

'Did you think your pitiful conjuring would stop me?' he snarled. 'Or that your sordid elixir would have enough power to command the spirits more forcefully than I, who have made this my life's work? Did you truly believe a little study and your name in blood on the front page would master its power? Is that what your father told you?' He brandished the book, holding it like a weapon. 'The book is mine,' he said, 'and it answers to me, in spite of your pathetic attempts to own it. Your father stole it, but the book was never his –

it has waited all these years, biding its time until it could come back to me, who knows how to harness its power.'

The sorcerer looked down at Mary, who was staring at him now in horror. Was it true? she thought. Had they been deceived?

'Did he tell you he could beat me?' Alexander asked. 'That his magic was equal to mine? If he did, then he lied.'

Terror swept over her in a shiver that she could not control, and her gaze swung wildly from one to the other as she balled her fists against the urge to flee, mindful of what lay beyond the circle's borders. Then Toby spoke, and she barely recognised the hardness in his voice.

'My sorcery may be no match for yours,' he said, 'but there are other ways than magic to destroy a man.'

Alexander stared for a moment of uncomprehending shock as Toby barrelled forward into the old man's bulk and smashed him to the ground. The wooden boards groaned and sagged as the two men crashed to the floor, and Mary leaped to her feet in panic, uncertain what to do. Toby was astride Alexander's chest and fighting to wrench the dagger from his hand, twisting at the arm, while the old man's other hand flapped in front of Toby's face, striving to grasp it. The knife swung dangerously in the air as they fought for its possession, and Mary hovered, watching, frozen in horror.

Slowly, by twisting Alexander's arm, Toby forced the old man to loosen his grip, but in the moment of letting go, Alexander managed to flick his hand to send the dagger spinning into the dark beyond the lines of the circle. In the instant that Toby's eyes followed it, the sorcerer made a frantic effort to grab Toby's face, and his fingers closed on the jaw, forcing his opponent's head upwards and away. There was a strength in the old man she wouldn't have guessed, Toby's youth and energy matched by the bulk and weight of age. They grappled, and Toby fought to get his hands to Alexander's throat, his face contorting in the force of the other man's grip.

Mary searched the ground in desperation for a weapon, but there was nothing she could use – no sharp edge, no heavy object. Her gaze slid to the dagger, just beyond the circle's edge. Did she dare?

She swung back to the men. Alexander was gaining ground, Toby's weight not enough to pin the old man in place, the balance turning. A few moments more and Alexander would be on top. She had no choice – she couldn't stand by and watch Toby die, but still she hesitated, mindful of the evil that lurked in the gloom, a memory of the ice in her blood. With a deep breath to force down the rising panic, she dropped to her knees at the line and reached her arms out of the safety of the circle to grab the dagger between her bound hands.

As one hand closed around the hilt, the bonds that held her wrists snapped in two with a crack. She stared wildly into the corners of the room, searching, but there was nothing to see but the dark. Then some cold force closed around one wrist, slimy and vice-like, and began to drag her from the circle's protection. She screamed and struggled and flailed with every ounce of her strength even as she felt it beginning to ebb, the chill surging through her body, freezing her limbs.

'Mary!'

Behind her she heard Toby's voice as though from far away. A moment later, his hand closed tight around her other arm, holding her fast. For three breaths she felt as though she were suspended between two worlds, opposing forces struggling for possession of her body, and she writhed with her horror of the thing beyond the lines that held her in its grasp.

Then she was hurled back into the circle, and Toby's body cushioned her fall, warm and strong with the force of earthly life. She squeezed his hand in thanks and he gave her a quick small smile. But the relief was short-lived, for the spirit they had conjured had followed them. She had breached the lines of protection and the shadow had slithered through the gap. A thick miasma filled the circle, with the shape of a daemon at the heart of it. She could feel death in its breath, and the reek of Hell oozed through the air as the shade drew itself up to full height. Like the Devil in a nightmare, she thought, come to take her soul. She held her breath as its gaze seemed to sweep the circle, and the memory of the sigil burned in her chest, fire and ice in her blood. Toby's arm tightened round her. She was conscious of the living heart that pumped beneath his skin, and the warm blood that ran through his veins as fear pulsed cold inside her, as the daemon swung its head toward her and fixed her with a stare. She gazed into the abyss, unable to tear her eyes away, pinned. For one long moment they hung in silent union, eyes locked until at last it broke the bond that held her, and slid its attention away to fix on the man beside her.

'Who dares command me?' The spirit's voice vibrated in her head.

'It was I that summoned you,' Alexander said, and even though the tones were rasped and breathless from the effort of the fight, his voice still exerted its old honeyed charm as he moved to stand beside them. In his hand he held the dagger. She had no memory of losing it – her last sight of it had been beyond the circle. She must have dropped it when Toby dragged her back. Terrified, she clung to Toby tighter. 'To offer the gift of a sacrifice.'

'In return for what?'

'The Elixir of Life.'

'He is willing?' The daemon's attention lingered on Toby and it licked its lips, as though anticipating a feast.

'He has broken a vow of obedience sworn in blood – his life is forfeit.'

Mary shuddered. She hadn't known about the vow. Was its bond more potent than Hecate's protection? Or the magic they had done together? Alexander's power surged in the presence of the evil he had conjured as a wave of darkness that rippled through the room, and in the next breath she saw the knife at Toby's throat. Instinctively, she took a small step away though her hand remained fast in his, gripping hard. Toby's breathing turned ragged and Mary saw the fear in his eyes as Alexander pressed the knife tip to the side of his neck, coaxing a thin line of blood to seep along the edge of the blade.

Hecate, help us! The words tumbled in silence from her lips. *Protect us.*

Beyond the window the clouds gave way before the pale luminescence of the moon, and somewhere close by a dog's howl echoed through the streets. Both daemon and sorcerer had forgotten her presence, their attention locked in the bargain they were striking, and she tore her gaze away to search around her once more for some kind of weapon.

Her gaze lit upon a small silver pentacle she hadn't noticed before, and the points of its star shone bright with the moonlight. The goddess, she realised, answering her call. But was it sharp enough? Would it do? In the right spot perhaps, where the flesh was soft. Letting go of Toby's hand, she reached for it and ran her thumb across a jagged point. It might.

There was no time for wondering. The knife pressed still against Toby's neck, and Mary dropped to her knees to kneel at Alexander's feet as she had done before at the brothel, but this time she had a weapon in her hand. She looked up – the sorcerer was oblivious to her presence, absorbed in his deal with the devil. Then, with all the strength of her fear and hatred, she thrust the point of the star into the soft underside of Alexander's scrotum, turning it, pushing, dragging it through the flesh to gouge and widen the wound. For Rosalind, she thought. Blood oozed, and she turned it again, understanding for the first time the pleasure in violence, the power that comes with inflicting pain.

Above her, the sorcerer's voice halted with a gasp and his head dropped to look down at her in shock, his eyes widening with surprise and pain and disbelief. When his legs began to buckle underneath him, his mouth gaped open with sudden fear and the knife fell to the floorboards with a clatter. Toby stooped to grasp it. The old man staggered, and Mary scrambled to her feet out of his way, seeking out Toby's hand in terror. Alexander fumbled at his groin to find the point of pain and his fingers closed on the pentacle, where it jutted from the wound. Mary waited, barely daring to breathe and willing the old man to die as he wrenched it from his body and the blood began to flood in earnest, pumping with a splash to the boards at his feet.

'You traitorous whore!' he hissed, as he dropped to the ground. 'I'll see you in Hell.'

For a long moment he knelt, swaying, head bowed, and she half expected him to rise again, animated with some infernal power, but after what felt like an eternity, he gave up the struggle for life at last, and his body slumped sideways with a thud. But his blind grey eyes still seemed to watch her from the lifeless face and she turned away to raise her eyes to the daemon, who was observing it all with a smile on his lips, teeth bared.

'Do you wish for the same knowledge?' it asked.

'No,' Mary breathed. 'I do not.' She wanted no truck with this scion of Hell, whatever it could offer her. She turned to Toby. 'Make it go,' she breathed. 'Please.'

He said nothing, and in the pause that followed she thought for one awful moment that he would accept the deal after all, lusting still for Alexander's power and knowledge. She waited, conscious of the struggle as the muscle in his jaw pulsed with the strain of the conflict.

'You can't!' She gripped his arm, trying to drag his attention towards her. ''Tis an evil thing. Make it go!'

He swallowed, still torn.

'If you love me,' she begged, and as he flicked his eyes towards her, a new fear billowed that his love would die with the sorcerer. But the look he gave her silenced her misgivings in a heartbeat. The old light coloured his eyes, and she knew that he loved her still. 'Please?'

He took a deep breath, then turned his head to face the daemon.

'Go now, Spirit, in peace,' he commanded, 'and take thy leave unto the place appointed for thee ...'

Mary breathed again and let the words wash over her. But she understood the daemon had staked its claim for Alexander's soul, and the knowledge made her glad.

Slowly, the spirit withdrew and as the fire began to flicker once more, the unnatural darkness that had pervaded the chamber light-ened to the shifting gloom of winter firelight. At the window the moon was shrouded once more in a mantle of cloud. Mary hugged herself, conscious now of the winter cold in the attic, the night air crisp and hard despite the fire. She had brought neither shawl nor cloak when Alexander had dragged her from the house.

When all trace of the daemon had gone, Toby began to pace the edges of the circle. She watched him, turning as he turned, aware of him again as a living body – muscles and sinew and bone, with warm blood that was vibrant within him. She remembered the knife at his neck, and the spirit's grip on her arm. They were still alive and unhurt, and relief washed through her in a wave so strong she sank to her knees. Then she began to tremble – she had killed a man, and her hands and dress were stained with his blood.

The thud of footsteps on the stairs beyond the door startled her from her thoughts. There was a loud knock and a man's voice called out. 'Master Alexander?'

A neighbour, she guessed, alarmed by the noise.

'Is all well?'

Fear seized her and she looked at Toby, who lifted a finger to his lips.

'All is well,' he called, in a surprisingly good imitation of the sorcerer's voice. 'Do not concern yourself. Some books fell, is all.'

There was no answer and they waited, holding their breath until they heard the thud of retreating feet.

They should go, she thought, before they were discovered here with a murdered man and no explanation that anyone would believe. Her gaze was drawn once more to the body that was curled and bloodless on the floor. He seemed shrunken in death, and it was hard to believe the old man before her now had wielded such power in his life. But his dead eyes still seemed to track her movements and she slid her gaze away, unnerved.

'The book,' Toby said. 'I must take the book.'

'Leave it here,' she answered. 'Leave it be, and have no more to do with it.' She wanted Toby the man, not Toby the sorcerer, who frightened her. 'It's brought you only suffering.'

He turned and took her hand in his. 'I cannot,' he said. 'It's my fate to have it, my connection to my father.' He smoothed an errant strand of hair from her face. 'Please understand, Mary. I'm bound to it.'

She could make no answer, for she did understand, though she wished his father had left him something different to find. She waited, impatient now to be gone, as he slid the book out from its place under Alexander's hand. Then he picked up the jewelled dagger and tucked it through his belt.

She raised her eyes to him with a questioning glance.

''Tis no good to him any more.'

She gave him a half-smile at that and, without a backward glance, they left, stepping with quick, light strides down the stairs, past the shut-up alehouse, and out into the murky dark of the street.

Chapter Thirty-One

TO UNPATHED WATERS, UNDREAMED SHORES

A way from the Wounded Raven they slowed their steps. Mary was weak with shock, still trembling, and when she regarded him with those deep brown eyes he knew so well, there was a new sadness in them, a darkness. She had killed a man and he wished it had been him that struck the mortal blow. He wrapped his cloak about her shoulders and kept his arm around her waist as they walked, supporting her. Her gait was unsteady against him, and it seemed a long walk home.

The house in Narrow Lane was a welcome sight. Light glowed behind the first-floor chamber curtains above the shop. Sarah would be waiting, he knew, anxious and afraid, and there would be spiced wine warming on the hearth. Had Nick stayed with her? Had she explained it to him? He lifted his fist to knock at the door, and the footsteps on the stairs that came to open it were not his mother's. The door swung open and Nick was there, a candle in his hand. In the flickering light he looked haggard and pale.

'Where in God's name have you been?' Nick peered into the night. 'Where's Sarah?' He stepped back to let them in and as they stood in a huddle in the hall at the foot of the stairs, Mary began to sway with cold and exhaustion.

'I must take her upstairs,' Toby said. 'She needs warmth.'

He half carried her to the first-floor chamber, and as he settled her on the cushions with a blanket before the fire, he could feel the other man's impatience for answers. Fear for his mother lit through him – it seemed all was not over yet. Weariness gave way to a new and restless energy. When he was sure that Mary was comfortable, he turned at last to Nick, and noticed the room's disarray. All the detritus from the wake remained across the table, which was still pushed up against the wall. Piles of plates and cups and empty wine jugs littered its surface. Briefly he wondered what had happened to Frances that she had gone and left such a mess.

'Where did you go?' Nick lifted his hands in gesture of exasperation. 'The whole household just disappeared without so much as a word. I know you bore my daughter little love, but it was her wake, for God's sake, and you owed her your respect ...'

'My mother came not with us,' Toby said. 'I left her here.' He swallowed, a new sense of dread creeping through his limbs. 'Where is she?'

Nick shrugged. 'I've not seen her. I assumed she was with you.'

Toby was silent, and lowered himself onto the stool at the hearth, close by Mary. She was sleeping now, and her breath was soft and regular.

'Where did you go?' Nick asked again, but Toby ignored him.

They needed to be away, he and Mary, and quickly. Toby had thought of little else since they left Alexander lying in a spreading pool of blood. In daylight, the neighbours would notice the stain across their ceiling. And if they failed to see it, the smell of his death would soon permeate the passages. Toby was known at the alehouse, and the widow who kept it had let him in that night: he couldn't trust to her befuddlement not to name him. For who would believe they acted in self-defence? He was an old man after all, and they had murdered him.

But now Sarah was missing, and he must find her.

'Tell me, God damn you!' Nick was growing impatient. 'I've waited here half the night for an answer.'

'It matters not.' Toby shrugged. 'But we must find my mother.'

Nick stared, and his fists balled and unballed in fury, but Toby was no longer afraid of him. Perhaps the other man sensed the change, because after a moment he sighed and took the second chair at the hearth. 'Where would she go?' he asked.

'Tom,' Toby answered, with sudden understanding. She would have gone to the Cross Bones to ask his help for their son. 'She would go to Tom.'

'Tom's dead.' Nick's incomprehension was written clearly in his look.

'I know …' He gestured to Mary. 'Wait with her till I return.'

Nick opened his mouth to protest, but Toby was already halfway to the door.

In the street, he took the torch from its sconce beside the door, and by its light he ran. The moon had remained behind its veil of cloud, and the sky was dark now and starless. The chill air stung his face and was hard in his lungs, but he warmed quickly with the movement, sweat on his back and beneath his hair. The city was starting to stir, and he could feel the new hum of wakefulness in the air by the time he reached the gate of the graveyard – the night was almost done and he was afraid. He paused, one hand resting on the gatepost – catching his breath, he told himself, though in truth it was more to gather his courage. Then, straightening his shoulders, he lifted the gate on its rusty hinges and stepped inside.

This time he found the grave with ease in spite of the dark, and his mother's still form beside it turned his heart in dread and sorrow. He bent to touch his hand to her cheek and felt for some sign of life, but her skin was quite cold, and no more breath issued from her pale and bloodless lips.

She had been the price to pay. One for one. She had offered herself to the Fates to save him.

He slumped down beside her and took one of her hands in his own, caressing the lifeless fingers as though to coax the living blood back into them. Such small and dainty hands, he thought. He had never really noticed them before.

Tears stung his eyes, warm against the coldness of his cheeks. He should have listened when she warned him of the danger. He should have known to trust her. And for his folly she had paid with her life. But she was with Hecate now, and with his father, the man she had loved. So perhaps she was at peace at last.

'Forgive me,' he murmured, blinking back the tears – there was no time now for grief. 'May Hecate see you safely home.'

Leaning over to kiss the stone-cold brow, he smoothed back the hair from her temple. The last time, he thought, that he would touch her. The last time he would look upon her face. He wiped his eyes, and forced his feelings deeper. Not now, he told himself. There would be time enough for tears in the days ahead. He would tell Nick to bury her here with Tom, and perhaps here in death she would find her happiness at last.

Then he got up from the graveside and, with a final backward glance of sorrow, he set his steps for home.

When Mary woke, the church bells were tolling, but in her half-asleep state she could not count the strikes. The fire was burning low and warm, and she was rested, her vitality returned. Turning on the cushions with a yawn, she looked for Toby, but her eyes found Nick instead. He was staring into the hearth, long legs stretched towards the warmth, a cup of something resting in one hand. It was impossible to read the expression in his eyes, but she was wary. She had felt his anger before, and he had had a hard night of things.

She stretched and he caught the movement from the edge of his eye.

'Good morrow, Miss Sparrow,' he said, with a tilt of his head. 'Are you recovered?'

She sat up and nodded, and the shadow of the night hovered in the corners of her mind. She gave him a smile, and searched for brighter thoughts. 'Where's Toby?'

'Searching for Mistress Chyrche.'

The recollection that Sarah was missing chased the last remnants of sleep from her head.

'And you ...?'

'I was charged to stay with you and keep you safe.' He gave her a wry smile that was redolent with his discontent.

'I thank you,' Mary said.

There was a silence, and Mary noticed again the blood on her hands and the stain on her skirts. She shuddered at the sight of them, and Alexander's blind dead eyes tracked her from his realm of death. Would she see him in Hell as he'd promised? It seemed likely – for all her faith in Hecate, the lessons from the orphanage were hard to shake off.

She said, 'Forgive me, but I must wash.'

Nick nodded, and she felt him watch her as she got up from the cushions and went to the door. In the doorway she turned back. 'If she can be found,' she said, 'Toby will find her.'

'I have no doubt.'

Then she ran down the stairs to the old apprentice's room where she kept her clothes in an chest that had once belonged to Toby's father. The wood was worn and smooth, and its connection to Tom had always made her glad.

When she had washed and changed into an unbloodied gown, she went to the kitchen for bread and cheese and ale, and took them upstairs to break bread with Nick. They sat together at the table in silence and she ate without interest, her mind turning again and again on their plight. They needed to be gone, to find a ship and safe passage away. It was only a matter of time before Alexander's body was found, and surely someone would make the connection. Someone would accuse them, and though she was desperate for news of Sarah, delay would have a dangerous end.

She gave up on the bread and cheese and took a mouthful of ale. Then she turned once again to Nick, who was still watching her with a look she could not read. She was losing her touch, she thought. Too many weeks away from the brothel.

'I have an errand I must run,' she told him. 'If Toby returns before me, tell him to wait. I'll not be long.'

'I am not your message boy,' he breathed. 'Tell him yourself.'

She took a deep breath and tried to remember he knew nothing of the night that had passed nor all that was at stake. No wonder he was resentful.

'Forgive me, Master Tooley. I meant not to presume.' He tilted his head to acknowledge her words. 'I cannot tell you what's taken place this night, and I doubt you'd believe me if I did, but please believe that Toby and I are in danger, and perhaps Mistress Chyrche too. I must go now, and do what I can to help.'

'And I am just to sit here and wait? To pass on messages?'

She swallowed, searching for the right words, still wary. 'I thought, sir, that you would be waiting for news of Sarah ...'

He smiled then, and nodded. 'I am at that. Go,' he said, 'do what you must. I will pass on your message.'

She curtseyed. Then, discreetly sliding Alexander's dagger from where Toby had left it lying on the table, she hurried once more from the room.

The night was cold, and she huddled into her cloak, her breath billowing in little puffs of mist before her face as she set off towards the river, footsteps heading for the Cardinal's Cap. The city was already awake and stirring and she kept to the shadows – she knew well how to move unnoticed in the dark. But she could hear the beating of her heart, and her mouth was dry.

The bawdy house was half-asleep. Most of the girls would be abed already, the night's business done. She slid in from the reeking yard behind the building and through the back door that led to the kitchen and to Madam's chamber. Tucked away from the common thoroughfare, it was quiet and secluded, with a private entrance from the rear. A slim line of light showed beneath the door, but no sound from behind it drifted into the passage and Mary whispered a silent prayer that Madam was alone. She paused to compose herself, straightening her skirts and smoothing down her hair. It was an automatic movement, the habit of years before her mistress. She almost laughed at herself for being nervous. All she had been through and Madam still had the power to frighten her.

Taking a deep breath, she rapped smartly with her knuckles, and when she heard Madam's voice, she turned the handle and entered. The room was just as she remembered. A dozen wax candles and a cheerful fire, bright cushions on a counterpane of coloured silk, and oriental hangings on the wall that depicted strange birds and flowers, and one with a dark-skinned maiden on a sun-drenched couch. Madam looked up from the ledger on her desk, and her eyebrows lifted in surprise and suspicion. 'Miss Sparrow,' she said. 'You are returned to us. You left without so much as a word.'

'Forgive me, Madam,' Mary said, 'but I was in danger for my life.'

Madam observed her with shrewd, hard eyes, and Mary waited, nervous as a child expecting a beating. Old habits, she thought, and drew herself up. She was no longer this woman's property.

'The old man?' Madam asked.

Mary nodded.

'And what brings you here now?'

'I …' She stopped, and took a deep breath. 'I am … in danger again.'

'How may I be of help?'

'I need passage on a ship, to anywhere, and quickly. For myself and one other.'

'You have money?'

'I have this,' she answered, and held out the dagger. The jewelled hilt reflected the candlelight, and the ruby glimmered like red wine before a fire. Madam's eyes brightened with greed and she reached out a hand, but Mary drew the knife back and kept it close.

'One of your captains, perhaps?' she risked.

Madam said nothing but turned on her stool to face the desk

once again, lips pursed in thought. From down the passage they could just hear a woman's voice from the brothel, but it seemed far away and the peace in the chamber was undisturbed. Mary waited for what seemed an age, and the thud of her heart was so loud she wondered if Madam could hear it. Finally, the older woman turned again.

'Give it to me,' she said. 'And I'll do what I can.'

'Thank you,' Mary breathed, holding out the dagger once again, and a sense of regret slid through her as the older woman's fingers caressed the jewels with pleasure. But jewels would give Mary nothing if she was swinging at the end of rope, and she had no other way to flee.

'Where will I find you?' Madam asked. 'When I have news.'

'The tailor's shop in Narrow Lane. Close by St George's church.'

Madam nodded as her gaze returned to the dagger in her hand, and she did not notice Mary leave.

Three days later, Mary stood on the deck to watch Amsterdam approach. It had been a rough crossing, a storm that had blown them off course and left most of the travellers too ill to leave their bunks. A cold wind whipped in the sails, through her hair, and the rope beneath her hand snapped taut, vibrating with the tension. The deck rocked underfoot, gently now, as she turned her face towards the wind. A Dutch wind, a Dutch sea. She scanned the water before them and the shore beyond, and found Toby in her thoughts, sleeping now below decks in the narrow space the captain had allotted them.

It had been simple in the end to arrange it. A favour owed, an exchange of coins, the greasing of palms. They had boarded the ship that very night, and sailed with the morning tide. Two sapphires from the dagger hilt were sewn into the lining of her bodice – Madam had struck a good deal, and she was grateful. She ran her fingers lightly along the seam, reassuring herself of their presence – it was all they had to start a new life in a new place.

Soon she would go below herself, to hide in cramped silence for the customs men, but she wanted to stay on deck a little bit longer in the fresh cold air that lifted her hair from her neck and dampened her skin with salt spray. Turning to look along the ship, she watched the sailors make ready for the slow draw into harbour, slackening the sails, spirits high with the thought of the shore leave ahead. Young men, she thought, with no cares to weigh at their spirits.

She smiled into the wind, full of wonder at this new world that beckoned, a fate she had never so much as imagined for herself. Bankside was a long way behind her now, her life there at an end, a new start on a foreign shore. Touching a hand to her belly, she caressed it, almost certain of the child that was growing within. Toby's child, she was sure.

Buildings loomed into clarity as pilot boats plied the waters ahead and merchantmen tugged at their anchors. She was almost home, she thought, and she should go below, but she tarried on deck a little longer, reluctant to leave its freedom. A pair of seagulls swooped close to the ship, cawing in raucous voices before they wheeled away to hover on the breeze above the waves. Mary watched them balance on the air, perfect, effortless, until a silent voice called them away and they turned as one, flapping their wings lazily to rise above the ship and out of sight.

Acknowledgments

I'd like to thank again the usual suspects who helped in the writing of this book. My husband Steve for his unfailing enthusiasm and support, Dr Louise Pryke for her encouragement, insight and inspiration, Jessica Gardner for proofreading and edits, and Deborah Frith for feedback. Thank you all.

Also by Samantha Grosser

SHAKESPEARE'S WITCH

A fortune told ...

When Sarah Stone foresees Will Shakespeare's latest play has opened doors to evil, she begs the playwright to abandon it. But Will refuses, aware the play is one of his best. And so rehearsals for Macbeth begin.

Forbidden desires ...

After her vision, Sarah fears for her life. A strange darkness seems to haunt the playhouse, and when Tom sets out to seduce the boy actor, John Upton, the boy sees the hand of witchcraft in his own forbidden desires for men. Then Sarah weaves a spell to win the lead actor's love, and John, terrified for the safety of his soul, begins to make his accusations.

The Spirits have spoken ...

As rehearsals continue, Sarah and Tom must struggle to convince John he is mistaken and that his sins are his own – their lives and the fortune of the play are at stake. But the Spirits have spoken – will the fate that Sarah foresaw come to pass or is their destiny their own to decide?

Available from all good online bookstores.

Also by Samantha Grosser

"Un-put-down-able! Dark, complicated and intense. I loved it!" - *Coffee and Ink*

"Shakespeare's Witch is, by far, one of the most intriguing and unique historical novels I've ever read." - *MacsBooks*

"Steeped in swirling, eerie darkness, there is romance, magic and sex, plus a touch of dark, grisly history." - *Chicks, Rogues and Scandals*

"Be prepared to be at the edge of your seat wondering what might happen next–and even when you think you know for sure, you might not be so certain after all." - *Juliette Sebock*

"I absolutely fell head-over-heels for this novel, would read it again in a friggin' heartbeat and want everything she ever writes for the rest of my natural born life." - *Pursuing Stacie*

"Samantha Grosser expertly explores a plethora of oft-studied Shakespeare topics: incest, duty, power, witchcraft, love, God, etc. The story of the novel itself evokes the bard with echoes of his dialogue and plot motifs." - *Amy's Booket*

"For those that enjoy their reads on the darker side and don't mind some sexy scenes, this is the book for you!" - *Passages to the Past*

"A refreshing look at the life and times of Shakespeare, and the creation and production of one of his greatest plays, Macbeth." - *Readers' Favorite*

Also by Samantha Grosser

THE KING JAMES MEN

England 1604

FAITH, FRIENDSHIP, LOVE, BETRAYAL

Two men, once friends, have long since gone their separate ways. But when the new King James commands a fresh translation of the Bible, their paths are fated to cross again.

Set against the background of the writing of the King James Bible, and inspired by the true story of the community who became the Mayflower Pilgrims, The King James Men is a vivid portrayal of the religious struggles of the age, and the price of being true to your faith.

Available from all good online bookstores.

About the Author

Historical fiction author Samantha Grosser has an Honours Degree in English Literature and spent many years teaching English both in Asia and Australia. Although she originally hails from England, she now lives on the sunny beaches of Sydney, Australia, with her husband, son, and a very small dog called Livvy.

facebook.com/samgrosserbooks

twitter.com/SamanthaGrosser

instagram.com/samgrosserbooks

CPSIA information can be obtained
at www.ICGtesting.com
Printed in the USA
BVHW031432210719
553928BV00029B/454/P